Also by Helen Yendall

A Wartime Secret

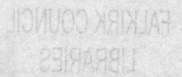

HELEN YEN _____ of short stories and a serial
published _____ .....s _____ ines over the past twenty years and
now writes female-focused WW2 novels. She's a member of the
Romantic Novelists' Association.

She studied English and German at Leeds University and has
worked in a variety of roles: for a literary festival, a university, a
camping club, a children's charity and in marketing and export
sales. But her favourite job is the one she still has: teaching crea-
tive writing to adults.

Although a proud Brummie by birth, Helen now lives in the
North Cotswolds with her husband and cocker spaniel, Bonnie.
When she's not teaching or writing, she likes reading, swimming,
tennis and walking in the beautiful countryside where she lives.

The Highland Girls at War

HELEN YENDALL

ONE PLACE. MANY STORIES

HQ
An imprint of HarperCollins*Publishers* Ltd
1 London Bridge Street
London SE1 9GF

www.harpercollins.co.uk

HarperCollins*Publishers*
Macken House,
39/40 Mayor Street Upper,
Dublin 1
D01 C9W8
Ireland

This paperback edition 2022

1
First published in Great Britain by
HQ, an imprint of HarperCollins*Publishers* Ltd 2022

Copyright © Helen Yendall 2022

Helen Yendall asserts the moral right to be identified as the author of this work.
A catalogue record for this book is available from the British Library.

ISBN: 9780008523138

MIX
Paper | Supporting
responsible forestry
FSC™ C007454

This book is produced from independently certified FSC™ paper
to ensure responsible forest management.

For more information visit: www.harpercollins.co.uk/green

Printed and bound in the UK using 100% Renewable Electricity
by CPI Group (UK) Ltd, Croydon, CRO 4YY

To the members of the Women's Timber Corps and the men of the Canadian Forestry Corps who worked in the forests of Scotland during WW2.

Chapter 1

Seffy stood in her stockinged feet in front of the bedroom window while Miss Lascard knelt on the rug, painstakingly hemming the awful green dress.

'Stand up straight, please, your ladyship. Shoulders back.'

Seffy sighed. She was slouching again. She tried to pull herself upright but could barely be bothered. She really didn't give a fig about the stupid dress. It could hang lopsidedly for all she cared. And as for the colour! Her pal Emerald would insist on green – of course everything had to be green – but this horrid shade of lime was an abomination. Perfect if you were dark-haired and olive-skinned, like the other bridesmaid, but Seffy was fair and freckled. It simply made her look ill.

The wedding wasn't for another fortnight and the whole thing could be called off, if Bertie's leave was cancelled. You could hardly have a wedding without the groom.

Seffy wasn't exactly over the moon about this marriage. She and Emerald, best friends since they were eleven, had always promised they'd have a "double wedding". They hadn't considered that they might not have fiancés at the same time. Emerald

1

couldn't possibly wait for Seffy to catch up; she was about to beat her down the aisle.

Still, at least the wedding was an occasion. It was somewhere to go and something to do and who knew what might happen or whom she might meet?

But for now – Seffy yawned – another dull day stretched before her, this tedious dress fitting her only appointment.

There was a sudden noise from downstairs. Seffy cocked her head. Wait a minute, was that . . . ? Yes! The oppressive silence had been broken by the sound of men's voices – deep and loud – drifting up from the hall.

'Oh, I say! That sounds like – yes! The twins are here!' Seffy cried, spinning towards the door and causing the seamstress to yelp as she was stabbed by a pin and the dress was yanked out of her hands.

'Please, your ladyship—'

'Quickly!'

Seffy flapped her hands and jiggled on the spot as Miss Lascard helped her out of the half-finished frock and into her day dress.

'We'll finish this later!' Seffy said. She hobbled out of the room and onto the landing, still pulling on one of her shoes. Oh, how the excited voices and laughter coming from the hallway below had cheered her up. Finally, some life in the old place! But what were the boys doing home? Term wasn't over yet, surely? Well, whatever the reason, it was a blessed relief they were here, filling the morgue-like house with merriment.

She stopped for a moment at the top of the stairs and bent down to peer at the scene below. Simpson was closing the front door; Father was shaking hands with Tol and Percy and slapping them heartily on the back. Mummy was flushed and squealing, as the dogs jumped up, barking and skittering on the tiled floor.

News! Good news! She tore down the stairs, one hand skimming the balustrade. Oh, don't say one of the boys had done something ridiculous, like fallen madly in love and got engaged on the spur of the moment. She'd rather it was almost anything than that. She was the oldest, after all; she should be first.

'What in heaven's name is going on?' She had to shout, over the din. When she reached the bottom of the stairs, she leaped over Trixie, her little Bichon Frise, who'd decided to sit with her back to the last step.

The laughter faded away and everyone turned to look at her. 'Well?' She put her hands on her hips. 'Do tell!'

'You tell her, Tol,' Percy said.

Ptolemy, the oldest twin, his face flushed, ran forwards and grabbed her hands. 'Seffy, you'll never guess! We've joined up!'

'Royal Air Force!' Percy added, proudly. 'And we've been accepted. We've said the oath of allegiance "to our Sovereign King and his heirs and successors" and everything!'

Seffy pulled her hands away, feeling a thud of disappointment. They'd enlisted! And they were merely passing through, on their way to their new, exciting lives. She was going to be left here alone again, twiddling her thumbs. 'But what about Cambridge?'

'Cambridge can wait,' Tol said. 'This is much more important!'

'Isn't it marvellous, darling?' Mummy said, a slight tremor in her voice that didn't quite match her words. 'It's so exciting! Can you imagine the boys in uniform? Now do come on, everyone, don't stand out here on ceremony. Through into the drawing room. Simpson's bringing champagne.'

'—yes, training overseas, in all likelihood,' Tol was saying to their father, as everyone drifted past her, including Trixie, who trotted off with the other dogs.

Seffy crossed her arms and glared at them all. Not that any of them noticed. Well, honestly! She might as well be invisible.

She was flabbergasted. The boys had joined up! They wouldn't be coming home for the summer, after all; they were leaving her here alone with the parents. She couldn't be pleased; it was a disaster. It was bad enough that Teddy and all her chums were disappearing off at a rate of knots to do exciting war work. She'd had a letter only this morning from Marguerite, boasting about her role as batswoman to an RAF officer.

And now the boys, too. It simply wasn't fair.

'And *my* big news is that I'm chief bridesmaid at Emerald's wedding in a fortnight,' she muttered to an empty hallway. 'Yes, big society wedding. An actual event, in actual London and a new hat and dress into the bargain. "Oh, really, Seffy? That is exciting. How marvellous!"'

But everyone had gone; she was talking to herself.

Simpson raised one eyebrow – how did he do that? – and gave her one of his looks as he marched across the hall, carrying a bucket of ice and a bottle of Bollinger.

'Will you be joining the rest of the family, Lady Persephone?' he asked, without breaking stride.

Hoots of laughter erupted from the drawing room. Oh, this was hopeless. If you couldn't beat them and all that.

She exhaled extravagantly. 'Oh, I suppose so.' She scooped up Trixie, who had deigned to reappear. 'Traitor,' she whispered in the dog's ear and then sneezed as Trixie's fur tickled her nose.

Even though it was only eleven o'clock, she could manage a glass or two of Bolly. Besides, her silent refusal to join the others had completely missed the mark; no one had even noticed.

She trailed behind Simpson as far as the open drawing room door and as he slipped inside to start dispensing drinks, she leaned on the doorframe, stroking Trixie and listening to the absolute fuss that was being made over the twins.

The thought of Tol and Percy as war heroes was rather disconcerting. They were mere boys; her little brothers. Only eighteen. She was the eldest and she'd always been the favourite. Oh, parents weren't supposed to have favourites, of course, but hers hadn't been able to hide their preference down the years and the boys didn't seem to mind. But now, suddenly, they were in the spotlight. Father looked as though he might burst with pride.

'The most vital crew member in a Bomber Command aircraft

4

is the navigator,' Percy said, apparently now an expert on all things airborne.

Father laughed. 'Ah, but the pilot's a pretty important chap too!'

'I'll say!' Tol said. 'It'll be good to get the first few ops under our belts. Apparently, it's during the first five and the last five ops that you're most likely to get the chop.'

Mummy's hand flew up to her mouth and she and Father exchanged anxious glances.

'Steady on, old boy,' Father said, his smile faltering. 'It'll be a while before you're out on missions. You've got to learn to fly the darned thing first!'

Mummy laughed a little too loudly. 'Yes! I should think that will take yonks!'

'Actually—' Tol started, but Father cut him off and gestured to Simpson to hurry up with the champagne.

'Come on, let's toast your success!' Father held his hand out for a glass.

"Success"? But they hadn't actually done anything! They'd enlisted and been accepted, that was all.

Soon, flutes of Bollinger were being passed around. Mummy was already giggling and she'd only inhaled the bubbles. The boys were getting louder by the second, Father was roaring with laughter at one of their quips and no, really, this wouldn't do at all.

'Ahem!' Seffy said, from her position at the door.

They ignored her. To be fair, they probably couldn't hear.

She put Trixie down on the parquet floor and picked up the mallet attached to Father's precious gong from the Far East, which stood just inside the door. She gave the gong a jolly good whack and the whole room was instantly filled with a satisfying boing-boing, reverberating sound. Two of the dogs put their heads back and howled. Everyone looked around, turning in their seats with startled expressions.

She had to wait a few moments, until the noise of the gong and the dogs had finally died down.

'Actually,' she said, stepping slowly into the room, 'I have some news myself!'

'Oh, darling!' Mummy raised herself up in her seat. 'Don't say—? Has Teddy—?'

Her mother's hopes were about to be dashed because Teddy Fortesque had not proposed before he jetted off to wherever he'd been posted. He hadn't been able to tell her his destination, of course – all very hush-hush – and heaven knew when she'd next hear from him.

'No, not that, Mummy,' she said, with a dismissive wave. 'No, the news is, I'm enlisting too!'

Tol laughed. 'You?'

'She always does this,' Percy said, shaking his head.

'What?' she asked.

'But you're a girl,' Tol said.

Percy sighed. 'You always steal our thunder!'

'I'm not stealing anyone's thunder! You've signed up and so have I. I'm about to, I mean.'

Her parents exchanged worried glances.

'But whatever for, darling?' Mummy asked. 'There's absolutely no need!'

Seffy stamped her foot on the rug. 'But there is! I have to! Women are conscripted now! Not you, Mummy, but all us bright young things. It's our duty. My call-up papers will be here any day!'

Mummy patted the empty place beside her on the velvet sofa. 'Oh, those. Come and sit down, darling, and have a drink. Daddy can get you off the hook. If you say you're working on the estate, that counts as war work. No need to enlist at all! You'll be out of it.'

Seffy felt her chest tighten. She thought she might explode with frustration. She'd been "out of it" since the blasted Blitz had begun and Father insisted she leave London and come up to Dalreay. She was thoroughly browned off with being "out of it". She was useless. What was the point of her?

The more she thought about it, the more her sudden decision made complete sense. She *should* be doing her bit for the war effort. She didn't have to wait to be called up; she could volunteer, right now. There must be something useful she could do. After all, the whole country – the whole Commonwealth, come to that – had rallied. She shouldn't be left out. She felt a moment's gratitude to the twins for giving her the push she jolly well needed.

'Come on, then, old bean,' Tol said, with a smirk, 'put us out of our misery. What are you going to do?'

Simpson was holding out the silver platter and Seffy took a glass of champagne and thanked him.

'As long as you're not thinking of the services,' Father said, firmly. 'I absolutely forbid it. No daughter of mine is going to ruin her good name by going into the services.'

'Gosh, no!' Mummy said, with a shudder. 'What about the WVS? You'd be rather good at that kind of thing, darling.'

Seffy rolled her eyes. Making tea, darning socks and shepherding evacuees? No thank you. If she was going to do her bit it needed to be more thrilling than that.

Mummy was patting the space beside her again but Seffy shook her head. She had more presence if she stood.

'Well, nursing's out for a start,' Tol said, helpfully. 'You can't join the FANYs because it's a well-known fact that you're a complete baby.'

'So, ambulance driving's out too,' Percy added.

'Oh, honestly!' Seffy said. 'Are you two ever going to let me forget? I fainted once, at the sight of blood – one single time – about ten years ago!'

'Did you, darling?' Mummy asked.

'Yes,' Seffy said, 'out hunting and not unreasonably, given that the bone of the chap's arm was actually sticking—'

'Enough!' Mummy held up her hand.

There'd been talk of Dalreay being requisitioned by the government and turned into a hospital for the duration. Seffy

7

had imagined the ballroom as an operating theatre and rows of patients' beds laid out in the gallery. She'd been quite entranced by the idea of wafting around, delivering glasses of water to grateful chaps and mopping brows. But she'd gone right off the idea at Easter, when Tol, home for the hols, had pointed out the likelihood of festering wounds, seeping sores and gallons of blood. The mere thought of it made her feel woozy.

No, the boys were right. Nursing was definitely out.

Oh, fiddlesticks! There hadn't been time to think this through. What could she do? If only there were a Hunting Corps or a Dancing Division. She was awfully good at those.

'Let's be realistic here, Seff, old girl,' Tol said, leaning forward and ruffling the ears of one of the dogs. 'What earthly use can you actually be? I honestly think, with the greatest of respect, that the fairer sex should simply stay out of it. Leave it to us chaps. You keep the home fires burning and all that.'

'Mummy, are you going to let him talk to me like that?'

But their mother laughed, holding the sides of her eyes with one finger of each hand, to prevent crow's feet. She was no good to anyone once she'd had a drink.

Seffy's gaze swept the room and landed on the framed family photographs arranged in neat rows on top of the Steinbeck piano.

There, at the back, was a faded picture of that funny old aunt they never saw – Dilys, her father's sister – dressed in Wellington boots and a sou'wester so huge it almost reached the ground.

'Didn't Aunt Dilys do something in the last war?' Seffy asked.

'Dilys? What's she got to do with it?' Father always got cross at the mere mention of her name.

Seffy had a vague memory, flitting at the edge of her mind, that Aunt Dilys had once done something worthy. If she could only think of it, perhaps she could do the same.

There! She had it. 'I'm joining the . . . er . . .' What in heaven's name was it called? 'The Land Army! For women! The Women's Land Army!'

'Army?' Mummy queried, fingering her pearl necklace.

'It's not actually an army, of course, dear,' Father said.

'The Land Army?' Tol asked. 'Why?'

'Why not?' Seffy said. 'I like fresh air. And gardening!'

Everyone laughed.

'Oh, Seffy, you are a hoot,' Mummy said. 'Please don't ever grow up, will you, sweetie? Stay exactly the way you are.'

'I hardly think swanning around the rose garden with a trug and snipping blooms for an afternoon's flower arranging counts as "gardening",' Father said. 'However—' he raised his hand '—I will concede that you might be on the right track there, with the Women's Land Army. I can probably pull a few strings and get you a posting at McCready's place.'

'But—!' Seffy almost choked on her bubbly. 'McCready's is just up the road. It's practically next door!'

'Precisely! You can still live here, safe and sound, where we can keep an eye on you! No need for a billet or any of that nonsense.'

Tol threw back the dregs of his glass of champagne. 'Milking cows and cuddling lambs. Yes, I can see you doing that, Seff.'

'But I don't want to live here! If I'm going to do it, I want to do it properly!'

Everyone looked at her doubtfully.

'We're only thinking of you. I'm not sure you could manage it, darling,' Mummy said finally. 'You're awfully . . .' Her voice trailed off.

'Pampered?' Percy muttered.

'You've led a very sheltered life,' Father said. 'Goodness, it would be like sending you into the lion's den!'

Seffy laughed. 'Hardly! It's the Land Army. Other girls can do it. I really want to give it a try.'

'Bet you ten pounds you don't last a month,' Percy said.

'I accept!' Her heart was racing. This was more like it. Excitement! A challenge! And she was only betting ten pounds. She could forfeit that if necessary.

'Let's make it more meaningful,' Father said. 'If you're really determined to go—'

'Oh, I am!'

'Then let's up the ante a little, shall we? You'll be earning a wage for the first and, let's face it—' he smiled '—probably the last time in your life.'

Seffy's eyes widened. 'Gosh yes, I suppose I will. Hadn't thought about that.' She rubbed her hands together. 'Goody! How much will they pay me?'

'I propose to stop your allowance,' Father went on. 'You shouldn't have an unfair advantage; you need to be on a level playing field with the other girls.'

'Quite right,' Tol said, grinning. Blast him and Percy. They were really enjoying this.

Seffy frowned. Stop her allowance? But how would she buy things? Oh, that was too bad. Would he really do that? This was rotten. Everyone was ganging up on her, trying to throw a spanner in the works.

Well, blow the lot of them! She'd show them all. She would join the Women's Land Army and jolly well do her bit and she *would* last a month. It was only four weeks, after all.

'Right. Seff. Ten pounds and no allowance. Do we have a deal?' Percy asked, standing up and holding out his hand.

Seffy stepped forward and shook it. 'Deal!' she said.

Chapter 2

15th May 1942, Glasgow, Scotland

Irene Calder was carrying Mr Fairley's third cup of tea to his usual table in the window when something outside caught her eye.

Rows of young women in identical khaki overcoats and brown felt hats were marching in formation down the street. Some were holding up banners on posts but they were at the wrong angle for her to read.

An elderly woman at a nearby table followed Irene's gaze. 'That'll be a recruiting march.' She rolled her eyes at her friend sitting opposite, to show what she thought of that.

Irene frowned. A recruiting march? This she had to see and there was no time to lose; they'd be gone in a minute. The bell jangled as she yanked open the door and ran outside, slopping tea in the saucer. Behind her, Mr Fairley was yelling, 'Oi, hen, where d'you think you're takin' ma tea?'

She stifled a giggle. The little devil on her shoulder was urging her on. Mr Fairley was a dour old so-and-so. Irene's charm, which never usually failed on any man, had never worked its magic on him. Let the miserable old sod wait for his tea.

She stood on the pavement and breathed in the cool morning air, so welcome after the steamy, stuffy tea room. The banners, held high above the girls' heads, were legible now.

BACK TO THE LAND

CALLING ALL WOMEN! YOU ARE NEEDED IN THE
FIELDS!
JOIN THE WOMEN'S LAND ARMY!

One of the passing land girls spotted the cup in Irene's hand. 'Don't mind if I do!' she said, breaking ranks to join Irene on the pavement.

'Here, help yerself,' Irene said.

The girl took the cup. The tea was so strong you could almost stand a teaspoon up in it but she didn't seem to mind. She gulped it down and gestured to Mr Fairley, who was shaking his fist at the window. 'He's not looking too cheery.'

'I dinnae care!' Irene said. 'He never is.'

They laughed. It was the first time in a while Irene had laughed so freely. She hardly even smiled these days. Jim was away at sea and last year their little house had been lost in the terrible bombing in Clydebank. Irene had been living with Ma since then and life seemed to be nothing but one long worry.

'Are you doing war work?' the girl asked.

Irene rolled her eyes. 'Aye, for my sins. That's no' my only job.' She nodded at the teashop. 'I work nights in munitions too. It's borin' as hell.'

'Leave it, then, and join the Land Army. It's never boring! And we've got the best uniform of all the women's services.' She scratched her collar. 'Although the shirts can be awful itchy.'

Irene hesitated. Oh, it would be wonderful to get out of the city. Jim would be proud of her and it'd be something else to write about in her letters. She had nothing to keep her here, after all: no bairns and no husband, for now, at least. Ma would pull a face but she could manage.

'How much do you earn?' Irene asked.

'Minimum twenty-eight shillings a week. Less board and lodgings.'

Irene bit her lip. It wasn't bad. 'Now, you're tempting me. I'm ready for a change. My husband's in the navy and I need a distraction, you know. My head's full of—' She shook her head. 'I dunno. I cannae stand much more of this. The Land Army, though . . .' She wrinkled her nose. 'It's farm work, am I right? See, I'm no good with animals. Coos and sheep and the like. I cannae abide them.'

The girl shrugged. 'There might be livestock. You have to be mobile and willing to go anywhere. And to pitch in.'

Irene could pitch in, all right; she wasn't afraid of hard work. But not with animals. The only time she'd ever been to the countryside as a wee girl, she'd been chased by a herd of cows and she'd never forgotten it. So, no, the Land Army was out. It had been a nice idea, for a fleeting moment.

The girls at the tail end of the march were passing by.

'Hey, you'd best be off, else you'll be left behind!'

The girl waved, wished her well and dashed off to join her friends.

Irene watched them longingly, as they headed down the street, the sound of their boots getting gradually fainter until they were gone. A delivery boy on a bicycle crossed close in front, almost knocking the cup from Irene's hands.

'Hey, you! Mind where you're goin'!'

She stared down the street – empty now – and felt a pang of regret. It would've been wonderful to get away from Glasgow but it wasn't to be. She knocked back the dregs of the tea and raised the empty cup at Mr Fairley. 'Cheers!'

His face was crimson. She couldn't make out what he was saying, although she could guess. She smiled. The air in the teashop would be blue and that'd be her fault, of course. They'd have to give him another warning.

For goodness' sake, why didn't someone else take him a cuppa? She wasnae the only waitress in the place. Where were Agnes and Jessie? He'd have a seizure in a minute.

'Hello! Me again!' The land girl was back, red-faced and out of breath.

'There's another part of the Land Army, a branch if you like – ha!'

Irene frowned. What was she goin' on about?

'It's new,' the girl continued. 'The Women's Timber Corps. I know they're looking for recruits.' She stopped to catch her breath.

'Timber Corps? What's that?'

'Working in the woods, chopping down trees for the war effort. We're supposed to be recruiting for the Land Army but the Timber Corps might suit you better? No animals!'

The girl fished in her coat pocket and brought out a sheet of paper, folded in half. 'Here's the application form. Tell them you want to be in the Timber Corps!'

'Dinnae bother sacking me!' Irene called out, as she burst back through the door, to the sound of the jangling bell. She put the empty cup on a table, reached round to untie her pinny and threw it down. 'I resign!'

Customers, the other waitresses and Mrs Mullins, the manageress, were all gawping at her. She was flushed with something: strength and purpose.

'Good for you, hen,' a customer muttered, finally.

'You're just having a bad day. You say that now, Irene, but you'll be back here again the morrow,' Jessie said.

'I will not!'

Irene unfolded the application form and held it up between her forefinger and thumb. It was a wee bit crumpled but she could press it between two tea towels when she got home. Then she'd fill it in straight away.

14

'I'm away to join the Women's Timber Corps!' she said, with a firm nod. That sounded good. She couldn't help but grin, seeing all their dumbstruck faces. 'See yous! I'll send you a postcard from the forest!'

Chapter 3

29th May 1942

'You're very well turned out,' the stern woman said doubtfully, peering at Seffy from behind her desk. 'I'm wondering, Lady, er . . . Miss Baxter-Mills, whether you'd be quite capable of mucking down?'

Seffy was perched on a hard seat in the middle of the room, facing an interview panel of two middle-aged women and an older man. She tucked her feet under. Perhaps the sandals and shirtwaister dress had been a mistake. She should have worn her riding clothes, for a more outdoorsy look.

'"Muck down?"' Seffy said. 'Oh yes, I'm sure I could.' She wasn't entirely sure how much "mucking down" she was going to be expected to do but she'd worry about that once she'd been accepted.

The woman's hair was pulled back into a severe bun. She reminded Seffy of Matron from school. She'd been raising possible objections to Seffy joining the Land Army from the start of the interview. This was the person she had to convince; the other two were eating out of her hand.

'You left school a couple of years ago, dear. What have you been doing since then?' the more sympathetic woman asked. 'It's just to give us an idea of your personality.'

16

Seffy smiled, grateful for the change of subject. Oh, but what could she say? She could hardly reel everything off. How she'd been "finished off" in Paris and Munich, until the rumblings of war necessitated her return and when war finally broke out, she'd been doing the season. Any chance of snagging a husband had been well and truly scuppered (unless you were Emerald, of course, lucky thing). All the soirees, lunches and parties had come to an abrupt halt. Young men – including Teddy, her "best hope", as it were – were getting drafted and suddenly no one had much appetite for fun.

She'd stayed in London for as long as possible but when the bombing got too awful, Father insisted she came up to Scotland. Since then, she hadn't done an awful lot.

'What have I been doing?' Seffy mused. 'Oh, this and that, you know. Country pursuits.' It sounded terribly lame.

'You're not in a reserved occupation, then?' the stern woman asked. 'We have to check.'

Seffy shook her head and winced as they continued to trawl through her application form. Oh, how she'd wrestled with the question, "Present occupation"?

"Debutante"? No, that was hardly the kind of occupation they had in mind and, strictly speaking, she wasn't a deb anymore, although, quite frankly, it had been a full-time job. The season was not for the faint-hearted. Stamina was required in spades for all those parties, balls and dress fittings, not to mention dashing up to town to meet pals.

In the end, sick of biting the end of her pen, she'd simply scribbled down, "Ready to serve king and country!" and hoped they'd overlook the lack of an occupation. Fingers crossed, they also had a sense of humour.

'Did Mummy serve? Last time?' the kind woman asked.

Seffy tried not to smile. Honestly, the thought of her mother doing anything other than barking orders at staff or occasionally rousing herself to pat one of the dogs or drink tea, was laughable.

They were waiting. The severe woman clearly didn't think Seffy's answer was going to be worth hearing. After a moment, she sat back in her seat and gazed out of the window.

'Er . . . no. No, my mother didn't serve,' Seffy said. Blast. The stern-faced woman looked back with a nod and scribbled something on her pad.

'But my aunt did!' Seffy added, decisively, hoping they wouldn't ask for more details.

They all sat forward.

'Land Army?' the man asked.

Seffy started to say yes and then thought again. No, come to think of it, that wasn't right. Not Land Army but something else. A picture floated into her mind: a sunny glade deep in a forest, thick trees all around and the sound of a gurgling stream. Where on earth had that come from?

'I think it might have had something to do with trees,' she said, hoping for the best.

'Ah!' The man slapped his hand down on the table and made Seffy jump. 'The Timber Corps! Although it was called something else then.'

'The Women's Forestry Service,' the serious woman said.

'Yes, that's it,' Seffy said. She was bluffing; she didn't have a clue. It had been yonks since she'd even seen Aunt Dilys. Gosh, she could barely remember her. For reasons that she couldn't fathom and had never bothered to investigate, Aunt Dilys was the black sheep of the family.

'The Timber Corps might suit you,' the woman said, begrudgingly. 'Given your background.' She nodded. 'Good. We'll put you down for the WTC.'

Seffy frowned. 'Not the Land Army, then?'

'There will be horses, you see,' the nice woman said. 'And you ride, don't you, dear? Country pursuits, you said? The horses are used for bringing the logs out of the forests. You might have the chance to work with them.'

Seffy nodded. She supposed there'd be people on hand, to help. After all, she'd never actually "worked" with horses. They were always presented to her tacked up and ready to go. She merely got on, jiggled around a bit and handed them back. Goodness, she didn't have a clue how to actually look after one.

'Splendid!' the kind woman said. 'Now you are completely mobile, aren't you? Happy to be posted anywhere? No relatives in the Highlands, which is where you're likely to be sent?'

Seffy hesitated. She had a vague idea that her aunt lived somewhere up there. But what did it matter? Their paths weren't likely to cross. No relatives, she confirmed and yes, she was completely mobile.

'Of course, you'll need to pass your medical.'

'But a strong, healthy girl like you should have no trouble there!' The old man leered at her across the table and then gave an 'Ouch!' as, presumably, one of the women kicked him. Quite right too.

'Does the Timber Corps sound like it might suit?' the kind woman asked.

Seffy liked the idea of the horses. She imagined herself leading a horse through the woods in dappled sunlight with butterflies fluttering around them. Perhaps, on her days off, she'd be allowed to go for a ride. The Highlands were supposed to be beautiful.

'Yes, it does. Absolutely. Put me down for that.'

Back home, Father was most put out that she was going to join the Timber Corps rather than the Land Army but Seffy told him it was a *fait accompli*. There was no backing out now. He muttered and grumbled and shook his head but, in the end, admitted defeat.

Mummy said, 'Caroline Mayhew's cook went to work for the Forestry Commission or some such organisation and I believe she spent the whole time planting out little seedlings.'

Baby trees. That sounded marvellous. *Yes*, Seffy thought, *I can do that.*

Chapter 4

15th June 1942, Glasgow Central Station

Grace McGinty stood alone under the clock at Glasgow central station, biting her lip and mithering. Had she come to the right meeting point at the right time? Was anyone else ever going to turn up?

She'd mislaid the joining letter from the recruitment office, so there was no way of checking. After turning the cottage upside down, she'd had to leave home without it. She'd read it so many times, she almost knew the letter off by heart but there was still a doubt in her mind.

Now, she scanned the concourse, looking for any likely-looking girls or someone from the Ministry of Supply – a man in a suit with a clipboard, perhaps. But none of the passers-by fitted the bill.

No one else was here.

Mother might have hidden the letter in a drawer or thrown it onto the fire. Grace wouldn't have put it past her. It would make Mother's day, to see Grace come home with her tail between her legs, having missed the train and the chance to join the Timber Corps.

'Now, we're fine, aren't we, Grace, just the two of us?' she'd say. 'How about you make us both a nice cup of tea?'

It was a miracle that Grace had got away at all and it was only because of Dougie and his encouragement that she'd dared.

The letter had come in the second post. Grace knew, from the official-looking stamps on the envelope, that it was her call-up papers. Finally! She'd started to wonder whether Mother had intercepted them, they'd taken so long.

She stuffed the brown envelope into the pocket of her apron. She'd go out later, once her chores were finished, and walk along the lane to the kissing gate and open the letter there. It was her special place, although if anyone knew, they'd surely laugh because she'd never kissed anyone in her life and wasn't likely to.

Mother bustled in through the back door, bringing in the smell of pigs and a cool draught from outside. 'Was that the post?' she asked, pulling off her boots. 'I could've sworn I heard Pat's bicycle in the yard.'

When Grace told her what the postman had brought, Mother's face fell.

'I was speaking to someone about that at church,' she said.

That was a turn-up; Mother never spoke to anyone, unless absolutely necessary.

'Aye,' she continued. 'If you're in farming – and goodness knows, if this isn't farming, I don't know what is – that counts as war work. They can't draft you! You can write away for something. An exemption, that's it. You can stay here, Grace!'

But Grace didn't want to stay here. Sometimes, lying in bed at night, listening to owls hooting and the wind howling around the cottage, she felt as though a heavy weight was pressing down on her chest.

It was awful lonely. She was twenty years old and life was passing her by.

Their nearest neighbour lived miles away. She could go for weeks without seeing anyone other than Mother and

21

Dougie-with-the-withered-arm, who helped them out on the croft. He'd failed the medical, so hadn't been called up.

'I have to go, Mother,' Grace said, as firmly as she dared, bracing herself for Mother's raised voice. 'I've asked Dougie and he can come every day, if you like.'

'Och, him!' Mother crossed her arms.

Grace had confided in Dougie: how she wanted to get away, do something worthwhile and experience the world outside the croft and village. He'd been all in favour. 'Good for you, Grace. Mind you stick to your guns! This place is too small for you.'

Mother was banging pots and pans on the range. 'What good will Dougie be to me?'

He was a good worker and Mother knew it. He brought in the cows and helped with the milking, lifting two churns with his one good arm without any bother; he mucked out the byre, fed the animals and, perhaps most importantly of all, he could handle Mother's moods. He ignored her when she was especially sharp and on the odd occasion she was nice, he was extra nice in return.

'Dougie could stay here,' Grace said, carefully. 'It would save time, not having to come in from the village every day.'

'A man? Living in this house? What would folk say?'

'He'd be a lodger, Mother, that's all.'

It wasn't so strange; after all, it was wartime. All kinds of people were living in all kinds of places. Evacuees were living in strangers' homes; land girls were billeted on farms. Grace wouldn't suggest getting a land girl. She couldn't inflict Mother on some poor unsuspecting townie; it would be a disaster.

'He could have my room,' she added.

Mother's head jerked up. 'Won't you be needing that yourself when you come back?'

Grace said nothing.

Mother sighed. 'Aye, well don't come greetin' to me when it doesn't work out. You're not one for people, Grace; neither of

us are. Folk let you down. You're best trusting no one but family.'
When Grace didn't answer, Mother said, 'Remember school?'

It was six years since Grace had left school. She'd hated every minute of it. She'd always been big and tall; she'd looked like a giant next to the other girls. And while it was bearable when they reached their teens and some of the girls caught her up, when they were younger, Grace was always left out of games.

She still had nightmares about the skipping in the playground. The rope they used was big enough for three or four girls to skip at the same time. You had to run in when the rope was high, timing it right so you were ready to jump when it hit the ground. But whenever Grace tried to join in, the girls turning the rope didn't lift it high enough and it snagged on her hair and slapped her forehead or cheek.

The rope would fall, the skipping stopped and everyone moaned that she was spoiling their fun.

Aye, she remembered school all right. A bundle of laughs that was. But it was a long time ago. Sure, it would be all girls in the Timber Corps but it wouldn't be the same. Would it?

A few days after the call-up papers had arrived, she'd been in the village shop buying cigarettes for Mother, when she'd spotted the feature about the Women's Timber Corps on the front cover of the local newspaper.

It had seemed like the answer to her prayers. She needed to be out in the fresh air but the Land Army wasn't an option: Mother would only say she might as well stay on the farm and she couldn't argue with that. It had to be something else.

'I'm joining the WTC,' she'd announced when she got home. And braced herself for a row.

Mother had frowned. 'What's that when it's at home? The Women's Tank Corps? I'll not see you in the services!' She tutted. 'Women in uniform, trying to do men's work.'

They wouldn't have her, in any case. Grace was sure of that. You had to be clever and polished for the services.

'It's the Women's Timber Corps,' Grace had explained. 'Felling trees.'

'Can't you do that round here?'

But she couldn't; that was the beauty of it. There were no forests around their small holding, only acres of rolling hills and the sea battering the rocks below their cottage.

Grace had applied to the WTC, passed the interview and the medical. Mother couldn't stop her: she was going.

Before she left, Grace had said goodbye to all the animals. Then she'd walked around the rickety old cottage for the last time, saying farewell to everything.

Farewell to the range that smoked and always needed blackening; farewell to the rooms with low ceilings, where she always had to stoop. No wonder she got backache. She'd spent half her life with her head bent and her shoulders hunched. It would be good to stand up straight at last.

'Mind your head on the eaves in that old room of mine,' she'd told Dougie. Mother had begrudgingly agreed he could stay.

And – oh, the relief – here they came at last, the other recruits, making their way across the station concourse towards the clock. They were carrying bags, accompanied by friends and family and calling out to one another – and even to Grace, 'Are you here for the Timber Corps?'

'Is this the place for the WTC?'

'Are you going to the forests too?'

Their excited blethering and laughter increased by the minute, as did the pile of luggage. Porters appeared and started to load it onto barrows, for transfer onto the train.

Grace let herself breathe and the butterflies in her stomach eased a little. This was really happening. She'd escaped – at least for a wee while. She was finally going to earn a wage; she was joining the Timber Corps. There were plenty of other worries whirling around in her mind but missing the group she was meant to join today was no longer one of them.

A swanky, fair-haired girl – English, by the sound of her and dressed in an expensive-looking suit – had just arrived in the company of a man who was carrying her suitcase.

'Is that your boyfriend?' someone asked and she shrieked.

'Goodness, that's the funniest thing I've ever heard!' She lowered her voice. 'That's Henderson, our ghillie. He's old enough to be my father! He drove me here. I know, tut, tut. Don't ask where we got the petrol!'

She shook her head and patted down her blonde curls.

'No, my beau's in the RAF. Training overseas,' she said, loudly enough for the whole station to hear.

Grace rolled her eyes. Was that girl really joining the Timber Corps? With that clipped voice of hers, she sounded like an actress or someone on the wireless. Grace couldn't imagine anyone less suited to working in the forest.

Mind, she wasn't the only one who looked as though she wouldn't last five minutes. The clothes they were wearing! Heels and tight skirts, a jacket with a fox fur collar – at least that would be warm – and good grief, there was someone in a hat with a veil attached. Clearly, that lassie thought she was off to a wedding not to the middle of nowhere for some hard grafting. Perhaps these girls had ticked the wrong box on the application form? It was summer now. Imagine how they'd cope when winter came to the Highlands and it was freezing cold, snowing and blowing a hooley?

Aye, well, it'd be interesting to see how they fared. Just as long as she didn't have to make up the slack when they failed.

The man from the ministry was here now, walking amongst the groups of girls, asking for names and ticking them off his list. Any minute he'd start ushering them along to the platform.

Grace watched as the fond farewells began. They might look ill-equipped for working outdoors but most of the girls had something Grace was definitely lacking: loved ones to see them off.

25

She felt a twist of envy as brothers and sisters, parents and grandparents and even a couple of men in uniform, hugged and kissed girls goodbye. Promises were made to write; entreaties rang out across the concourse to: "Keep well and safe!" and "Have fun!"

Grace shoved her hands in her coat pockets and tried not to mind that she was here on her own.

Mother wouldn't have made the journey to the station even if she'd begged her. Or she'd have only come to persuade Grace to give up this foolhardy notion and come back to the croft where she belonged.

A ginger lass was standing nearby with her similarly red-headed parents and a gaggle of children. They must be the girl's younger brothers and sisters and they were all in tears and hanging on to the girl's skirt as though they might never see her again.

Grace stiffened as a pretty, dark-haired girl sidled up to her. She'd seen her arrive at the station earlier with a woman that she assumed must be her mother. After a few minutes, the older woman had been sent on her way with a no-nonsense peck on the cheek and now she, too, was standing on her own.

'Hello, I'm Irene Calder,' the girl said, holding out her hand. 'Mrs,' she added. She was older than most of the others: mid-twenties, at a guess.

They shook hands. Mrs Calder's was soft, Grace noticed.

'Grace McGinty,' she said. She cursed her mother every time she had to tell someone her name because she was the least graceful person she knew. She was tall and clumsy and it was like a cruel joke, christening her "Grace". She yearned for a plain, ordinary name, like Joan or Pam. Something that didn't mean anything else and that didn't highlight what you weren't, every time someone said it.

Irene Calder was looking her up and down. 'You'll dae all right at this, I reckon,' she said, in a broad Glaswegian accent.

Grace winced. This petite woman, wearing high heels and a slick of red lipstick and who looked like she'd stepped off the cover of a magazine, was surely about to make her feel rotten.

26

'Dinnae look so worried, hen,' she continued. 'I only meant, you've got the physique for it. That's nae bad thing! You'll be taking the work in your stride, is all I was thinking. How tall are you? Five eight?'

'Five nine,' Grace mumbled.

'Lucky you. I'd give anything to be tall! I might have been a ballet dancer or a fashion model, if I'd been tall. I have to try to make up for it with these.' She lifted her shoe to show an elegant high heel. How on earth did she manage to walk in those? It must be like wearing stilts. 'I'm average height for a woman,' she went on, 'but I dunnae like it.' She nudged Grace and grinned. 'I hate being average at anything!'

They shared a smile. Perhaps Grace had misjudged her. Irene Calder was awful pretty – and she had a pretty name, too – but she didn't seem the type to look down her nose. No, she seemed kind and she was chatty which was a good thing. It meant Grace didn't have to worry about filling any long silences.

'Anyways, hen, what made you decide to do this? Join the Timber Corps?' she asked.

Grace shrugged. 'I'm used to the land. I couldn't stand being in a factory.'

'No, me neither. I mean, I did, for a while. I was working in munitions but I hated it. The noise! Nearly drove me barmy.'

Grace nodded and looked down at her feet.

They waited in silence for the man from the Ministry of Supply to reach them.

Irene Calder tapped her foot and then turned away, to talk to another girl standing nearby.

They chatted for a minute then, 'What made you enlist?' the girl asked Irene.

Grace could have kicked herself. What was she thinking? She should have asked Mrs Calder about herself. Why had she enlisted and where did she stay, when she wasn't off up to the Highlands?

She'd got it all wrong. No wonder the woman had turned away and found someone else to speak to. Grace had missed her chance to make a friend.

Chapter 5

At the station, Henderson, the ghillie, stuck to Seffy's side like glue until it was time to head for the platform and board the train. Father's orders, no doubt. It jolly well served him right when someone asked if he was her beau and he blushed scarlet.

Thanks to Henderson cramping her style, she hardly had chance to exchange a word with the other girls but she managed to tune in to some of their chatter. They were exchanging names, home towns and details of where they'd worked before.

Gosh, it was quite astounding. She'd never considered the different jobs women had before. This lot had been domestics, factory workers, shop assistants and hairdressers. Someone had worked in a tearoom, another in a city centre hotel. Nothing wrong with that, of course. Goodness, how would the world run without women doing those jobs? But they were all "townies"; they weren't like her.

Soon, she and the other recruits were piling onto the train and, before it even set off, Seffy's compartment was full of excited Scots voices: soft lilting tones as well as the harder accents of the Glaswegians. The "Weegies", as they called themselves.

Seffy recalled Mummy's advice before she'd left home. 'Don't throw your Englishness about too much, darling. The Scots can be a little touchy. Conquered race and all that.'

She glanced at the girls around her and then up at her suitcase in the rack opposite. The luggage label dangling down from the handle read: *Lady P. Baxter-Mills*. It mightn't be a good thing to be English and titled in her new role. She was going to stand out from the others like a sore thumb.

As the train started to pull out and the girls waved to their families standing on the platform, Seffy had an idea. Perhaps she could disguise her accent? She'd always been a dab hand at impersonations. At school, her take off of Miss Denton and Miss Wilcock had been triumphs. She'd had constant requests to mimic them.

Of course, she wasn't that familiar with Scottish accents – she only heard those of the staff at Dalreay – but how hard could a Scottish burr be? She only had to roll her r's, say "wee" instead of "small" and speak in a higher pitch. It would definitely help her fit in. It might even be a lark, to reinvent herself.

The other girls were settling into their seats now and the excited clamour had died down.

'Has anyone worked in a forest before?' Seffy asked, in her best Scottish brogue.

They stared at her.

The girl in the seat opposite frowned. 'Are you Irish?'

'Noo,' Seffy said, with a plummeting heart. 'As I said, I was only wondering, if any of you had done this kind of thing before?'

'No, wait. You're Swedish, am I right?' another girl asked.

'You talk awful strange!'

She couldn't do it; not while they were all staring at her like this. Oh, blast. This hadn't been one of her best ideas. Now they'd probably think she was making fun of the way they spoke.

'Actually, I'm English,' she admitted, in her normal voice, wincing and wishing she wasn't.

'Aw, never mind. No one's perfect!'

'Someone has to be, eh?'

Everyone laughed and Seffy joined in, relieved.

'Has anyone worked in a forest before?' she asked again. Nobody had.

'What about you?' someone asked.

'I've never swung an axe in my life,' Seffy said. 'I've only swung a handbag!'

At least she'd managed to make them all laugh.

These girls were rather nice and certainly better than some of the others at the station, who'd sounded rather rough around the edges.

Fingers crossed she wasn't going to be expected to bunk up with any of them.

Farrbridge, the Cairngorm Mountains, Scotland

It was a long journey up to the Highlands and the girls dozed for much of it, exhausted by the early start and their initial burst of "Timber Corps fever". Then there was an uncomfortable ride in a lorry from the station, packed in like sardines.

Once they arrived in camp, Seffy was rather hoping for a rest and an early night but Miss McEwen, their new supervisor who'd met them off the train, had other ideas.

They assembled in the dining hut for a disappointing supper of potatoes and burnt rabbit stew, after which uniforms were to be distributed for those in need. Some of the recruits had apparently been to a training camp and had arrived from there that morning. They already had their uniforms.

Seffy felt rather put out. This was the first she'd heard of any training camp. Over supper she checked with the other girls on her table and was reassured to find she wasn't the only one who'd been excluded. It was rather a poor show. She'd make an official complaint, once she knew who to complain to.

'I wouldn't fret too much about missing the training, hen,' a girl sitting opposite, said. 'We were up at the crack of dawn every day and it was awful hard work. Look.' She held up her hands, which were covered in scratches and blisters.

Seffy winced and turned away. Yuck. If she hadn't been absolutely famished, it would have put her right off her meal.

The girl laughed. 'We arrived this morning and they had us felling, sawing logs and loading up the lorry. We only finished an hour ago. No rest for the wicked, eh?'

Gosh, that did sound tough. In contrast, Seffy had done nothing today except sit on a train.

'I'm going to be working with the horses,' she told the girl. She wouldn't be felling trees. Seffy's hands would, with any luck, stay blister-free.

Perhaps it hadn't been such a bad thing to miss out on the training course, after all. If there were girls here with more experience than her, she might be able to take a back seat. That would suit her just fine.

The uniforms were laid out according to size on trestle tables at the back of the dining hut and Miss McEwen instructed the girls to take two pairs of breeches, socks, a fawn shirt, pullover, tie and a beret each. The berets had a natty little fir tree badge. The pullover, tie and beret were all green. Emerald should join the WTC, Seffy thought. She'd be in heaven.

'Ooh la laaa!' One of the girls had grabbed a beret and put it on at a jaunty angle.

'Once you've got those, there are overalls, jackets, boots and sou'westers over here!' Miss McEwen yelled. 'I suggest you keep your uniform for best.'

'Best?' Seffy queried. She couldn't possibly imagine a situation when these odd garments might be thought of as "best".

'For when you're representing the WTC,' Miss McEwen said, sharply. 'At church, for example, or on a march. For day-to-day work, you've got your overalls and jackets.'

Once they had their kit, Miss McEwen read out the names of the girls allocated to each of the three dormitories. They were primitive-looking wooden huts – all, apparently, named after famous Scots: Burns, Carlyle and Stevenson.

'Right, away to your dorms,' the supervisor said, once the final name had been called. Seffy had to swallow her disappointment: she wasn't with any of the girls she'd met on the train.

Blast. If she'd thought about it sooner, she could have slipped Miss McEwen a few coins to ensure she was put in her dorm of choice. It was too late now. And somehow, she didn't think Miss McEwen would take too kindly to a request to move.

'Put on your boots and overalls and assemble here again in twenty minutes! We'll take a wee walk in the forest before dark. To acclimatise yourselves!'

Seffy yawned as the other girls filed past, out of the dining hut. Mightn't they, she asked Miss McEwen, acclimatise themselves in the morning, after a decent night's kip?

'No, you may not! There's still plenty of daylight left and some fresh air will do ye the world of good.' Miss McEwen glanced at her register. 'I'm guessing you must be Lady Baxter-Mills?'

'That's right. I'm going to be working with the horses.'

'Are you now? We'll see.'

Seffy's chest tightened. That didn't sound very promising. 'Is there any reason I wasn't invited on the training course?' she asked. She actually wasn't that bothered any longer but it was a matter of principle.

Miss McEwen shrugged. 'I'm not admin, so I cannae tell you for sure. Something to do with the date you enlisted, perhaps. But you're here now; you'll learn on the job. Dinnae fret!'

Seffy frowned. She wasn't "fretting" but this was turning out quite differently from what she'd expected.

'And another thing, you'll be known as Miss Mills from now on.'

'I don't think so—' Seffy started, but one look at the supervisor's narrowed eyes made her stop.

'That title of yours is too much of a mouthful to be shouting out in the forest and besides—' Miss McEwen dropped her voice '—if you want to get on here, my girl—' she pronounced it "girr-ul" '—you'll take my advice: work hard, keep your head down and forget any airs and graces. Understood?'

Well, really. Who did this woman think she was? Seffy had never been spoken to like that in her life. But before she could reply, Miss McEwen turned away and called out to a dark-haired, older girl. 'Mrs Calder? A word, please.'

Seffy's shoulders slumped. Oh, blast. She was too cross and worn out to start an argument now. There'd be time, over the coming days, to get matters straight. 'Which hut am I in again, please?' she asked.

The supervisor sighed and glanced down her list. 'You're in Stevenson, at the far end.'

Seffy nodded her thanks, flung open her suitcase and stuffed as much of her new uniform as she could inside. She quickly refastened the buckle and raced out of the hut, trailing her sou'wester and with one boot tucked under each arm.

She might not have got the dorm she wanted but at least she could get the best bed.

The other recruits were meandering over the grass in twos and threes, loaded up with their belongings. Some of them were inspecting the washroom. As she hurried past, Seffy glanced through the open door. It looked positively primeval. There were rows of sinks, lavatory cubicles and – thank heaven for small mercies – what appeared to be a small shower. One of the girls emerged from the washroom yelling, 'There's nae bath! Not even a tin one!'

No bath! There must be some mistake. How could they possibly survive without a bath? This place was a nightmare; she might seriously have to think about going home.

Seffy overtook her dawdling roommates and burst through the door of Stevenson hut, the first to arrive.

Gosh, this was basic, too. There were eight army cots, four on each side, with one flat pillow and a thin grey blanket on each. There were Tilley lamps for light and a wood-burning stove in the centre. Seffy took the bed nearest to the stove.

It wasn't lit, as it was summer but who knew how chilly it might get at night or later, when winter came? Winter: that wasn't an inviting thought. But it was months away. This whole ridiculous war would most likely be over by then; the twins and Teddy would be back from the RAF, safe and sound, and Seffy would be at home. Or, even better, in London, having fun.

She hauled her suitcase onto the end of the bed and threw herself down onto it as the hut door creaked open and two other girls staggered in, weighed down with luggage and uniforms.

'I've bagged this one!' Seffy cried, sprawled out, victorious.

'Bully for you.' It was the dark-haired girl that Miss McEwen had been speaking to as Seffy left the dining hut. She let her bag fall to the floor with a thump, then she fished in her jacket pocket and threw a pair of socks, none too gently, at Seffy. 'You dropped those.'

Charming! Seffy caught them and flashed an ironic smile of thanks.

Clearly, she and this girl were not going to get along.

The others started to arrive. They chose a bed each and Seffy tried not to mind that the only bunk that remained unchosen was one of those next to hers.

Introductions were made. The girl who'd come in with the sock-thrower was Miss Ferguson, a freckled redhead, who seemed to know everything and had an awful lot to say for herself. Next was Miss Wallace, a wiry little thing who requisitioned the bed on one side of Seffy's and confessed that she used to be a land girl.

'The land girls hate us and vice versa,' Miss Ferguson said, pushing up her spectacles. 'I'm glad you saw the error of your ways.'

35

'They hardly "hate us". There's a bit of friendly rivalry,' Miss Wallace said.

'It's more than that! They think we've got the soft option and they're green with envy that we can do piecework and earn more than them.'

Miss Wallace smiled. 'Well, that's true about the piecework. That's not the only reason I swapped though: the Timber Corps uniform is better!'

There were four or five other girls but too many names and faces for Seffy to be bothered to remember. It would take a day or two. In fact, unless things perked up a bit, she might even give this Timber Corps up as a bad job, pack her bags and go back to Dalreay before she got to know everyone.

'Erm . . . I'm Mills,' Seffy said, reluctantly, when it was her turn to introduce herself.

'Miss Mills? Are ye sure? Or would you prefer, "Your Royal Highness?"' the dark-haired girl asked.

Everyone laughed.

'I'm only joshing with you, hen,' she added. 'You do sound like Princess Elizabeth, though. Ye can take a joke, can't you?'

What could Seffy do but smile like a good sport and act as though she could?

The girl was called Mrs Calder. She emphasised the "Mrs", as though they should all be impressed. Miss McEwen had apparently just made her "leader girl" which must be some kind of forewoman. Well, she needn't think she was going to start bossing Seffy around. She'd joined the Timber Corps to get away from being told what to do, thank you very much.

'I expect being "leader girl" is rather like being a prefect at school,' Seffy said. She didn't think it at all: she was only trying to break the ice.

Mrs Calder shrugged. 'Aye, well at my school we didnae have prefects. We were lucky to have paper and ink.'

Miss Ferguson, the redhead, was impressed. 'Well done,' she

said. 'You've been promoted already and you've only just arrived! Your husband will be proud of you. Is he serving?'

Mrs Calder brightened at the mention of her husband. 'Aye, he's away at sea. He's an ordinary signalman but there's nothing ordinary about ma Jim. He was my childhood sweetheart, the love of my life. I'm only doing this to distract me, until he comes home.'

She sighed and bowed her head for a second. Then she seemed to pull herself together and looked up with a smile. 'Now, listen up, girls!'

Goodness, she was issuing orders already.

'We're gonna be living and working close together for a while, so let's forget the formalities, shall we? My name's Irene.'

'Jean,' the redhead said, promptly.

'Josephine. But you can call me Joey,' the former land girl said.

'Enid.'

'Morag.'

'Grace.'

'Seffy,' Seffy said, firmly. 'Not Steffi or Saffy or Siffy. It's short, if you must know, for Persephone.' She braced herself for more quips but none came.

'Aw, I think it's a lovely name,' Joey said, and Seffy smiled at her, gratefully.

'You're English, aren't you?' Irene said. 'So, what're you doin' in Scotland?'

Seffy shrugged. 'I live here. At least, some of the time.' Ouch, that was a mistake. Could she have made it any more obvious that she had more than one home? 'Our family seat's in Ayrshire,' she added, without thinking. Double ouch.

'Your "seat"? What, like a lavatory seat?'

There was laughter all round, yet again. Seffy sighed. She supposed she'd asked for that but honestly, was this girl going to make her the butt of all her jokes?

Irene glanced at her watch. 'Make haste, girls, we've got to get changed. We're going for a walk, remember!'

The girls hurried to put on their overalls and unpack as best they could. That was something else that was sorely lacking: storage. They only had a small bedside table each. They'd have to leave most of their belongings in their suitcases under the beds.

'Do you have children, Irene?' Jean, the redhead asked.

Irene was older than the rest of them and married, so it seemed a reasonable question, but Seffy noticed her grimace before she answered.

'No, I don't. I could hardly have volunteered for this if I had weans at home. I have enough trouble lookin' after meself! Once you get to know me, you won't be able to imagine me with children!' She laughed. 'And kiddies today, they're wee wild scamps, aren't they? No, thank you very much!'

The hut door was flung open and in marched Miss McEwen, followed by a young girl with hunched shoulders, carrying a large bag.

'Nice to hear some laughter,' Miss McEwen said, sounding anything but happy herself. 'Here's the final recruit for your hut: Mrs Ellis, just arrived from Aberdeenshire. There's a bed for you, dear, next to Miss Mills.' She looked around. 'Don't be late now. We're all meeting in—' she checked her watch '—seven minutes!'

Once she'd marched out, the girls peered at the newcomer.

She was so slightly built she looked like a child. How on earth was she going to fell trees? A puff of wind would blow her down and oh, she looked so miserable. She had a face, Seffy thought, that would turn milk sour.

'What's your name, hen?' Irene asked, gently. She could be kind then, when the mood took her. 'Apart from Mrs Ellis, I mean. I'm Irene.'

The girl muttered something and placed her bag down on the end of the bed.

'What did she say?' Seffy asked.

'Hazel,' Irene said. 'She said her name's Hazel.'

'Are you really married?' Jean asked. 'If you don't mind me saying, you look awful young.'

Hazel nodded but didn't answer. There were dark rings under her eyes as though she hadn't slept for a month.

The girls exchanged glances and raised eyebrows. She was a queer one, all right. Why had she joined the Timber Corps, Seffy wondered, if she was clearly so unhappy to be here?

Irene clapped her hands. 'Come along, everyone, look sharp or our names will be mud. Boots and overalls, quick as you can!'

Seffy looked down at her black leather boots and curled her lip. They looked like something a man would wear and yes – she poked them – as she'd suspected, they were rock-hard.

But Jean, who seemed delighted by everything, was thrilled at her new acquisition. 'Marvellous! I've never had a new pair of boots before! Nobody else's foot has ever been in these boots before mine!'

Irene rolled her eyes. 'Aye, well don't be too happy, hen. They're as hard as nails and they'll probably cripple you for weeks.'

Once they were changed and even the new girl, Hazel, had managed to rouse herself sufficiently to put on her overalls and boots, the new recruits followed Miss McEwen in single file out of the camp clearing and into the forest. It was nine o'clock but still light. The sun was low in the sky, sending shafts of golden light through the trees, so that everything seemed to glow.

Their voices rang out through the evening air, as girls exclaimed over the queerness of wearing slacks and the comfort – or lack of it – of their new boots.

Seffy sighed and shoved her hands in her pockets as they were led along a dirt track, which gradually disappeared as they went deeper into the woods.

Today had been beastly. She hadn't kept a diary for years but if she did, she'd have written: **Best forgotten!** in big bold lettering across the page for June 15th.

She'd been slighted and made fun of, disappointed by the primitive accommodation, missed off the training course and she might not even be working with the horses. She was certainly not in the mood to chat to whoever was walking near her, so she plodded on in silence.

An hour later, they were still walking and Seffy's boots had started to rub.

'What's that?' someone asked.

It was a tumble-down wooden shack, set against a rocky incline, in a clearing at the edge of the forest. The slate roof was intact and when Irene pushed open the door and Seffy and a few others followed her inside, it was surprisingly cosy: dry and warm. There was a stone floor, a fireplace and two bare rooms with a cobwebby window in each.

'I know!' Jean said. 'It's a bothy. They're for workers to live in or to use. Shepherds and such like. The deerstalker from the estate probably used it, in times gone by.'

It was a sweet little place and Seffy felt her mood lift.

'With a woman's touch, it could be actually be more comfortable than our hut,' she said, pursing her lips. She took a few steps forward, into the room at the back. 'Yes,' she mused, 'if this place was furnished . . . a bed there, with a feather mattress, a chest against the wall, a Turkish carpet on the floor and some pictures on the walls – oh and a gramophone – it would be perfectly habitable! I might even come and live here myself!' She spun around, laughing but there was only silence and emptiness behind her.

The other girls had gone. They must have slipped out without her noticing.

She'd have to hurry after them. She didn't want to get lost. They must be miles from camp now. The light was fading and the woods looked the same in every direction: nothing but trees, bracken, ferns, moss and lichen-covered stones.

But first . . . she bent down and took off her horrid men's

boots. Then the socks too. She wriggled her red, sore toes. That felt better.

She didn't care what anyone thought: she would walk back barefoot, over the carpet of pine needles on the forest floor. All of her was hurting – inside and out – and at least she could do something about her feet.

Chapter 6

Sergeant Callum Fraser of the Canadian Forestry Corps sat on the hard-baked earth with his back to the Nissen hut, watching the sun go down.

The only thing missing was a cold beer, but there was no alcohol allowed in camp and he'd gotten used to that rule pretty quick. He wasn't much of a drinker, in any case. If he did nothing else in his life, he'd vowed to stay sober and true.

He was surrounded by fellas sitting nearby or lying on the grass, smoking cigarettes and shooting the breeze. A couple of them were reading letters from home, occasionally smacking a midge on their forearm but not taking their eyes off the pages for a second.

Private Adams – Tom – was trying to explain the queer big British coins – the pennies and shillings – to the saw doctor, Stefan Goodman, with little success.

'Look, there's twelve pennies in a shilling and twenty shillings in a pound. Got it?'

'But why twelve and why twenty? Who came up with those dumb figures?'

Adams laughed and slapped his thigh. 'Well, how the hell should I know?'

Callum smiled and let their banter drift around him, happy to be sitting here, doing nothing.

He shook his head when the pontoon players sitting up at the wooden table asked if they should cut him in.

He inhaled the warm, pine-scented evening air. Three months on and he still found it hard to believe he was really here, four thousand miles from home, in Scotland. He felt comfortable in a way he couldn't explain to anyone, not even to himself. Ma's folks, the Lennoxes, were from here; it was the old country. The guys would rib him something rotten if he ever said it aloud but he felt at ease here, close to his forebears.

'Hey, Sarge!'

It was Verne Blumenthal, waving his letter in the air. Verne was one of the thirty or so guys in the company from Invermore, Callum's hometown. They were practically related: Verne was married to Missy's sister. Callum didn't care much for Verne, so he gave the faintest nod to show he'd heard him.

'My wife says Missy ain't had a letter from you in months!' He tapped the sheet of paper in his hand. 'And I'm instructed right here, to tell you to write her ASAP!'

Callum closed his eyes and didn't reply.

'Shut up, Verne.' That was Gordy speaking. 'Sarge probably wants to write saucy stuff but he's trying to think of a way round the censor. So that's held up his letter writing. Ain't that the truth, buddy? When you're writing to your best girl you don't want some officer you know reading over your mail!'

The men whooped and laughed, delighted by the thought of "saucy stuff" and by Gordy's daring to say it. Callum shrugged and held up his hands in a gesture of surrender, grateful to his pal for the distraction.

The censor wasn't the reason his letter writing had slowed to almost nothing in the last few weeks. But it was easier to let the men think that, than have them guess the truth.

'Hey, misters! Got any candy?'

Callum opened his eyes. It was a bunch of scrawny kids from the village. They were braver these days; they'd stopped hiding behind tree trunks. Now they ventured out to the camp in gangs, bold as anything and stood watching the guys, wide-eyed.

The company and the kids had kind of adopted each other.

At first, the fellas had found it hard to make out what they were saying but they'd gotten used to the Scottish accent and, oh boy, it was nice to see the kids' eyes light up when they were offered gum or a candy bar, or when they begged for more tales of "red injuns" and derring-do.

One of the men stubbed out his cigarette, went inside the hut and brought out a bag. 'What's the magic word?'

'Please, mister! Please!' the kids chorused and the next moment, they were scrabbling around in the dirt, as the private threw them a bunch of goodies.

'There you go! And then I guess it must be your bedtime!'

'Yeah, home you go!'

'And don't "haste ye back!"'

The guys laughed. They were joshing; they liked the kids really.

Callum felt bad sometimes, thinking about how little the locals round here had while they had a ton of stuff: plenty of good food and cooks to do something with it. But then, he'd been the same when he was a kid: scratching around in the dirt, 'specially after Ma died. And at least the company tried to share it out, as much as they could.

'Remember, guys,' he'd told the fellas more than once, 'if anyone invites you to their home for a meal, go easy. Don't eat too much. All their food's rationed. Got it?'

The novelty of being stared at and appreciated like they were movie stars had pretty much worn off by now. But Callum had liked it while it lasted; being someone special. He wondered how long the company would be here. A while yet, he reckoned. They'd not long finished building the camp and the mill and putting in the roads, after all. There sure were a lot of trees to fell.

He wasn't in any hurry to get back on that ship again. Jeez. He shook his head at the memory. He'd never been so sick in his whole life. Ten days crossing the Atlantic and he'd been just about ready to jump overboard. He felt so dog rough he wouldn't have cared if a German sub had torpedoed them. At least the misery would have ended. The voyage had been months ago but the memory was as clear as day. The thought of doing it all over again made his stomach heave. No, despite what he put in his occasional letter home to Missy, he was more than happy to stay here a while yet.

Gordy's head shot up. 'Whoa up! The cavalry's arrived!'

It was Private Matthews, tearing into camp, dust flying from his boots, arms flapping, red-faced. The fellas yelled and laughed. It was quite a spectacle. Matthews was on the chubby side. He sure wasn't made for running.

'Hey, what's up, fella? You seen that there Loch Ness monster?' Gordy asked.

Matthews had reached them now. He bent and put his hands on his knees, wheezing, until someone took pity on him and slapped his back a few times, hard. Eventually he managed to get the words out.

'GIRLS!' he announced. Now he had their attention. 'Girls!'

'Where?'

'Back there, in the bush!'

Callum laughed as one or two of the fellas stood up and looked around. It was as though they were expecting the girls to come floating out from the trees like nymphs or sylphs or whatever forest spirits were called.

Matthews, still gasping, jabbed his finger in the direction he'd just come. 'Thought I was dreamin' at first. Then I heard their voices, like the coos of a dove, you know. And then giggling, like a gurgling brook.'

The guys were doubled up with laughter now.

'Quit the poetics, will ya, Matthews, and just tell us. And

if you're making this up, I'll swing for you! Where are they? These girls?'

'They're back there, like I said. In the bush. Leastways, they were an hour or so back. And, here's the best part: they're felling trees!'

The laughter stopped. The men looked at one another and frowned. That wasn't true. Women didn't fell trees. They couldn't. Had Matthews been on the liquor? He had to be kidding, right?

'I swear,' he said. 'I swear on my ma's life. There are girls, working in the forest, a couple of miles that way. I saw them with my own eyes and after, I asked an old fella in the village. He says there's more of them coming tonight, to fill up the camp. They're working for the government and—'

His words were drowned out as the fellas started yelling and talking all at once. Callum hadn't seen them this excited in a while. Not since they'd arrived in Scotland and climbed aboard the train to the Highlands, so grateful and happy to be on dry land again.

Now, they were almost jumping on the spot, like they had springs on their boots. And Gordy was the most excited of all.

'Say, they could come to the fete next month!' he said, eyes wide. 'We need to let 'em know. Because they mightn't know about it. If they're new in town and all?'

Callum nodded. He couldn't see any harm in that. The whole village would turn out for the fete, after all. The more the merrier. 'Yeah, sure,' he said. He smiled as Gordy slapped his thigh and let out a whoop. Gordy hadn't even seen these girls yet. For all anyone knew, they might be a figment of Matthews' imagination.

Callum had known Gordy Johnson since school days. What he lacked in height – for a woodsman, he was pretty short – he made up for in personality and energy. He was smart. If he'd played his cards right, he could have made corporal, no doubt, but he was the joker of the gang. He liked sending the village laddies on errands for a "long stand" or a tin of tartan paint; he'd gone to the mill once or twice to fill the head sawyer's cap with

46

sawdust. His latest trick was nailing someone's mug of coffee to the bench and doubling up at the guy's reaction.

Yeah, he could be good fun, Gordy.

But they were only pals when they were off duty. When they were working, representing the CFC, Callum was the sergeant and Gordy was the private. And Callum would never let him forget it.

'OK, fellas, let's all calm down some,' Callum said, standing up. 'We've got our work and these woodswomen, or whatever they call themselves, have, presumably, got theirs.'

'I sure would like to see a girl fell a tree!' one of the guys said and the others whooped and hollered their agreement, shaking their heads at the very idea of it.

Gordy tutted. 'Boy, the British must be desperate, if they're getting women to do men's work.'

'That's why they need us!' Verne said.

Callum nodded. 'Yep. They sure do and that's why we answered their call for help. But I will not be best pleased – and neither will Lieutenant Coomber—' the men quickly sobered up at the sound of his name '—if we catch any of you fellas over there, in that neck of the woods, where you're not supposed to be. Girls or no girls. Got it?'

The guys mumbled their agreement, kicking at the ground, clearly not happy. Callum wasn't happy either. His sense of ease and calm had gone. He might've known it wouldn't last: this had all been going too well. They'd set up camp, got the equipment and the fellas working just fine and now, if Matthews was to be believed, there were women playing at lumbering in the forest.

If his men worked well and kept on top of things and the lieutenant was happy, Callum was in line for promotion.

And nobody nor nothin' was going to stand in his way.

Chapter 7

Although she wasn't exactly keen on the posh English girl in her dormitory, Grace felt bad about leaving her behind.

It had been Irene's idea. She'd tiptoed to the bothy door, putting her finger to her lips, while Seffy was in the back room, blethering on about what she'd do to the place. No doubt she lived in a mansion and the bothy was like a little playhouse for her.

Irene had beckoned to Grace and the others and they'd trotted out and hurried through the forest to catch up with Miss McEwen.

'It's only a bit of fun,' Irene said, as they glimpsed the other recruits ahead of them through the trees and started to speed up. 'We won't lose her completely.'

But it was mean. Grace knew how it felt to be left out and teased. Irene was the first girl Grace had spoken to at the station and she'd been friendly. But you wouldn't want to get on the wrong side of her. She knew the way Irene was picking on Seffy wasn't right but, to her shame, another little voice in Grace's head was saying, *But better her than you.*

Miss McEwen and the group of girls had stopped in a clearing. 'Come along, stragglers!' she yelled. 'Who else have we lost?'

'One more coming up behind us,' Irene said. 'She's back there in the bothy.'

Miss McEwen huffed. 'Miss Mills, I've no doubt?'

One of the girls from their hut – Enid – was sitting on the forest floor with little Hazel, who'd been the last to arrive. When Enid saw Grace, Irene and Jean, she said something to Hazel and got up to join them. She pulled them away from the main group.

'It's about Hazel,' Enid said, quietly. 'She told me the reason she's in such an awful state. Her husband was killed last month in a raid.'

Irene's hand flew to her mouth. 'Dear God,' she murmured. 'And we were asking her if she was really married because she looked so young.'

'The poor wee doggie as well.' Enid's voice was cracking. 'The three of them were in the shelter and Hazel ran out to fetch something from the house and while she was away—'

'—the shelter took a direct hit?' Jean finished.

'Aye, that's about the size of it.'

The girls shook their heads in disbelief and were silent for a moment.

Poor thing, Grace thought. No wonder she was so sad.

'Was he no' drafted? Her husband?' Irene asked.

'No, he worked in the harbour. Reserved occupation.'

'But why has she come here, to do this?' Irene said. 'I dinnae understand it. She's in no fit state. She's a wee slip of a thing with no strength in her and she's grieving summat awful.'

Enid glanced back at Hazel. 'Her folks thought being out in the fresh air, in nature, you know, would help her get over it.'

'Nonsense! How can nature help you get over summat like that? I tell you now if my Jim . . . if the worst happened . . .' Irene swallowed '. . . I'd never get over it. Never.'

Their supervisor's voice was ringing out through trees. 'Ah, there you are, Miss Mills! Nice of you to join us! Now what on earth have you done with your boots?'

'Come on,' Irene said. 'Her ladyship's caught us up.' They moved back towards the rest of the group. 'Little Hazel's going to need our help over the next few weeks,' she added. 'So, let's all be 'specially kind to her, eh?'

She hardly needed to say it, Grace thought. But what about Seffy? Oughtn't they tell her what had happened to Hazel, to stop her putting her foot in it? Her bare foot, judging by the looks of her now.

Grace tried to catch up with Seffy as they marched back to camp but she was steaming ahead, weaving through the trees, a boot in each hand. Judging from her stance and her set mouth, she wasn't in the mood to speak to anyone.

That night, Grace was the first to bed.

She spent a quick five minutes in the washroom. She splashed her face with cold water and cleaned her teeth. Then, she got undressed under the grey blanket and turned in, pleased that she'd picked the bed tucked away in the farthest corner of the hut.

The other girls – even little Hazel – spent an age in the washroom and then wandered around the hut in their vests and pants, putting curlers in, slathering on face cream from pots of *Ponds* and generally taking forever to complete their ablutions.

Darkness finally fell and, as they turned off the Tilley lamps and settled down for the night, Jean piped up with a suggestion. 'I vote we change the name of this hut!'

There were creaks as girls moved in their cots, turning towards her.

'What should we change it to?' Joey asked. She shone her torch towards Jean, making shadows on the wooden walls. Jean was propped up on her elbows. She put up a hand to shield her eyes from the light.

'The huts are all named after famous Scottish men,' she said. 'Rabbie Burns, Robert Carlyle and Robert Louis Stevenson. It's no' right. We should change ours to a woman!'

'But why?' Joey asked.

Grace had wondered the same but hadn't dared ask.

'What does it matter?' Irene said. Her voice became muffled as she turned over in her bed. 'Honestly! If that's all you've got to fret about!'

Jean sighed. 'Apart from the foreman, there isn't a man around here for miles.'

'Worse luck,' Joey said.

'And we're the Women's Timber Corps. Why should our hut be named after a man?'

To her shame, Grace couldn't think of a single famous Scottish woman but no doubt Jean would have some ideas: she was awful clever.

She'd told them all earlier how she'd been due to go to university to study maths, of all things, but had put her studies on hold, to help the war effort.

'I don't mind at all,' she'd said. 'As someone in government said – I think it was Bevin: "It's better to suffer temporarily than to be in perpetual slavery to the Nazis."'

Grace's stomach clenched; she didn't know who this Bevin fella was but what he'd said made sense. To be a slave! It didn't bear thinking about.

'Actually, it was my father's idea,' Jean added. 'That I should put university on hold.'

Imagine that! A father who encouraged you to do your bit, rather than a mother who put obstacles in the way.

Grace didn't have a father. Or at least, not one she remembered or that Mother ever talked about. All she knew was that her da had died when she was a baby. As a child, whenever she'd tried to ask about him, Mother had snapped at her and changed the subject. Eventually, she'd stopped asking.

'What famous Scotswomen were you thinking of, Jean?' Morag asked.

'Mary Somerville, the Queen of Science? She helped discover Neptune. Or Frances Wright? She campaigned for the abolition of slavery. Anyone else got any ideas?'

There was silence. Jean had shamed them all with her knowledge. Grace was surprised the English girl, Seffy, hadn't piped up. But then she heard the sound of gentle snoring coming from her bed.

'I know! What about Flora Macdonald?' Joey suggested. 'The woman who helped Bonnie Prince Charlie escape?'

'Aye, that's not a bad idea,' Jean said. 'She was imprisoned and went to America and all sorts. She was brave and she led quite a life.'

'And isn't that what we'd all like?' Joey said. 'To be brave and to lead quite a life?'

The others murmured their agreement.

'Come on, let's take a vote on it,' Jean said. 'All those in favour of "Macdonald" say "aye"!'

'AYE!'

'Was that everyone? Except Sleeping Beauty, over there, of course,' Jean said. 'Grace, are you in? I couldn't hear you from here. Did you say "aye"?'

Grace lifted her head from the pillow. 'Yes,' she said. 'I did.'

She was in; she was one of the gang. It was going to be all right.

Chapter 8

Seffy woke up with a jolt.

The room was in semi-darkness. Where was she? Then she remembered: the long train journey up to the Highlands, the awful girls in her dorm, the boots that pinched and this basic wooden hut in the forest.

Perhaps the light seeping in at the curtain edges had woken her, or else this ridiculously uncomfortable bed. The mattress was so thin she could feel the slats of wood in the bedframe pressing into her back.

But no: it was the sound of crying, coming from the next bed.

She took hold of the edges of the thin excuse for a pillow and wrapped them round her ears. If she didn't get her eight hours a night, she was no good to man nor beast. Oh, this was no use: she could still hear it.

A minute later, unable to stand it any longer, Seffy leaned over and prodded the girl's shoulder. 'Hazel, isn't it?'

The girl stopped sniffing long enough to murmur, 'Yes.'

'I'm awfully sorry, Hazel, but I'm afraid I need my beauty sleep. Which you are currently preventing. I expect all of us feel like crying. We're a long way from home, tired and lonely. But crying really won't help. It won't help you and it's certainly not helping – aagh!'

A firm hand had slapped down on Seffy's head and grabbed a handful of her hair.

'YOU!'

Seffy instantly recognised that accent; it was the horrid leader girl, Irene, and she was furious. 'Come wi' me, now!'

It was an order, not a suggestion.

'Aw! Get off! Let go, then!' Seffy complained, pushing Irene's hand away. Still half asleep, she clambered out of bed and reluctantly followed Irene to the washroom. The other girls were stirring, some of them were sitting up in bed, watching. Seffy couldn't imagine what was going to happen. Were she and Irene going to have an actual fight? In their nighties?

Irene was leaning against a sink, in her long blue nightdress, with a face like thunder. She rounded on Seffy the moment she came in. 'Do you realise, you've woken everyone, with your loud la-di-da voice?' she said, jabbing her finger in the air. 'And, as for wee Hazel, have you no feeling, at all? No compassion? Ma God, you're a hard—' She stopped herself, with some effort and shook her head.

Seffy rubbed her eyes. It was a relief that Irene was only attacking her verbally but this seemed awfully unfair. "No compassion?" What did she mean?

'I don't know what you're talking about,' Seffy mumbled, making her way to a sink. Perhaps if she splashed some water on her face, it might help.

'Well, let me put you in the picture,' Irene said. 'Hazel, that poor lassie, the one you're yelling at, for crying, is in mourning! Her husband was killed last month in an air raid, in front of her. Do you know what I'm talking about now?'

Seffy had turned on the tap but she turned it off again and faced Irene.

How dreadful. But it explained Hazel's strange behaviour. Seffy held up her hands. 'I'm truly sorry. That's terribly bad luck. But how was I supposed to know?'

'Aye, well now you do! So, stop being such a witch! Understood?'

Seffy gave a reluctant nod. A witch! She'd never been called a witch in her life.

Irene swivelled around and stormed back into the hut, letting the door swing behind her.

Seffy looked down. The stone floor was soaking wet. And dirty. She was standing ankle-deep in a puddle of water. She leaned on the sink and looked at her reflection in the mirror. Gosh, what a fright. She did actually look rather witch-like. Her hair, where Irene had grabbed it, was sticking up at right angles and her face was pale and puffy.

But how should she have known Hazel was a widow? Horrible word that, "widow", worse even than "spinster". But really, she wasn't a mind-reader. The others might have warned her. Perhaps they'd been discussing it as they walked back to camp this evening. Seffy had walked back on her own.

She'd suspected the other girls might not like her; why else would they have run off and left her alone in that bothy? But Irene clearly hated her.

Seffy felt the back of her head and winced. Irene had really given it a hell of a yank. She'd had run-ins over the years at school with other girls but nothing like this. She wouldn't be surprised if a clump of her hair hadn't come out in Irene's hand.

There was nothing else for it. In the morning she'd find a telephone box. She'd reverse the charges, call Father and ask him – beg him – to remove her from this awful place, *tout de suite*. She couldn't bear it any longer. She'd find some other way of assisting the war effort. Something that didn't involve spartan living conditions and horrid girls.

Oh, but hold on a sec.

Father would take great pleasure in saying, 'I told you so!' And the twins – RAF heroes in the making – would tease her mercilessly; probably for the rest of their lives.

Seffy sighed. No, she couldn't throw in the towel after only one day. It would be a rather poor show. She turned the tap. It squeaked and spluttered and finally ejected a trickle of brownish water. She grimaced, then splashed some on her face. She took a deep breath. No matter how awful it was – and so far, it was the worst experience of her life – she'd have to stick it out for a little while longer.

Chapter 9

'Breakfast in fifteen minutes!' Irene yelled, walking round the hut, shaking the beds of those who hadn't stirred when the alarm clock went off.

When Miss McEwen had made her leader girl yesterday, she'd given Irene the alarm clock ('Although banging a spoon on a bucket also does the trick.') and a whistle for signalling the start and end of tea breaks.

It felt good to be singled out, so early on. And it wasn't only because she was older than the others. She'd told Miss McEwen about working nights in a munitions factory, in charge of thirty women and that had clinched it.

Apparently the recruit Miss McEwen had in mind for leader girl had got TB and couldn't come to the camp. 'So, you're my new choice, Mrs Calder. Don't let me down.'

'Do I get more money?' Irene had asked, with a tilt of her chin.

'An extra ten shillings and a badge for your sleeve.'

'Then I'll do it.'

Irene had reached Seffy's bed and she shook it especially hard until the mop of blonde hair moved and the girl yawned loudly and stretched. It was only a few hours since they'd faced each other in the washroom and Irene was still seething.

Little Hazel was already up, seemingly none the worse for wear, despite crying half the night. Irene gave her a sympathetic smile.

'Come on, hen,' she said, 'you'll feel better with some breakfast inside you.'

Their first camp breakfast was nothing to write home about: tea without milk and watery porridge. Even at that miserable teashop in Glasgow they'd had enough milk for tea and as many cups a day as Irene had wanted.

As for the porridge: it looked like dirty washing-up water. When she thought about the delicious creamy porridge Ma managed to make, regardless of rationing – always with a sprinkling of salt and sugar and so tasty and filling, it set you up for the day – Irene's mouth watered and she had a sudden pang of longing for home.

No, that wouldnae do at all. She must not think about home now; she must focus on the tasks ahead.

'Right, come along, girls!' she said, getting up from the dining hall table. She was given a firm nod of approval from Miss McEwen, who was standing by the door, arms crossed. 'It's time to go and meet our foreman!'

The recruits gathered in a clearing outside the huts, kitted out in their overalls and boots, berets and headscarves.

Jock the foreman climbed down from the driver's seat of a lorry stacked with logs the size of telegraph poles. He was oldish but lean and strong-looking, with a shock of grey hair and a grizzled beard. And two middle fingers missing from his left hand.

He cast an appraising eye over the girls, shook his head and slapped his forehead theatrically.

'They've sent me bairns! Cack-handed bairns too, I've no doubt. It would've helped if you'd had training before ye came!'

Bloomin' cheek. Irene wasn't a bairn and she didn't care that she hadn't been trained; it couldn't be that hard. She'd soon pick it up.

Miss McEwen gave an uncharacteristic smile. 'Jock, some of the Glasgow girls have felling experience. Miss McGinty here, for one.' She nodded at Grace from Irene's hut, the shy lassie with the mass of dark hair. 'And we've some trained measurers. Miss Ferguson, for instance.' She nodded at Jean. 'The girls who've been on the training camp can help the others, if needs be.' She slapped Jock on the shoulder. 'Dinnae fash yourself, man. It'll all be fine!'

Jock didn't look convinced but he rubbed his hands and addressed the girls. 'Right, listen up. Miss McEwen's only with us for a wee while, then she'll be away to another camp, so make the most of her, do you hear?'

No one answered.

'Do YE HEAR ME?'

'YEEEES!' the girls yelled back.

'What's all the wood for, anyway?' one of the recruits asked, gazing up at the logs on the lorry. 'Building houses?'

There was a murmur of disbelief and a few giggles.

Jock rubbed a hand against his grey beard, with a rough scraping sound. 'Noo,' he said, slowly. 'These logs were felled by your colleagues here yesterday, afore most of you arrived. And is that what you all think? That we're felling trees for houses?'

'No!' Jean piped up. 'It's more important than that.'

'Pit props, for the mines,' someone else added.

'Aye, that's right.' Jock looked down at the girl who'd asked the question about building houses. She was looking sheepish and probably wished she'd stayed quiet.

Irene craned her neck for a better look at Jock. She hadn't given a thought to why timber was so important to the war effort and as leader girl, she should know.

'Since Jerry invaded Norway – you heard about that, did you, hen? Aye, well since then, there's been a shortage of timber. We used to get lots from those Norse fellas. It's mostly needed for pit props for the mines, as that lassie said. For propping up the roofs of the tunnels.' He pointed to the logs stacked high on the lorry. 'Without these, the mines will close. If the mines

59

close, the whole country'll grind to a halt. We'll have no power. No heat, no light. So, they're important, these bits of wood.'

'It's not only for the mines, though, is it?' Jean said.

Irene smiled. She was as bright as a button, that one. And not afeared of showing off her learning, either. Good on her.

'Go on,' Jock said.

Jean pushed her glasses up her nose. 'The timber's needed for railway sleepers too and telegraph poles and building ships and planes and the charcoal's wanted for explosives and gas-mask filters and—'

'Enough, enough!' Jock said, holding up his hand and laughing. 'You get the idea, am I right? This timber is vital to the war effort and that means your work here is very important!'

Irene glanced around at her fellow recruits. He had their attention now, all right.

There was another use for timber that she'd wondered about: coffins. Surely the wood was needed for coffins, too? And crosses for graves? She shook her head, glad no one had mentioned those. It would have brought everyone down in an instant. She'd brought herself down now, thinking it. How she wished she could keep those dark thoughts at bay.

'Can anyone drive a car, by the by?' Jock asked.

'Me! I can!'

It was the English girl, Seffy, stretching her arm up, leaping in the air and generally making a scene. Irene rolled her eyes. She might have known that one would have a driving licence: she had the money for it. She was an actual lady, born with a silver spoon in her mouth, spoilt and no doubt wealthy. Irene had overheard Miss McEwen calling the girl "Lady Something-Something" yesterday in the dining hut and then taking her down a peg by telling her she'd be known as "Miss Mills" from now on.

What she was doing here, mixing with the hoi polloi? Irene hadn't said anything to the other girls but she wondered how long it would take "Miss Mills" to start trying to lord it over them all.

Irene glanced around. No one else had put their hand up to say they could drive. Like her, they probably caught a bus if they wanted to go anywhere. Or cycled, or walked.

'Have you ever driven a wagon?' Jock asked Seffy. 'A flatbed lorry, for example?'

Seffy pulled a face. 'No, but I have driven a Rolls-Royce and they're absolutely massive!'

She'd made them all laugh, at least. They probably thought she was joking. But Irene could imagine the English girl behind the wheel of a Rolls-Royce. She'd probably travelled overseas too and met royalty and never had a day's worry in her whole life.

Jock smiled. 'Aye well a lorry's even bigger, hen, but the principle is the same. I might need you to drive timber to the sawmill or the station from time to time.'

'I'll give it a go,' Seffy said.

Fair enough. At least the girl had cheered up since yesterday, when she'd been in a proper sulk. Perhaps she wasn't a completely lost cause, after all.

Miss McEwen stepped forward, arms folded over her ample bosom. She was dressed in Timber Corps breeches and a fawn Aertex shirt. She looked approvingly at the girls. 'You all look much better in your work clothes,' she said. 'I watched you arrive at the station yesterday and very fancy you looked, in your heels and dresses and furs collars. All dolled up to the nines.'

The laughter stopped when Miss McEwen glared at them. She wasn't trying to be funny. 'I even heard a tight skirt rip at the seam as someone was hauled up into the lorry.'

At that, there was yet more laughter and an embarrassed shriek from the girl concerned. Even Miss McEwen allowed herself a faint smile.

'So, that's what you wore and that's what you thought about when you were civilians. But listen up, girls, I've got news for you: you're not civilians anymore. You're a task force, you're soldiers of the forest, you're the lumberjills!'

61

Lumberjills? The girls frowned at one another and then looked questioningly at the supervisor.

Someone dared ask, 'What did you call us, then, Miss McEwen?'

'You've all heard of lumberjacks, I'm sure,' she said. 'Well, you're women, therefore, you can't be "jacks".'

'But we can be "jills",' Jean said. 'Lumberjills! It's a super name!'

There were murmurs of agreement. Aye, Irene thought, it's no' bad.

When the voices had finally quelled, Miss McEwen spoke again. 'So, now you all understand, I'll say it again: you're the lumberjills. What are you?'

The yell went up and it was like a battle cry. Irene yelled it louder than anyone, feeling a sudden swell of pride. Tears pricked her eyes and all her dark thoughts disappeared in a flash and it felt good; very good indeed.

'We're the LUMBERJILLS!'

Later that morning, deep in the forest, Jock taught them how to identify different types of trees and how to lay in and fell. Irene straightened up and wiped her brow with the back of her hand. She was already sweating.

If she was finding it tough, how were the smaller girls coping? She watched as wee Hazel bent to pick up an axe from the forest floor and staggered back a few steps. 'It weighs a ton!'

Jock nodded. 'Seven pounds, to be exact.'

'Seven – oh!' Hazel let the axe drop to the ground. 'I'll never be able to do anything with this!'

'Ye can! Small folk like you can fell trees because it's not about muscle, it's about technique and how you handle the tools. You have to let them do the work. Here, look.' He picked up the axe that Hazel had dropped. 'If you slide your hand down the shaft like this, you'll increase the momentum of each stroke. Your sink cut – think of it as a triangle, if that's easier, ladies – should be pointing the way you want the tree to fall. And as low as possible!'

He swung the axe deftly a few times and made the cut in the base of the tree.

Grace and Morag were chosen to take either end of the long crosscut saw and place it into the dip. 'Come on, now, pull it back and forth between you!'

It took about ten minutes, kneeling on either side of the trunk and pulling the saw. The girls managed to build up quite a rhythm; Morag only muttered and cursed a couple of times.

'Can you feel the tree startin' to move? Aye, well then you need to come away, stand back. And then one of you – who's brave? Come on, one of you needs to go forward and give it a shove.'

'I'll do it,' Grace said, stepping forward.

The tree creaked and then – whoosh – down it went.

Everyone cheered and someone started to sing, 'Amazing Grace, how sweet the sound . . .'

Then they sang, 'For she's a jolly good feller, she's a jolly good feller, she's a jolly good feller . . . ! And so say all of us!'

Jock nodded. 'Aye, well let's hope we don't have a sing-song every time a tree's felled, eh? But what did ye all forget?'

The girls looked at him blankly.

'You forgot to shout "TIMBER!"' he said, for about the tenth time that day. 'And now, work your way along the trunk, sawing off the branches. I'm away to see to another gang, so I'll leave you to your own devices for a wee while. Don't do any damage to yourselves while I'm gone!'

Hazel sighed and gazed mournfully at the felled tree. 'Do you think it hurts when we chop them down? I feel sorry for them.'

Irene and Grace looked at each other, wide-eyed.

'Better no' let Jock or Miss McEwen hear you say that,' Irene said. Honest to God. Trees, with feelings? She couldn't cope with thinking about that now. 'Imagine it's the trees doing their bit for the war effort,' she told Hazel. 'And besides, did you no' hear Miss McEwen say that more trees will be planted, to replace these?'

The big lassie, Grace, was sawing away at the branches of the felled tree with gusto. She actually looked like she was enjoying herself. 'Snedding!' she declared. 'That's what this is.'

Grace had told Irene she'd lived on a croft all her life, so unlike most of them, she was used to working outdoors. She'd even felled trees before. No wonder she wielded the tools like fairies' wands.

Irene frowned and glanced around. She couldn't shake the feeling that they were being watched.

Perhaps it was just the strangeness of the place making her feel this way. The pine trees, taller than houses, stood like sentinels as far as the eye could see and although it was a sunny afternoon and there were glimpses of blue through gaps in the tree canopy, it was shadowy here. She shivered; it was chilly too.

There! She'd heard a rustling sound in the nearby bushes. 'Did you hear something?' she asked Grace.

Grace shrugged. 'Probably just my stomach rumbling.'

They were hungry. Not merely peckish but starving. They'd had nothing since breakfast and that porridge had been more like gruel.

Posh Seffy had poked at it with her spoon and pulled a face. The girl was irritating, there was no doubt, and Irene could happily have clocked her last night when she'd been so mean to Hazel. But she couldn't let the girl work a full day in the forest without some breakfast inside her.

'Here, eke it out a bit. Use a wee spoon and eat it slowly,' she'd said. 'It's no' the best porridge but it'll fill you up.'

Seffy hadn't replied but she'd nodded, held her nose and eaten it.

A twig snapped. Followed by something that sounded like a giggle.

Irene turned around. 'Hey! Come out, whoever you are!' Seconds later, two boys of around nine or ten emerged from the undergrowth. 'Come on. Over here. Are there any more of you?'

The other girls had stopped working and they watched as the heads of two more boys bobbed up, making a total of four, standing in the middle of the ferns, shamefaced.

They were scruffy little beggars in short trousers and threadbare pullovers, with dirty faces and knees and tousled hair that clearly hadn't seen a brush for a while.

Irene wiped her hands on her overalls. 'What d'you think you're doing? We should be charging you a penny each to watch the show! It's dangerous here! We're chopping down trees! What would I say to your mother if one fell on you?'

The boys glanced at each other, then the tallest spoke up. 'We thought you were spies, missus.'

The girls laughed.

'Spies, is it?' Irene said. Even she had to smile. 'And exactly who do you think we'd be spying on, in the middle of a forest?'

There was a pause, then, 'My grandpa says you're no good,' one of the boys ventured. 'That you cannae do it.'

The girls stopped laughing.

'Aye,' Irene agreed. 'He could be right. For now, there's no telling where the trees might fall. Forwards, backwards, any way they please. And if you're there, hiding in the bracken, one might just land on you!' She clapped her hands and made them jump. 'Then what?'

'We'd be squashed,' one lad said.

'Flat as pancakes,' another added.

'Exactly! So, run along now and stay out of these woods, do ye hear me? AND,' Irene called after them, as they scampered off with obvious relief, 'we're no' experts yet but we'll soon be as good as any lumberjack! Tell your grandpa to put that in his pipe and smoke it!'

Moments later, a girl's sing-song voice rang through the woods. 'Ali, Jimmy, Tommy! I'm going ta skelp yer wee behinds when I get a hold of you!'

The voice got louder until the girl finally appeared. She was a skinny thing, not that much older than the boys. 'Hellooo!' she said. She was breathless, from running. 'I'm looking for my wee brothers. Have you seen them?'

The girls told her in which direction the boys had headed and she thanked them.

'They thought we were spies,' Irene said.

'Aw, I know you're not spies,' the girl said, as she turned to go. Then she added, shyly. 'You're lumberjills.' Her eyes were shining. 'And I think you're wonderful!'

Chapter 10

At the end of the first week, Miss McEwen paired Grace up with the English girl, Seffy. Hopefully it wasn't a permanent arrangement because she really was a daft coo.

'Goodness, it looks like something from a torture chamber,' she said, staring at the long crosscut saw on the ground, as though she'd never seen one before. She must've been shirking 'til now; that was probably the reason Miss McEwen had put her with Grace.

She gingerly stretched her hand towards the row of vicious-looking teeth. 'Do you suppose they're awfully sharp?'

Grace pulled her back . 'Stop! You'll have your fingers off before we even start! Here, grab hold of the other end and let's give it a go.'

They heaved the saw into the dip Grace had made with an axe. Then they knelt down on either side of the tree and tried to pull the saw back and forth between them. It kept getting jammed. Finally, it was wedged so firmly that nothing would shift it. Grace sat back on her haunches with a sigh.

'Does it need oiling?' Seffy asked, peering down. 'Honestly, I didn't imagine we'd be doing this kind of thing!'

Grace rolled her eyes. 'What did you think you'd be doing?'

'Not this! It's brutal.' Seffy looked down at her hands. 'I've broken four nails already.'

'Here!' Grace threw a pair of gloves at her.

'They're too big!' she replied, tossing them back. She yawned. No doubt she was glad the tree was resisting them; any excuse to stop work. 'I thought there'd be men!'

Grace let out a hollow laugh. 'Men?'

'Yes, men doing the hard work, like chopping down the trees. I thought we'd—'

'What? Stand around looking pretty? All the men have gone off to war. Remember that, the war?'

Seffy tutted. 'Sarcasm, my father says, is the lowest form of wit. I actually have two brothers and a boyfriend out there, preparing to fight the Luftwaffe. I'm hardly likely to forget there's a war on!'

Grace blushed and felt rotten then. She mumbled an apology. She was getting as bad as Irene. But there was something about Seffy that seemed to invite snappiness.

And she was still blethering on about the lack of men.

'I thought they'd find chaps from somewhere. They haven't all been drafted. There must still be a few older fellows around, with some life left in them. I imagined them doing the donkey work and we'd follow behind, cutting off the branches.'

'Snedding,' Grace said.

'Yes, I thought we'd do the snedding, light bonfires, that sort of thing.' Seffy paused. 'And make tea!' She laughed. 'Oh dear, does that sound pathetic?'

'Aye, it does! There are no men, d'you hear? There's only us and if we don't get moving, we'll still be here at midnight. Let's try again.'

Grace got back into position, at the base of the trunk.

With obvious reluctance, Seffy started to pull herself up too.

'Need a hand, ma'am?'

The girls froze.

68

The voice – a deep man's voice, not Scots nor English but something foreign-sounding – had come from somewhere behind Seffy. The girls swivelled around, all thought of trying to saw the tree gone.

A broad-shouldered, stocky man stepped out from behind a tree a few feet away. He wasn't tall but he was solidly built and dressed in baggy denim dungarees and a white shirt: work clothes. He pulled off his cap respectfully and gestured at the saw.

'Can I help, ladies?' American, in his early twenties, Grace guessed. His eyes and teeth were bright against his tanned face and he was smiling. Where in heaven's name had he come from? A moment after she'd told Seffy there were "no men", one had appeared, like magic.

Seffy scrambled to her feet.

'Need a hand?' he asked again, stepping nearer. 'Oftentimes when the blade gets stuck like that, it only needs a good kick and it'll start behaving.'

Before Seffy could speak – and, no doubt, gratefully accept his offer – Grace answered for them both. 'No, we don't need a hand!'

It came out harsher than she'd intended and she saw the stranger jump back, startled.

In a softer voice, she added, 'Ta very much but we can do it ourselves.'

She was still kneeling. She looked up at Seffy and jerked her head to call her back to work. 'Yanks,' she muttered.

'Hey! Who're you calling a Yank?' The man raised himself a little taller, grinning. 'We're not from the States; we're from Canada.'

"We"? There were more of them? What on earth were they doing here?

Grace shrugged. 'America, Canada. You're all Yanks to me.'

'That's not awful friendly, ma'am, if you don't mind me saying.' The smile never left his face. 'It's like someone calling you "English". You wouldn't care much for that, would you?'

'No, I would NOT!' Grace agreed, shooting a look at Seffy.

Oh, why didn't he clear off? Why did everyone assume they couldn't do the work? They could, if only folk would give them a chance.

The man was pulling his cap back on. He tugged down the peak, gave a resigned shrug and winked at Seffy. It wasn't surprising he hadn't winked at Grace; she'd hardly given him a warm welcome.

'Thanks awfully for your kind offer,' Seffy said in her clipped tones, 'but Grace is right. This is our job and we have to do it ourselves.'

'Gordy?' It was another American-sounding voice, calling from somewhere amongst the trees.

'Over here.'

So that was his name. Gordy, short for Gordon, Grace supposed.

The owner of the voice appeared out of the woods. He was taller than the first man and he was chewing gum. He slapped his pal on the shoulder and stared at the girls. He didn't have the same nice manners as his friend. 'Hey! Land Army girls!'

'We are NOT!' Seffy and Grace said simultaneously. They looked at each other in surprise and smiled.

'We're WTC: Women's Timber Corps,' Seffy said, in a particularly snooty voice. 'And who exactly are you?'

Grace had to bite her lip so as not to smile, as the two men gawped at her. They'd probably never met anyone like Seffy before.

The nice man shrugged. 'Same as you. We're woodsmen. Only you're woods*women*, I guess.'

'We're lumberjills,' Grace corrected.

'Delighted to make your acquaintance,' the gum-chewer said, giving a little bow from the waist. 'I'm Private Le Measurier and this here's Private Johnson, at your service, ladies! We're CFC, Number Thirty-Four Company, Canadian Forestry Corps.'

'You ladies new in town?' Private Johnson asked.

Seffy nodded. 'Yes, I suppose you could put it like that. We arrived on Monday.'

70

'We've been here since spring,' Le Measurier said. 'We've built a camp and a mill and a road through the forest. We brought a load of equipment over: caterpillars, sulkies, angle dozers, drum winches. The whole shebang!'

'Gosh, how impressive,' Seffy said. 'It's practically an invasion!'

Grace wondered if she were dreaming. Canadian lumberjacks in Scotland? She wanted to know why they'd come and how long they'd be staying but she was too shy to ask. She kept her eyes down, firmly fixed on the saw, to show she was waiting to start work again.

But the men seemed in no hurry to leave.

'We're felling trees a couple of miles back in the bush,' Johnson said, nodding at the forest behind them.

'Rather a long way from your patch then, aren't you?' Seffy said, archly. 'Are you lost?'

They laughed and Johnson looked sheepish. 'To tell the truth, ma'am, we heard a rumour there were women working in the woods so, yeah, I guess it's a fair cop. We wanted to see for ourselves.'

'Well, now you've seen!' Seffy said.

How did she do it? How did Seffy have such an easy way of talking to men? Of course, she had a beau – they'd had to hear all about the marvellous chap last night, as they lay in bed. And she had brothers, too. They were in the RAF and they had queer names like hers. Perhaps having brothers helped.

Grace often wished she wasn't an only child. If she'd had a big, happy family they could have shared the burden of Mother. Life would've been easier. Yes, a brother or a sister who was more like a friend. That would've been something.

She watched now, as the Canadians and Seffy chattered away. She'd talk all day, that one, if she got the chance, and no work would ever be done.

Private Johnson, the smiley one, seemed nice. Not nice in that way. Grace could never step out with someone like him, someone shorter than her. They'd look ridiculous and everyone would mock them. But she liked his easy manner. He had an open face and when he laughed – which he often did – his eyes sparkled. Even though Grace wasn't joining in with the chatter, every few seconds he glanced over, as though he were trying to include her.

They were making lots of noise, so it was hardly surprising that some of the girls working nearby started to appear. Irene was one of the first. Jock would have something to say if he came back and caught them all standing around, wasting time.

'Say, there's more of you!' Johnson said, doffing his cap again. 'Hi there, ladies!' And he introduced himself and Le Measurier.

'My, we're havin' lots of visitors, aren't we, girls?' Irene said. 'The other day it was the wee boys and today, it's—' She paused and beamed at the woodsmen. 'You!'

The fellows kept looking back into the forest behind them and although their smiles never wavered, they seemed awful jittery.

Seffy must have noticed too. 'Is anything wrong?' she asked. 'Only you keep looking around, as though you're expecting someone.'

There was an awkward pause, the men glanced at one another and then Le Measurier spoke. 'It's our sergeant, ma'am. He ain't awful keen on us talking to you ladies. Frat— something . . .' He scratched his head.

'Fraternising,' Johnson said, nodding. 'He doesn't want any of that. He's told us, in no uncertain terms.'

Seffy crossed her arms. 'Why on earth not?'

'Aye,' Irene said, hands on hips and pretending to be affronted. 'What does he think we'll do to you?'

Everyone laughed but before the woodsmen could answer, a man's voice, calling out 'Johnson!' from the forest behind them, made them jump.

Le Measurier cursed and apologised in the next breath. Grace had to smile. Even when these men swore, it sounded quaint and really not wicked at all.

They were looking left and right and didn't seem to know where to turn. It was comical and it was making the girls giggle.

'That's him, I assume?' Seffy said, shaking her head. 'Oh goodness, you're for the high jump now, chaps!'

With a glance and a nod at each other, the men took a running jump at two of the nearest trees and started shinning up them, wrapping their legs around the trunks and pulling themselves up, as effortlessly as a couple of monkeys.

Grace clasped her hands to her mouth. It was like something from a comedy film. Everyone laughed and she couldn't help but join in.

They managed to disappear into the treetops at the very moment their superior strolled through the trees and stopped dead, a few feet from where the girls were standing.

Grace had been expecting someone older, in his thirties, perhaps, but their sergeant was a similar age to his men, no more than about twenty-five. He was tall and broad-shouldered, his walk slow and steady, his face, beneath its cap, was serious.

If he found it odd that a gang of women were in the forest with axes and saws, he didn't show it. 'Afternoon, ladies,' he said, without smiling. He tipped his cap. 'Somethin' funny going on?'

Clearly, he'd heard them laughing. No one answered. The mood had changed from light-hearted to sober, the moment he'd arrived. Grace was desperate to glance up and check whether the men were completely hidden but she didn't dare.

'Ma'am,' the sergeant said, nodding curtly at Seffy, as though she were in charge. Irene coughed and moved forward.

He lifted his cap half an inch from his head in greeting. 'Sergeant Fraser, Number Thirty-Four Company, Canadian Forestry Corps.'

'Oh, fancy that!' Seffy said. 'We're a corps too. Women's Timber Corps.'

'With respect, ma'am,' Sergeant Fraser said, after a pause. 'We're not the same kind of "corps". We're infantrymen. Soldiers.'

73

'Well, we're soldiers of the forest, aren't we, girls?' Seffy said.

No one answered, so Grace cleared her throat and piped up, 'Yes, we are!' And then blushed bright red as everyone looked at her.

'Who's your commanding officer?' Seffy asked the sergeant, with a tilt of her chin. A few of the girls gasped. When he frowned at the question, she added, 'Just in case, at some future date, we need to make a complaint.'

You mightn't take to her, at least not at first, Grace thought, but you had to admire the English girl. She could be fierce; as fierce as Irene, in her own way. She wouldn't take any nonsense from the fellow.

He was nodding slowly. 'I sure hope that won't be necessary, ma'am. But you could always ask to speak to Lieutenant Coomber.'

'Lieutenant Coomber?' Seffy repeated. She said it differently to him: "lef-tenant" instead of "loo-tenant". 'Thank you, I'll remember that.'

'You'll have to excuse her,' Irene said, butting in, all smiles. 'She's English!'

Everyone, except Seffy, laughed. Even Sergeant Fraser managed a tight-lipped smile.

'WAAAA!' A screech of despair had come from somewhere within the forest but too far away to see who'd made it.

'That'll be Enid. Or Morag,' Irene muttered, rolling her eyes. 'That pair cannae get the hang of that flamin' saw, no matter how many times I show them.'

Everyone cocked their heads, listening for the rasping sound of the crosscut going successfully back and forth. But all they could hear were more howls of frustration, followed by hysterical laughter.

Sergeant Fraser looked unimpressed. 'Sorry to interrupt your work,' he said, 'but have you ladies seen any of my men? I'm a couple of fellas down. Reckon they're playing truant.'

There was silence. No one wanted to lie but no one wanted to give the men away.

He sighed. 'Ladies, it's a pretty straightforward question. Have you seen them? Yes or no? May I also add that my men oughtn't to be here, in this part of the woods. It's out of bounds and if they have been here, I sincerely apologise. We certainly won't be disturbing you again. So, have you seen 'em, lurking around?'

Seffy spoke up. 'Lurking?' She put her finger to her chin and pretended to think. 'No, I don't think so. We haven't seen anyone, have we, girls?'

'No, we haven't,' Irene said.

The sergeant tipped his fingers to his cap and gave a quick nod. Thank goodness, Grace thought. He was leaving and the men would only have to wait a minute or two, then they could come down.

But as he turned to leave, a fir cone dropped from one of the branches and fell with a soft thud onto the forest floor, a foot or so from his hobnail boots.

Grace and a few of the other girls gasped.

He stood stock-still and stared at it for a moment. Grace braced herself for the inevitable, but after another couple of seconds, he walked on, back the way he'd come.

The girls exchanged relieved glances and one or two dared to look up into the trees. Irene put a warning finger to her lips.

But it was all for nothing. The sergeant didn't look back or stop walking. He simply called out, 'OK, gentlemen, I'm countin' down from ten . . . TEN!'

Och no! He'd known they were there all along!

The girls looked up in dismay as the trees above them shook and seconds later, the men appeared, feet first, shinning down the trunks, like sailors sliding down the mast of a ship. They thumped down onto the ground simultaneously, as the sergeant's voice, getting ever fainter, was calling out, 'SIX!'

They wiped their sticky, sap-drenched hands on their dungarees, grinned ruefully at the girls, tipped their caps and raced after him. But there was a spring in their step. The shorter one gave a little jump to the side, his left leg coming up to touch his right. It made the girls giggle.

Then, they were gone. The forest closed around them and the girls erupted into laughter and exclamations of delight and surprise. Woodsmen, imagine that! And all the way from Canada! Goodness, it was the other side of the world! Did Jock and Miss McEwen know? Why hadn't anyone told them there were Canadians working in the forest?

Grace stood up and kicked the end of the crosscut saw. It shifted a couple of inches and she gave a satisfied nod. He'd been right, Johnson. A good kick was all it needed. She walked over to one of the trees the men had climbed, leaned against the trunk and gazed up into its branches.

Wee Hazel was standing nearby. 'Quite something, weren't they?' she said and Grace sent a silent thank you to the men for putting a smile on Hazel's face. 'I couldn't climb a tree like that in a month of Sundays.'

'Me neither,' Grace said, tilting her head back further. 'It's about sixty feet tall and there are a few knots and ridges in the bark but mostly, it's as smooth as a telegraph pole.'

'Do you think they really are soldiers?' Hazel asked.

Seffy heard her and spun round. 'No, I don't! They might call themselves a "corps" but proper soldiers? They can't be! Did you see any sign of a uniform? Or stripes on that sergeant's sleeve? They chew gum! Goodness, they're like something out of the Wild West!'

'I thought they were rather dishy,' Irene murmured.

'What soldiers? Who's dishy?' Enid asked, emerging from the trees with Morag in tow.

'That sergeant was arrogant,' Seffy said. 'Didn't you see the disdain on his face?'

'I thought he was all right, myself,' Irene said. 'Just because he didn't tug his forelock to you, eh? Mind, I wouldn't want to get on the wrong side of him. I bet those two laddies are getting a right dressing-down for "fraternising" with the likes of us!'

Grace bit her lip. She hoped not. That meant they wouldn't come back and she'd a sudden longing to see that fellow Johnson again.

Enid wiped her brow with the back of her hand. 'What have we missed?'

Irene laughed. 'You've managed not to saw your fingers off then, girl? Come on, we'll tell you all about it in the tea break.' She glanced at her watch and then blew hard, three times, on her whistle.

'Soldiers?' Morag was asking as everyone downed tools. 'Who's seen soldiers?'

Seffy shook her head. 'No one! Honestly, if they're soldiers, I'll eat my hat!'

Chapter 11

'They found you then,' Jock said, a few minutes later, as the girls gathered around the fire for tea. 'The Canucks?'

Seffy frowned. '"Canucks"?'

'Aye, that's what they call themselves, the fellas from Canada. I thought you girls might've had a bit of peace for a wee while yet but they soon sniffed you out, eh? There's a whole company of them working on the laird's estate upstream from here. Couple of hundred men.'

'Two hundred? That's nearly seven each!' Jean said, grinning.

The lumberjacks had been a pleasant distraction from the hard work of felling trees, Seffy supposed. The first two, at least. They'd been rather nice and up for a chat, and the panic on their faces when they'd heard their sergeant approaching had been hilarious. Even grumpy Grace had laughed.

But as for that Sergeant Fraser fellow! "With respect, ma'am", indeed! Whenever anyone said that – especially a man – it always meant the complete opposite.

The memory was making Seffy's jaw tense. He'd been so sneering and dismissive. The others hadn't noticed but it had made her want to challenge him. Asking for the name of his superior officer had probably been a step too far – she'd noticed

Irene pulling a face – but she wanted him to know she was watching him.

He was clearly better educated than the other two, and at least he wasn't chewing gum, but he'd been dressed like them in dungarees and a loose white shirt. He was, in essence, a lumberjack. Hardly anything to write home about.

But the other girls could talk about nothing else for the whole tea break and those who'd missed out on the excitement wanted to know every detail.

'Their sergeant was awful handsome,' Irene said, 'Like he'd stepped down from the silver screen!'

'Was he?' Seffy murmured. 'Can't say I noticed.'

What she had noticed – with some satisfaction – was the way Irene had stepped forward, removed her beret and flicked her hair back, all to no avail: Sergeant Fraser had paid her absolutely no attention.

He was a grump, a complete misery. Who could find that attractive? Seffy thought about Teddy, with his foppish hair – all close cut now, no doubt – and his grin and his sunny nature.

Yes, that was the kind of chap she liked. She couldn't be doing with moodiness.

The other girls might have been impressed, but that sergeant had been nothing but a dark cloud coming over the horizon. In contrast, her Teddy was like a sunbeam. And she knew which she preferred.

The Canadian men were nothing more than labourers; the kind of chaps who worked on her father's estate; the sort she'd ride past on her morning hack and hardly notice.

Irene was sitting cross-legged on the ground near Seffy. 'You know, girls,' she said, 'those Canadian boys actually came to scout us out! They must've been very disappointed! Well, look at us! We're sweaty—'

'Glowing!' Seffy corrected.

'*Sweaty* and grubby,' Irene continued. 'We've no make-up, our hair's windswept, we're dressed like ragamuffins and – not that they got close enough to notice – we're probably more than a wee bit whiffy!'

The girls groaned and laughed. A few of them sniffed their armpits.

Aside from the "sweaty" reference – ladies, after all, didn't sweat – Seffy was inclined to agree with Irene for once: the girls were hardly looking their best. What would dear Teddy think, if he could see her now? She'd even followed the other girls' example and rolled up the legs of her overalls to make shorts and she had dirty knees from kneeling at the base of the trees.

Jock blew on his tea and frowned. 'Those boys shouldna be this far into the forest, though. They weren't felling trees, were they?'

'No,' Seffy said. 'But they were awfully keen to help us. I'm happy to say, we declined their kind offer.'

'Miss Mills has got the right attitude,' Miss McEwen said, to Seffy's surprise. 'Be friendly to the Canadian boys but don't get too close. They're out for a good time, because who knows what will happen tomorrow?'

'But what are they doing here?' Seffy asked. 'This isn't their war. Their country's not in danger of being invaded. I don't understand.'

'They answered our call for help. They want to do their bit. Our king is their king too, remember,' Miss McEwen said.

'There's plenty of work for all of us; it's a mighty big estate,' Jock said. 'The forest stretches from here, the whole length of the loch and then up towards Dornoch Hill. Once they've finished logging here, they'll move on, as you girls will too. Did they not say at your interview that you needed to be mobile?'

Seffy nodded; she remembered now.

'Dinnae fash yourself, lassie,' he said. 'We've got months of work here. You'll no' be moving on for a wee while yet.'

Seffy tried to smile. Jock was trying to reassure her but the thought of staying here for months was hellish. She was desperate to move on to somewhere more comfortable, where they didn't have to work like Trojans and where she might have a chance of making a few chums. Chums definitely made life more fun. Gosh, what she'd give to have her best pal Emerald here with her now.

The others were still bleating on about those blasted Canadians. She couldn't bear it. She took her tea and moved away, to sit on a tree stump in the sunshine near Joey, from her hut, the hut which had been rechristened "Macdonald", for reasons that no one had taken the trouble to explain.

Soon Seffy's ears were pricking up. Joey had her job! How had she not known this before? Joey was working with the horses. Seffy overheard her telling a couple of other girls how she had to attach chains to logs and run alongside, as the timber was dragged out of the woods.

'You have to be fair nimble!' Joey said. 'I have to jump the chains and swerve between the trees the whole time. I never stop!'

Seffy sidled up to her. 'How did you swing that?' she asked.

Joey looked puzzled. 'I didnae "swing" anything. I worked with horses over near Forres, on a farm, before I came here. I drove the plough and the cart. It's not easy, if that's what you're thinking. Look.' She held up a bare leg. 'I'm covered in bruises.'

Seffy nodded. She'd take those bruises over broken nails, blisters and the sheer effort of swinging an axe or trying to pull one of those blasted saws through a tree trunk, any day. It wasn't fair! Everyone else was getting the good jobs. Jean was a measurer, although you had to be frightfully clever to do that, so that definitely counted Seffy out; Irene was leader girl, promoted as soon as she set foot in the place and Joey was working with the horses – something that Seffy had more or less been promised at her interview. It felt like the other girls were officers, while she was still a foot soldier.

She nudged Joey. 'How much will you take for it? Working with the horses?'

Father always said everyone had their price. Joey didn't look the type to have pots of cash; Seffy was sure she could be persuaded. 'I'll buy it from you.'

Joey turned to look at her. Her big brown eyes were incredulous. 'You cannae do that!'

'No, you're right. We'd best wait until Miss McEwen leaves the camp or we'll get a ticking-off. But once she's gone, we could do a swap. Horses for felling. What do you say?'

Joey laughed and shook her head. 'You're incredible! Do you think you can waltz through life buying anything you want? Just because you've got money?' She'd raised her voice and a few of the girls sitting nearby were watching them, curiously.

Joey's eyes narrowed and her voice became harder. She put her face up close to Seffy's. 'I don't want to give up ma job. It's not for sale!' She got up and went to rinse out her cup in the bucket, leaving Seffy sitting alone.

Be like that then, she thought. Why had Joey taken such offence? She was pally with Enid and Morag and if she swapped to the felling gang, she could spend all day with them. Plus, she'd have extra money from Seffy in her pocket, into the bargain.

Oh, but how much might Joey have wanted? Seffy didn't actually have a huge amount of spare cash. She couldn't remember a time when she'd had to even think about money, or the lack of it. But Emerald's wedding last month had been an expensive do: new hat, hairdo, outfit, hotel, champagne. It had fairly wiped her out and, of course, there was no allowance from Father anymore.

Oh, blast. She should have kept her mouth shut and not said anything to Joey about swapping jobs.

Now that was someone else she'd upset.

Chapter 12

Saturday 20th June 1942

Dearest Emerald – or should I say, Mrs Bertrand Jamieson!!!

I hope you and Bertie are well and had a perfectly wonderful honeymoon, all two days of it. Better than nothing, I'm sure.

I've been at the camp for a whole five days now (feels like five years) and it's Saturday. Hallelujah, a half-day!

We've just got in from the woods, after lunch around the fire: beetroot pieces – that's sandwiches to you and me (perfectly horrid but – top tip – the beetroot makes a rather good lipstick).

Now, I'm stretched out on my bed writing this, totally fagged out, hardly able to move.

Where shall I start, dearest Emmie? It's awfully tough, being in the Timber Corps. Long story but I'm not working with the horses after all and I tried to swap with someone but no go. However, I AM to be allowed to drive the lorry which, I've persuaded myself, is almost as good.

I have actually been taught how to fell a tree. And I can do it. (Just about!) Can you imagine? I can hardly believe it myself. So, that's the good news. The bad news is: I've never worked so hard in my life. Remember that trip to the

Languedoc, when we picked grapes, for a lark? Hellish, wasn't it, and we only lasted a day? Well, think of that and times it by about a thousand.

I'm getting muscles on my muscles. Before we're finished, I'm going to have the build of . . . I don't know . . . a builder! Or a navvy. I've already got blisters from the horrid, ill-fitting boots and I ache from head to toe, as though I've been in a fight. (Talking of which, I was nearly in a fight – on the first night – with a tough Glaswegian in my dorm. It didn't actually come to fisticuffs in the end but she pulled my hair and called me a witch and now we do our very best to avoid one another).

Weather-wise, it's actually warm here. As I write, we've got all the windows open and a jolly nice breeze is wafting through. But, the others say, just wait until winter, when there'll be ice on the inside of the windows and we'll all get chilblains and bronchitis, so that's something to look forward to!

And talking of the other girls, they're . . . well, they're not half as friendly as I'd hoped. (Especially the one who called me a witch!) So don't worry about anyone usurping your position as "Best Friend".

I'm doing my absolute best but I seem to offend someone every time I open my mouth. They're completely lacking any sense of humour. Perhaps that's a Scots thing?

I've been trying to make them laugh. Remember Fiona-three-fiancés, who had to label her engagement rings to ensure she didn't go out dancing with the wrong chap, wearing the wrong ring? I know, a hoot! Well, they didn't find that funny at all.

And Daphne Richmond and that awful fellow she was with? Whatsisname? She had such a pash on him! She was totally cracked on him, wasn't she? Remember how I did her a favour by luring him away?

They didn't find that story entertaining either. Not in the slightest.

I'm in a blue funk – there I've said it. I've put off writing to Teddy or the parents because I don't want to sound down in the dumps but I'll have to do it soon else they'll worry. It's hard to keep up a cheerful tone but at least with you, I can be myself.

Do write and tell me how married life is treating you, but please – I beg – not a word about ladies' luncheons or choosing soft furnishings. Do remember, some of us are working!

Love as always, write soon.

Your friend,

Seffy xxx

PS: Almost forgot: everyone (except moi!) got awfully excited this week when we discovered a company of Canadian lumberjacks working in the woods, not far away. We actually bumped into some. They look and sound terribly glamorous but appearances can be deceptive! To my mind, they're gum-chewing, rather uncouth chaps. They haven't made another appearance so far and I'm hoping they'll leave us well alone. However, something tells me we haven't seen the last of them!

Chapter 13

The door to the hut burst open as Seffy was dotting the final exclamation mark in her letter.

It was Jean and she was panting. She pushed her spectacles up and took a deep breath. 'Good news! Tea dance in the village, this afternoon! And a bring-and-buy! In aid of "Warship Week"!' She frowned. 'Or perhaps it's the "Troops' Comfort Fund"? Anyway, something worthy.'

Irene, who was also lying on her cot, propped herself up on her elbows. 'How do you know?'

'I've just bicycled past the poster in the shop window and whizzed up the hill to tell you. We should support it! Let's all put on a frock and go!'

The others grunted and sighed; no one seemed particularly keen.

'It's all right for you, Jean, swanning around, measuring trees,' Morag said, sitting up. 'We're grafting all day. And you have a bicycle for getting around. No wonder you've the energy for dancing.'

Morag flopped back down on her bed. It was true that as a measurer, Jean didn't have to do the same hard physical work as the rest of them, but there were more diplomatic ways of saying it. Morag was miserable. "Crabbit", as they said up here. Compared to her, Irene was a little ray of sunshine.

'Aye, Morag's right,' Joey said. 'We're all fair scunnered! We need to rest!'

Irene swung her legs off the bed. 'Don't be so dull, you lot!' She marched around the hut, tweaking the other girls' feet. Seffy pulled hers in just in time. 'There'll be plenty of time for restin' when you're six feet under.'

Seffy winced and glanced at Hazel. Honestly, if she'd said that, Irene would probably have grabbed her hair again and called her a witch.

Although Hazel had rallied a little since she'd arrived and was managing the odd smile, she was still mostly in a world of her own. Everyone was tiptoeing around her, being careful what they said.

But Irene had got away with it. Hazel seemed to be dozing on her cot, so she probably hadn't heard the insensitive reference to being "six feet under".

'Come on!' Jean said. 'At least dancing's not rationed! It'll be fun! We could meet some villagers. Make new friends?'

Seffy looked up. 'All right, I'll come,' she said. As she wasn't likely to make chums here, she might have more luck in the village.

'Good,' Irene said. 'Now, what about the rest of you? You know, there's always a chance some of those Canadian laddies might be there!'

Enid, Morag and Joey suddenly found they had the energy to get off their beds. They started rooting around in their bags for something to wear.

'What about you, Hazel, hen?' Irene asked.

Hazel's eyes flickered open for a second. She shook her head. No one tried to persuade her otherwise.

'Grace?' Seffy called. Grace was sitting cross-legged on her bed. She was the only one so far, apart from Hazel, who hadn't made a move to get ready.

'I don't dance,' Grace said.

'What do you mean?' Seffy asked. 'Everyone dances!'

Grace squirmed. 'I don't.'

'But there must be one dance you like! If you don't foxtrot, then perhaps the tango and if you don't like the waltz then there's the—'

'For God's sake,' Irene said. 'Are you going to list every dance in the world? We'll be here all day. Leave the girl be! She doesnae want to come and that's the end of it! Grace and Hazel are staying here; the rest of us are going. End of story. Everyone who's coming, get yourselves ready, NOW!'

The village hall was an uninspiring one-storey wooden building set on a patch of grass across the road from the shop.

The door had been propped open with a chair and there was a flat cap laid out on it. The girls dropped their pennies in as they filed inside.

Children were tearing around, sliding on the wooden floor and a gramophone was playing a crackly recording of "Roll Out The Barrel".

The babble of voices they'd heard on their approach fell silent, and all heads turned in their direction.

It was mostly old chaps, seated on wooden chairs around the edge of the hall and women in headscarves and pinnies, laying out sandwiches on a trestle table. There were – thank goodness – a couple of younger women, about their age. Land girls? Yes, Joey gave a cry of delight as she recognised them.

There was no sign of anyone male between the ages of about seven and seventy. Definitely no Canadian lumbermen. It didn't bother Seffy, of course, but the other girls were going to be awfully disappointed.

Gosh, this was going to be a dull affair. It certainly didn't seem like a good hunting ground for potential pals. She felt inclined to walk straight out again, picking up her penny on the way. But bossy Irene was behind her. When Seffy turned, she and Irene came face to face. Irene made a twirling "turn around" gesture with her finger and gave her a none-too-gentle shove in the back.

Jean was saying 'Hullooo!' to everyone and introducing herself. The old men leaned forward in their seats, cupping their hands to their ears. She had to get up close and yell. 'WE'RE WORKING IN THE WOODS!'

'Oh aye? Is that right?'

'Lassies? Lassies as lumberjacks? Now, that I have to see!'

'You cannae do it, hen. You don't have the strength.'

'Actually,' Jean said, 'it's not all about strength; there's technique too, you know. And being canny with leverage and pivot points.'

Jean sounded jolly knowledgeable but most of the old fellows couldn't hear her and those who could, weren't convinced.

'What does that foreman of yours have to say about it? He had some good men working under him before they were drafted. Aye, very good men indeed.'

'And now,' Irene said, joining in, 'he's got some very good girls instead!'

One of the chaps shook his head. 'It's nae job for a decent woman.'

Jean sighed and pulled Irene away. 'Come on. We're wasting our time. Shall we dance?'

Irene laughed. 'I thought you'd never ask!'

Seffy leaned against the back wall with her arms crossed, trying to look unconcerned and not at all like a wallflower. Morag and Enid had also paired up for the foxtrot and were twirling around the floor. They looked very different, wearing summer dresses, instead of their usual breeches and boots.

Joey was dancing with one of the land girls she knew.

Nobody had asked Seffy.

She'd learned ballroom dancing at school but it had been terribly dull, as there were no men, apart from their elderly dance master and the girls had danced with one another, like today. Occasionally a dance was arranged with the nearby boys' school but it was excruciating, attempting the Viennese Waltz with a spotty juvenile who didn't want to be there either.

Things had improved during the season, once she'd left school. There were men, for one thing; dozens of handsome men. And Seffy had to admit, Mummy had been right.

'You'll thank me for all those dance lessons one day, darling,' she'd said, 'when you're spinning around the floor with the most dashing man in the room!'

Seffy had had the most wonderful time and it helped that she was a super dancer.

'Light on her feet and easy on the eye', as she'd overheard a chap say once and she was quite sure he'd been talking about her.

It had been such fun but none of the men meant anything, of course, because for as long as she could remember, Teddy Fortesque had been the chap for her.

Dear Teddy. He was mad about her, and her parents approved because he was the son of their dearest friends, so it would be a kind of "alliance", once Teddy got round to popping the question. But he had other things on his mind, like fighting the Luftwaffe. She would have to be patient: all in good time.

'Persephone?' an upper-class English voice cut into her thoughts, making her jump. 'Is that really you? Wh-what on earth are you doing here?'

For a few seconds, Seffy couldn't place the middle-aged woman in a flowery apron standing in front of her. But then, in a flash, she realised who it was: Aunt Dilys!

She was a slightly shorter, younger version of Father. Dilys was his sister, after all, so it was hardly surprising that they looked alike.

Seffy couldn't remember the last time she'd been in the same room as Dilys but there was no mistaking that Roman nose and pointed chin. They looked super on Father – quite distinguished – but those features were rather too severe for a woman's face. Even in the midst of this queer family reunion, Seffy felt a pang of disappointment – and pity – for Aunt Dilys. She really was rather plain.

'Oh, hullo! Aunt Dilys?' Seffy stood on tiptoe and gave her aunt a kiss on her powdery cheek. 'Yes, it's me,' she added, unneccesarily. 'I did wonder whether I might bump into you!'

Dilys seemed incredulous. 'But why? Goodness, how many years has it been? I only recognised you because you're the image of your mother when she was your age. What are you doing here?' She cast a furtive look around the hall. 'Are your parents with you?'

'Gosh, no! I'm *toute seule*, as they say. I'm here with the Timber Corps, Aunt Dilys! I'm a lumberjill!'

Her aunt visibly blanched. 'The Timber Corps?'

'I know, isn't it a hoot? I'm as surprised as anyone but one has to do one's duty! I'm usually in overalls, of course. This—' she tugged at her dress '—is a rare treat! Didn't Mother write? Must have forgotten. She's been in a total tizz since the twins and I enlisted. Hardly knows if she's coming or going.'

Dilys frowned. 'What does your father have to say about it all?'

'Oh, he's pleased as punch with the boys and furious with me. He didn't mind the idea of the Land Army. Probably imagined me as a wholesome milkmaid! But at the interview, they offered me the WTC.' She shrugged. 'And despite his protestations, I stuck to my guns and here I am!'

Dilys still looked dumbstruck. 'The Timber Corps? Well, well. And how are you finding it?'

'Outrageously hard!' Seffy said, rolling her eyes.

Her aunt nodded. 'I wonder how long you'll stick it?'

Seffy was taken aback. That was rather caustic. It was on the tip of her tongue to tell her aunt that, in actual fact, the only reason she was here was because of her and that stupid photograph on the top of their piano.

'Well . . . I . . .' she started. 'The thing is, I've got a bet with my brother—'

'Perseus or Ptolemy?'

'Percy. He reckons I won't last a month and I want to prove him wrong.'

Dilys pursed her lips; she seemed distracted. But perhaps she was always like this. From the occasional comments her parents had made over the years, Seffy had concluded that her aunt was, at best, eccentric; at worst, loopy.

'Are you at the camp in the forest?' Dilys asked, focusing on Seffy again. 'You're not far from me. I live on the road that runs past the camp.' She yawned. 'I suppose I should invite you for tea.'

She might sound more enthusiastic. Seffy was tempted to say, 'Oh really, there's no need, Aunt.' But it would awfully rude and she couldn't let standards slip completely, so she made an encouraging murmur instead.

Dilys fished a scrap of paper and a pen out of her apron pocket and jotted something down. 'Here's the address. Drop me a line when you're ready and we'll make arrangements.'

Seffy smiled and took the chit. '"Ballykinch House"', she read. 'Lovely. Thank you so much.' She popped it into her handbag, praying that both she and Dilys would quickly forget this conversation had ever taken place.

'Aren't you dancing?' Dilys asked, nodding at the other girls, who were dancing now to "Boogie Woogie Bugle Boy". Some of the village women were up on the floor too and one or two children, although they clearly didn't know the steps.

Before Seffy could answer, she added, sharply, 'No, I don't suppose this is your cup of tea at all. Can't think why you came.'

Why did her aunt have to be so abrasive? Gosh, she was as prickly as a porcupine.

Seffy could hardly say she'd come looking for friends but as the hall was full of children, old men and middle-aged women, it had been a complete waste of time. A duffer of an event, in fact.

'Actually, some of the girls were hoping the Canadian lumberjacks would be here,' she said. 'Not me! I'm practically engaged!'

Dilys pursed her lips. 'Hmm, of course you are. Well, your colleagues are out of luck, as you can see. The Canadians are infantrymen, as well as lumberjacks. "Sawdust fusiliers" they call them in the village. On Saturdays they have military training.'

So, they were soldiers, then. Of a kind.

'You tell your pals to be careful,' Dilys went on. 'Those Canadian boys have already turned a few girls' heads. They've got money and they like to throw it around. But don't fall for their lines. Before you know it, they'll be heading back to where they came from. Now—' She looked Seffy up and down. 'Did you bring anything for the bring-and-buy?'

Seffy shook her head. She hadn't and neither had any of the others.

'Well, never mind,' Aunt Dilys said. 'You can at least do the buying part. Everything's laid out on the table over there.

Seffy was still thinking about Dilys' comment, about the Canadians, turning girls' heads. It was the second warning she'd had. Miss McEwen had said something similar. The other girls – her "colleagues" as Dilys called them – were hardly Seffy's chums but she should probably warn them. Jean, for example, could easily be swept along by a smooth Canadian's chat. She seemed awfully naïve in spite of her intelligence.

Dilys gave a sudden start and raised a forefinger, as though remembering something. She shot off into a room at the back of the hall without another word.

When she returned, seconds later, she was holding a plate laden with delicious-smelling pastries. 'Take those round, will you, Seffy? Make yourself useful.'

They looked and smelled marvellous. Surely they couldn't be . . . ?

'Sausage rolls!' Dilys announced. 'Mock,' she added, in a quieter voice. 'Mostly haricot beans and pastry.'

As there wasn't much else to do, Seffy took the plate. Once Dilys' back was turned, she popped one of the sausage rolls into her mouth. Ouch, it was hot; just out of the oven. Then she ate another, for luck. She meandered over to the other side of the hall, dodging the dancers and put the plate down on an empty table. There, people could help themselves. She wasn't a waitress, after all.

When there was finally a break in the music, Seffy grabbed Irene and Jean and suggested they might want to come and browse the "bring-and-buy" table. If they didn't, Dilys would reappear and start chivvying them. They only needed to buy one thing between them, she said, to show willing.

Luckily the items laid out on the tressle table weren't too expensive. There was a jar of marmalade, a punnet of raspberries, a half-chewed straw hat, a paperback and a tea strainer.

'There's not much left,' the dour woman sitting behind the table said. 'Did ye bring anything yourselves?'

Jean shook her head and apologised.

'We ought to have brought something,' she murmured, as she picked up the romance novel and handed over her money.

'But what?' Seffy asked. 'A branch, or a few fir cones? Or a log! We could've brought some firewood.'

Jean wrinkled her nose. 'It's hardly our wood to give away.'

Irene took the book from Jean and looked at the title. '"Princess Lily-of-the Valley",' she read. 'Fancy that: it's about you, Seffy!'

Seffy rolled her eyes. Ha ha, very funny.

The woman standing behind the table had been listening. 'Are you the lassies working on the laird's estate?'

'Aye, we are,' Jean said. 'We're the lumberjills! I'm Jean Ferguson, pleased to meet you.' She extended her hand but the older woman made no move to take it.

'It's beyond me, why they've sent good men away and brought in lassies to do their work. Criminal, that's what it is.' The woman walked off, shaking her head and muttering.

'So much for making new friends!' Seffy said, laughing. Jean, normally so cheery, was looking awfully glum. Seffy gave her shoulder a reassuring pat.

Meanwhile, Irene had made a beeline for the old chaps sitting around the edge of the hall. She was perched on a chair next to one of them. In moments, he was chuckling at something she'd said and slapping his thigh. What on earth could be that funny? As he laughed harder, he began to cough and wheeze. The woman from the bring-and-buy bustled over and shooed Irene away.

Jean was watching too. 'They hate us,' she said.

'They don't hate you,' Aunt Dilys said, bustling up from behind, with another plate of pastries. 'They simply have to get used to the idea of you. They've never seen women doing men's work before. You're like wee wild beasties, running around with no parents keeping you in check.'

Seffy laughed. She rather liked the idea of being a "wee beastie".

'And they're worried you'll be a bad influence on their youngsters,' Dilys added. 'One of the village girls wants to join you, I understand, and she's only just left school. Her mother's against it but she's determined.'

'You seem to know an awful lot about it,' Jean said, 'if you don't mind me saying.'

'Oh, this is my aunt,' Seffy said, suddenly remembering her manners. 'This is Jean – erm, sorry, I've forgotten your surname.'

'Ferguson.'

'Jean's a measurer, Aunt.'

Dilys looked impressed. 'Are you indeed, my dear? Clever girl. Jolly good. Mock sausage roll?' She proffered the plate and Jean took one and thanked her.

'My aunt was – at least, I think so – weren't you a once a lumberjill yourself, Aunt Dilys? During the last war?'

Her aunt's face closed down. 'I don't know what you mean,' she said, coldly. 'And in any case, it wasn't called that in my day.'

Jean was reaching out for another mock-sausage roll but her hand fell into the air.

Aunt Dilys had stormed off.

* * *

95

The girls were in a low mood when they finally left the village hall and trudged back up the hill to their camp. The lane was quiet, except for the tweeting of birds overhead, so they walked three abreast.

The gramophone had broken after half an hour, so apart from a few minutes spent dancing – with each other – early on, there hadn't been much to do. The tea and sandwiches had soon run out and the welcome, they all agreed, hadn't exactly been warm.

'Everyone thinks we're useless,' Morag said. 'Maybe they're right.'

'No,' Enid insisted. 'We can do this. We passed the medical and the interview. They wouldn't have sent us here if they didn't think we could do it.'

'Aye, but the villagers didn't exactly roll out the red carpet, did they?' Irene said.

'They're suspicious because we wear slacks and we're doing men's work,' Jean said. She pushed up her glasses. 'It's not ladylike. They're worried we won't be chaste or monogamous.'

'She means,' Irene said, 'they're worried we'll turn into tarts.'

'It was the same in the Land Army,' Joey said. 'The farmers' wives hated us; they thought we were man-eaters. They'd change our slogan from "Back to the land!" to "Backs to the land!" but honestly, we were too fagged to think of anything like that!'

That raised a laugh.

'And to think my father was worried about my reputation being ruined if I joined the services,' Seffy said, shaking her head. 'It seems, as women, whatever you do for the war effort, people get the wrong idea.'

'We need to prove we're not all bad,' Jean said. 'That we're just ordinary girls.'

Speak for yourself, Seffy thought. She was the daughter of an earl; she was anything but ordinary. But now wasn't the time or place to say it.

'And the Canadian boys didn't even show up,' Enid said, pulling out her bottom lip.

'Ah – and I know why!' Seffy said, pleased to finally know something that the others didn't. 'They're on manoeuvres at weekends, apparently. Military training. Running round with rifles, that kind of thing.'

'So they *are* soldiers, then!' Irene said, triumphantly.

Seffy pulled a face. 'That bunch? They might call themselves soldiers but I wouldn't rely on them if Jerry comes! They'll hide up in the trees!'

'Oh, I don't know.' Jean tilted her head and gazed dreamily into the distance. 'I can imagine them handling guns. When they talk in that lovely drawl of theirs, they sound exactly like gangsters in the films.'

'I almost forgot,' Joey said, holding up her finger. 'All this talk of fighting's reminded me: we've been challenged to a tug of war!'

'That'd better be a joke!' Irene said.

'Who's challenged us?' Enid asked.

Joey side-stepped up the lane, swinging her arms and giggling. 'My pal Alice, the land girl I was dancing with. There's a fete next month, with games and contests. She asked if we wanted to challenge the land girls to a tug of war!'

Everyone except Jean groaned.

'Noooo!' Enid said, shaking her head.

'They're our rivals, the Land Army,' Jean said. 'We have to do it!'

'We cannae do it,' Irene said, shaking her head. 'We need all our strength for learning how to be expert foresters and proving everyone wrong.'

'Aye,' Morag agreed. 'It's all right for the land girls, collecting eggs and milking cows. They've got it easy.'

Joey had flushed bright red.

'What?' Irene demanded.

Joey winced. 'I told her we'd do it.'

'Right, well you can un-tell her!' Irene said. 'Let her ask the girls from the other huts. Some of them might be up for it. There's no way we've got time – or energy – to organise ourselves into a team.' She suddenly glanced behind and yelled, 'Watch out!'

The girls screamed and leaped into the hedgerow, as a truck roared past, tooting its horn. There were dozens of swarthy uniformed men hanging out of the open back.

'Who are they?' Joey asked.

'They're POWs,' Jean said. 'See the red circles on their jackets? They're Italian prisoners!'

The men were calling out, blowing kisses and scrambling over one another to get a better look at the girls.

'*Bella, bella!*' they shouted, pointing at Irene and whistling. They were throwing pieces of paper out of the truck.

Seffy huffed. What a performance! It wasn't exactly seemly.

But the others thought it was a hoot. They ran around the lane, laughing, picking up the notes, which appeared to have been written on lavatory paper and waving back at the men.

'Aw, give them a wave, hen!' Irene said but Seffy crossed her arms and raised her eyebrows. How unpatriotic! Let the others do what they liked; she wasn't going to wave and smile at the enemy.

The truck disappeared around a bend in the lane.

The excitement had only lasted for half a minute but it had certainly cheered the other girls up.

'They might have given us a lift!' Irene said, laughing. The truck had looked pretty full to Seffy but presumably Irene wouldn't have minded squashing up. Old, young, in uniform or civvies, Irene did seem to rather like the chaps.

'What does it say?' Enid asked Joey, who was trying to decipher the note she'd retrieved from the hedge.

'Dunno. It's in Italian.'

'Billet-doux,' Morag said, nodding. 'Probably filth.'

Irene laughed. 'I do hope so!'

Jean was gazing into the distance. 'I expect they were captured in North Africa,' she mused. 'And now they're working on the farms.'

'Perhaps they'll be sent to work with us,' Irene said. She fanned herself with her hand. 'It would be terribly distracting, though. We wouldn't get a stroke of work done!'

'They didn't look too glum, did they?' Jean said. 'For prisoners? We probably made their day. Don't expect they've seen girls for a while. And perhaps they don't mind being here. It's probably better than being on the front.'

'They liked you, Irene, didn't they?' Enid said.

Jean glanced at Irene: they were walking side by side. 'Yes, you look Italian, Irene, with your dark hair. Perhaps you reminded them of their sweethearts back home.'

Irene gave a nonchalant shrug but she was clearly pleased. 'Aye, perhaps. Shame they weren't at the tea dance, eh?' She sighed. 'There's a definite lack of men in these parts.'

Jean frowned. 'There's a definite lack of men everywhere!'

'But what about the Canadians?' Enid asked.

Irene shook her head. 'No, forget them. Their sergeant made it very clear they're under strict orders to keep away from us!'

'But you told us they might be at the tea dance,' Enid pointed out.

'I only said that to get you to come out. And it worked and now we've seen those Italian fellows, I'd say we've had a good time. No, girls, I think we need to face facts: while we're here, we're going to be doing an awful lot of dancin' with each other!'

Chapter 14

Sunday 21st June 1942

Dear Teddy,

Well, I've arrived in camp and it's peculiar and frightfully Scottish. Och aye the noo!

As for the uniform . . . ! Thank heavens you can't see me. I know you'll say I'd be perfect even in a sack (and the overalls are rather like wearing a sack) but in the actual uniform, I look as though I'm off to a gymkhana! Shirt, cord breeches and boots. Very fetching, I'd rather have had a stylish WRENS outfit but you know how Father was against the services. (He didn't want me exposed to "the ways of the world" apparently! Don't laugh. He's only trying to protect me. You know I've always been a Daddy's girl. I expect I always will be.)

But at least I've escaped!

The parents are wonderful of course but it's nice not to have them breathing down my neck for once and while I wouldn't, for a moment, compare what we're doing here, to what you chaps are doing up in the air, it's rather satisfying to feel that one is doing one's bit, at last.

100

There is something I should tell you: there are chaps in the forest. There's absolutely no need to worry ("fret", they say here) or be jealous. We saw a truckload of POWs (Italian) yesterday, off to work on the farms and there are Canadian lumberjacks on the other side of the estate. They caused quite a stir amongst the other girls but I am more than resistant to their apparent charms!

Let's be honest with each other, dear Teddy, shall we, in the weeks and months ahead? You're certain to cross paths with girls at some point – WAAF women too I expect, once you're back in Blighty – and I'd hate for either of us to string the other along, so let's be truthful.

That's all I wanted to say. Oh, and I can hear you now, chuckling at me and saying, 'Chin up, old girl!' And so, that's what I shall do: keep my chin up.

Keep well and safe, my darling. I miss you terribly.

Love from,

Seffy

xxx

Sunday 21st June 1942

Dear Mummy,

Just back from church and as Sunday is our day of rest, thank goodness, I've finally got a moment to write.

I hope you and Father are well. Please send him my love but keep schtum re: what I'm about to say. He'll only say "I told her so" and I honestly couldn't bear it.

The truth of the matter is, I'm not sure I'm cut out for this Timber Corps lark. There must be easier ways of doing one's bit.

It's incredibly hard. We're up at 7 a.m. (it gets light here at 4 a.m. so I suppose I should be grateful they don't make us start then) and we don't finish until five o'clock, by which *time I'm fit to drop. Perhaps I'd have been better off in the WVS, after all.*

On the plus side (I've been desperately trying to think of something positive) the weather's not bad, for Scotland. No rain (hurrah!) and it's warm and only slightly midge-y.

But, the food's atrocious, the portions are minuscule and I honestly don't think I can stand much more. You couldn't possibly send an emergency food parcel, could you? No, on second thoughts, I mightn't be here to receive it. I hate to be a giver-upper but I think Percy might be getting his £10, after all.

Oh, almost forgot! I bumped into Aunt Dilys yesterday at a little event in the village! Small world and all that. She sends her love to you both. She's invited me for tea, which will be super.

All my love – kiss Trixie for me,
Seffy xxx

She read the letter through. Gosh, it was a litany of complaints. And there were a couple of white lies. She hadn't gone to church, of course – none of them had. Someone had suggested it, half-heartedly, but they'd all plumped for a lie-in instead.

The part about Aunt Dilys wasn't true either. She hadn't sent her love but perhaps she would have, had she not stomped off the moment Seffy mentioned her having once been in the Timber Corps. It had been frightfully odd; as though Dilys was ashamed or didn't want to be reminded of it.

Gracious, this letter was hardly going to cheer Mummy up. It was more likely to bring on one of her heads. She hadn't been in the best frame of mind when Seffy had left home to join the corps.

'First the boys, now you,' she'd said, tearfully, as Henderson pulled up in the car, to take her to the station. It turned out Mummy had merely been putting on a brave face when the boys announced they'd enlisted.

'Inside, I wanted to die,' she confessed. 'I wanted to hug them and beg them not to go.'

Remembering that now, Seffy sighed, ripped up the letter – never mind the paper shortage – and started again.

Sunday 21st June 1942

Dear Mummy,

    I hope you and Father are well.

    Just back from church and as Sunday is our day of rest, I've got time to write and let you know that I'm having the most wonderful time . . .

Chapter 15

'Ma'am, you might wanna think about movin'.'

Seffy stiffened. She recognised that voice: it was him again, that Sergeant Fraser, from last week. From the sound of him, he was standing a few yards behind her. So much for not disturbing them again.

'I beg your pardon?' she asked, without turning around. She was putting a dip into a tree and it was taking all her concentration. Grace had nipped off into the woods to answer a call of nature and Seffy was determined to finish before she returned.

Seffy's axe was wedged firmly in the trunk and she'd been so intent on pulling it out, she hadn't heard him approach. She planted her feet wide, bent her knees, grasped the axe handle tightly and gritted her teeth as she tried to yank it free.

She could sense him waiting and watching. No doubt about to make some unhelpful remark. Oh, this was useless. She stopped tugging, released her grip on the axe and turned.

Their eyes met. He was gazing at her without a flicker of interest. It was queer; most men went all silly around her. But not him.

'You should move,' he said, more forcefully. His cap was low on his head and he hadn't tipped it to her this time. His voice was calm and perfectly polite but really, what right did he have, to tell her what to do?

Seffy huffed, put her hands on her hips and took a step towards him. 'We absolutely will not!'

She had a good mind to make good her threat and put in a formal complaint. This was harassment. He was only a sergeant, after all. There were plenty of ranks above him and the Timber Corps had every right—

She screamed as he suddenly ran, launching himself at her and grabbing her around the waist. They fell onto the ground with a thud and rolled to the side, crushing bracken and ferns. The world turned green and brown. Nearby, with a great whooshing sound, followed by an earth-trembling crash, a tree fell to the earth.

The forest floor had actually bounced.

She was winded. The closest she'd come to this feeling was being catapulted off a horse. WHAM! The shock was the same. But when one was thrown by a horse, there wasn't a six-foot man involved, his limbs tangled in yours, his weight pressing down on you from behind.

Seffy took a gulp of air and closed her eyes, braced for something else – the full force of a ten-foot branch, say – to hit them. It would be the end of everything.

But nothing happened. A wave of relief washed over her. Her life hadn't flashed before her, the woods were quiet again. She opened her eyes. She was alive. Overhead, a red squirrel scampered along a branch, its tail waving like a flag.

Wait a minute, though. What was this? She was lying on the ground with a strange man, closer than if they were dancing a waltz.

'Get OFF me!' she said, struggling against him.

Fraser loosened his grip on her waist but didn't make a move to get up. 'Shh,' he whispered. 'Wait a sec. Let's give 'em a fright.'

'OH, MA GOD!'

That was Enid's strident voice. She and Morag had been working together not far from Seffy and Grace. They must have been responsible for sending the tree plummeting in the wrong direction.

'We've killed her!' Enid said. 'NOOO! She was here, wasn't she? English Seffy? Look, there's her axe still stuck in the tree. But where's she gone? Oh, God. She's not under there is she? Look and see if her boots are sticking out. Morag, go on! I cannae bear to!'

There was a minute's silence, presumably as Morag searched the felled tree for any sign of Seffy. The sergeant's chest was pressed up against her back, she could feel the thud of his heartbeat and his warm breath on the nape of her neck.

'No sign of her,' Morag said, dully.

'Well, she can't have disappeared!' Enid gasped. 'What if the force of it flung her up into the canopy? She's maybe stuck up on a branch somewhere?'

Behind her, Fraser moved, making the bracken rustle. He made a muffled noise. Was he actually trying not to laugh?

She aimed a kick at his shin with her boot. 'It's NOT funny,' she whispered. It was hard to whisper in an angry tone so she pushed herself away from him, as much as she could and hoped she'd made her feelings clear.

A blade of grass was tickling her nose and threatening to make her sneeze. This was ridiculous! How did she get herself into these scrapes?

'How terrible!' Enid said. 'I know none of us likes her but you wouldnae wish this on anyone!'

Oh, that stung. Seffy had suspected she wasn't popular but to actually hear one of the girls say it was hurtful.

Fraser was nudging her. 'OK. Enough now,' he whispered.

He shifted and she felt a soft breeze on her back, instead of the warmth of his chest against her. She heard him jump to his feet, making the other girls gasp. What would they think of her, emerging from the undergrowth with a Canadian woodsman? But then, they didn't even like her, so why should she care?

Seffy rolled off her side and took his outstretched arm. He pulled her up with such strength that she almost banged straight into him.

She turned to face Enid and Morag. 'Surprise!' she said, painting on a smile. 'Here I am!'

Morag frowned. 'What're you doing down there?'

Enid ran around the felled tree – gosh, it certainly was a whopper – and, to Seffy's surprise, enveloped her in a hug. 'Oh, thank God you're all right!' She glanced suspiciously at Fraser and then back at Seffy. 'You are all right, aren't you? What a relief! We were going out of our minds with worry!'

Morag stared glumly at the tree. 'It was supposed to land over there.'

'And we forgot to shout "TIMBER!"' Enid added. 'Again!' She put her hand up to her mouth. 'Oopsie.'

Seffy was covered in pine needles and bits of fern. She brushed them off, amazed to find that nothing hurt. Despite having been flung to the ground, most unceremoniously, she appeared to be in one piece.

'He could probably tell us what we did wrong, couldn't you?' Enid asked, nodding at Sergeant Fraser. 'What must you think of us, eh?'

He grimaced and gave a non-committal shrug. 'Ma'am,' he said, 'I don't have the words to tell you what I'm thinking.'

Both times they'd encountered him in the woods, now, Enid and Morag had been doing something stupid with a saw or a tree. It was infuriating but it was hardly any wonder he thought so little of the lumberjills.

Enid took off her beret and scratched her head. 'Don't tell Jock, will you, Seffy? We'll be put on probation. Or sent home!'

'Seffy?' Fraser said. 'Is that your name?'

Was he laughing at her again? It certainly hadn't taken long for his polite veneer to drop.

'Actually,' she said, emphasising her English accent, 'my proper given name is Lady Persephone Baxter-Mills.' She knew she sounded haughty and uppity but quite frankly, amongst these people, none of whom even liked her, she didn't give a hoot.

Fraser gave a low whistle and doffed his cap. 'Should I bow? "Perse-phoney"?' He tried out her name, putting the stress in all the wrong places.

Seffy sighed. She supposed she'd asked for this.

'Phoney?' he said. 'Your name's really "phoney"? Hmm, that figures.'

'Excuse me? What's that supposed to mean?'

He merely tipped his finger to his cap in a half-salute and walked around the rogue tree, shaking his head. And in the next moment, he was strolling off into the woods, looking for all the world as though he owned the place. 'My pleasure, by the way!' he called out, raising a hand and not looking back.

'Oh, blast. I didn't thank him,' Seffy murmured.

'Did he save you, then?' Enid asked. 'I wondered what you were doing in the undergrowth there. He's rather handsome, isn't he?'

'You could always run after him and say thanks,' Morag suggested.

Run? Even if Seffy wanted to run, she couldn't. Her legs suddenly felt wobbly, like jelly. Goodness, it was hardly surprising: she'd nearly died. She sat down heavily on a tree stump and held her hands tightly in her lap, to stop them shaking.

Grace had returned and was looking at the three of them, puzzled.

'What was he doing here? What's going on?'

'Gosh,' Seffy said, looking down at the tree that had almost floored her. It had landed inches from where she'd been standing. 'I was practically . . . I mean, if that tree had hit me—'

'I'm so sorry,' Enid said, wringing her hands. 'I really am.'

'Will someone tell me what's happened?' Grace asked.

'The tree came down the wrong way,' Seffy explained. 'It was an accident. I don't think they were trying to kill me, were you, girls?'

Enid shook her head frantically. Morag didn't look so sure.

'Don't worry,' Seffy said. 'No harm done! Listen to me, I sound like Jolly Jean! No, but really, it's fine. I'm not hurt.'

Her pride was rather dented, though. It was painful to discover the others really didn't like her at all.

'You won't tell Jock?' Enid asked, again.

'Of course, I won't. I'm not a snitch.'

'Thank you. We owe you, Seffy.'

'And are you really a lady?' Morag asked. 'Is that like a princess or a duchess?'

Oh, blast. She'd been keeping that a secret but of course, the girls had been there when she'd announced her real name to Sergeant Fraser. Her cover was blown.

'Look,' Seffy said, 'let's make a pact, shall we? I won't mention this to Jock—' she gestured to the fallen tree '—if you two forget you heard me say anything about being a lady.' She nodded at Grace. 'That includes you now.'

Enid and Morag glanced at each other.

'We promise, don't we, Morag?'

'Aye. Cross our hearts and hope to die.'

Seffy wrinkled her nose. 'You might want to think of a different expression, Morag, given what's just happened.'

Grace shook her head and went to pick up her saw. 'I don't have a clue what any of yous are talking about,' she said, 'but let's get to work and get these branches off the tree.'

Seffy gazed again at the pine in front of her. It was as wide as a telephone box and as long as a ship. She must have been stupid not to realise Sergeant Fraser was trying to warn her it was coming down. She thought he was telling her to get out of the forest but actually, he'd been trying to help.

Oopsie, as Enid would say.

Chapter 16

'Come!' Captain Graham called and Callum entered his office.

Boy, it was smoky in here. He saluted and then put his hand to his mouth and coughed.

Graham looked up from his oversized desk and frowned. 'You? Where's Coomber?'

'I offered to come speak to you, sir, instead of the lieutenant. To explain.'

Lieutenant Coomber had been more than happy to let Callum take his place; no one wanted to spend time with Graham if they could avoid it.

'Want one?' Captain Graham pushed forward a pack of Sweet Caporal cigarettes but Callum shook his head.

'All righty, explain away!' Graham said. 'Why did you fail to meet your target last week?' He flicked a nicotine-stained finger at a sheet of figures on the desk. 'Your men are five per cent down, Sergeant.'

Callum nodded. 'There are women working in the woods, sir. It's kinda distracting.'

Captain Graham laughed. 'Gee, I've heard some excuses for poor performance in my time—!' He shook his head. 'Sure, I know about the ladies. And I'm guessin' they could be mighty distracting if you let 'em. But the secret is, Sergeant, not to let 'em! Or shall I arrange a transfer to the mill, so you won't have to be . . .' he paused '. . . distracted?"

'No, sir.'

It was a feeble excuse but it was the truth. Despite his best efforts, the fellas kept sneaking off to chat to the girls. They'd gone doll dizzy. He'd taken to patrolling the woods, near where the lumberjills were stationed, trying to catch the guys out. That's what he'd been doing this morning, when he'd shoved snooty Miss Phoney out of the path of the falling tree. Perhaps he shouldn't have bothered. She was probably filing a complaint against him with Lieutenant Coomber right now, for daring to touch her high-class body.

Graham swivelled in his seat and spread his hands. An inch of ash from his cigarette dropped onto the rug. 'So, whadda you want me to do about these women, Sergeant?'

He wouldn't tell Graham about the incident this morning. He'd want to know what the hell Callum, the bush foreman, was doing in that neck of the woods; he'd accuse him of losing control of his men.

Callum shook his head. 'They're gonna get themselves hurt, sir. Their equipment's basic; they use horses to pull the timber out. They don't know what they're doin' out there.'

There was an ashtray on the desk, next to a framed photograph of the king and queen. Graham stubbed out his cigarette, sat back and folded his hands across his stomach. 'Everyone knows lumbering's dangerous as hell. I've seen fellas injured and worse. I'm sure you have too.'

'Sir.'

'I'm not about to start telling the British how to run their affairs. Their men have gone off to war. Hell, they're fightin' for their liberty! If they think ladies can do the job and ladies wanna have a go, then I say, let 'em!'

'But, sir—'

Graham leaned across the desk. 'They know the risks! They

won't be here long, Sergeant, mark my words. Come winter, they won't be able to stick it. How many little ladies are there?'

Callum shrugged and did a rough calculation based on the gangs he'd spotted around the forest. 'About thirty, sir.'

'And are they cute? Or do they look like Amazon women?'

A picture of the ice-cool blonde, Seffy, flashed into Callum's mind. He had to admit, she was pretty; pretty in a way that made his stupid heart go pitter-patter. It was crazy because he didn't even like her. He pushed the thought away. 'Amazon women? Oh no, sir, they're pretty enough.'

But what did this have to do with anything? He might have known telling Graham about the women foresters would be a waste of time.

The captain was scratching his chin. 'Now, don't go thinkin' you're off the hook, Sergeant, because I ain't happy about that low tonnage. It's your responsibility to keep the men away from distractions in the forest, right?'

Callum nodded. 'Yes, sir.'

'But, outside of work, well, you can't deny, Sergeant, that a few more cookies decorating this place wouldn't do any harm. It'd keep the fellas happy!'

'I suppose, sir.'

At least he hadn't got yelled at as much as he'd been expecting. The captain was in an unusually good mood. Maybe he'd got mail from home. That and payday were always guaranteed to cheer a fella up.

'It's your duty, Sergeant,' he was saying, 'to keep those men of yours happy . . .'

. . . *It's your duty* . . .

Duty. Oh boy. He knew all about that. Duty had gotten him into big trouble.

Those words reminded Callum of Mike and his last night in Invermore before he and the guys had left for their training in Quebec.

112

The town had held a shindig for all the fellas who'd enlisted with the CFC. There were quite a few headed for Europe. Brothers had persuaded brothers, friends had encouraged friends and co-workers had agreed to enlist together in the Forestry Corps.

That night, the beer was flowing and the liquor too. Everyone was steamin', as the Scots would say.

It was near the end of the party – getting on for 2 a.m. – and most folk had drifted off home, when Missy's dad – Mike, as he'd told Callum to call him recently – came over, slapped him on the back and told him he was like a son to him.

'I feel kinda bad,' Callum told him, ''bout uppin' sticks and leavin'.'

That wasn't completely true. He was feeling a twinge of guilt, but mostly he was looking forward to the adventure, to seeing another part of the world: Scotland, where his grandparents had emigrated from.

Being with the CFC was a proper job, after so long scraping a living. And he'd be getting away from the sawmill, too. Mike had got him the job at the mill and in no time at all he'd been made foreman. He should be grateful but he hated the place.

''Course, it's not gonna be forever,' Callum added. 'I'll be back, God willing and all.'

He was hoping Mike would say something like, 'It's OK, buddy. There are some things a man's gotta do. If I was twenty years younger, I'd probably be doing the exact same thing,' but instead, he was quiet.

The silence between them was heavy. Callum knew something was coming and he wasn't too sure how he felt about that and whether he was gonna like it.

Mike said, 'There is something you can do. Something that I think you should do!' His face – flushed with beer – loomed up close to Callum's. 'Something that'd make us all – me and Barbara and Missy – especially Missy – very happy.' He staggered a little and then rested his arm on Callum's shoulder. 'You could say, it's your duty, boy . . .'

113

'So, what do you think, Sergeant?' Captain Graham was saying now. Callum shook his head and brought himself back to the present.

'Beg pardon, sir?'

Graham sighed. 'Hell, I knew you weren't listening! You had a dreamy look in your eye. I said, how about you invite some of those woodswomen—'

'Lumberjills, sir. That's what they call themselves.'

The captain waved his hand. 'Whatever. How 'bout you invite them to the camp sometime, for one of the cinema nights? And dancing? Say, get 'em along to the fete next month?'

He nodded. 'That's a swell idea, sir.'

'So, you'll arrange it?'

'I will, sir.'

'Good. Dismissed! Oh – and, Sergeant.' He slapped his hand down on the sheet of figures on the desk. 'Gals or no gals, don't let this shortfall happen again, d'you hear?'

'Yes, sir.' Callum saluted and left the office.

As he walked past the quartermaster stores and the orderly room, back to the sergeants' mess, his thoughts returned to that last night at home . . .

When Missy's pa, Mike, had said, 'You could say, it's your duty, boy . . .' Callum had laughed.

He'd thought maybe Mike was going to ask if he'd look up one of his relatives when he got to Scotland; a few of the townsfolk had been asking fellas to do that. Or perhaps he wanted him to bring back a bottle of the hard stuff? But Mike hardly drank – it was another thing that separated him from Callum's real pa – so no, it most likely wasn't that.

'I think you should ask Missy to marry you, son,' Mike said.

His first thought was: *No, no way.* He didn't like people telling him what to do. Leastways, not then. He'd changed over the nine months he'd been in the corps and away from home. He was used to taking orders now.

But after that rebellious first thought, Callum had remembered all the things Missy's family had done for him and how, without them and their kindness, he'd most likely be in jail. Or dead.

Mike had been especially good to him. A kind of surrogate father. Now, he wanted Callum to marry his daughter, Missy.

Callum had nodded. He guessed he owed him one.

Chapter 17

They'd been at the camp for two weeks and, to her surprise, Seffy had started to wake early, before the shrill call of Irene's alarm clock or the even shriller call of Irene herself.

She'd never been an early riser but it was rather nice to start the day gently, to the sound of birdsong in the trees outside.

That morning, when she woke, she heard the light drumming of rain on the hut roof. The fine weather had finally broken.

No one else was awake. She slipped out of bed and peered round the blackout curtain. Rain was coming down steadily and there was a low mist on the ground. Not necessarily a bad thing: perhaps they'd be excused work today.

No such luck. Later that morning, damp and miserable, the girls spent their tea break huddled under a makeshift shelter: a tarpaulin sheet, draped over a wooden frame. They were wearing their sou'westers for the first time. It had been a struggle to get the bonfire to stay alight. Wisps of smoke were rising from it now and there was little sign of a flame.

Jock had spotted a makeshift necklace around Morag's neck: a ring on a piece of wool. 'No jewellery when you're working, girls! Have I not made that clear?' he said.

While the others argued about whether Jock had ever told them to remove their jewellery, Seffy was reeling from the surprise discovery that moaning Morag was engaged.

It only went to show, there was someone for everyone. Perhaps Morag was cheerier when she was with her fiancé, or perhaps they simply enjoyed being miserable together.

Jock insisted it was too dangerous to wear jewellery when they were working in the woods. He urged them to imagine what might happen if a locket or a ring snagged on a saw or a branch.

'I can tell ye some gruesome tales of accidents in the sawmill!' he said, and when the girls shouted him down, he laughed. 'All right, all right! I see you don't have the stomachs for it. But all the proof you need, is this.' He held up his hand with the two missing fingers and the girls shrieked and shuddered.

'Thank goodness we don't have to work in the sawmill,' Enid said.

'Ah, that reminds me!' Jock said, looking around. 'Where's Blondie?' Seffy knew he meant her. Charming. Not only was she not allowed to use her full title, now she had to put up with a silly nickname.

'I need you to drive the wagon down to the sawmill this afternoon, once it's been loaded up,' Jock said. 'Reckon you can do it?'

Seffy's stomach flipped. She'd been full of bravado when he'd asked if she could drive a truck but now she wasn't so sure.

'I don't know where the sawmill is,' she said. She wasn't going to admit that she had absolutely no sense of direction. And the weather today was atrocious. She imagined sheets of water on the windscreen and not being able to see more than two yards ahead.

'I'll go with her,' Irene said, to Seffy's dismay. 'It'll make a change from felling.'

Irene was the last person she wanted with her in the cab. Even in the small confines of Macdonald hut, they managed, for the most part, to avoid each other. It would be impossible in the lorry.

And it was clear she wasn't coming out of the goodness of her heart: she merely wanted to get out of work and out of the rain.

117

Seffy held her breath, praying Jock would say no.

'As long as we don't have to unload the timber at the other end,' Irene added.

Jock shook his head. 'Not on your own. There are fellas at the sawmill who'll give you a hand.'

'Might I go too?' Jean asked.

Jock rolled his eyes. 'It's a wagon, not a charabanc! It's not a day trip you know! All right, then. You two can go with Blondie. But no riding on top! It's too wet; those logs'll be slippery. Right, Mrs C, blow your whistle – that's tea break done. I'll see the three of you at the wagon at two o'clock sharp!'

At two o'clock, it was still raining and pairs of girls from another gang were loading the last pit props onto the flatbed truck. They took one end each, yelled, 'One, two, three!' and swung the timber up onto the stack.

Jean had forgotten her beret and her wet hair was plastered flat onto her head.

'Look at you, hen,' Irene said, laughing. 'You're drookit!'

'Drookit?' Seffy queried.

'Soaked,' Jean translated. She shrugged. 'I'm not bothered. As my grandpa used to say, "The rain is God's way o' cleanin' the coos!"'

Irene smiled. 'Ah, that's the way. Nothing can bring you down, eh!'

It was true: on the whole "Jolly Jean" lived up to her nickname and Seffy was grateful she was with them. Jean and Irene could chatter away and leave her to concentrate on driving the lorry.

Irene looked up. 'Now, here comes Jock, at last!'

It was a long way up into the cab and it was a stretch just to reach the step but finally Seffy managed to haul herself up into the driver's seat. Jock got in on the other side, to give her a few pointers.

The seat was rock-hard, the cab smelled of sawdust and oil, and the steering wheel was huge – like the wheel of a ship. The pedals, when she pressed down on them, were stiff.

'Aye, you'll need to press hard,' Jock said. The gear lever was an old thing and it took a few attempts – and she had to use both hands – to even get it into gear.

'Now, there's a knack to driving this beast,' Jock said.

'You don't say,' Seffy said. 'Oh, goodness. I'm not going to have to double declutch, am I?'

'Doubledy what? No, hen, it's not that old. Firstly, pull out the choke before you start the engine and don't forget to push it back in again after a wee while.' He spent a few minutes running through the vagaries of the vehicle, until Seffy's head was spinning. Finally, he said, 'Right, are ye ready to give it a go?'

Seffy swallowed. At least she was high up and had a good view from here, despite the rain splattering on the windscreen, but the truck was so big, it was like being in charge of an elephant.

And it was quite a responsibility, with all those precious logs loaded onto the back, the result of hours of back-breaking work. Jean and Irene were squeezed together in the seat next to her and were watching closely. She couldn't get this wrong.

'I cannae drive so it's no use asking me anything,' Irene said, holding up her hands.

The engine was chugging and the whole lorry was vibrating. At least it was facing the right way and she didn't have to turn it around.

Nothing happened when she lifted one foot from the clutch and pressed down with the other on the accelerator. 'Gie it laldy!' Jock yelled through the open window.

Seffy could only guess what that meant and she pressed harder. At last, the lorry started to move, jerkily at first, jolting Irene and Jean and making them scream. There were ruts and dips in the forest floor and it was hard going. At times the lorry rocked so much, Seffy feared it might tip over but Jock was yelling encouragement from behind and finally, they reached the relatively smooth surface of the lane. Seffy managed a two-handed gear change and they set off.

'Keep going straight down this road,' Jean said. 'I know where the sawmill is.'

Irene announced she'd received a letter from Jim that morning. She pulled it out of the pocket of her sou'wester and read it while they were driving along, complaining the whole time that it was making her want to boke.

'You do look awful peely-wally, Irene,' Jean said.

For goodness' sake, Seffy thought, as she peered out through the rain, why not simply stop reading the blasted thing, then? Everyone knew reading in a vehicle made you feel sick. But she bit her tongue. The last thing she wanted was a row. If she said anything, Irene would be bound to blame her queasiness on Seffy's poor driving.

'Aw, now, listen to this!' Irene said, holding up the letter. 'Someone in Jim's unit is trying to get compassionate leave. No one's died or been bombed out but he's told his CO that it's time he went home and started a family. And Jim told him, "It's compassionate leave, Sonny, not passionate leave!"' She laughed loudly.

'What else does he say?' Jean asked. 'Oh, it's left here, Seffy, at the crossroads – that's right.'

'Right?'

'No, left! That's it.'

Seffy pulled the huge wheel round, already feeling the muscles in her arms start to complain, while Irene groaned dramatically.

As soon as they were back on the straight, Irene rallied again and returned to her letter.

'Jim's asked his CO if he might grow a set.'

'What does that mean?' Jean asked.

'It means, grow a beard! Next time I see him I might not recognise him: he'll look like a proper Jack Tar! I cannae wait!'

'Ooh, it'll be awful tickly when he kisses you,' Jean said, giggling.

'And he says – now, this is funny – that if the beard turns out to be no good, say, if it's too straggly, he'll be asked to shave it all off! Can you imagine the shame?'

Irene laughed hard and wiped the tears from her eyes. She was as tough as old nails – and sometimes rather mean – but she did seem awfully fond of her husband. It must be hard, not seeing him for so long and having to rely on the odd letter, to stay in touch.

On the way back from the sawmill, the truck, emptied of its timber, was much easier to drive and Seffy could relax a little. The conversation in the cab turned to chaps.

'Are you courting, Jean?' Irene asked.

Jean said she was but it was nothing serious and she'd be quite happy to throw the chap over if anyone more interesting came on the scene.

Irene turned to Seffy. 'And what about you?'

'Yes, I am,' Seffy said. She'd told the girls about Teddy one night when they were all chatting in bed before lights out. Irene obviously hadn't been listening.

Irene sat forward in her seat and glanced at Seffy's hands on the wheel.

'Engaged?'

She shook her head. 'I think perhaps Teddy was on the verge of popping the question but then he got called up like everyone. I expect he wants to wait now, until the international situation calms down a bit.'

She was braced for a sarky comment but to her surprise, Irene simply waved her hand and said, 'Well, there's plenty of time.' That letter from Jim had put her in an unusually expansive mood. 'Mind, I was only sixteen when I got married. A child bride, like wee Hazel! But when you've met your one true love, you just know, don't you?'

They were heading up the hill now out of the village, and the rain was streaming over the windscreen. Visibility was poor and Seffy had slowed down and was leaning forward in her seat.

'STOP!' Irene screamed.

Seffy braked hard. The lorry skidded through the puddles and finally came to a juddering halt in the middle of the lane.

'What?' Seffy could see nothing ahead but the pewter-grey sky and rain like stair rods. Perhaps she'd been about to hit a deer or worse, a pedestrian?

Irene was turning in her seat and gazing out through the cab window behind them. 'Canucks! Look!'

About eight men, in caps and great coats, their heads bent against the driving rain, were racing up the road towards them.

'How did you know they were there?' Jean asked, bouncing on the seat.

'I saw them on the side road. Tall, young men – what else could they be? We'll have to give them a lift back to their camp. They'll be soaking!'

Before Seffy could object, the first of the men had reached the lorry and started to pull himself up into the back. 'Mighty grateful, sir, thank you!' he yelled.

The girls looked at each other and laughed.

'I think you'll find that's "ma'am"!' Seffy called back through her open window.

There was a pause, then: 'Permission to climb aboard, ma'am?'

That was more like it. 'Permission granted!'

It wasn't part of her duties, to transport Canadian woodsmen around, but Seffy supposed she should do the honourable thing and deliver them back to their camp. They'd still get wet – the back of the truck was open to the elements, after all – but it would save them a long walk.

As the rest of the men jumped up into the lorry, making it shudder and shake, Irene wound down her window and called to them in the back. 'What're are you doing out in this?' The rain blew into her face and with a yelp, she quickly pulled her head back inside.

'Truck broke down at the station!' came the reply.

'It don't like the Scotch weather! That's the second time!' another man yelled.

122

Irene and Jean laughed. Gosh, they were so keen on the Canucks. It wouldn't have surprised Seffy if they suddenly decided to sit in the back with them, rain or no rain.

'Thank you, ma'am.' A deep voice on her right, at the window. It was him: Sergeant Fraser, standing hunched in his great coat, rain bouncing off his cap. His blue eyes widened in surprise when he saw Seffy behind the wheel. 'Oh, it's you,' he said.

Her stomach lurched. It was only, of course, because the last time she'd seen him, he'd flung her to the ground, as though they were in the Wild West rather than the wilds of Scotland. All rather melodramatic. She squirmed now at the memory of them lying there in the grass, hiding from Enid and Morag, cuddled up like two birds in a nest. How mortifying. She hoped he hadn't told anyone; she couldn't bear it.

She painted on a smile. 'Yep, it's little old me!' She lowered her voice. 'Erm . . . Thank you, by the way, for the other day. I didn't get chance to say it, when you . . . er . . . and I apologise.'

Gosh, this was ridiculous. She was tongue-tied. She was never tongue-tied.

'Hey, Sarge, can we get going? We're drowning back here!' one of the men yelled.

Sergeant Fraser put up his hand. 'Sure, in a minute!' He turned back to Seffy and nodded. There was no reading the expression on his face. 'Apology accepted.'

Goodness, this felt awkward. And she couldn't even get away from him. They were inches apart and despite the rain and his men's discomfort, he didn't seem in any hurry to move off.

Fraser turned his head and gazed at her windscreen. 'Say, don't you have windshield wipers on this thing?'

Seffy shook her head. 'No. There is one, but it's temperamental. Only works if you speak nicely to it, apparently. And even then, not all the time.'

She knew what he was thinking: that as well as being mere women, not up to working in the woods, they didn't have the right

123

equipment. Their lorry was old-fashioned and barely roadworthy but at least it hadn't broken down.

'Your truck gave up the ghost, I understand?' she said. 'So much for all that fancy gear you've brought with you across the Atlantic!'

He nodded wryly and bit his lip. 'Yeah. We'll send someone out to fix it when we get back to camp.'

'Sarge! Have mercy!' one of his men yelled.

The rain was bouncing off the ground now and drumming on the roof of the cab. He started to move towards the back of the lorry.

'Sure you want to risk it?' Seffy asked. 'With me in the driving seat?'

'I'll take my chance!' he called back. Seconds later he was aboard and someone thumped on the roof to tell Seffy she could set off.

She glanced at the other girls, grateful they'd been too busy flirting with the boys in the back to hear her conversation. It might have taken some explaining. Enid and Morag seemed to have kept their side of the bargain; no one had mentioned Fraser saving Seffy from the falling tree. As far as they were all concerned – if, indeed, anyone was remotely interested – the only time Seffy had spoken to him was the day his men had shinned up the trees.

They drove a few miles down the road, splashing through large puddles. When the men banged on the roof to be let off, Seffy braked and pulled in. Gosh, this was like driving a bus and stopping to let your passengers off. All she needed was a clippie to take the fares and she'd be in business. She smiled; it was rather good fun.

Fraser appeared at her window again and tipped his cap in thanks. The rain had eased a little but it was still coming down hard. 'Say, do you ladies know about the Dominion Day fete? On the eighteenth?'

Seffy looked blankly at Jean and Irene and they all shook their heads.

'It's our national day, when we celebrate being Canadian,' he said. 'Strictly speaking, it's tomorrow, July first, but we're on manoeuvres for the next few weekends, so the fete's been put back.'

Jean's eyes lit up. 'Ah yes, the fete! I know what you mean now.'

Some of the Canadian boys had gathered behind their sergeant and they started chipping in.

'There'll be contests and games and a ton of food. The whole of Farrbridge'll be there!'

'They love us in the village!'

'Especially the lassies!'

Seffy rolled her eyes. Sergeant Fraser turned and presumably gave his men a "look" because they instantly calmed down. He turned back. 'We're hoping you ladies will come along. Will you?'

'Try stopping us!' Irene said, leaning forward in her seat, smiling broadly. Honestly, she was keen with a capital K.

'And there's a tug of war contest!' one of the boys said, his face appearing suddenly at the side of the window. 'We'll be competing against other companies in the area. You could take on the land girls!'

Sergeant Fraser elbowed him gently out of the way. 'That's right,' he said. 'There's a tug of war. D'you wanna put a team forward? I'm guessing not.'

Seffy frowned. That was rather presumptuous of him but actually, he was right. The girls had discussed it after the bring-and-buy sale and they'd all agreed: they didn't have the time or energy to take part . She knew absolutely what the answer was.

'NO!' she said.

At exactly the same time as Irene and Jean cried, 'YES!'

Chapter 18

At supper that night there was a mixed reaction to the news of the tug of war.

Morag frowned. 'But we said we wouldn't do it!'

'True,' Irene said. She waved her hand dismissively. 'But it's a lady's right to change her mind! Come on, it'll be fun.'

It would be more than fun, Irene thought: it was a chance to mix with the Canadian boys again. She'd been starved of affection for so long, after all. Meeting these tall, athletic boys, firstly in the forest and then again, today, out in the truck, flirting with them – and feeling a thrill as they flirted back – had reminded her that she was still young and pretty. The war had ground her down. She was only twenty-five but some days she felt as though she were nearer fifty.

Jean thumped the table. 'But we have to take it seriously! The Land Army are our sworn enemies!'

The others laughed.

'Jean, you read too many adventure stories. Joey used to be a land girl and she's awful nice!' Enid said.

'Why, thank you!' Joey waved from the other end of the trestle table.

'And,' Irene said, 'I'm only here because a friendly land girl told me about the corps.'

But Jean wasn't having any of it. 'Mostly, they're beastly about us. I'm out and about more than you lot and I hear them. I want to slay them! So, please, can we all do our absolute best? Now, the anchor's critical. It needs to be someone big. Grace, it has to be you. Agreed?'

Irene winced. That was hardly diplomatic.

'A tug of war team is like a chain,' Jean continued. 'It's only as strong as its weakest link.'

'There's no point putting me in, then,' Hazel said. 'I'm too wee.'

'Aye, you're like a sapling,' Morag said. 'And Grace is like an oak that's been growing for hundreds of years. Sturdy and strong.'

'Thanks very much,' Grace said.

Irene rolled her eyes. This wasn't going well. 'I'm sure,' she said, 'we can find a place for you in the team, Hazel.'

Seffy was toying with her supper: she didn't know the value of good food, that girl. She looked up from her plate and waved her fork in the air.

'Perhaps Hazel could be our coach. Like a cox in the boat race! Little chap who sits in the front of the boat, barking orders? I've seen it at Henley Regatta.'

Irene pulled a face. 'Henley whatta?'

'Never mind. The point is, he's in charge. Oh and at the end – it's such a hoot – they throw him into the river! But we won't do that to you, Hazel; don't look so worried!'

Irene exhaled. Hazel as coach? Yes, that might work. For once, her ladyship had thought of others and had come up with a good idea.

'Could I do it?' Hazel asked, doubtfully.

'Oh yes!' Seffy said. 'Like rowing, it's all about timing. You need to get the team into a rhythm. I've never done it but I'm sure a tug of war's not simply about pulling madly. Does anyone want these carrots, by the way? I can't stand them, although they're

127

supposed to help you see in the dark, which is jolly useful in the blackout.'

'Carrots used to be purple,' Jean said. She pushed her spectacles up. 'And yellow. And white.'

Irene shook her head. 'Never mind the carrots! This tug of war is a fortnight on Saturday, so we don't have much time.'

Jean stood up, pushing her chair back.

Irene looked up at her. 'Where are you going?'

'You're right, there's no time to lose,' Jean said. 'I'm away to the Canucks' camp, to see if they'll lend us a rope. So we can practise. Hazel, why don't you come with me and we'll ask them for a few tips!'

When Jean and Hazel returned later that evening, they were full of what they'd seen and heard.

'The Canadians' camp is incredible! They've got everything!' Jean said. 'A cookhouse, an ablution hut with hot and cold showers, sergeants' quarters and a mess, officers' quarters and a mess, an orderly room, a medical hut—'

'And,' Hazel interrupted, 'they have teabags!'

The other girls looked at one another and frowned.

'They were sitting round the fire, using them in mugs,' she added.

'Imagine!' Jean said. 'A little bag, with tea in it. And a string, to pull it out! You put one in the mug, pour the boiling water on it—'

'—and leave it to brew for a minute or two. We took ours out straight away and it was too soon. It hadn't had chance to do its magic.' Hazel screwed up her nose. 'When you take it out, it does look rather like a dead mouse but the tea wasn't half bad.'

Irene laughed. 'Well, I used to work in a teashop in Glasgow—' she could barely believe she'd ever done that; it felt like a lifetime ago '—and I can assure you the customers wouldnae take to "teabags" there. No, they might be useful out in the forest, but they'll never replace a teapot and strainer.'

'Anyhow,' Morag said, 'apart from drinking tea and having a guided tour of the camp, did you find out anything about the tug of war?'

'Ah yes,' Jean said, raising a finger, as though she'd just remembered. 'There are eight on a team. So, that's the seven of us and I've roped in Belinda – pardon the pun – from Carlyle hut. As well as the eight pullers, there's the coach.'

Hazel smiled and nodded.

'The coach is the only one allowed to address the team and is in the arena with the judge. It's the best of three goes.' Jean pointed to a coiled rope on the floor next to her feet. 'A very charming Canadian, a captain no less, gave us that. Captain Graham, his name was.'

'Grabber Graham?' Joey asked.

Jean frowned. 'What?'

Joey shrugged. 'One of the land girls mentioned him. Said he had "octopus arms" but wouldn't tell me any more.'

'Aw, don't spoil it, Joey,' Irene said. 'I think Jean's got a crush on Captain Graham, haven't you, hen?'

Jean blushed. 'I wouldn't go that far. But he's awful nice. He's high up too. He's second-in-command of the whole company!'

'After the major,' Hazel said, nodding.

Irene laughed. 'No scratching his initials with a love heart into the bark of a tree, now, Jean. We'll be keeping an eye out!'

Jean managed a wry smile.

'He called her "Red",' Hazel said. 'He did pay her an awful lot of attention.'

'Anyway,' Jean said, still blushing furiously, 'he sent one of his men to the stores to find us that rope. So now we need to go and practise.'

The girls looked at one another.

'Do you mean now?' Seffy asked, yawning.

Jean glanced at her watch. 'It's only nine thirty. Come on! We've got ages yet, before it gets dark.'

Chapter 19

It was Saturday afternoon and work had finished for another week.

Enid, Morag and Joey were still toasting their cheese sand-wiches on the camp fire; the other girls had come back to Macdonald hut and collapsed onto their cots.

'What are "members of the Dominion Forces"?' Hazel asked. She was lying on her stomach, leafing through a copy of *Woman's Weekly*.

Seffy pursed her lips. 'I'm not sure. What else does it say?'

'Jean, do you know?' Hazel asked, calling down the hut. 'There's an article here about "Getting to know Americans or members of the Dominion Forces".'

Seffy felt rather snubbed. If she'd known the context, she could probably have worked it out but Hazel had ignored her and gone straight to genius Jean.

'It means the Commonwealth forces,' Jean called back. 'That includes Canada, of course. Do tell us what it says!'

Hazel read from the magazine, '"Don't treat them as strangers, make them welcome and give the lie to the wrong impression that we're an insular people. Remember, their ways of life are quite different to ours and don't make a joke of what might appear to be their 'funny' ways. Some of the ways we do things might appear funny to them".'

'Aye,' Irene said. 'Climbing trees, that's one of their funny ways!'

Everyone laughed and Seffy returned to the list she was writing: "The Pros and Cons of Teddy Fortesque."

Pros:

1. Known him forever, a safe bet, no skeletons in the cupboard!

2. Parents would be over the moon.

3. Is sweet on me. Unlikely to get bored or to stray.

4. V. handsome = gorgeous children. Would make a good father.

And now for the cons. She twirled the pencil between her fingers. There was only one but it was a biggie.

Since the excursion to the sawmill in the truck, Seffy had been mulling over what Irene had said. She'd married Jim at sixteen and never had any doubt that he was her "one true love". But what did that actually mean? How were you supposed to know? Seffy tapped the pencil against her chin. Then she wrote:

Cons:

1. Not sure whether he's my "one true love".

Grace walked past, a towel slung over her shoulders. 'Anyone tried the shower lately? Is it still a freezing cold trickle? No, don't tell me, it'll spoil the surprise.'

'At least we've got running water!' Jean said. 'We don't have to wash in the burn!'

Irene looked up from her knitting. 'Gi' it a rest, will you, Jolly Jean. There's no bright side where that shower's concerned!'

'I'd give anything for a bath,' Grace said mournfully. 'I feel so mawkit.'

'Me too,' Irene said. 'Can you imagine lying back in hot water and soaping yourself down with Lux?'

'Aye! And washing your hair with a whole sachet of Drene!' Hazel said.

Seffy was only half listening. She was still thinking about her list and wondering if she should balance it out with another "con" or two. The words were out before she could stop them. 'My aunt's got a bath,' she murmured.

When she looked up, everyone was staring at her.

'What? What're you all looking at? Have I got porridge in my hair again?'

Irene stood up, hands on hips. 'Where exactly is this aunt and her bath? If they're down in England-shire, that's no use.'

Seffy felt a moment of doubt. She'd never actually been to Dilys' house. But it was bound to have a bath, wasn't it?

'Is it the same aunt who was at the tea dance? The bossy one?' Jean asked.

Seffy nodded, hoping that "bossy" wasn't going to count against her. 'She lives around here. I've got the address somewhere. It's only a couple of miles away.'

'But they won't post you near kin,' Jean said, 'in case you keep going AWOL to see them.'

Seffy vaguely remembered being asked at her interview whether she had relatives in the Highlands but honestly, what did it matter now?

Irene narrowed her eyes at Seffy. 'How much does this aunt of yours love you?' she asked.

In no time at all, they were marching along the dusty road in what Seffy hoped was the right direction, towels tucked under their arms.

'Your aunt won't mind you bringing a few pals home!' Irene had said with a firm nod. Before Seffy could object – they were hardly all "pals", for a start – the others were whooping with delight and grabbing their towels from the washroom.

Hazel held up a bar of soap. 'I'll bring this!' she said, eyes gleaming.

Seffy hadn't been in touch with Aunt Dilys since the tea dance two weeks ago and thought it quite likely that her aunt could send the whole lot of them packing. But the bath might be her best chance of getting the girls on side. It was a risk she was prepared to take.

And besides, there wasn't much else to do on a Saturday afternoon.

But as the minutes ticked by and they still hadn't come across Aunt Dilys' place, Seffy's confidence started to drain away. Much like water down a plughole, in fact.

It was a warm day and the quiet country lanes buzzed with insects.

Occasionally, one of the girls yelled as she was bitten by a midge. If they were turned away – or couldn't find the house – they'd return to camp sweatier and dirtier than when they set off. Seffy could imagine how popular she'd be then.

But finally – thank goodness – they found it. A moss-covered stone at the entrance bore the name "Ballykinch House" and as they walked down the drive, Jean said, 'Gosh, it's an actual castle! It's got turrets and everything!'

'It's not as big as—' Seffy stopped herself and the others looked at her, curiously. 'As some,' she finished, lamely. She'd been about to say it wasn't as big as her parents' place in Ayrshire. Which was true but too boastful, she'd realised just in time.

The house was set back fifty yards from the road. It was built from grey granite that sparkled in the sunshine and was surrounded by perfectly manicured green lawns.

Hazel nudged Seffy. 'You didn't tell us your aunt lived some-where so grand!'

Seffy nodded, vaguely. She could hardly admit she'd never set foot in the place. They'd think she came from a right rum family. It was rather queer that they never saw Aunt Dilys; she was Father's only sister, after all. But her parents had never offered an explanation for their lack of contact and she'd never asked them.

'Are you sure this'll be all right?' Hazel asked. 'Five of us, turning up, begging for a bath?'

'Oh, yes,' Seffy said, crossing her fingers for luck. 'It'll be abso-lutely fine!'

As the girls cooed over the house, Seffy scanned the rows of narrow dark windows for signs of life. It seemed awfully quiet.

The huge wooden door was covered in metal studs. When there was no answer to a polite rap with the knocker, Seffy resorted to pounding on it with her fist and pressing her ear against it, hoping to hear approaching footsteps.

Finally, she had to turn and face the girls and admit. 'I don't think she's at home.'

Everyone groaned.

'All this way for nothing!'

'Nooo, it can't be true!'

Grace threw herself down on the neatly mowed lawn and tugged at tufts of grass, shaking her head. 'Might have known,' she muttered.

Seffy's heart sank. She'd failed. Now they thought she was full of false promises. Oh blast. She hadn't thought this through. "Impetuous and impatient" – that's what her school reports had said. She should have waited until she'd got a proper invitation from Dilys to bring the girls here.

She stepped back and gazed up at the solid stone walls and the narrow windows. If only there were some way of getting in. Perhaps they could scale the ramparts? Although there was a risk of getting arrested. Miss McEwen, she suspected, would take a dim view of a lumberjill with a criminal record.

She had a sudden idea. Oh, it was probably useless but it was worth a go. She plunged her hand into the ornamental pot to one side of the door, gently pushing the petunias and marigolds to one side. She prodded the dark earth around them – there! With a triumphant smile, Seffy brought out a long, silver key.

'How did you know that was there?' Irene asked, sounding impressed for once.

'We hide ours in the same place. Must be a family tradition!'

Seffy didn't admit it was actually the key to the summer house that was kept in a pot by the door. They didn't need a key to the main house because they had a butler to open it.

She hesitated, her hand hovering over the keyhole.

'Are you sure this is all right?' Hazel asked.

'Aye,' Irene said. 'I would nae be too happy about folk I didn't know rampaging around ma house!'

Seffy exhaled. Hopefully there wouldn't be any rampaging. They were each going to take a bath, nothing more. Of course, it wasn't quite the done thing, to let yourself into someone's house, uninvited. But what else could she do? She couldn't let the girls down. With any luck, Aunt Dilys would be away for the weekend. They might be able to come and go without anyone being any the wiser.

Seffy went to insert the key into the keyhole but the door moved and started to creak open. A golden Labrador squeezed its way through the gap and bounded out to greet them, tail wagging.

Thank goodness, it wasn't Aunt Dilys who emerged behind it but another middle-aged woman, dressed in an artist's smock. She was dainty, with grey ringlets and a sweet, kind, face.

'Oh, hullo,' Seffy said, holding up the key. 'I won't be needing this then. I'm—'

'I know exactly who you are.' The woman took the key with a smile and put it into her pocket. 'You're Persephone. Dilys' niece.'

Who was she? A housekeeper, perhaps, or a lady's companion?.

'I'm Marigold,' the woman said, in a broad Scots accent. 'I knew you when you were a wee girl. You've still got the same lovely blonde hair. You stayed with Dilys and me once.'

'Did I?' That couldn't be true. Seffy had no memory of that at all. She was desperate to ask more but she could sense the other girls around her, listening intently.

Irene coughed.

'Erm, is my aunt in?' Seffy asked.

'No, she's not here.'

What should they do now? Wait?

Marigold started to usher them inside. 'You look hot and thirsty, girls and I've just the thing: homemade lemonade! That's Goldie, by the way. Oh, he loves visitors. So do I, for that matter. We don't get many! Come in, come in, we don't bite!'

Seffy lowered herself into the bathtub, averting her eyes from the colour of the water and the soapy scum mark around the edge. She tried not to think about the four bodies that had used it before her.

The water was barely warm. It had probably been hot when Hazel had taken the first bath but now it was tepid. And grey.

They'd let Hazel go first, telling her it was because she was the smallest and cleanest. But in truth, it was because Hazel's aches and pains seemed worse than anyone's. As well as sore limbs and backache, of which they all complained, Hazel had a tender stomach and a pain in her chest. 'Right here,' she said. Where her heart was.

Seffy exhaled and stretched out in the tub, vowing to never, ever take a bath for granted again. At home, she would often spend a whole evening – and gallons of bubble bath – soaking in the tub and washing her hair. She would fiddle around for ages afterwards with setting lotion, hair nets and kirby grips.

Even if she had that equipment now, she wouldn't have the time or energy to use it. Most nights, she collapsed into bed and slept, appropriately enough, like a log.

This bath wasn't perfect but it was an especially memorable one. Goodness, the lengths she'd had to go to! But she'd done it and all before Aunt Dilys got home. There was a definite satisfaction in that.

Seffy picked up the slender remains of the bar of soap and washed her hair, which was matted and sticky with tree sap.

She squinted at the black five-inch line, the measure beyond which, Marigold had instructed, the bath was not to be filled because hot water was rationed. But this could hardly be classed as "hot". She pulled out the plug, allowing some of the dirty water to gurgle away.

It was so loud; someone was bound to hear, so she only let it run for a few seconds. She pushed the plug back in and listened. From the kitchen below, the murmur of voices and the occasional laugh continued.

She turned the tap and a delicious burst of hot water rushed out. She let it run for as long as she dared, keeping a careful watch on the black mark on the tub, then turned off the tap and lay down again.

Oh, this was utter heaven. She could already feel the awful aches melting away.

As she closed her eyes, he popped into her thoughts: the Canadian, Sergeant Fraser. It was ridiculous, how often she thought about him. It must be the novelty factor. She'd never met anyone like him. He was handsome, she supposed, if you liked your men tall and muscular with a cleft chin and serious blue eyes. Yes, she couldn't deny he was quite easy on the eye. But she preferred her chaps to be rather more cultured.

The boys in her set – Charles, Rupert, Louis, Emerald's Bertie and Teddy, of course – were all so unfailingly polite and charming and impeccably dressed. You'd never catch them chewing gum or speaking anything other than the king's English.

They were wonderful, they absolutely were.

But oh – were they, perhaps . . . ? No, that was terribly disloyal. Seffy pushed the thought away but it bobbed up to the surface again. Were the chaps of her acquaintance perhaps just the tiniest bit dull?

Nonsense! Especially now they'd all enlisted. As Father said, when he'd been gushing over the twins and the RAF: the experience would make men of them.

Oh, what was that? She sat up. Heavy feet were pounding up the stairs and thudding along the corridor towards her. Seffy grabbed the closest thing – a yellow sponge – and held it in front of her chest, like a small, ineffectual shield.

The footsteps were getting nearer. Any moment now . . .

She screamed as the bathroom door was flung open so hard it banged against the wall.

Aunt Dilys was filling the doorway, wearing slacks and a thick sweater, despite the sweltering heat. She had wild, windswept hair and her face was white with anger.

'What do you think you're doing?' she cried. 'Out! Right now!'

Seffy froze. Did she mean this very second?

'Aw, leave the lassie be,' said a voice behind Dilys. It was Marigold. 'She's not doing any harm.'

Dilys spun around. 'If you call breaking and entering "not doing any harm"! She's a spoilt little madam, that's what she is!' She nodded and crossed her arms. '"The child is father to the man"!'

Seffy gasped. What on earth did Dilys mean?

She couldn't sit here like this, in cold dirty bath water, a moment longer. Marigold said something and as Dilys turned to answer her, Seffy grabbed her towel, which was draped over a nearby chair, stood up and wrapped it tightly around her. That was better.

'Did I stay with you, Aunt Dilys, when I was little?' she asked. Diversion tactics – that's what was required. 'Marigold said I did.'

Dilys looked taken aback. She frowned. 'Yes, you did.'

'Without my parents? But why?'

Some colour was returning to Dilys' face and she had calmed down somewhat.

She sniffed. 'When the twins were born. Your mother was unwell.'

'What kind of unwell?'

'I'm not sure; I've never had a child. But sometimes, it can leave one feeling . . .' Dilys cast around for the right words.

'Not quite oneself?' Marigold suggested.

Dilys nodded. 'Yes. Rather blue. Unable to cope. The twins were born early; they were awfully sick. And then, there was you. You weren't exactly over the moon about having two new brothers.'

Seffy frowned. Why hadn't anyone told her about this?

'I did find it rather droll, at the time,' Dilys said. 'What did they expect, I asked your parents. After all, they'd given you a name that means "bringer of destruction" and "one who brings chaos"?'

Dilys and Marigold laughed.

Seffy frowned. 'But I thought Persephone . . . wasn't I named after the beautiful goddess of spring?'

Dilys was getting into her stride now. 'My brother – your father – said there was nowhere else they could send you. They didn't want a stranger – a nanny – in the house and your mother needed peace, to recover. So, they asked if I'd take you.'

Seffy frowned. 'What? They sent me away?'

'Your father was worried you were going to do something.'

'I'm sure he was simply being overcautious,' Marigold said quickly.

The world seemed to be tilting on its axis.

'What kind of something?' Seffy asked.

'He was concerned that you might hurt the babies,' Dilys said.

'What?' This couldn't be true. Why would her aunt make up something so awful?

'You had . . . he thought you'd been pinching them, making them cry. Oh, it was perfectly understandable. You were a spoilt little girl, the centre of your parents' universe and suddenly there were two new siblings, competing for your attention.'

'We used to sing a little song about you, didn't we, Dilys?' Marigold said. 'You know, the nursery rhyme. "There was a little girl, who had a little curl, right in the middle of her forehead. And when she was good, she was very, very good but when she was bad, she was horrid!"'

Seffy could hardly breathe. Was this true? She'd been a horrible child! So awful that Mummy and Father had sent her away. She hadn't always been their favourite, after all. She'd been a problem. Perhaps nothing had changed and she was a horrid grown-up too. No wonder the other girls didn't like her.

'So . . . I'd have been, how old?'

'Three years old,' Dilys confirmed.

Old enough to remember.

'Did you take me into a forest?'

Dilys pursed her lips. 'Yes. Not here, but nearby. We walked slowly, you and I, and we looked at everything and we breathed in the woody forest smells. We touched the bark of the trees, we sat on logs, kept perfectly still and silent and watched the deer. We listened to the birdsong all around us. The sunlight played through the trees. And we dipped our toes and fingers in a stream.'

Dilys was getting choked up; her anger had disappeared.

It was as though a piece of the jigsaw puzzle had slotted in. That was why Seffy had fleeting memories of the forest; that was the attraction of the trees. It all made sense now.

'I'm very sorry,' Seffy said. 'About this—' She waved down at the bathtub. She seemed to spend her whole life either apologising or thinking about apologising. 'But I didn't do any breaking and entering,' she said, firmly. 'And we'd walked two miles to get here. I'd promised the girls—'

'You had no right to promise anything!' Dilys said.

Her aunt was right of course and perfectly entitled to be furious. What on earth had she been thinking? Since she'd left home and become a lumberjill, Seffy had lost all reason and common sense. But she could hardly admit the pathetic truth: that she'd brought the girls here for a bath because maybe, after almost three weeks here, she wanted to stay, after all. And she wanted them to like her.

'Marigold said we could,' Seffy added, in a small voice, hoping she wasn't getting the poor woman into trouble. Goodness, the mood Aunt Dilys was in, she might sack her.

'Well, Marigold would say yes to anything!' Dilys snapped. 'You've taken advantage of her good nature.'

Behind her, Marigold was silent.

'I'll get dressed now and come downstairs and perhaps we can talk about this more sensibly, Aunt.'

Dilys nodded. 'Agreed. I must say, I'm amazed to find you still here. In the Timber Corps, I mean. And you can tell your pals that they'll simply have to miss out.'

'But the other girls have had their baths,' Marigold said. 'Seffy's the last.'

Dilys sniffed. 'Hmm. Drew the short straw did you?'

Seffy shook her head. 'No, Aunt. I offered to go last.'

'It was here or the burn, Dilys,' Marigold said.

'What?' Dilys said, glaring at Seffy. 'Is that true?'

Behind her aunt, Marigold nodded vigorously at Seffy.

'Well, yes, we were rather desperate. You must remember yourself, Aunt, from when you . . . er . . . you worked in the woods—'

'I never said I did!'

Seffy winced. 'No. Sorry. But you must . . . What I mean, is one gets filthy. If we weren't able to take a bath here, we'd have no choice but to have a dip in the burn.'

That wasn't true but it seemed to have done the trick. Dilys was suddenly completely calm. 'You mustn't swim in the burn. Or in any of the lochs. Do you hear me? They're deep and dangerous.'

'And full of pike!' Marigold added.

Dilys nodded. 'The next time any of you needs a bath, come here!'

Later, as the girls walked back to camp, with damp hair and damp towels under their arms, Seffy felt a shift in their attitude towards her. It helped that they were in a good mood. They were clean, refreshed by Marigold's lemonade and they'd spent time in the garden, playing with the delightful dog.

And they seemed to have taken to Dilys.

'She's nice, your auntie,' Hazel said.

'Aye, for an Englishwoman,' Irene agreed. 'But I do wonder if she's quite all there. You know, if she's right in the head.'

She pronounced it "heed". Seffy felt a sudden protectiveness towards Dilys. Yes, she was a funny old bat but perhaps there was a reason for it.

'You know, I think my aunt was in the Timber Corps or the Land Army last time,' Seffy said. 'But she won't talk about it. She completely denies it! But I've got the evidence: we've got a photograph of her at home. I know she was there!'

'Perhaps something happened,' Jean suggested. 'When she was working in the woods? And she's trying to forget about it?'

Seffy nodded. It was a possibility. There was something of the wounded animal about Dilys. It was a mystery. But before she left the forest for good, Seffy was determined to unravel it.

Chapter 20

The next day was Sunday and Irene seemed awfully keen for the Macdonald girls to go to church.

Seffy sighed. Sunday was their only day off. A day for rest and relaxation, catching up on sleep, washing clothes, writing letters home. She didn't want to spend a couple of hours of it trudging down to the village and sitting through a boring sermon.

'We didn't go last week!' Joey pointed out.

'No, we were too fagged out,' Morag agreed.

Irene had been ready for the past hour. She was all kitted out in the full Timber Corps uniform. She sat on her bed, checking her lipstick in a compact mirror. She looked up. 'What d'you think all that bathing was for yesterday, if it wasn't to prepare us for going to church?'

'Some of us didn't have a bath,' Morag said. 'When me and Joey and Enid got back from lunch, you'd all gone without us.'

Thank goodness for that, Seffy thought. Aunt Dilys' blood pressure couldn't have coped with another three lumberjills sneaking into the house.

'Irene, I think you look super,' Jean said. 'You must show me how you curl your hair like that. I can never get mine to stay.'

'You've lovely hair,' Irene said, which was kind, if untrue. Jean's hair was a beautiful colour but no straight-as-a-die hair like that could ever be described as "lovely". It was a wonder she'd never considered a perm.

'Hazel wants to go to church, don't you, hen?' Irene said, playing her trump card. 'It gives her comfort.'

That was it, then: decision made.

'But I'm only coming on one condition,' Seffy said, 'that if I fall asleep during the service, you won't nudge me awake.'

It was another warm sunny day and, to the girls' surprise, the main street through Farrbridge was lined with people. There was an air of expectation, as though they were waiting for a carnival.

As the girls – dressed in their lumberjills' breeches and shirts, boots and berets – wandered through the crowds, they spotted Jock with his "missus". He waved to them across the street.

The girls were chattering away when Jean put her hand up for silence. 'What's that noise?'

Hazel gave a little yelp, covered her head with her hands and ducked down behind a nearby wall. Jean pulled her up gently and hugged her. 'Sorry, Hazel. I didn't mean to startle you. I'm sure it's nothing bad!'

The sound was getting louder. But the street was still empty.

Then they could make it out: it was the crunching sound of boots on the road, the unmistakeable sound of marching.

'Here they come!' someone yelled.

The villagers were straining to see and jostling for position. The mothers of children playing in the street, called out to them and pointed down the road.

Now the girls could see what all the fuss was about.

It was the Canadians. Dozens of them. No longer lumbermen but soldiers, marching in perfect formation and wearing smartly tailored khaki uniforms and caps. Goodness, some of them were even carrying rifles. As they approached, their buttons, badges and belt buckles glinted in the morning sun.

'Glad you came now, girls?' Irene asked. 'Church parade. First Sunday of the month. Now, isn't that a sight for sore eyes?'

Jean grinned. 'It certainly is. Don't they scrub up well!'

'I can hardly believe it's them!' Joey said. 'But how did you know?'

Irene tapped her nose. 'A little birdie told me.' She nudged Seffy. 'See, they are soldiers!'

Seffy gave Irene a quick, ironic smile. It was true; she'd been wrong. They'd only ever seen the boys wearing baggy dungarees and shirts, or overcoats in the rain. Now, they were transformed. Gosh, they were like creatures from another planet. She had to smile. Even when they marched, they did it with a kind of swagger. They definitely knew the effect they were having.

Oh! Her stomach swooped away. That was him: Sergeant Fraser. Or was it? He looked so different out of his work clothes. But yes, it was him: she recognised his cleft chin. He did look awfully handsome. As he marched past, their eyes met for a second.

The girls had edged their way through the crowd to the kerb, close enough to see the pride in the men's eyes and the smiles that, try as they might, they clearly couldn't contain. The locals cheered and waved and some of the children called out to chaps they knew who had, no doubt, been free with their gum and candy.

'That's full dress uniform they're wearing,' said an old chap standing nearby, leaning on a walking stick. He had to raise his voice over the sound of so many marching feet. 'They'll have been inspected before they marched out from camp.'

'Inspected? By whom?' Jean asked, not taking her eyes off the soldiers as they swept past.

'By their CO of course, Major Andrews. Woe betide any man whose tunic isn't perfectly pressed!'

'Aren't they bonny?' an elderly woman said. She was clutching her handbag to her chest, her rheumy eyes bright as a bird's. She nudged Seffy. 'If only I was twenty again!' She chuckled and her tiny body shook.

Seffy smiled at her. That was her age: twenty. Perhaps she'd be like that old dear herself one day: standing on the sidelines, wishing she was young again. Maybe she should pull herself together, stop wishing she was somewhere else and make the most of this time. It wouldn't last forever.

A younger woman – presumably the old woman's daughter – was standing nearby. 'We had two of them billeted with us, didn't we, Ma, while they were building their camp last spring? Alfred and Ernest. Friends, from the same town. So polite and well brought up. We're writing to their families now and they're so grateful we're looking out for their boys. Well, you would be, wouldn't you? They still come to us for the occasional Sunday lunch.'

'They don't eat much, mind!' the old lady said.

'Aye, we couldn't understand it at first. Big strapping lads, they need their food. But they were under strict instructions not to eat too much! See, what I mean? Well brought up.'

Morag was the only lumberjill who didn't seem impressed. She glanced around at the excited villagers and tutted. 'Look at them! They think these fellas are heroes but what about us? Do you think anyone knows what we're doing? Or cares?'

'Apparently,' Enid said, 'Lord and Lady Lockhart have been out to the Canadians' camp more than once, to inspect them.'

'Well, that's just typical,' Morag said. 'They haven't even called in to pass the time of day with us!'

Seffy was tempted to say, perhaps the laird was worried about a tree falling on him, if he went anywhere near Morag and Enid, but she thought better of it. They mightn't see the funny side and besides, they'd had almost two more weeks' training since the incident with the falling tree. She was sure they were much better foresters now.

* * *

146

Grace had never seen so many men in her life. Since the war had begun and all the young men had been drafted, there were hardly any fellows to be seen, anywhere. So, this was quite a sight. They were dozens of them: young and handsome. You'd have to have a heart of stone not to be at least the tiniest bit smitten.

As the men marched past, eyes firmly fixed on the horizon, Joey and Jean made up a game and started to play, "Spot the film star".

'Of course, we can mostly only see them in profile, so it's difficult to judge,' Jean said.

'There! Cary Grant! The spitting image!' Joey said.

'Och, I'm sure Cary Grant's taller.'

'Yes, but the face. It was him to a tee!'

Enid joined in. 'Look! On the far side. A dead ringer for Leslie Howard!'

'Ooh, yes! Ashley Wilkes!' Joey said, with an excited squeal.

'And there's Mickey Rooney!' Jean said.

Grace's head spun around. Where? She blushed; she shouldn't have made it so obvious. But the Canadian boy she'd liked since she'd seen him climb the tree almost three weeks ago – Gordy Johnson – had freckles and an impish grin and that's exactly who he reminded her of: Mickey Rooney. She'd been thinking about him ever since that day and hoping he might reappear.

She craned her neck to see where Jean had pointed. Yes, that was him. Even in his uniform, she recognised him instantly. He caught her looking and – oh! He winked at her! Then, in the next moment, he'd swung his arm and marched past.

Grace held her breath, not daring to move a muscle, expecting the girls to start teasing her any second. Someone would surely have noticed that wink? But no one was paying her any attention. The other lumberjills were laughing and pointing, their attention fixed firmly on the men. For once, she was grateful for their silliness.

* * *

147

Irene watched the Canadian boys march past with a lump in her throat and a sense of longing. If only this was the crew of Jim's ship, home at last at the end of the war and she was waving a Union Jack flag and bursting with excitement, scouring the bearded faces for her man. She'd give anything for that.

'They'll take their caps off inside church, won't they?' Jean asked suddenly, interrupting her thoughts. 'They're bound to. And we'll get a better look at them. Come on, let's go and get a good seat!'

Irene pulled Jean back by her shirt sleeve. 'Hey! A word. You're not off to the pictures. It's the church and folk round here take it seriously. A little decorum, please!'

Irene wasn't religious but she'd noticed some of the women in the crowd giving them disapproving glances, as the girls exclaimed and laughed over the soldiers. They were in their lumberjill uniforms, after all; they needed to be making a good impression, not confirming the villagers' opinion that they were good-time girls.

Half an hour later, as they sat on the hard pews with a good view of the soldiers seated up near the altar, Joey whispered, 'Going to church has never made me so happy.'

'Aye,' Enid agreed. 'All my prayers have been answered!' They pressed their faces into their open hymn books to smother their giggles; a woman in the pew in front turned round and shushed them.

'And that's not even all of them,' Jean said, eyes shining. 'The whole company wouldn't fit in the church, so they take it in turns. Those who don't come to the village have a service outdoors, conducted by their own chaplain.'

'How much time do you spend hanging around that camp, Jean Ferguson?' Irene asked.

Jean's eyes were wide. 'Sometimes I bump into them in the forest and we have a chat, that's all. They're lonely – lonesome, they call it – and homesick.' She nudged Irene. 'That's the one I like: Captain Graham. He's the one who got us the rope for the tug of war. Can you see him, at the end of pew? With the pips on his sleeve?'

Irene frowned. 'Aye. Be careful, Jean. He's far too old for you.'

'But I like older men,' Jean said, airily.

Irene bit her lip and tried not to smile. Jean might be as bright as a button but she was hardly worldly-wise. Irene doubted whether she had much experience of men. But she didn't want to embarrass the girl, so she simply nodded.

The minister looked down from the pulpit at the large congregation and announced the next hymn. Rather appropriately, it was "Onward Christian Soldiers".

After the service, the girls gathered around Hazel as she lit a candle in memory of her husband, Angus, and then another for Prince, who'd died with him in the raid.

'Do you think that's allowed?' she whispered. 'Lighting a candle for a dog?'

Seffy steadied Hazel's hand until the wick of the little candle had taken light.

'Definitely,' she whispered back.

At supper that evening, Seffy's beret was served up to her on a plate.

'Here, you might need salt and pepper,' Enid said, pushing the shakers across the table.

The other girls in the dining hut were nudging each other and pointing.

'Don't you remember, Seffy?' Irene said. 'The first time we met those Canadian laddies, you said if they were soldiers, you'd eat your hat?' She gestured to the plate. 'Well, be my guest!'

Everyone laughed. To be fair, even Seffy managed a wry smile. She lifted the beret up to her mouth and pretended to take a mouthful.

'Aye, that'll do, hen,' Irene said. 'Good girl.'

* * *

149

That night, as the girls lay in bed, having their usual chat before lights out, Enid said, 'That wasn't a bad sermon today. I mean, it wasn't boring, was it? When the minister asked about our idea of heaven, it really made me think.'

There were murmurs of agreement, then Hazel spoke up. 'I know what mine is. My idea of heaven.'

'Go on,' Irene said.

There was a long moment while the girls waited and Hazel seemed to be gathering her thoughts. Eventually, her clear voice rang out through the hut.

'There's a steep hill near home, where we always used to walk. It's a long hard climb but it's worth it because when you reach the top you can look down into a lochan.'

'What's a lochan?' Seffy asked.

'It's a wee loch. This one is as blue as anything,' Hazel replied. 'As blue as the Saltire.'

'And that's where you used to walk?' Seffy asked. 'You and Angus?'

'And Prince. Aye. My idea of heaven is the three of us there, walking together in the sunshine.'

There was silence.

What a change, Irene thought, in wee Hazel in these few short weeks. She was still sad of course, but she was brighter than she'd been when she arrived. Maybe there was something in it after all: maybe nature had helped her heal.

Finally, Seffy spoke. Her voice sounded as though it was cracking. 'That's lovely, Hazel,' she said. 'I expect Jean's idea of heaven is a 200-page maths book! Or a ten-hour science exam!'

'Actually,' Jean said, 'you're wrong. I'd like to travel to America and see the redwood trees. That would be my idea of heaven. And measure them, obviously.'

Everyone laughed.

'Irene, what about you?' Jean asked.

Irene didn't speak for a moment; like Seffy just then, she was a little choked up. But then she said, 'Mine's an easy one. My Jim coming home from sea, safe and sound. That's my idea of heaven. That'll do for me.'

Chapter 21

Grace glanced up at the two flags flapping on poles at the entrance to the fete: the Scottish St Andrew's white cross on a blue background – and, next to it, the Canadians' striking red ensign flag.

Her stomach twisted. It was the Dominion Day fete. She was nervous about the tug of war but there was something else: the Canadian boys would be there today. She'd almost certainly see Gordy Johnson again. And this time, she might even pluck up the courage to speak to him.

The weather was good – fine but not too hot – and folk of all ages were swarming around the fields. It looked as though the whole of Farrbridge had turned out. Some people had dressed up for the occasion in their Sunday best but there were farm labourers too, who'd clearly come straight from the fields in their mud-splattered work clothes. And there were scores of children running around, laughing and squealing with excitement.

Everywhere Grace looked, there were men in uniform: Canadian soldiers, tall and loud, flirting with girls, laughing, slapping one another on the back and handing out candy to the kiddies. But there were strapping young men in baggy shorts and vests too, limbering up for the various contests that would be taking place between the companies today.

Grace scoured their faces but none of them was Gordy. It was two weeks since he'd winked at her as he marched past during church parade. Oh, but had he, really? It had all happened in a flash: he could've been winking at someone else. Another lassie, standing behind her, perhaps?

Oh, stop now. She'd been tormenting herself with thoughts like that for almost a fortnight.

And she hadn't told a soul.

As the girls meandered past the various stalls – the coconut shy, horse-shoe throwing, a "pin-the-moustache on Adolf Hitler" game – Jean read from the fete programme, listing all the events they'd missed.

Unlike the Canadian boys, the lumberjills hadn't been given a day's holiday: it had been work as usual that morning.

'We're too late for the log hurling and softball, whatever that is,' Jean said, 'and we've missed the heats of the sawing contest, the chopping contest and three soccer matches.'

'That's football,' Joey said.

'I know, silly,' Jean replied, pushing her playfully.

They'd reached an open grassy area near a fence.

'Shall we have our picnic here, girls?' Irene suggested. 'Not,' she added, 'that we're going to eat much, I dare say.'

'Perhaps we'd better wait until after the tug of war?' Jean suggested. 'We might feel more like eating then.'

Enid huffed and put her hands on her hips. 'You can do what you like but I'm starving and I've spied a ton of food over there!'

'Oh yes, the Canadian camp's kitchen is putting on a spread, apparently,' Jean said.

Enid and Morag didn't need telling twice. They were away to see what they could find in an instant, while the others spread out a couple of blankets, sat down on the grass and got out their cheese pieces. They had almost two hours until the tug of war competition.

After a while, a young girl wandered over to speak to them. She looked vaguely familiar.

'Hello, I'm Flora,' she said.

Irene recognised her. 'We met you a few weeks back, looking for your wee brothers in the forest.'

'Aye, that's right,' she said. 'I'm going to be joining you soon! I'm going to be a lumberjill too!'

'Are you now?' Irene said. 'You're awful young.'

She shrugged. 'I left school last year and I've been working in the ironmonger's 'til now but I hate it. Your foreman's agreed, so long as I live at home, so I'll bicycle in every day. Do you all chop down the trees?'

Irene pointed at Jean. 'No, this one's a measurer. She works out the tonnage of timber we've felled, so the laird can be paid and, more importantly, she works out what wages we're due. She knows what trees will make telegraph poles and she's so good, she can calculate a tree's dimensions simply by looking at it.'

Flora's mouth fell open. 'Golly! How do you do that?'

Jean peered at her over her spectacles. 'I dunno. It just comes to me. I was good at arithmetic at school, too. I always knew the answer straight away.'

'And she gets paid more than the rest of us, which made us hate her at first—' Jean pretended to slap Irene's arm '—but we've forgiven her now and actually, I think she deserves it.'

'I'm useless at sums,' Flora said, cheerfully. 'I'm always giving folk the wrong change in the ironmonger's.'

'Me too,' Seffy said. 'Not the ironmonger's but the sums bit. Ask me to add a crown, ten bob and two shillings and I'll always be sixpence short.'

'You're in the tug of war later, is that right?' Flora asked.

The girls exchanged nervous glances. They'd been trying to forget about it.

'Aye in a mad moment, we signed up,' Grace said.

'And we're as ready as we can be,' Irene said, firmly. 'We've practised so hard, we've worn holes in our gloves and Hazel here – she's our coach – well, she's gone hoarse, with all the shouting.'

Hazel nodded ruefully. 'It's true,' she whispered. She pointed to her neck. 'I'm saving my voice for later.'

As Flora waved them cheerio and wished them good luck, Enid and Morag returned from their foraging.

'You should see the tables! There's so much food, they're almost collapsing,' Enid said. 'Go and get some before it disappears.' She licked her lips. 'Some of it's queer though.'

'Aye, spam,' Morag said, frowning.

'And I've just eaten potato salad for the first time ever!' Enid said. She smacked her lips. 'It was good.'

'Hey, girls!'

They all looked around and Grace's heart missed a beat.

It was him, Gordy Johnson, striding towards them with another couple of Canadian boys she didn't recognise. They were wearing long shorts and vests, along with their boots and lumberjack caps.

Grace sat on her hands, then crossed them in front of her and, finally, she grabbed the programme from Jean and pretended to flick through it.

'Hey there, ladies,' Gordy said, as he reached them. He tipped his cap. 'All set for the tug of war? Say, we'd love to come and cheer you on but our heat's at the exact same time. So, I just wanted to come and wish you the very best of luck!' He pointed at them and grinned. 'My money's on you!'

The girls thanked him. Grace kept her head down and bit her lip. She hoped that was merely a turn of phrase; she didn't want anyone's money on them.

Soon they were only minutes away from their turn in the spotlight. It was time to walk over to the arena and get ready for their first pull.

'We don't have heats, like the Canucks, do we?' Joey asked.

Jean shook her head, grimly. 'Nope. There's only us and the land girls, with one team each. It's sudden death!'

'Ready then, girls? Let's go!' Hazel said, getting up.

155

Grace frowned. There was something missing. 'Who's got the gloves?'

Joey was folding up one of the blankets. 'Not me,' she said. 'I thought you had them, Jean.'

'I did,' Jean said, frowning. 'I definitely had them. I put the bag in the basket at the front of my bicycle . . .'

They looked around. The bicycle had gone.

They couldn't think where it might be. The only folk who'd been anywhere near them this afternoon were young Flora and the Canadian boys.

'And none of them had the bicycle when they left us. We'd have noticed,' Irene said.

The truth was, it could have been anyone. The bicycle had been propped up on the fence behind them and someone could easily have taken it while the girls were distracted.

Hazel smacked her hand against her forehead. 'What'll we do? You've not trained without gloves!'

Grace looked at her hands. Like the other girls', they were covered in cuts and bruises. They didn't bother with gloves when they were working in the forest. But they needed them for the tug of war, else they'd get friction burns from the rope.

'Can't someone run back to camp and get more gloves?' Morag asked.

But there wasn't time. The tug of war was due to start in ten minutes.

'Quick,' Irene said, 'everyone spread out and look. And check the ground too, in case the gloves have fallen – or been thrown – out of the basket.'

The girls ran around the field, searching for the bicycle with the basket of gloves and asking everyone if they'd seen them.

But no one had and now it was too late. The call came over the tannoy, for the women's tug of war.

* * *

156

Grace, as the strongest – the anchor – took her position at the back of the line.

'Pick up the rope,' the judge instructed. He was a dour old Scotsman in a navy kilt who looked most unimpressed at having to judge a women's competition. 'Then both teams move back, until the rope is taut.'

Grace glanced around at the few spectators, in case she recognised anyone. Judging from the cheers that had gone up when the land girls' team had been announced, most people were rooting for them. The Timber Corps had only received one cheer, from young Flora, who was leaning over the fence, watching them intently.

'Hurrah!' she yelled, when their name was called and then blushed and squirmed as folk stared at her.

'Take the strain,' the judge said, his hands held high above his head.

'Come on, girls, you're stronger than them,' Hazel said, walking down the line. 'Let's show them! You can do it!'

'PULL!' the judge called, dropping his hands to his sides and the girls immediately leaned back and pulled on the rope with all their might.

Grace gritted her teeth. This was awful: it felt completely different, pulling the coarse rope with bare hands. Only seconds into the bout, Morag, in front of her, yelled out in pain and sat down hard on the grass.

'GET UP!' Hazel yelled. Morag staggered to her feet. If she stayed down longer than three seconds, they'd be disqualified.

'Come on, you can do it!' Hazel shouted again.

But they couldn't.

They lost the first bout in hardly any time at all.

Irene cursed.

'Any more bad language like that, madam,' the judge said, 'and you'll be out.'

But it was the best of three pulls, so there was still a chance.

Hazel did her best to encourage them, running up and down the line and calling when they should pull. But within moments of starting the next bout, they could literally feel it slipping through their hands.

The land girls, buoyed up by their easy victory in the last pull, dragged the lumberjills over the central line, to win a decisive second bout.

The third – and last – was no better, in fact it was worse.

Moments after they started to pull, it was Seffy's turn to cry out in pain. Their rhythm had gone, they toppled over one another, Irene cursed again, the judge blew the whistle, waved his flag and jabbed his finger at them.

They'd been disqualified!

'Oh damn!' Morag said, as she slipped on the grass and lay there, prone and not bothering to try to get up. 'Never mind, they can't disqualify us twice.'

The girls lay on their backs, arms across their faces, panting too much to speak. Like a load of skittles that had been knocked down, Grace thought. A few feet away, the land girls danced in jubilation, hugging each other and waving their arms in victory. The small crowd that had gathered to watch, applauded politely.

'Those flamin' land girls are as pleased as punch,' Jean muttered, hugging her knees. She started removing grass from her breeches in a series of hard slaps.

Punching something hard was exactly what Grace felt like doing. She clenched her fists. She'd bet a pound to a penny that those land girls had something to do with the missing gloves. She felt rotten about letting wee Hazel down. She'd put her heart and soul into this stupid tug of war and Grace had wanted to do it for her.

Eventually, Irene sat up and clapped to get their attention. 'Come on, girls, chin up. We did our best but it wasnae to be. Come on now and shake hands with the winners.'

It was the last thing they felt like doing but they roused themselves and stood in a line, ranging from the smallest, Hazel, at the front, to Grace at the back, ready to congratulate the land girls.

'What does Miss High-and-Mighty think she's doin?' Irene said, crossly. 'Oi, come and shake hands!' she yelled.

Seffy was still sitting on the grass, the rope coiled around her, nursing her right wrist. She was fighting back tears. 'I can't,' she said.

'You! Come on!' Irene said, stomping over to her. 'You cannae let us all down now. Don't be such a bad sport!'

Something flared in Grace's chest.

'Stop!' she yelled at Irene. 'Will you just stop now? You've done nothing but pick on the girl since the day we got here! Can't you see she's hurt?'

Irene turned slowly, staring at Grace in disbelief. Grace could feel the eyes of the rest of the team on her. She could hardly believe it herself – she never shouted – but that had been building up for some time.

Grace stepped out of line and walked over to Seffy, crouching down to speak to her. Her hand looked swollen and sore. 'What've you done? Never mind, now. Come on, the land girls are waiting. Let's get this over with. Shake with your left hand. Could you do that?'

Seffy sniffed and nodded. Grace helped her up and they joined the team. Through gritted teeth, they muttered, 'Well done,' and shook hands with the members of the other side.

'Right, forget about that now,' Irene said, when the torture was over. 'Shall we go and see how the Canadian fellas got on? Hopefully, better than us.'

They made a solemn little troop, trudging over the field.

'Hey! There's my bicycle!' Jean said, pointing ahead.

Young Flora was wheeling it towards them. 'Is this yours?' she asked. 'I spotted my brothers playing with it, the wee terrors and I ran after them and got them to admit they'd taken it from the "wood chopping lassies". So, I guessed that was you.' She winced. 'Sorry about the tug of war.'

Irene shook her head. 'Call me a bad loser but I still reckon there was sabotage involved. But at least you've got your bicycle back, Jean.'

Jean was kneeling down, examining it closely. 'Aye, but the pump's missing. And there's no sign of any gloves. They were here, in the basket.'

Flora was wringing her hands. 'I'm sorry. You'll not want me joining the Timber Corps now, will you?'

'Don't fret,' Grace told her. 'It's all water under the bridge now.'

'What's water under the bridge? How d'you get on, girls?' It was Gordy again. He'd taken off his cap and his eyes were bright against his tanned face.

His smile faltered. He must have seen their slumped shoulders and dejected faces. 'You lost, right? Unless you're kidding me? No? Oh, that's too bad! I'll bet you worked real hard for that, too.'

'Aye, we did,' Irene said. 'But no matter. We did our best. Especially wee Hazel here, our super coach.'

'How did you get on?' Grace asked Gordy. It was the first time she'd ever spoken to him and she hoped he couldn't see her blushing.

He grinned. 'We won! The heats, the final, everything. The fellas are over the moon! Say, come join us, if you like, girls. We're over there in the far corner of the meadow. We've got a ton of food and drink and you can drown your sorrows with a Pepsi or two. What d'you say?'

'Aye,' Irene said, 'we will, thanks. That's the best offer we've had all day.'

Chapter 22

Seffy's wrist was agony. As she and the other girls headed towards the Canadians' picnic, she supported it carefully with her other hand.

It was her own stupid fault. Frustrated, in the final bout, she'd wrapped the rope around her hand, hoping to secure a better hold. When the rope was suddenly yanked, hard, she'd felt something snap.

Perhaps it was a sign. She was too feeble for the Women's Timber Corps. She'd done her month here now; she'd won her bet with Percy. Maybe it was time to call it a day.

Aunt Dilys was marching purposefully across the field towards them, swinging her arms but otherwise looking quite ladylike for once, in a dress and straw hat. Marigold – similarly attired – was having to run to keep up with her. Goldie was on a lead, trotting by her side.

'Why the glum faces? What's happened?' Dilys asked.

'We lost the tug of war,' Seffy said, dolefully.

'Goodness, is that all? I thought someone had died. I wouldn't be too upset. After all, it's hardly what one would call a sport.'

'It IS a sport!' Seffy wailed. She hated Dilys. Why did she have to rub salt into the wound? Why couldn't she be kind and consoling?

161

'Actually,' Jean said, 'tug of war used to be an Olympic sport. Until 1920.'

Dilys sniffed. '"Used to be". That's the point. Oh, Persephone, here.' She grabbed Seffy's shoulder and spun her around and Seffy yelped as her wrist was jarred. 'I'd like to borrow you for a second. There's someone I'd like you to meet.'

Seffy could hardly refuse. She told the other girls to go on without her but before they had a chance to walk on, Joey gasped. 'Oh, look! That's HER! Lady Lockhart. And his lordship, wearing his actual kilt. The chief of the clan!'

A noble-looking older couple were meandering across the meadow in their direction. The woman – presumably Lady Lockhart – was rather a head-turner, even at her age. She was slender and pretty, dressed in a pink suit with a matching hat and the man with her – the laird – was wearing a blue tartan kilt and long grey socks.

Aunt Dilys practically stepped out in front of them, giving them no option but to stop. 'Your ladyship,' she said. 'I wonder if I might introduce you to my niece?' Gosh. Seffy had never heard Dilys speak in such a simpering tone.

She could sense Irene's disapproval behind her. Morag was probably rolling her eyes too. After the progress she'd been making with the girls lately, it was too bad.

Once the introductions had been made, comments exchanged about Seffy's parents – whom, it transpired, the Lockharts knew – and amazement expressed that Seffy was working in the woods and what a game gal she must be – the Lockharts moved on.

'Now, why don't you come along with us and watch this baseball thingamajig?' Dilys suggested to Seffy. 'It sounds intriguing.'

Seffy shook her head and glanced around. There was no sign of the other girls. 'No, thanks, Aunt. I'm not really in the mood. To top an absolutely miserable day, I've done something to my hand.'

Marigold peered at it. 'Oh, my dear. It's awfully swollen. Look, Dilys! I think she needs some ice and a bandage on that.'

Dilys' gaze was focused across the meadow. 'Marigold was a VAD in the last war,' she said, dismissively. 'Ergo, she's frightfully interested in injuries.'

Seffy shrugged. 'I expect it's only bruised. It'll be fine.'

She didn't want any fuss and she wanted to get away. She made her apologies and left.

When she finally joined the others in the far meadow, Irene was stretched out on the grass, chatting to a group of Canadian boys. She turned to look at Seffy. 'Ah, here she is,' she said. 'Did you ask if the Lockharts would come and inspect us, like they've done for these fellas?'

Her tone was scathing, as though she already knew the answer and Seffy's heart fell. 'No,' she said, 'I didn't, I—'

But Irene had already turned away.

Goodness, that was unfair. Who'd said anything about asking for an inspection? As it was, Seffy had spent the whole conversation with Lady Lockhart grimacing in pain. She'd felt obliged to offer her right hand to her ladyship when they were introduced and even though the handshake was limp, it had been agony. As they made polite small talk, all Seffy could think about was the searing-hot pain shooting through her arm.

But there was no point trying to explain that to Irene now.

'Come and sit with us, Seffy,' Grace said, making room on the picnic rug she was sharing with one of the Canadians.

Seffy sat down gratefully and the chap introduced himself as Gordy Johnson.

'Ah, I remember you. One of the tree climbers!'

'Yes, ma'am. And there's the other one – Jean-Paul – talking to your pal.'

Seffy glanced around. The blonde Canadian and Irene were sitting very close. 'And is your charming sergeant here?' she asked.

'Oh, sure, he's someplace.'

Within seconds, she'd spotted him, sitting apart from the others, leaning back against the trunk of a horse chestnut tree. He raised his hand in greeting and she nodded back, not daring to move her injured wrist. He was dressed in civvies, like the others but unlike them, he was still wearing his army cap. Always on duty, she supposed.

'He was real good today, our Sarge,' Gordy said, following Seffy's gaze. 'Got us over the line a couple o' times.'

As she and the other girls sat in the warm sunshine, drinking cool Pepsi and laughing with the dozen or so men around them, the memory of their disastrous performance in the tug of war started to fade away.

The boys were in high spirits after their victory over a neighbouring company and their good mood was infectious.

'Say, what do you ladies know about our homeland, about Canada?' one of the boys asked.

'Yeah. It's a Dominion Day fete after all, so we have the right to ask!'

'It's big, there's lots of snow and you have Mounties,' Joey said, with a firm nod.

'And you all speak French,' Enid added.

'Not exactly, ma'am. If you're from Quebec, then you speak French, but we're from all over. JP's from Quebec. But we've got herring chokers and bluenosers too and I'm from BC.'

Enid almost went cross-eyed trying to work out what he'd just said. 'I see,' she said, politely.

The Canadian's eyes were twinkling. 'Do you know where that is, Miss? BC? British Columbia?'

'Of course!' Enid said, glancing around. She was probably wondering if genius Jean was nearby, to help her out. 'Well, I'm from Greenock,' she said, decisively. 'Do you know where that is?'

'Touché!' the boy said.

Enid slapped him on the arm. 'I thought you didn't speak French!'

'Is it really cold there, all the time? Like the Arctic?' Hazel asked.

'It's pretty cold in the winter but we have hot summers. Hotter than here, that's for sure.'

'Are there polar bears? And walruses and penguins?' Hazel asked.

The guys laughed.

'Only polar bears in the far north. We do have grizzlies though!' Gordy said.

All the men laughed.

'Oh, here we go!'

'Go on, Gordy, tell 'em all about it.'

Gordy started to regale them with a story of how he'd been chased through the woods by a bear.

'You must never surprise a bear,' he told them. 'Clap shout, sing, yell. Let 'em know you're around. A surprised bear is a dangerous bear. They can run as fast as a horse! Black bears, you know, back home, they're ten a penny. If you yell they usually get outta the way but this was a grizzly—'

'You could always have climbed a tree,' Grace said, blushing.

Gordy smiled at her and held her gaze for a second or two.

'Good idea, in theory, but—' he held up a finger and winked at her '—bears can climb trees, you know! And remember, just because you can't see a bear, it don't mean they ain't around!'

Grace laughed and as Seffy watched her and Gordy Johnson, she realised something: they couldn't take their eyes off each other.

'Who are those fellas?' one of the Canadian boys asked suddenly.

A couple of young men were walking across the meadow a few yards away, hands in their pockets, deep in conversation. They stood out because they weren't in uniform or sportswear, even though they were young and looked strong and able-bodied.

'They farmers?' someone asked.

'Nah,' came the reply. 'They're conscientious objectors. Conchies.' The man's tone was scathing. 'They won't do military service.'

The Canadian boys muttered amongst themselves and the jolly atmosphere of a moment ago disappeared.

'Some of those COs work in the bush, with us,' Gordy told Seffy and Grace. 'Clearing up behind us, burning leaves and branches, that kinda thing. I don't have a problem with them but some of the fellas do.'

'That's because they're selfish cowards, Gordy,' one of the men said, overhearing.

'Irresponsible.'

'Yellow-bellies . . . a danger to society.'

'Nazis . . .'

Nazis? Seffy frowned. That didn't make sense. Oh, she didn't like this at all. Some of the boys were getting quite worked up. One or two had got to their feet and were glaring at the men, with clenched fists. The conchies had quickened their pace and were glancing back occasionally, clearly nervous.

'That's ENOUGH!'

It was Sergeant Fraser. He'd left his position against the tree and his mouth was set; he was furious.

'Cut it out! Sit down and quit that now! I expected better from you!'

There was silence. The men turned and sat back down on the grass. Some of them put their heads down. Hopefully, Seffy thought, in shame.

'What day is this, fellas?' Fraser asked.

There were a few indecipherable murmurs, then Gordy said, more clearly, 'It's Dominion Day, Sarge.'

'Yeah, this is Dominion Day. It's a holiday, a day to honour our homeland. We're supposed to be getting along, having fun not a fight. Understood?'

'Yes, sir,' one or two murmured.

There was another uncomfortable silence. Sergeant Fraser pulled off his cap and rubbed his forehead, as though he were getting a headache.

Gordy cleared his throat. 'Say, did I ever tell you 'bout the time I was chased by a *black* bear . . . ?' Everyone laughed and groaned and someone threw a bread roll at his head.

The party mood was back, in full swing.

Sergeant Fraser threw himself down on the grass next to Seffy. He snatched up a blade of grass and started to chew the end.

'Hungry?' she asked.

He didn't answer.

'That was horrible,' Seffy said, 'for a few minutes, back there. Gosh, I thought they were going to launch themselves at those poor conchies. It was a relief, I can tell you, when you calmed them all down.'

He gazed ahead and gave a small shrug. 'Yeah, well I can't stand bullies.' He said it with such force, Seffy thought it must be personal. Not that she could ever imagine someone like him being bullied.

He was looking down at her hand and frowning. 'What did you do?'

'Oh, it's nothing.' She'd forgotten for a moment not to move it and pain shot through her wrist, making her wince. She should have taken up Marigold's offer of some ice.

Fraser sat up and touched it gently and Seffy yelped and pulled it away.

'That looks real bad,' he said.

Her hand had swollen up to almost twice its normal size. Suddenly she felt rather queasy.

'What did you do?' he asked again.

She sighed and prepared to be ridiculed. 'I wrapped the rope around my hand in the tug of war. I know, it was stupid. I wouldn't have minded quite so much if we'd actually won the blasted thing. But we lost. We were terrible. I'm sure you've heard.'

He rolled his eyes. And now he was standing up. Oh, that was it: he'd had enough of her again. Any moment, he'd be marching off, shaking his head. No, he was looking down at her and holding out his hand. 'Up. Come on, you need to get that looked at, ma'am.'

'Where are you off to?' Irene asked, tearing her eyes away from the chaps surrounding her and frowning up at them as they walked past.

Seffy shrugged. 'Apparently I have to see the medic. About this – ow!' She held up her hand, gingerly. 'And I daren't disobey!'

She followed Fraser across the field, trying not to lose him as they dodged people strolling past the stalls and tents. Every few yards, he passed someone he knew – a villager or one of the troops – and he nodded and greeted them all by name, without once breaking his stride. He was business-like and serious, occasionally muttering, 'Over here, ma'am,' when she went to turn in the wrong direction.

It was his holiday today, after all and although he was doing the gentlemanly thing and taking her to the medic, Seffy couldn't blame him for wanting to get it over with as quickly as possible.

'I guess this is all my fault,' he said, when the crowds had finally thinned a little and they could walk side by side. He wasn't being sarcastic this time; he sounded genuinely sorry. 'After all, I encouraged you to enter the tug of war contest.'

That was true, he had. She could picture him still, standing at the lorry window, rain dripping down his face.

'Oh, never mind,' Seffy said. 'Someone had already mentioned it. I think we'd have done it anyway.'

'You, though?' he said, glancing at her.

'Me though, what?'

He shrugged. 'I'm surprised you wanted to do the tug of war.'

Not this again. He thought she was prim and proper and snooty into the bargain.

'Turns out, I can't resist a challenge,' Seffy said. 'Actually, I was surprised that you also lowered yourself to do it, Sergeant.'

He smiled. 'Guess I can't resist a challenge either.'

A few minutes later, as they sat outside the medic's tent, waiting to be called in, he said, 'You won't be able to work for a while. Not with that hand. There's a name for that.'

Seffy laughed. 'Is there?'

'Men do it in the field.'

'"The field"? What, like farmers?'

'The *battlefield*.' His tone was scornful. Seffy wished they'd never started this stupid conversation but there was no going back now. 'Malingerers,' he said. 'Some men shoot themselves—'

She gasped. 'What?'

'Nowhere too bad – not the head, obviously, or the chest – but maybe the leg or sometimes the arm.'

'So they can't fight?'

'Yep. They get taken off duties, carted off to hospital. They're out of action for weeks, sometimes months. Sometimes they never go back to their company.'

Seffy looked at her swollen hand and then back at him. Was this his idea of a joke? Or was he trying to shock her?

'Are you saying you think I did this on purpose? To avoid work? You can't be serious?'

He shook his head. 'I'm only saying, there's a name for that.'

There was silence for a second, then he asked, 'How come the other girls don't like you?'

Seffy bit her lip; he certainly didn't beat about the bush. 'Is it that obvious?'

'No, leastways, not to me. But that day in the woods, when the tree nearly got you, one of the other girls said something about no one liking you.'

Seffy felt tears sting the backs of her eyes at the memory. She swallowed hard – which was actually quite painful.

'They didn't like me,' she admitted, 'when we first arrived. I didn't fit in. I was different and it wasn't only because I'm English. And there's still one girl in particular who'll never be my chum.'

She shrugged. 'But I've been trying awfully hard. And things are definitely looking up now.'

Callum nodded slowly. 'That's good. They were probably just jealous.'

'Oh, but why? I don't have any more money than them.'

He looked as though he were going to say something else but stopped himself and shrugged. 'But look at you. You've done all right. You haven't thrown the towel in.'

That sounded terribly like a vote of confidence. Goodness, this man was a strange one. Talking to him was like being on a merry-go-round: up and down and never quite knowing where one was.

'No,' Seffy agreed. 'I haven't. Although, to be honest, I've been wavering about whether or not to stay from the moment I got here. It's—' she shrugged and gave a rueful smile '—not been easy.'

Fraser looked at her. 'But you're gonna stay, right?'

It was ridiculous but he sounded genuinely interested in the answer. And as though he were hoping she would.

Seffy nodded. 'Yes. Despite everything, I've discovered a stubborn streak! I'm going to show them all. Or at least . . .' she looked at her swollen hand '. . . I was going to, until this happened.'

He was trying to be kind. Not many people had been kind since she'd arrived at Farrbridge. Certainly not Miss McEwen or Irene or Aunt Dilys. Grace had been kind today, when she'd stood up to Irene. That was the first time any of the girls had taken her side. It was something to be grateful for.

Fraser sighed. 'I'll be honest, I didn't have you down for a – what do they call you? A lumberjill?'

'What then?'

'I see you more as a "reclining on a chaise-longue while someone feeds you grapes" kinda gal.'

Seffy smiled. He didn't think an awful lot of her. 'Actually,' she said, 'what you've described is my mother, down to a tee.'

'There you go! What do they say? If you wanna see the girl

in twenty years' time, look at her mother?' He inclined his head. 'I rest my case.'

Seffy laughed. 'I am not that bad! I'll tell you something about my mother: she holds down the corners of her eyes when she laughs so she doesn't get laughter lines!'

'Really? That's crazy!'

'Isn't it?'

They laughed and then sat in silence for a minute.

'Isn't it queer to think that if it wasn't for the war, none of us would have met?' Seffy said. 'I'd never have known any of these girls, the lumberjills. And we wouldn't have even known you chaps existed. You'd still be over there in Canada, doing whatever you do. Chopping down trees, I suppose.'

He laughed. 'I run the sawmill for a – for a guy there. But yeah, we're woodsmen. That's what we do, in peacetime. What about you? If you weren't a lumberjill, what would you be doing?'

Seffy didn't want to say. She'd have finished the season and she'd probably be planning her wedding to Teddy Fortesque. Engagement announcement in the *Times*, wedding in Westminster, honeymoon on the continent. It was all mapped out. Children, of course, all being well. And looking after the home. Managing servants. All the things they were taught at finishing school: how to entertain, how to talk to people, etiquette and titles, how to get out of cars without flashing your knickers, how to mix a cocktail.

It all seemed so silly and trivial and unimportant now. There was a war raging and people were being killed and captured and no one knew how or when it would all end. No, her life, without a war, was too shameful to admit.

She shook her head. 'Heaven knows! This and that!'

'You wouldn't be working though, would you?' he said. 'You're not like the other girls. Oh, it's not only how you talk. You're a classy dame, as we say back home.'

171

'"A classy dame"? I've been called some things in my time but that's a new one on me!'

The tent flap was pulled back and the medic's head popped out. He frowned at them, as they laughed. 'Does someone here need medical assistance?' he asked, doubtfully.

'Oh yes, me,' Seffy said. She carefully held out her hand for inspection. She'd forgotten all about the pain for a few minutes.

'Right, I'll leave you in the lieutenant's capable hands,' Fraser said. He stood up slowly and tipped his cap.

Seffy thanked him – this time she remembered. She couldn't help wishing he would stay.

That night, as Seffy climbed into bed, careful not to bang her hand, which was wrapped up tightly in a bandage, Irene called across the hut.

'His name is Callum! Callum Fraser. What d'you say to that? He could be a Scotsman!'

'Who?' Seffy called back.

Irene chuckled. 'You know very well who, my girl.'

That was a surprise. Irene, being nice for once.

Seffy lay back, staring up at the wooden roof, feeling . . . what? Happiness. Yes, that's what this unfamiliar feeling was.

She'd been wondering about his full name and now she knew, it was like possessing a little part of him. *Callum Fraser.* She said it over and over in her head.

It was a good name, a strong name. It suited him.

She smiled as she thought back to this afternoon.

They'd actually had a proper conversation. And although he'd teased her and all but accused her of being a shirker, something made her think that he quite liked her. And strangely, against all the odds, she quite liked him too.

'Night night!' Jean called out.

'Sleep tight!' Seffy called back. 'Don't let the bed bugs bite!'

Chapter 23

'You're no good to us here,' Miss McEwen said, when Seffy gave her the doctor's certificate. She'd been signed off work for at least a month. The wrist wasn't broken but it was badly sprained. 'I expect you're over the moon,' the supervisor added, dryly. 'You might as well go home and come back when you're more use.'

"Go home"! Those words would have been manna from heaven when Seffy had first arrived. She'd been desperate for an excuse to leave – and she probably wouldn't have come back – but not now.

Home would be dreadfully dull compared to this. She was worn out, with a tiredness that seeped into the bones and a few days' rest wouldn't go amiss but leave? No, thank you.

She looked at Miss McEwen. 'I don't want to go home,' she said.

The supervisor's eyes widened in surprise. 'And what good'll you be here? You can't drive the truck, fell trees or haul logs.'

'No, but I can make the fire for tea breaks, do some snedding and burn sticks for charcoal.'

Snedding, using a sharp knife and with her left hand, was probably not her best idea but Miss McEwen nodded. 'Aye, all right.' She turned to go and then stopped. 'You know, Miss Mills, when you arrived, I'd have put money on you not lasting the week, so—'

'So?'

'So, well done.'

Praise indeed. She'd lasted more than a week: she'd lasted five weeks, in fact. She'd won her bet with Percy. If only she didn't have a wonky wrist, she'd write straight away and tell him he owed her ten pounds.

Joey had offered to do her correspondence, when she came back from the medic tent, all strapped up.

'I can be your secretary and you can dictate your letters to me. I can't do shorthand, mind, so you'll have to speak slowly.'

It was awfully kind of Joey – she and Hazel were the two sweetest girls in the hut – but Seffy couldn't accept. Aside from all the white lies she'd have to include, she'd have to reveal her parents' address: an actual castle. How would she live that down?

'You're going to be a lady of leisure for a wee while, then,' Irene said, when Seffy announced she'd be staying in camp until her wrist healed. 'You can go and take tea with Lady Lockhart now.'

'I shan't,' Seffy replied.

She went to take tea with Aunt Dilys, instead.

'Shall I be mother?' Dilys asked, reaching across the table for the teapot, which Marigold had brought out into the garden on a tray, complete with bright yellow tea cosy. Marigold was sitting with them which was awfully good of Aunt Dilys. Mother would rather die than have staff sit in on a tea party.

'How's that hand of yours, dear?' Marigold asked. 'Still unable to work?'

Seffy nodded and held up her bandaged wrist. 'I feel rather useless. Although I'm managing to do bits and pieces.'

'I'm surprised you didn't go home and wait it out there,' Dilys said. She was cutting up the carrot cake now and putting slices onto plates. 'Well, if there's anything I can do,' she said, vaguely.

'There is something, actually,' Seffy said. 'Would you mind writing home for me? I could try using my left hand but Mummy will think I'm drunk. Could you send her a quick note on my behalf, telling her what's happened and that I'll be in touch as soon as I can write? I'll give you the address.'

'The address? There's hardly any need for that!' Dilys snapped. She pounced on a petunia in a nearby pot and started to dead-head it with vigour. 'Dalreay Castle was my childhood home too,' she said, without looking up. 'I rather think I know the address, thank you very much!'

Seffy swallowed. Yes of course. How could she have forgotten? Aunt Dilys and Daddy had grown up in the place. So why, she wondered, did Dilys never show any inclination to come back?

After they'd finished tea and were sitting, replete, on their seats, as bees buzzed around and the fountain in the ornamental pond tinkled softly, Seffy broached a subject she'd been wanting to tackle for a while.

'Aunt, I wanted to ask you about your time with the Land Army. Or the Timber Services. Which was it?'

Marigold flinched and Dilys, who'd been looking quite relaxed until that moment, stiffened. 'I have no idea what you mean. You must have confused me with someone else.'

Seffy reached into her bag and produced her evidence. 'What's this, then?'

It was the photograph of Aunt Dilys. Before she'd damaged her wrist, Seffy had written to Mummy requesting it and Mummy had duly sent it. It was clearly Dilys, although it had been taken years ago when she was a similar age to Seffy. She was standing in a forest, holding an axe and wearing a huge sou'wester. There were other girls on either side of her but the photograph had been cut, presumably to fit the frame, and they'd been sliced in half.

Dilys snatched the photograph from Seffy and for one awful moment, it looked as though she were going to rip it up.

'Where did you get this?' she demanded.

'It's been in a frame on our piano, with all the other family photos, for as long as I can remember.'

Dilys stared at the picture and a range of emotions seemed to flash across her face.

'Shall I fetch your spectacles?' Marigold asked, quickly rising from her seat.

'No! I can see it well enough.' Dilys turned to Seffy. 'Quite the little detective, aren't we?' Her voice was calm but cold. 'You're right, I was in the Women's Forestry Corps, last time.' She sniffed. 'It wasn't here though.'

Seffy felt guilty; this was clearly painful.

'It was in England. In Devon,.' Dilys continued.

Marigold bit her lip. 'Dilys, no, don't. Don't go through all this again.'

Dilys had seemed to be on the verge of saying more but she stopped, abruptly. 'It wasn't a very happy time of my life,' she said. She handed back the photograph.

Once, Seffy would have said something crass like, *Gosh, I know what you mean! I've never worked so hard or ached so much!* but she could see the hurt and pain etched clearly on her aunt's face and she stayed silent. Whatever had happened, it was much more than sore muscles and a few blisters.

Chapter 24

'What about here?' Enid asked, stopping next to some rocks and pointing down into the burn.

'No, too shallow,' Grace said. 'You can see the stones on the bottom. It'd be hardly worth getting in.'

At this time of year, it didn't get dark in the Highlands until after they'd all gone to bed. After supper, the girls had started to go down to the burn for a splash around and to cool down. It helped soothe the itchy midge bites on their legs, too.

Tonight, Irene had suggested going further along, away from their usual paddling spot, so they'd tramped along the bank for half an hour or more.

'A wee bit further,' Irene said.

They walked for a few more minutes and then, in the distance, they heard strange yelling sounds. There was silence again for a moment or two and then the yelling started again.

'What in heaven's name is that?' Enid asked.

'Sounds like someone being murdered,' Morag said.

'No, it's yodelling!' Jean said. 'Make haste! Let's go and find out!'

Irene knew exactly what it was – JP had told her what the fellas often got up to on a Sunday night – but she said nothing.

The girls made their way towards the source of the noise and as they rounded a bend in the burn, it all became clear.

There was a swing over the water – a huge truck tyre attached to a rope, suspended from a branch – and a group of Canadian boys were taking it in turns to swing from it.

The boy on the tyre now was beating his chest and calling out the Tarzan yell. 'Aah-eeh-ah-eeh-aaaaaah-eeh-ah-eeh-aaaaah!'

'Now, isn't that a sight for sore eyes?' Irene murmured, as they got nearer. She pretended to fan herself. 'I may have to call for smelling salts!'

They'd been spotted.

'Hey, girls! Howdy! D'you wanna come have a go?' It was the young private who'd taken a shine to Grace – Gordy.

Jean-Paul smiled. 'Yeah, it's your turn, ladies! If you can fell a tree, you can swing on a rope!'

Irene smiled back. She'd talked to him for a while at the fete last weekend. He was awful young but she'd taken a shine to him. She liked his manners and the way he listened carefully to everything she said, laughed at her jokes and paid her compliments. She liked him even more with wet hair and wearing nothing but knee-length shorts.

'You carry on for a moment, fellas,' Jean said. 'Show us how it's done.' The girls had stopped a few yards away and they giggled as JP grabbed the tyre with one hand and jumped up onto it with ease. His pal then pulled the tyre back and released it, like a catapult in a sling.

'Tarzan! The one, the only!' he yelled as he swung across the burn, leaped off effortlessly onto the other bank and landed neatly, arms aloft. Then he waded his way back through the water and up onto the bank again.

'You're hardly Johnny Weissmuller!' Irene shouted. She turned back to face the girls, crossed her eyes and pulled a face, making them all laugh. In truth, the boy looked as good as the film star, even without a loincloth or long floppy hair.

'I suppose we might as well have a go,' Enid said, shrugging nonchalantly.

'Aye. We've got as much right to splash around in the burn as them,' Joey pointed out.

'Absolutely!' Jean agreed.

Irene smiled. They were eager. Even little Hazel.

Of course, with her strapped-up hand, Seffy couldn't do it but the chances were, Irene thought, even without an injury, she'd have wrinkled up her nose at the idea of swinging on a tyre. She thought she was too good for the Canucks.

Grace looked reluctant too. She was staying firmly at the back of the group and as the others argued good-naturedly about who should have the first swing, she stayed silent. Irene felt a pang of sympathy for her. Grace was shy.

Grace sat down on the bank to make her intentions absolutely clear: they wouldn't get her on that tyre for love nor money.

The other girls were being instructed as to the best way to climb onto the tyre and how they should position themselves if they wanted to try jumping off onto the opposite bank.

She shuddered as she imagined the boys helping to heave her up, then pulling the tyre back with difficulty, complaining how heavy she was. Imagine if the rope snapped when she was halfway across the burn? The thought made her go hot inside.

No, she'd stay safely here and watch the others.

Gordy was demonstrating the best swinging technique and Grace shifted to one side, to get a better view and gasped as he lost his grip and dropped into the burn with an almighty splash.

He disappeared. For ten seconds and then longer. The boys were shaking their heads and laughing but the girls were peering into the water, anxiously looking for any sign of him. It wasn't more than about three feet deep. Where could he have gone?

Perhaps he'd hit his head on a rock? Grace was starting to

wonder if anyone was going to rescue him, when his head popped up, eyes closed. He made a spout of his mouth and blew a fountain of water a foot up into the air. Everyone laughed and Grace smiled with relief.

'You did that on purpose!' Hazel said. 'You didn't really fall.'

'Sure,' he said, as he scrambled nimbly back up the bank. 'I was only fooling around!'

Grace felt strangely cheered that her favourite hadn't really fallen in, that he could swing just as well – better, in fact – than some of the others. He wasn't actually that short, either; the rest of the fellas were just big.

When he flexed his arms, his biceps were just as big as theirs. And he seemed to be something of a leader. She'd noticed it at the fete too, when he'd invited her to share his rug and he'd told those funny stories about being chased by bears. They all listened when Gordy spoke.

Jean was the first on the tyre, squealing as two of the boys pulled it back and then let go, giving her an extra push as they did so. Gordy supervised for a few minutes, making sure the boys knew what they were doing and then he wandered over to where Grace was sitting. His hair was sticking up like a crest; he was drying himself with his shirt.

Grace's stomach turned somersaults. He was blocking her view of the swing now. Perhaps he hadn't even noticed she was sitting there, quietly on the bank? As he stood over her, cold water dripped onto her leg.

'Oi!' she said.

'Oh, I beg your pardon!' He took a few steps away. *No, don't go,* she thought, wishing she'd stayed quiet.

'It's no matter,' she said, quickly. 'I'm not made of sugar! But maybe you need to dry yourself a little more.'

He threw himself down on the grass in a pool of sunlight. 'If I sit here, I'll dry out real soon.'

'You're soaked!'

He laughed. 'I sure am. Sometimes I just let myself fall. It's kinda refreshing. In any case, I'm more like Cheeta than Tarzan!'

Grace smiled uncertainly and Gordy narrowed his eyes and peered at her. 'Say, you do know who Tarzan is, don't you?'

Grace shook her head.

'And Cheeta? The chimp?'

She shook her head again.

'Jeez!' He laughed. 'Don't you have the movies in Scotland?'

Grace smiled. She liked the way he pronounced "Scotland". ''Course we do, in the towns. But I live on a croft in the middle of nowhere. There are no cinemas nearby.'

He didn't pester her to go on the swing; he seemed quite happy to sit with her and watch the others from a distance.

Grace exhaled. She felt calm around him. He didn't seem to expect anything from her.

She racked her brain for something to say. If she didn't speak soon, he'd think she was an idiot or that she didn't want to talk to him. Any second now, he'd get up and leave.

'Why did you come here? To Scotland?' she asked, suddenly hitting on a topic of conversation.

'Well, it sure wasn't my idea! I was happy back home in BC. Things are tough there since the Depression and there ain't much work but I got by. It was my pal, Callum – that's Sergeant Fraser—'

Grace looked around.

'Oh, he's not here right now,' Gordy said. 'Anyhow, he was the one who persuaded me to enlist. "Europe?" I said, "but they're in the middle of war!" And he said that was the exact reason why we should go; they – you – needed us. Some other fellas from our town – that's Invermore – had already enlisted and Callum said it would be an adventure and he said, didn't I want to see some place other than home? "It's a big wide world out there, Gordy!" And he said I needn't worry because we wouldn't have to fight, that we'd be lumbering, like back home. Though . . .' He hesitated.

Grace leaned forward. 'What?'

'Well, I ain't so sure about that now. I've heard of other companies getting disbanded and all the men sent to join combat units.
Sometimes – like yesterday, with the conchies – it feels like the
fellas are just itching for a fight.'

Grace hoped that wasn't true. Jock had told the girls how
much the country needed timber. Surely, with this whole forest
to clear, the Canadians would stay for a while yet?

'But you're still glad you came, aren't you?' she asked.

'Oh, sure! I'd worked all over before I did this. On logging
camps, living in bunkhouses, dirty and draughty with leaking
roofs. You had to rent a mattress from the company but most of
us used branches off the trees instead. Compared to all that, the
CFC is luxury. The pay's good and the conditions and the food.
We used to get beans to eat, the whole time. And now of course
– there are you girls, too. Life's looking pretty good!' He sighed.
'But . . . I have to admit, I've been pretty homesick. Canada's a
helluva way away. It takes weeks for mail to arrive, so you can
go a while without hearing from your folks. And you worry, you
know, in case something's happened?'

Grace nodded, feeling her heart go out to him. But it hadn't
occurred to her to be worried about Mother; not at all.

As Gordy spoke, he pulled at bits of grass in front of him.
She liked the way she could just throw out a question to him
and he'd catch it and run with it. She dreaded "conversation"
because she didn't know how to do it. She wasn't "chatty". But
Gordy made it easy.

'But yeah, it's good here,' he said. He glanced up at her, shyly.
'Specially now.'

Grace kept her eyes on the girls and the fellas on the swing.
Little Hazel was on there now, screaming wildly and swinging like
a maniac; even the boys were telling her to hold on a little tighter.

Gordy shuffled a little nearer, still sitting cross-legged in the
patch of sunlight. 'Say are you warm enough there, Gracie?

You're sittin' in shadow. If you move a couple of inches to your left, you'll be in the sun.'

He'd called her "Gracie". She moved along.

'How're you enjoying working in the forest?' he asked. 'Kinda different ain't it?'

Grace nodded. 'I like it. I've done some felling before.'

'Oh, sure, I can tell. The way you cut in? I was watchin' you the other week. You did it real good.'

Grace blushed, so taken aback she couldn't speak. He'd been watching her? Her mind raced. Perhaps this was all a joke or maybe he had a bet on with the other fellas. Seffy had been talking about her brothers the other night and how they'd bet on anything: which raindrop would hit the bottom of the window first, anything. Perhaps that's all this was. He couldn't be serious about liking her, could he?

Seffy leaned against a boulder on the riverbank and watched the others on the swing. It looked like fun; she'd have liked to have a go but there was no way she could do it, with her hand all bandaged up like this. Goodness, she could hardly do anything. She'd had to ask Joey to help her dress again this morning.

But she was glad the other girls were joining in and showing those Canadian fellas what they were made of. It was a shame Callum, as she now thought of him, wasn't here to see it. The girls were strong and lithe, like gymnasts. It was rather impressive. If he saw it, he might even revise his poor opinion of them. Although he'd probably think Hazel was being reckless rather than brave. She was like a wild wee beastie, when it was her turn on the swing: holding on with one hand, leaning right back and laughing when the fellas warned her not to. It was as though she didn't care what happened to her. Seffy held her breath as Hazel leaped off the tyre, arms and legs spread like a starfish and exhaled again when she landed safely on the other bank.

Gordy had made a beeline for Grace, just as he'd done at the fete. Seffy tried to watch surreptitiously. They were so sweet together; it was lovely to see them getting on so well.

She could be grumpy and rather abrupt but Grace was a nice girl, really. Just a little awkward. She'd probably not had much of a life, living on that isolated farm in the middle of nowhere. Oh, the thought of a possible romance in the camp was so exciting, it sent a little shiver down Seffy's spine.

Jean sat down on the rock next to her. 'Some of these boys are French-speaking. From Quebec,' she said. 'The one Irene's talking to, Jean-Paul. He's one. You've been to France, haven't you? You said you'd spent time in Paris. Why don't you go and talk to them?'

Seffy shook her head. Oh, this was mortifying. She could order wine and say please and thank you in French, of course, but little more.

'To be perfectly honest, I can hardly speak a word,' she admitted. 'I was sent to Europe to be "finished" and dragged back again when it looked like war. I'm afraid I spoke English the whole time.'

But it was rude, she realised that now, not to at least try. What had she been doing with all these marvellous opportunities? She'd been sleep-walking through her life until now.

'We've tired of the tyre!' Joey announced, laughing. She threw herself down on the bank. 'Aw, that was great fun. I didn't think I'd have the energy but it's like dancing. No matter how exhausted I am after a day in the woods, I can always manage to dance!'

'Watch out, here comes Mr Killjoy,' Irene said.

Seffy looked around: it was Callum Fraser, dressed in his work clothes: dungarees, white shirt and boots. His cap was low down on his head. He stood nearby, calling out the men's names and waving at them.

Seffy's chest tightened. Oh, this was mean. They were enjoying themselves and now that they'd all stopped swinging, there might be time for a chat and a laugh before the sun finally went down.

184

'They're not working,' Seffy said, sharply. 'They're off duty. You can't call them back to camp.'

He looked at her. 'It's late. They've got an early start, ma'am.' He glanced at her arm. 'Unlike you.'

'We're almost done, Sarge,' one of the boys said. 'One last swing for Buddy, all right?'

'All right,' he agreed.

Callum was looking past her now – which was insulting in itself. Men of her acquaintance didn't usually do that. He was staring at Grace and Gordy, who were still sitting a couple of feet apart on the grassy bank, deep in conversation.

'Oh, I'd leave them be, if I were you,' Seffy said. 'They're getting on splendidly.'

'Johnson!' he called out, ignoring her.

Honestly, what a meanie. And to think she'd started to like him, after the fete. But he was being a complete spoilsport.

Gordy had turned at the sound of his name and was getting up now and preparing to leave Grace.

Callum nodded at Seffy's hand. 'How's it doing?'

She had no inclination to tell him. What business was it of his?

'It's fine, thank you,' she answered, frostily.

He cleared his throat. 'We've got a cinema evening at camp next Saturday.' He was being formal with her again. As they'd sat outside the medic's tent at the fete and he'd teased her about being a malingerer, he'd let his guard down. She'd liked the chap she'd glimpsed then. But now he was being distant again. Blast. She didn't like Sergeant Fraser; she only liked Callum.

'A cinema evening? Oh, yes?' She wasn't going to make this easy for him.

'Yes, we'd like to invite you ladies.'

'And what is the film?'

'The picture? It's "Gambling on the High Seas" and after the show there'll be dancing 'til midnight, music provided by Mr Kielty's gramophone records.' He gave a small ironic bow.

Seffy nodded. 'Thank you. I'll ask the girls and see what they want to do.'

She knew they'd jump at the chance to go to the camp for a film and a dance – it would be a real treat – but she was determined not to seem that keen. Let Sergeant Fraser stew a while.

'I've gotta go,' Gordy said. Was it Grace's imagination or did he seem reluctant to leave? 'Sarge is calling us in. Here, I made you something.'

Grace took it and her stomach swooped. It was a neat little daisy chain bracelet. She looked up to thank him but he was already off, striding away, lost now in the group of boys who were picking up their shirts and waving goodbye to the girls.

'Haste ye back!'

'So long!'

'See you soon, ladies!'

She would put the bracelet on now, before the others spotted it. She worried for a moment that it might be too small. She didn't have delicate little wrists like the other girls but Gordy had judged it perfectly. Carefully, oh so carefully, she put her hand through the flowers and held out her arm, to admire it.

When she got back to the hut, she'd take it off and ask Jean if she could borrow one of her books. Then she'd press the flowers between the pages and keep them forever.

The sun was going down and a bright shaft of sunlight hit her face. Grace lifted her chin towards it, closed her eyes. And smiled.

Chapter 25

One of the fellas came up with the idea in the canteen, as they sat eating stew and dumplings. One word and one word only, to describe each of the lumberjills they'd met.

'Grace?'

Callum tensed, hoping no one would say something mean, something that'd make Gordy see red. He sure wasn't in the mood to break up a fight right now. He'd been working real hard today, he was tired and hungry. He wanted to have his supper in peace.

'Friendly!' he suggested, getting in first. He ate a forkful of stew and glared at the other men, daring them to contradict him.

'Yeah, Grace sure is friendly,' one of them said. 'I don't mean *that f*riendly,' he added, glancing at Gordy. 'You know, I mean, she's a nice girl.'

'Irene's friendly,' Tom said, meaningfully, looking at Jean-Paul, who stared straight back at him, giving nothing away.

'Yeah, look, they're all nice girls, OK,' Callum said, 'but let's not get carried away here, fellas.' He was looking directly at Gordy, who wouldn't meet his eye. He took another forkful of stew and washed it down with some water.

'What's that supposed to mean, "let's not get carried away?"'

Gordy asked. He'd finished eating and was moving his knife back and forth over the gravy on his plate.

Callum let his fork drop with a clatter. The guys around him looked up.

'OK, for a start, we don't know how long they're gonna stick around. You really think they'll still be working the woods come winter?'

A few of the guys shook their heads and muttered. They could see he had a point.

'They won't last,' Callum said. 'Or the British will see they've made a mistake, trying to use women to do a man's job and they'll send 'em all home. So, guys, you might wanna save yourselves a whole lotta—' he wanted to say "heartache" but that wouldn't do, not for these fellas '—*trouble*. Be friendly an' all but don't go doing anything dumb like falling for one of those girls.'

He looked at Gordy again but there was no telling if he was listening. His head was down.

Callum shrugged. 'Take it or leave it, that's my advice.'

He'd pulled Gordy away from Grace the other night at the rope swing because the way they were looking at each other was making him uneasy. She was probably nice as pie but Gordy was rash and Grace was the first girl he'd been sweet on here. Or maybe, ever. Gordy was the little brother he'd never had. He was like family. And, something he'd learned from Missy's folks: you looked out for family. He didn't want Gordy to make the same mistake as him, rushing into something without thinking it through.

They'd be seeing more of the lumberjills over the next few weeks. There was the dance at the weekend, for one. It was kinda inevitable that there'd be flirting and romances. The Timber Corps girls were young and pretty, like he'd told Captain Graham, and the guys were only human. They were lonesome and a long way from home. There were no parents, or wives or girlfriends around. Hell, they could do anything they liked.

But no attachments. He would do his best to put a stop to that. *Sure, have some fun, fellas,* he thought *but don't let it turn into anything serious.*

He had other reservations about the British girls. If their own men hadn't been sent off to war, would they be quite so keen on the company guys? And did the fact that the fellas had loot: money, cigarettes, candy and gum – and were so free with them – add to their attraction?

Take the shapely, older girl, Irene. She was married but you'd never guess it, the way she carried on with some of the guys and especially with JP. It was obvious she had a thing for him. Maybe it was just a way of killing time, of focusing on the present rather than the past or the future. They were all trying to do that, of course. But, somehow, it didn't seem right.

'Jean?' someone suggested, moving on with the game.

'Smart.'

'Sure, she's one smart cookie, that one.'

'Seffy?'

'Classy!' Gordy said.

'Spoilt,' Callum said, at the same time.

The guys laughed.

Callum shook his head. 'You know, her real name's something fancy. Lady something or other. She's like one of those charity ladies who come to town to do good works. You know the kind I mean?'

'Oh, sure,' one of the fellas said. 'Rich ladies, filling their time. And they wear white gloves.'

Callum nodded. 'That's it. White gloves, so they don't have to touch anyone and they probably breathe through their mouths so they don't have to smell nothing bad.'

When Ma passed away and Pa turned to drink, one of those charity ladies had tried to put Callum in an orphanage. He'd been seven years old.

He felt a twinge of guilt, calling Seffy "spoilt" in front of all the guys. It was true, she was pretty spoilt but she was a ton of other things too. She was brave and funny and sharp as a tack. He couldn't help liking her and he hadn't quite worked out why.

'Joey?'

'Which one's Joey?'

'Josephine. Dimples. Cute.'

'Remember what the chaplain told us last week at the service,' Gordy said, 'about how to treat women? The local women, as well as the lumberjills? "Treat them as you would treat your best girl back home, as you would want another army, in your country, to treat your sweetheart and your sisters".'

Callum nodded at him. It was worth reminding the men of that. Good job, Gordy.

'Hazel?'

'Who's Hazel?'

'The little wild one! Remember her, on the swing?'

'Oh yeah.' Gordy thought for a second. 'She was kinda crazy that night. Oh, but she's sad. She's one sad lady.'

'Her husband was killed, I heard.'

'Yeah, that's right.'

The mood around the dinner table changed. The cheerful banter dried up and everyone was suddenly deep in thought.

'D'you think we did the right thing, coming here?' Wally Mitchell asked from the end of the table. Wally asked that question at least once a day. And he always wanted to talk about home, which wasn't good because it made the guys feel blue.

Callum stood up, pushed back his seat and picked up his tray to return it to the hatch. 'Give it a rest, will you, Wally?' he said and then, to the others, he said, 'Anyone up for a game of pool?'

Later, as Gordy handed Callum a cue in the sports room, he said, 'That girl, Gracie?'

'Grace? What about her?' Callum asked.

'I'm gonna ask her to marry me.'

'Don't,' Callum said.

'Why not?'

'You know the saying, "The girl you fool around with is not the girl you marry"? That's why not.'

Gordy bit his lip, bent over the pool table and pocketed the eight ball.

'You lose,' Callum said.

Gordy straightened up and banged the end of the cue on the floor. 'I am not foolin' around! What d'you take me for?'

Callum nodded. 'OK, calm down. You're not foolin', I get it. Just wanted to be sure, pal.'

Chapter 26

'I won't be coming,' Grace said, when Seffy told the girls about the invitation to the film and dance night at the Canadian camp. 'I'll stay behind and mind the place.'

There was nothing to "mind", of course, but she wouldn't budge.

Seffy couldn't understand it. Everyone knew Grace didn't like dancing but didn't she want to see Gordy again? Boys needed a little encouragement; Seffy didn't need one of the women's magazines to tell her that.

She'd watched Grace and Gordy on Sunday night, at the riverbank and it was clear how much they liked one another. If Grace didn't go to the dance on Saturday, he'd wonder what he'd done wrong. Seffy considered saying something along those lines but stopped herself. It wasn't her place; Grace might take offence.

'Shall I stay with you, Grace?' Seffy asked, in a small voice. 'After all, I can hardly dance with my wonky wrist.'

Grace waved away her suggestion. 'Och, no. That's kind but don't miss out because of me.'

Seffy smiled gratefully; she could go now with a clear conscience. She was looking forward to the evening. She couldn't remember the last time she'd been to the pictures and she was dying to see the Canadian barracks. Since their visit, Jean and Hazel hadn't stopped talking about how wonderful they were.

Her excitement had nothing to do with the possibility of seeing Callum Fraser again, of course. She was still cross with him for breaking up their jolly gathering at the stream – or rather, the burn, as the others called it. If he was at the dance, she'd go out of her way to avoid him.

The huge Nissen hut where the entertainment was to be held was in the centre of the Canucks' camp, in a forest clearing and surrounded by trees. The girls oohed and aahed as they walked inside.

'Everything the Canadians have is bigger and better than anything we have,' Joey said.

At one end of the hall, rows of wooden seats had been laid out, facing a large white screen. There was even a projector set up on a table, for the film.

'Golly, it's like a real cinema!' Enid said.

The hall was crowded with uniformed Forestry Corps men, as well as villagers, land girls and lumberjills from other huts. Some folk had already started to take their seats for the show.

There, standing in the middle of them all, was Gordy Johnson. His face lit up when he spotted them and he weaved through the milling throng, until he reached them.

'Grace isn't here, Gordy, I'm sorry,' Seffy said, thinking it was best to put him out of his misery straight away. His face fell and she patted his shoulder.

Silly Grace, she might well have missed her chance now. There were lots of pretty girls here tonight and once the dancing started, Gordy might find another potential sweetheart: someone who wasn't playing hard to get.

* * *

193

Later that evening, Seffy watched as Irene sashayed back to her seat, pestered by chaps who wanted the next dance. She was laughing and shaking her head, insistent that she wanted to sit the next one out.

She and Irene weren't exactly bosom buddies but Seffy had to admit, the girl had a marvellous figure: she went in and out in all the right places and walked perfectly upright, with her chest thrust out, unapologetically.

The others had spotted Jean trying to walk like Irene earlier – "all slinky", as Joey described it. But she'd soon stopped, when Morag asked her whether she was feeling all right or whether she'd strained her neck, looking up at all those treetops. Seffy had learned how to carry herself in deportment and she could still recite the tutor's instructions. "Imagine a string attached to the crown of your head, pulling you up into a straight line, stomach in, bottom under, swing your arms gently but not like a soldier on parade and for goodness' sake, girls, smile!"

But she hardly ever remembered to do it. Mummy was always telling her not to slouch but to "stand up straight!"

Irene had almost certainly never had a deportment lesson in her life. She was a natural.

'Don't you think she has a look of Vivien Leigh?' Jean asked, as she joined Seffy and they watched the effect Irene was having on the men. 'I think she's beautiful.'

'And you're clever, Jean. The cleverest girl I've ever met and that counts for a lot!'

Jean sighed, unconvinced. 'I'd rather be beautiful,' she said.

Seffy gazed around the hall, at the jitterbugging couples. It might only have been coming from a gramophone but the music was loud and it was so warm in here, that the windows were steaming up.

'Oh, off you go!' Seffy said to Jean, as someone asked her to dance, pulling her into his arms and onto the dance floor before she'd even had time to say yes.

'Care to dance, ma'am?'

Seffy shook her head at the chap who was asking and held up her bandaged hand. It was a good excuse for turning them down. If her partner was gentle and didn't swing her around too much, she could probably manage it, but she didn't want to dance with any of the fellows who'd asked her.

Irene threw herself down on the seat beside Seffy and stretched out her legs. 'Woo, I'm done in!' she said, wiping a wisp of hair from her face. 'I can't remember the last time I danced so much.'

Seffy wondered if the chap Irene had been dancing with most of the night – Jean-Paul – knew she was married. Irene wasn't wearing her wedding ring.

'Now, don't you start,' Irene snapped, following Seffy's gaze. She extended her left hand. 'I've not forgotten my Jim! This is a wee distraction, that's all. When I'm dancing, I cannae think about anything other than the music and the steps. It's the only time I'm not dwelling on the worst case. You must know how it feels. Didn't you say you had a sweetheart in the forces?'

Seffy pursed her lips. It wasn't the same. *She* wasn't married. And besides, she couldn't, in all honesty, say she spent every waking moment worrying about Teddy. Perhaps she was uncaring but she could go whole days without thinking about him at all.

Irene patted Seffy's arm. 'If you have to think about it that hard, hen, the answer's probably no.'

Jean was grinning as she was escorted back to her seat. Her partner dropped her off and seconds later, was whisking Irene up onto the floor.

'These fellas are so noticing!' Jean said. 'They notice how your hair's done, your frock, your shoes. They comment on it all and say how nice you look. What a breath of fresh air, after Scottish men!'

Enid, who was standing nearby, nodded. 'The fella I was with a minute ago even noticed my ears. Said they were like little pink shells!'

Seffy was acutely aware of one fella who wasn't noticing anything. Or perhaps he was noticing everything? It was hard to tell. She'd been watching him out of the corner of her eye for most of the night: Callum Fraser.

Why had he bothered coming to the dance, if all he was going to do was lean against the back wall, scowling? Perhaps he was merely there to keep an eye on his men?

An announcement was made: the next dance would be a "ladies' choice". Jean and Enid clapped their hands in delight and raced off, to choose partners.

Oh, to heck with it. Seffy was bored and out of humour. She hadn't had a single dance all night. She stood up and marched over to Callum, who was still standing alone. "Chattanooga Choo Choo" was playing; she loved this tune.

'Are you going to stand there all night, Sergeant, with a face as long as a fiddle, or are you going to dance with me?'

He looked startled for a moment, then he nodded at her bandaged wrist. 'What, you wanna dance one-handed?'

Seffy shrugged. 'Why not? It's only one hand. The rest of me is absolutely fine!'

He bit his lip and smiled. 'It most certainly is.'

Oh goodness. That must have sounded as though she were inviting a compliment. Blast. She'd messed up. If only he'd get cracking and put out his arms, so they could move onto the dance floor, this awkwardness would end.

They might even be able to laugh about her clumsy demand that he should dance with her.

He hesitated, clearly considering her request. Then he shook his head. 'You'll have to excuse me, ma'am. I'm sorry but I'm not in a dancing frame of mind.'

He pushed himself off the wall and strode away, past the twirling couples.

Seffy gasped. She could barely believe what had happened. He'd actually turned her down. "Not in a dancing frame of mind!" Could he have made it any clearer that he couldn't stand her?

She stood facing the wall, clenching her fists and fighting back tears, not daring to turn around. Everyone was probably staring. She felt so utterly stupid.

Oh, thank goodness. Another soldier had appeared at her side and asked her to dance. Never mind that it was supposed to be a ladies' choice, none of that mattered now.

'Thank you,' she said, with feeling. She could have kissed him.

'Irene sent me!' he said, gesturing behind him. Oh, wonderful. Irene had not only seen her moment of mortification but had taken pity on her and relinquished one of her spare men.

'Do be careful with my hand!' Seffy said and the boy nodded.

He was a good dancer, to be fair and at least, as she moved around the floor with him, she could force a smile and keep the tears at bay.

Another lesson learned. She'd never asked a man to dance before and she would never, ever do it again.

Once the truck had picked up the other girls and she had the camp completely to herself, Grace put a blanket down in the clearing, stoked the fire and settled down in front of it.

It was still light and warm so she didn't really need the fire, but there was a comfort in the sound of logs cracking and the smell of woodsmoke.

She didn't mind being here alone. Before she'd joined the WTC, she'd been used to her own company. And at least, now they'd all gone to the dance, no one was badgering her to go with them.

It was too difficult to explain that she wasn't good with busy places or crowds. The noise and the need to chat and smile, and prove that you were enjoying yourself, was a strain. She'd rather sit here, quietly, alone.

And there was something else: fear. She'd fallen for Gordy Johnson and it was too much to hope that he'd fallen for her too. He was going to break her heart. Better to stop things now, before she got too tangled up.

She sat cross-legged and watching the dancing flames and wondered how the others were all getting on at the dance.

A sudden noise from the woods snapped her out of her daydream. A twig cracked; there was a rustle in the undergrowth.

It was too loud to be an animal.

Someone was there.

Grace grabbed a branch from the pile of brushwood nearby and dipped it into the flames. It caught immediately and she held it aloft. There; if she needed it, she had a weapon.

A man's voice called out, 'Gracie, don't be scared. It's only me. It's Gordy!'

Gordy! She put her hand to her chest. What was he doing here? 'Are you trying to give me heart failure?'

It had come out sharper than she'd intended but he'd scared her.

He was wearing his uniform, his cap held in both hands, wincing apologetically. Instantly, all her fear and annoyance disappeared.

'Sorry!' he said. He was standing on the other side of the fire, talking across the flames. 'Didn't mean to sneak up on you like that. But you weren't at the dance, so – I brought the dance to you.'

No! Had he come here, expecting her to twirl around the clearing with him?

Grace shook her head. 'Look, I won't dance. I can't. I tried a couple of times and I nearly killed my poor partner!'

They laughed, a little too loudly, a little too long. Perhaps he was nervous too.

'Is that all?' Gordy asked. 'You don't like to dance? See, I was worried I'd said something wrong, at the brook? And that's the last thing—'

'Oh, gosh, no,' Grace said, quickly. How could she tell him this was all new and terrifying and that she still couldn't believe someone like him – kind and funny and popular – would be interested in someone like her? 'No, it was nothing like that.' She shrugged. 'I don't like dances much. I feel all wrong.'

He nodded. 'OK. I'll remember that. Grace doesn't dance. As my ma always says, you can't be good at everything.'

'Your ma sounds nice.'

'Oh yeah, she's great. You two would get along. I know it. I wrote her about you. In my last letter home.'

Grace felt the ground sway beneath her feet. 'Did you? What did you say? No, don't tell me. I mightn't want to know!'

They laughed again.

Gordy pointed at the burning log in Grace's hand. 'Say, are you gonna hold on to that thing all night?'

She'd forgotten she was even holding it. She tossed it into the flames and it landed with a thud and a hiss, throwing up sparks.

'You're missing the film. And the dance,' she said. There was a moment when he didn't speak and she held her breath.

'I'm not missing anything.'

'Do you want to come over here and sit down?' she asked. Was that awful forward? But there was no one else around and she was feeling brave.

They sat on the blanket together, like they had at the fete, only this time they were alone. Gordy asked if she minded if he unbuttoned his tunic because it was warm here, by the fire?

She shook her head; no she didn't mind.

She wished it wasn't summer. It wouldn't be dark for hours yet. She needed the darkness, to hide her blushes.

'Hey, do you want to come a little nearer?' he asked.

Grace shuffled along the blanket and he shifted too, so that they ended up with Gordy sitting behind her, his legs on either side of hers.

'Here, lean back.' His breath tickled the back of her neck as he spoke. Grace leaned back against his chest and it felt good. More than good: perfect.

Remember this, she told herself, wishing she could freeze the moment forever. Because things like this didn't happen to her and it might never happen again. She'd never been on her own with a boy, a boy who seemed to like her, who'd come all this way through the woods to find her.

Gradually, the sky grew darker, until the stars were bright pinpricks of light above them. They put more wood on the fire.

An owl hooted in the trees behind them.

She felt Gordy tense behind her. 'Say, did you hear that?'

'Tawny owl,' she said. 'Actually, it's two. The male and the female, calling to each other.'

She exhaled and wondered whether it was a bad thing to bless the war, even if only for a moment? Yes, it was a sin, no doubt. But without the war, she wouldn't be sitting here now, with this boy from the other side of the world. She'd be at home on the croft with Mother, wondering if that was all there was to life.

They were almost asleep, it was pitch-black and the fire had gone out when Gordy suddenly stirred. 'Say, that sounds like the lorry,' he said.

Was it really that late already? Gracie stirred, stretched her stiff limbs and rubbed her eyes.

The girls were back.

'I'll go grab a lift back to camp,' Gordy said, pushing himself up. 'I had a real nice time, Gracie,' he said softly. 'Hope you did too.'

He reached down, took her hand and planted a kiss on it. He squeezed it gently and as the girls' laughter and babble of voices reached them, he slipped quietly away.

Chapter 27

'Hey, Miss Mills! Might I have a word, please?'

It was a few days after the dance – the non-dance, in Seffy's case – and here was Sergeant Fraser, striding through the forest, calling out before he'd even reached her. Come, no doubt, to torment her again.

Seffy's wrist was still bandaged but, as she'd promised Miss McEwen, she was keeping herself busy. She was in the clearing, tending the fire. She'd filled the billy cans with water from the burn and now the water was boiling, ready for the girls' imminent tea break.

It was tricky, getting the fire to light, and she was still learning the knack of it. She ignored Fraser for a minute and let him wait for her response. It was no more than he deserved. She put another bundle of twigs onto the flames and stood back, coughing, as smoke billowed into the air.

'Good afternoon, Sergeant,' she said, wiping her good hand on her overalls. 'Gone AWOL have you? I think you'll find that you're out of your area. Again.'

She was still cross with him for refusing to dance with her and she doubted he'd come to apologise or offer an explanation. But as it was just the two of them, much as she wanted to, she couldn't exactly ignore him.

'Good afternoon, ma'am,' he said, pulling off his cap. 'Sorry for yelling.'

He did sound rather contrite, so that was something. He blinked as the smoke swirled around them and Seffy braced herself. No doubt the wood she'd used was too damp. But he didn't mention it.

'TIM-BERRRRR!' A girl's voice rang out from somewhere deep in the woods, as another tree was felled.

'I have something to ask,' he said. 'Would you mind asking Irene if, next time, she could please dance with some of the other guys?'

Seffy thought about this strange request for a moment. 'I'm not Irene's boss; Irene does as she likes.'

He sighed and kicked at a pine cone on the forest floor. 'Yeah, well, she's not exactly sharing out her favours—' He put his hand up to quell Seffy's indignant shout. 'OK, let me rephrase that. You know as well as me, there aren't enough ladies to go round. So, it would be fine and dandy, if Mrs Calder – she is married, right?'

He was making a point but Seffy simply nodded. She wasn't sure where this sudden loyalty to Irene had come from but Irene was a lumberjill and a Macdonald girl too, so that probably accounted for it.

'OK,' Callum continued, in a more considered tone, 'it would be nice, if Mrs Calder – Irene – would dance with other men, not just her favourites. It's driving the fellas nuts. They're crazy, for her, I mean.' He shrugged. 'I can understand it. She is the prettiest lumberjill, so it would be kinda nice.'

Ouch, that stung. Irene the "prettiest"? Seffy supposed that was true but still, did he have to say it? Was it gentlemanly to say such a thing? No, it was not. She burned inside. There was a challenge in those blue eyes of his. Was he goading her, hoping for a reaction or – more likely – was he simply uncouth?

She took a breath, determined to stay calm. 'I'll see what I can do, but I'm probably the last person Irene will listen to. And while we're making requests, here's one for you, Sergeant. We've got a new girl in our gang. Flora. She's a local lass. Used to work at the ironmonger's but now she's joined us.'

'Ironmonger's?' he pronounced the word slowly, as though he'd never heard it before. 'What? Is she a blacksmith?'

Seffy laughed. 'No! She didn't actually work with iron. That's the name of the shop.'

He shook his head. 'And what does this shop sell?'

Goodness, now he was asking. There was an ironmonger's in the nearest town to her parents' place and on occasion she'd glanced in the window as she trotted past en route to more interesting shops. 'I think they sell pans and things. Nails and brooms and – oh, I don't know. Things for fixing things!'

He laughed. 'Right, I get it. We call that a hardware store. What do you call it again? An iron—?'

'An ironmonger's,' Seffy said. She supposed it was quite amusing. Especially if he'd seen how small Flora was. The thought of her as a blacksmith was rather droll.

'Anyway, Flora is awfully young,' she said. 'Can you please ensure your men are aware? And no matter how much she might flirt and . . . ahem, encourage them, she's strictly off limits, out of bounds, a no-go area!'

He nodded, serious as always. 'Understood.'

'And if I see any of them so much as within two feet of her, I won't be held responsible for my actions!'

Callum held up his hand and his eyes flashed. 'I said, "understood". We're not animals, you know.'

He'd lied, of course. About Irene being the prettiest. She was pretty enough, in an obvious kind of way, but she didn't do anything for him.

No, this was the prettiest lumberjill, standing in front of him now: the cool girl, the ice queen, Miss Persephone Baxter-Mills. Wow, that really was quite some name. He'd only been kidding when he'd messed around the other week and called her "phoney" because – oh, hell – he was such a cliché. He was the kid in the schoolyard who pulls the girl's braids because he wants her to notice him.

This was the girl who set his pulse racing, made him stutter when he spoke and feel kinda dumb and inferior sometimes when she looked at him down her haughty little nose.

This was the girl he didn't dare dance with.

He could still remember the softness of her skin and how good her hair had smelled when he'd pulled her to the ground, back in June. He'd suggested they lie there a little longer, to worry the other girls, but in truth, he didn't care about teaching anyone a lesson, he'd just wanted to be there, close to her, for as long as he could.

He was trying real hard but he couldn't get her out of his head. From the moment he'd first seen her, with her dungarees rolled up into shorts and legs that seemed to go on forever and that way she had of . . . he shook his head. Enough now. Enough.

'You're not animals, no of course not,' she was saying. 'I simply wanted to make things clear. About Flora. Now, was there anything else, Sergeant? Only, I'm rather busy.'

He grinned and nodded slowly. '"Rather busy", making the tea?'

'Oh, tea's a very serious business,' Seffy said, prodding the flames with a stick and sending out even more blue smoke. That wood was green as hell. 'Even without milk or sugar – and we have neither – it's one of the highlights of the day.'

'Sure. "Everything stops for tea", right? How's that hand of yours doing?'

'This?' Seffy asked, holding up her bandaged wrist. 'Oh, I'm still happily malingering!'

Callum laughed. She didn't take herself too seriously, you had to give her that. He felt mean about Saturday. He should've danced with her. But she was dangerous; he was trying to keep away.

From somewhere deep within the forest, a whistle blew.

'That's tea break,' she said. 'The girls'll be here any minute. If you've nothing else to say, Sergeant, I'm sure you've got work to do and I certainly need to get on.'

He nodded, pulled his cap back on and turned away, before he said something he might regret; before he made a goddamn fool of himself.

Chapter 28

'Do you wanna read the letter I wrote my folks last night?' Gordy asked Grace. It was mid-August, two weeks after their evening in front of the fire and they were spending Sunday afternoon fishing at the loch. Or rather, Gordy was fishing and Grace was sitting quietly, watching him.

When the girls had talked about their ideas of heaven, a while back, Grace hadn't joined in. She hadn't known what to say. But now she knew: this was it. The water was crystal clear and sparkling in the sunlight, the sky was as blue as forget-me-nots and the hills across the loch were purple with heather.

And she was in love.

Gordy hadn't caught anything; the fish weren't biting, apparently, but he didn't seem to mind.

'If I catch something though, we have to eat it, OK?' he'd said. 'I'll cook it over a fire. You can't catch something and then not eat it. It's a waste; it ain't right.'

Grace nodded. She agreed with him. She agreed with him on most things.

Now he wanted her to read his letter. Wasn't that too private, like reading someone's diary? But it was one of the things she loved about him: he wanted her to know everything about him.

'Come on, Gracie, please,' Gordy urged. 'My English ain't too good and you can tell me if I've made errors and stuff.'

Grace said she would, although she was hardly a shining example of letter writing. Her letters to Mother had dwindled to almost nothing over the last few weeks. She hadn't mentioned Gordy at all because heaven forfend she should be having a good time. She was courting! For the first time in her life, Grace was stepping out with a boy. Mother wouldn't approve of that.

Instead, on the odd occasion that she wrote home, her letters were about work and how many tons of timber they'd felled, how the trainer, Miss McEwen had left now to go to another camp, how they'd taken part in a tug of war competition and lost.

Mother wrote about church and the weather and how the hens were laying. She never mentioned Dougie, even though Grace asked after him. Perhaps he wasn't at the croft anymore? She wouldn't blame him if he'd left. Even a quiet, patient man like Dougie could only take so much.

Grace took the letter that Gordy had pulled out of his pocket and started to read. It was so different from the letters she and Mother exchanged, she felt like crying.

'No, not like that Gracie, please. Read it out loud. Then I can read along with you.'

She laughed. 'All right. Is this a test, to check whether I can read?'

'Aw, you caught me out!' He looked suddenly serious. 'Say, you can read, can't you, Gracie?'

He was joking. She went to smack him with the paper but stopped, in case she ripped it. He couldn't send a torn letter back home; this was something precious.

She shielded her eyes from the sun with one hand and with the other, she held up the letter and read:

Saturday 15th August 1942

Dearest Ma,

 Well, I guess it's been a while but I've been thinking about you all.

 By the time you get this letter, you'll probably have gotten the harvest in. I hope you got it in fine. Write me how much corn and wheat you made. You know I like to know that stuff. It makes me feel less homesick.

 But, I ain't so homesick anymore, to tell the truth. I been meaning to tell you for a while now but a few weeks back, I met a girl, a real nice Scotch girl here. She's working in the woods too. She sure is a honey, though she don't think that about herself.

Grace stopped reading and looked up at Gordy. They smiled at one another.

'Go on,' he said.

 She's a homely kinda girl and sweet as apple pie.

"Homely". Grace supposed she was. She wasn't posh like Seffy or womanly like Irene or clever like Jean. Men didn't have an urge to protect her, like they did wee Hazel. No, she was "homely". Was that a good thing or bad? It sounded plain and ordinary but Gordy didn't seem to mind. She read on.

 Gracie is her name. You know, Ma, I never felt like this 'bout no one before. When I'm not thinking about you all, it's Gracie who's in my mind the whole time. It's like she lives there. Ain't that a thing? Guess that's what they call being in love. I dunno because I never was in love before but I guess I am now.

 Anyhow, thought you'd like to know and it might make you happy, Ma, to know that, all these miles away, I'm not

lonesome and though I miss you all, I got something here
that's good. And winter's coming in the next couple of months
but the fellas say it won't be so cold here as BC, so that's a
good thing too.

Write me soon with all the news from home, won't you, Ma?
Missin' you a LOT.
Your loving son,
Gordy

The whole letter had been about her. Gordy *loved* her.
Grace hardly dared look up. She felt shaky, as though she
wasn't really here, on this grassy bank in the sunshine, alone
with this wonderful man. Was she really "sweet as apple pie"
and a "honey"? It was as though she'd been reading about
someone else.

'Do you think it's all right? The letter?' Gordy asked, nonchalantly. He flicked the fishing line back and cast it out over the water.

Grace nodded but he wasn't looking at her. 'Gosh,' she said,
quietly. 'Did you mean all that?'

He turned and looked at her. 'Every. Single. Word. And is
it OK, Gracie? I mean, I don't wanna send Ma something that
might not work out and get her all excited and happy, you
know, and—'

She reached over and stopped his talking with a soft kiss on
the lips. And then another. His right arm jerked suddenly. 'I – got
a bite,' he managed to say between kisses. 'Ain't – that – darned
– typical?'

Once Gordy had reeled in the fish – a trout, he said – and
they'd stopped laughing about their incredibly bad timing, he
looked at her. 'Marry me, Gracie?'

She pulled away and stared at him. She shook her head, not
daring to believe it.

'Marry me!'

There. He'd said it again.

Grace laughed. 'But we hardly know each other!' Her heart was hammering in her chest and despite her protestations she'd never been so glad of anything in her whole life.

'So what? We can spend the rest of our lives getting to know each other. How 'bout that? You can come home with me, to Canada. When the war's over, that's when you'll come.'

It sounded as though he had it all planned.

'What d'you say, Gracie? You'll love it there.' He frowned as something occurred to him. ''Course if you don't think you can leave your folks, then we'll stay in Scotland. It'll be hard but I'd do it for you. What do you say?'

No, she had no folks to stay here for. She'd go to the ends of the world with him. It wouldn't matter where it was. As long as she was with him, she'd be all right.

There was silence for a moment, then Gordy cast another line and gazed out across the loch.

'Will you stop fishing for one moment and ask me properly?' Grace said.

He dropped the line into the water, fell onto one knee and took hold of her hand. 'Grace McGinty, love of my life. Will you make a poor woodsman very happy and consent to be my wife? Hey, that rhymes! I'm a poet! I made a poem!'

'Oh, you!' Grace said, laughing and shaking her head. 'Yes of course I will. Yes, yes.'

Chapter 29

When Grace got back to Macdonald hut later that evening, the girls were lounging on their beds, knitting, reading and writing letters.

Enid was reading out from her magazine. 'It says here, "Smile brightly the first two times he looks at you and then the third time, look very sad".'

Jean held her pen aloft and looked up. 'Whatever for?'

'"So he can come and ask you what's wrong"! That's good. I'm goin' try that. And here's another good one. "Boys' feet point towards you if they like you." Fancy that!' She looked up from the page. 'Oh hello, Grace, I didn't see you there for a minute. Did you have a nice afternoon?'

Grace nodded. She didn't want to appear too smug but good grief, what a relief not to have to fret about that kind of thing. Gordy's feet, she was sure, would always be facing her.

'Ears are coming back into fashion!' Joey announced, from her *Woman's Own*. 'The Liberty Cut. It's short and it will show your ears but apparently, we mustn't be afraid! "In the name of utility, the locks must fall!"'

Everyone laughed.

'I certainly won't be doing that,' Joey said, slapping the magazine shut. She touched her curls. 'I like my long hair!' She looked at Grace standing in the doorway and her eyes narrowed. 'You look different, Grace. Like you're going to burst. Has something happened?'

Everyone stopped what they were doing and stared at her.

'Aye, you could say that,' she said. 'Gordy's asked me to marry him.'

The hut immediately filled with screams of delight, that brought girls from the other two huts running to the Macdonald windows within seconds.

'What's going on?' one of them asked.

Jean pointed across the hut. 'Amazing Grace is getting married! To one of the Canadian boys! We're assuming you said yes, Grace! Am I right?'

Enid and Joey were holding Grace's hands, jumping on the spot and demanding all the details of the proposal.

'Aye,' Grace managed to say, as Irene swooped in and landed a kiss on her forehead.

'First in the camp to get engaged,' Jean said proudly to the girls at the window. 'And from Macdonald hut, too!'

'Did you say yes straight away, hen?' Irene asked.

Grace nodded. 'I didn't have a moment's doubt.'

'Aw, that's the way. I was the same. You know when you've found your one true love. I'm over the moon for you, I really am.'

'When's the wedding?' Jean asked. 'Gosh, you'll have to start your bottom drawer straight away!'

'Not until we get permission from Gordy's commanding officer,' Grace said.

'The major? But he won't refuse, will he?' Morag asked.

'Och, no. It's a formality. But they have to do some checks. They'll make sure Gordy's not in debt and that neither of us is married already, that kind of thing. It'll take a wee while. And I have to produce a letter from a "responsible citizen" vouching for my character.'

Morag pulled a face. 'I dunno who you'll get to do that.'

'My aunt would do it for you, Grace,' Seffy said, glaring at Morag. 'If you like.'

Grace nodded gratefully at Seffy. She wanted to be married as soon as possible but there were hoops and hurdles to get through first. Gordy had told her that if they married without permission, Grace wouldn't be eligible for any widow's allowances, should the worst happen. And the army might not pay for her passage to Canada, when the time came.

'Let's all start saving clothing coupons!' Jean said.

'Aw, yes,' Irene said. 'If you can get the material, hen, I'll make your dress. I'm a dab hand with a needle, even if I do say so myself! And it's unlucky to make your own wedding dress, as I'm sure ye know!'

Grace smiled. 'It'll be a few months yet, before there's a wedding. Springtime, perhaps. And then, when the war's over, I'll be moving to Canada.'

A couple of the girls gasped.

'You'll never come back. You'll never see your family again,' Morag said, darkly.

'But you'll be making a new family, over there, won't you, Grace?' Irene said, brightly. 'It'll be a wonderful adventure.'

'You'd go all that way, to a strange country? And leave everything behind? Your whole life?' Joey asked, eyes wide.

Grace nodded. Joey didn't understand: Gordy was her whole life.

'You'll have a refrigerator in your house,' Irene said. 'And you'll never be short of nylons or gum!'

The girls were being so kind and sweet. Grace felt a swell of love and gratitude for them all.

'I'm so happy for you,' Seffy said. 'Gordy clearly adores you. But what about your mother? What'll she say about you moving thousands of miles away? Mine would have forty fits.'

Grace swallowed. She'd been trying to push thoughts of Mother to the back of her mind. She was the only possible fly in the ointment.

213

'Gordy's due some leave soon. We're going to tell her then,' she said.

The sooner, the better. But she wasn't looking forward to it. Mother was not going to be happy.

Chapter 30

Three weeks later, in early September, there was another dance at the Canadian camp.

At ten o'clock Grace stepped out of the dance hall and inhaled the cool night air. It was dusk. Still another two hours to go until the end of the dance.

She'd only agreed to come because Gordy was her fiancé now and they shouldn't be apart, but events like this were a trial.

It was so hot in there and the three-piece band was loud. She had no inclination to dance but Gordy couldn't refuse when other girls asked him. There were dozens of other available fellas but Gordy was a good mover and they knew they'd be safe with him.

'You don't mind, Gracie, do you?' he asked and every time, she shook her head. But she did mind. She felt like an out-of-place lump, standing against the wall, watching the others.

Jean had been dancing all night with Captain Graham. It didn't seem fair that Jean was allowed to have a favourite while Irene's preference for the tall, blonde Jean-Paul had been noted and commented on. Seffy had told her that, according to Sergeant Fraser, it was making some of the men jealous.

Irene had rolled her eyes; she didn't like to be told what to do.

She'd been dancing with other men tonight but she kept drifting back to Jean-Paul.

Poor Seffy had been looking out of sorts all evening, sitting at the edge of the dance floor, her wrist still strapped up, saying no to all requests for a dance. Grace would go back inside and ask if she wanted to get a lemonade in a second.

Oh, what was that? She'd heard a noise in the bushes. A deer or a badger, perhaps? No, there were voices: a man and a woman. They were enjoying themselves out there amongst the trees, no doubt. Which was more than she was. She'd go back inside now, in case they caught sight of her and thought she was a Peeping Tom.

She crept back towards the dance hall but something made her stop. The sounds were louder now. There was a sharp cry, the man murmured something indecipherable, in a coaxing tone and then, quite clearly, a girl's voice said, 'NO!'

Grace jumped and listened hard. The woman was saying something else but her voice was muffled, as though she were being kissed. Or as if someone had their hand over her mouth.

Oh God. She should run and get help. But she might've got it all wrong; it could simply be a courting couple having fun. Grace didn't know much about necking; she and Gordy had never shared more than a chaste kiss.

The light was fading fast and it was getting harder to see. Grace felt her way between the trees, getting nearer to the source of the sounds, stumbling every few yards on roots and branches. She could hardly hear the music from the dance band anymore.

There they were. A slight girl in a pale-coloured dress was pinned against a tree by a uniformed man. His back was towards Grace. There was no telling who they were.

But it was clear the girl was struggling to get away, twisting her head from side to side to avoid his kisses and trying to push him off.

'Oi, you! Gerroff her!' Grace yelled but the man took no notice. She ran forward, yanked at his shirt and thumped his back. He

216

didn't even look round but lashed out with one arm and almost sent her flying.

'Clear off!' he said. 'We're just having a bit of fun, ain't that right, Red?'

"Red"? That meant something but Grace was in too much of a panic to remember what. She couldn't think straight.

The girl was panting from the effort of resisting the man. She was barely managing to say, 'No' and 'Stop'; her voice was getting fainter. He pulled her towards him, hooked his boot around the girl's ankle and they fell backwards onto the forest floor with a hard thud. There was the sound of material ripping. My God, was he tearing off her clothes?

Grace kicked frantically at his legs but they were all tangled up with the girl's. It was no use; she'd have to run and fetch someone. But then the girl managed to yell, 'Help me!'

Jean? That had sounded like Jean. Grace had seen the pips on the soldier's sleeve; he was an officer. And Jean's nickname was "Red". It was Jean and Captain Graham.

Grace kicked him in the ribs. 'GET OFF HER!'

But he merely grunted and swore under his breath and he was still on top of Jean.

She had to do something else. Think, think! It was almost dark now under the canopy of trees. Grace's foot knocked against something on the ground and she bent to pick it up. A branch. It was heavy, a foot long, about three inches thick. It would do.

There was no time to think. She held it up. Jean managed to let out an ear-piercing scream.

Grace leaned forward and hit the captain on the back of the head, as hard as she could.

'Did you hear that?' Irene asked, stopping dead on the path. 'Back there. It sounded like a girl shrieking.'

Jean-Paul reached back and took her hand. 'Nah. It was nothin', honey. Probably a fox. You know, there's all kinds of queer noises in the forest at night.'

But not a noise like that, Irene thought. It had been otherworldly. It had sent a shiver right through her.

He tugged her hand gently and they moved forward.

'Where're we going, anyway?' Irene asked. She felt a wee bit woozy. Jean-Paul had bottles of beer hidden in the bushes outside the hall – all the guys did, apparently, even though it was against the rules – and he'd persuaded her to have a few sips.

'It'll help you relax, sweetheart,' he'd said.

She'd laughed at that because she didn't need drink to help her relax. She was having a ball. Who wouldn't be, surrounded by attentive fellas, the air filled with loud, foot-tapping music, dancing her cares away?

Then Jean-Paul told her he knew someplace they could be alone.

And now here she was, walking through the woods with him, in the twilight, doing something secretive and forbidden. This was silly. Had she completely lost her heed, skulking around like a lovesick lassie? As for Jean-Paul: he was a nice fella but he wasnae much more than a bairn himself.

She was on the verge of telling him she wanted to turn back when the wee devil who sometimes sat on her shoulder, started whispering. Who knew, it said, what lies around the corner? The world's gone to hell in a handcart; you might as well enjoy yourself while you've got the chance.

Jean-Paul had stopped.

'Aw, I know this place,' Irene said. In the spooky half-light, it looked like a gingerbread cottage in a fairy tale. 'It's the wee bothy!'

She pushed everything out of her mind: the scream she'd heard back there, her life in Glasgow: the teashop, the munitions factory, her bombed-out house, Ma, the constant fretting, the stupid war. Jim.

'Is this all right, then, honey?' Jean-Paul said, pushing open the bothy door.

'Aye, as long as there's no spiders!' Irene said, giving a throaty laugh. 'I cannot abide the things.'

'No spiders, I promise.'

He took Irene's hand and led her inside.

Seffy pushed past the girls queuing for the lavatories and stood in front of the mirror, to retouch her powder and apply lipstick.

'Don't mind me,' said one of the girls she'd jostled.

'Charmed, I'm sure,' said another. They rolled their eyes at each other.

Oh, blast this infernal wrist of hers. It was a damn nuisance. She couldn't even put on her lipstick properly and there was no one around to ask for help.

'What's up, hen?' one of the girls asked. 'Your fella dancing with someone else?'

Seffy thought of Callum Fraser. Not that he was her fella and never would be. As usual, he wasn't dancing with anyone. He was skulking around the hall as though he were on duty. Perhaps he was. A couple of times she'd spotted him sitting up near the band, tapping his foot in time to the music.

She should just forget about him; the stupid man put her in a funk, every time. He wasn't worth the bother. She was fed up; she wanted to go back to camp.

The door opened and Grace appeared, clearly looking for someone. She was stony-faced. 'Quick,' she murmured, when she spotted Seffy. 'Come with me.'

They were attracting curious glances from the girls in the lavatory queue, so Seffy quietly followed Grace out into the main hall. They made their way around the edge of the dance floor, dodging the whirling couples. Gordy was amongst them and Seffy saw him turn his head and watch them curiously, as they slipped outside.

It was almost dark and the sound of the band quickly faded until it was only a faint beat in the distance.

'What's the matter? Where are we going?' Seffy asked, quickening her pace to keep up. Grace didn't answer and marched resolutely on, deeper into the woods.

Finally, they reached a girl, crying and crouching over a man in uniform, who was lying on his front. Jean! Her dress was half torn off. The man wasn't moving. He was either asleep or . . .

'What's happened?' Seffy cried, running forward. This looked serious. Why had Grace summoned her, of all people, to help?

Grace scratched her head. 'It's all right, I don't think he's dead. Though he deserves to be. He's got a lump the size of an egg on his head and he's out cold. We can't leave him here.'

The very thought of it! An injured man? Had Grace and Jean gone completely mad?

'Who is it?' Seffy asked.

The girls jumped at the sound of approaching footsteps. It was Gordy – and then Callum, close behind. What a relief. They could take charge and sort out this awful mess. Why hadn't Grace fetched them in the first place?

'You shoulda come and got me, Grace,' Gordy said, echoing Seffy's thoughts.

The boys carefully rolled the unconscious man over onto his back. Callum opened one of his eyes and shone a torch into it, while Gordy felt his wrist for a pulse.

'What's the story here?' Callum asked, in a low voice. Gordy stood up, scanning the forest and checking behind them, making sure they hadn't been followed.

'I hit him,' Grace said, defiantly, folding her arms. 'With a branch.'

'Sshh,' Gordy said. 'Keep your voice down, Gracie.'

'You hit him? Why?' Callum asked.

Seffy was aghast. It was as though the three of them – Grace, Jean and this man – had had some kind of fight.

'I had no choice! He was attacking Jean! He wouldn't stop.'

Jean was shaking and crying. Her glasses were broken and she was twisting them in her hands. Seffy pulled off her cardigan

220

and put it around Jean's shoulders. 'Is that right, Jean? Was he hurting you?' she asked gently and Jean nodded and cried even harder.

'See this, three pips?' Callum pointed to the unconscious man's sleeve. 'That means he's a captain.'

Seffy winced. 'Important?'

'Yep.'

Grace shrugged. 'What's that got to do with it?'

'It was . . . maybe it was my fault,' Jean said, between sobs. 'I might've given him the wrong idea. He asked me to come outside for some fresh air but I thought he wanted a kiss. That's all. But he tried . . . he wanted more.'

Seffy rubbed her temples and sighed. 'This is all Irene's fault.'

'Why?' Grace asked.

'Because Jean worships her. She even tries to walk like her. And now look what's happened.'

'No, you're wrong.' Grace nodded at the unconscious man. 'It's not anyone's fault except his.'

'Jeez, he's coming round,' Gordy whispered. It was true: the captain was stirring and moaning.

At least Grace hadn't put him in a coma or actually killed him. The thought of that was too awful to contemplate. But if he opened his eyes and saw them staring down at him, guilt written all over their faces, what would happen? It would be Jean and Grace's word against his. They'd all be in the most awful trouble.

'Come on, buddy,' Gordy whispered to Callum. 'Let's get him up and back to his bunk. You girls get along to your camp, pronto. Don't breathe a word. Don't let anyone see Jean like that.'

But Callum didn't move.

Gordy had placed his hands under the captain's arms and was trying to drag him. He was a big man, almost twice Gordy's size. He must be a dead weight. 'Callum?' he asked and when he got no answer, 'Sergeant Fraser?'

221

Callum wasn't going to help him. Seffy's head was swimming; this was a nightmare. She thought she might faint. If she didn't have this blasted injured wrist, she'd help Gordy herself. What were they going to do?

Gordy set the captain back down. 'Don't spill the beans, buddy,' he said. 'You can't tell no one about this.'

Callum's jaw was set and his eyes were troubled. 'But what about Jean? Doesn't she want to report this? It's assault.'

He had a point. If they swept the incident under the carpet in order to protect Grace, there'd be no justice for Jean. This awful man would get away with what he'd done.

'He's right, Jean,' Seffy said. 'We should report this to someone.'

Jean was getting more upset. She shook her head. 'No, no I can't. I can't go through it. Don't make me!'

The captain moaned again and put his hand up to his head.

'Hurry up, come on,' Gordy whispered to Callum. 'We've gotta do something with him damn quick! Just – don't say anything, buddy, right?'

Callum's sigh filled the night air and when he spoke, his voice was cold. 'I must. It's my duty.'

'What d'you mean, your duty? You heard Jean. She don't want to report it!' Gordy said. He wasn't bothering to whisper anymore.

'Is that right, Jean?' Seffy asked, pulling the crying girl closer to her. 'Because if you do, we'll help you all we can.'

'I don't mind, Jean,' Grace said. 'He shouldn't get away with it.'

Jean sobbed and shook her head. 'Noo,' she wailed. 'I just want to forget all about it.'

Seffy looked at Callum. He was rubbing his face with his hands, clearly still undecided. 'You can't report this,' she said. 'Grace'll be in the most awful trouble.'

'Yeah! I mean, who're they gonna believe?' Gordy asked. 'The girls or the captain? No offence, ladies, but—'

'No, you're right,' Seffy said. 'We have to protect Grace! She

222

was only trying to stop the brute. Any of us girls would have done the same.'

Callum pulled his hands away from his face and took a deep breath. 'Look, I get that this young lady doesn't wanna make an official complaint,' he said, nodding at Jean. 'But there's still been an incident here tonight. A senior officer has been injured.'

'Yeah, but it's Graham and—' Gordy started.

'—whatever you think of him or whether he had it comin' to him, that's immaterial! It doesn't change the facts.' He glared at them all. 'I have a duty to report this!'

Chapter 31

The next morning, after a sleepless night, Seffy announced she was going to church and Irene said she'd come too. It was the first Sunday in September: church parade for the Canucks. Perhaps they could find something out.

Last night, Seffy and Grace had put Jean to bed and when the others had finally returned from the dance, they'd told them the whole sorry story.

'I feel terrible about what happened,' Irene admitted as she and Seffy walked down into the village. 'I shoulda been keeping a closer eye on Jean.'

'You're not Jean's keeper, ' Seffy said. 'She's a grown woman, after all.'

But there was no consoling Irene. She shook her head. There were dark rings under her eyes as though she'd hardly slept. 'No,' she said, biting her lip. 'I shoulda been there, watching out for her.'

Jean was understandably shaken and upset but Seffy was sure she'd be all right. It could have been so much worse if Grace hadn't come to the rescue. It was Grace that Seffy was more concerned about now: she'd hit a man so hard, she'd knocked him out. A captain, no less. She might be in the most awful trouble.

'Is Grace still going to her mother's tomorrow?' Seffy asked.

Gordy and Grace had leave to go to Grace's home, to announce their engagement. But Grace thought she should cancel the trip, after what had happened, in case it looked as though they were running away.

Irene nodded. 'Aye, I told her she should go. Heaven knows when they'll ever get leave at the same time again. She has to act normal, as though she's done nothing wrong. Because she hasn't.'

As the soldiers marched past, through the village, Seffy scanned their faces, praying for a miracle: that she'd see Captain Graham amongst them, right as rain and suffering from nothing more than a bump on the head and a touch of amnesia.

She spotted Callum but although she was sure she'd seen a flicker of recognition in his eyes, his mouth was set and he didn't acknowledge her as he swept past. He was probably wishing he'd never set eyes on her or any of the lumberjills.

Captain Graham was nowhere to be seen.

After the service, the congregation spilled out onto the church steps and into the graveyard. Troops and villagers stood around in small groups, chatting. Seffy knew she and Irene probably only had a minute or two before the order came for the men to move out.

She nudged Irene. 'Let's split up, as they say in all the best detective stories. You mingle with the boys over there and listen out for any gossip about you-know-who. I'll make a beeline for Sergeant Fraser.'

Her stomach swooped away as she said his name. She wasn't looking forward to this conversation.

'Are you the only lumberjill here today, representing the corps?' a sharp voice said, at Seffy's side.

It was Aunt Dilys, in an alarmingly large hat. Seffy stood back before the pheasant feather at the front poked her in the eye.

'Oh hullo, Auntie. Yes, we are rather thin on the ground today. Some of the girls . . . erm . . . aren't feeling too well.'

Marigold peered around Dilys' large frame. 'Aye. There's a nasty bug going around. It'll probably be that.'

Seffy raised her finger. 'Would you excuse me for one second, please? There's someone I need to speak to.'

She'd spotted Callum, turning away at the end of a conversation with the rector and she marched up to him, blocking his way.

'How is he?' she murmured.

Callum's eyes widened in alarm. 'Shh, keep your voice down. Come over here.'

As they moved away from the others, to stand beside an angel-topped monument in the graveyard, one of the other Canucks spotted them.

'Wayheyy!' he called out, nudging one of his pals and grinning. Callum muttered, 'Shut up, Verne.'

'Friend of yours?' Seffy asked.

'Hardly.'

Callum turned his back on the men and crossed his arms. 'Look, I can't talk to you about this here.' He looked drawn and tired and she felt a flash of pity for him. He shrugged. 'There's nothin' to tell. I don't know anything.'

'But you haven't spoken to anyone about what happened, have you?' Seffy asked, bracing herself for the answer.

Last night in the forest, Gordy and Callum had urged the girls to leave, to go back to their camp while there was still some light and they'd acquiesced. The longer they stayed there, the more likely it was that they'd be spotted. And Jean was shivering and distraught: they needed to get her back to the hut.

The men had assured them they'd deal with the captain. Seffy had wondered all night what that meant.

'Have you?' she asked again. 'Said anything?'

He gave the smallest shake of his head. 'Not yet.'

'I think you're a good man, Sergeant,' she said, flooded with relief. 'You want to do the right thing. You stand up for bullies; you help maidens in distress.' She raised her eyebrows, hoping he'd smile back but instead, he glared straight ahead, expressionless. She stepped closer to him and lowered her voice to a whisper.

'Grace is a lovely girl. She doesn't make a habit of hitting people with branches and—'

'I won't give the names. Of the girls,' he said. 'I'll just say, Graham was getting fresh with a girl, another girl hit him. But I dunno know who they were.' He shrugged. 'I've been thinking about it all night. It's the best I can do.'

Seffy's stomach plunged. 'But you can't! That won't help!' She wanted to grab him by the tunic and shake him. 'There'll be an investigation. Everyone saw them dancing together. Jean'll be hauled in and questioned and it'll all come out. Grace's part in it too. This could ruin her life. Gordy's as well.'

The sound of a bugle filled the air. The call to fall back in line and start the march back to camp.

Callum turned and looked at her. Although there were people all around, shouts and laughter and someone even slapped him playfully on the back as he passed by, it was as though it were just the two of them. The crowd fell away.

'I'm pleading with you,' Seffy said, 'for the sake of my friend and yours—' she assumed they were friends: Gordy had called him "buddy", more than once '—and, for all that's good, in this otherwise pretty rotten world. Please, do the right thing, Callum.'

His face was impassive. He tipped his cap at her and moved off to join his men without a word. She could only hope that she'd done enough.

Aunt Dilys tapped Seffy on the shoulder as the men moved into formation. 'That looked like rather a serious tête-à-tête,' she said. 'Is everything all right?'

'Perfectly,' Seffy said, with a quick nod. She couldn't involve Dilys. Irene had sworn everyone in the hut to secrecy; they'd agreed not to breathe a word to a soul.

Dilys was narrowing her eyes, as though she didn't believe her.

'You look quite wrung out, dear. As though you could do with Sunday lunch. Or a cup of tea, at least.'

Seffy shook her head. It was tempting but she had to get back to the girls.

'Thank you, but perhaps another time.'

Dilys nodded and went to turn away.

'Aunt, do you think honesty is always the best policy?'

Dilys frowned. She peered out at Seffy from under her huge hat. 'Good grief, no! Can you imagine if we did nothing but tell each other the truth? Exactly what we thought? There'd be chaos, carnage, mayhem! We lie to protect one another's feelings most of the time.'

Seffy nodded. That was true enough. She kept telling Teddy in her letters that she missed him but that wasn't strictly true. 'And if you're lying to protect someone who's done the right thing but might get into trouble?'

Dilys nodded. 'Then I think that's all right too.'

Chapter 32

Early on Monday morning, Grace and Gordy were on the train, travelling north to visit Mother.

'Did you write your ma and tell her we were coming?' Gordy asked.

Grace hadn't. She'd thought it better to turn up unannounced and take her mother by surprise.

'Don't fret. She'll be there,' she said. It wasn't market day or Sunday, when Mother always went to church, so where else would she be?

It was a dreich day, which matched Grace's mood. Through the dirty train windows, the hills and vast swathes of moorland were a blur of mist and rain.

This trip had been Gordy's idea and Grace had taken some persuading. Gordy wanted to do things properly and as Grace didn't have a father, he was determined to ask Grace's mother for her hand in marriage. Which was quaint and sweet and very romantic: everything that Mother wasn't. Grace could only imagine how she'd react. And what if she refused Gordy's request? What would they do then?

It might have been better to say nothing and announce they were married when it was too late for her to disapprove. But Grace couldn't do it. She was Mother's only child, after all. It would've been too cruel. It might have caused a rift that would never heal.

She was dreading what lay ahead of them and fretting about what might be happening back at the camp. If only she could stay on this train forever, cuddled up close to Gordy and never having to face either situation.

Military police might even now be swarming around Macdonald hut, looking for her. Or they might be on the platform when she and Gordy arrived at the station, waiting to arrest her.

'Shall we go AWOL?' Grace whispered. She was only half-joking. If only they could elope without the need for anyone's permission or approval and put Saturday night behind them. Before Gordy could answer, she added, 'What if he dies?'

'He won't.' Gordy squeezed her hand and she tried to smile back. He glanced around the carriage, checking that the man opposite was asleep and that the soldier and the girl in the corner were too busy whispering sweet nothings, to pay them any attention.

'Graham's a numbskull and his head's rock-hard,' he said, quietly. 'When me and Callum carried him to his bunk he was moaning and cursing but he was all right. If anything was amiss, we'd have heard by now.' He nodded, a little too vigorously. 'Dontcha worry, honey. He's gonna be fine.'

They walked up the lane from the station towards the cottage and it felt strange. Here she was, with a lovely man – her fiancé – less than three months since she'd left home. They were holding hands but as she got nearer to the cottage and there was a chance they might be seen, she let her hand slip out of his and gave him an apologetic little smile.

Mother and Dougie were sitting side by side at the kitchen table, with their backs to the window. That was something, considering Mother's objection to Dougie living in and taking over Grace's bedroom while she was away. Dougie was still there then; Mother hadn't driven him away.

'Is Dougie your stepfather?' Gordy had asked, on the journey.

'Och, no, he's the hired help.' There was a good chance they wouldn't even see him, she'd added. He'd most likely be out working in the fields. But Grace had hoped he would be there. Dougie was an ally.

'He's also about twenty years younger than my mother,' Grace said. 'She's – she was quite old when she had me.'

'That doesn't matter, does it, honey?'

She'd only told him so Gordy didn't get a shock when he saw Mother, with her greying hair and stooped figure. Weeks had passed since Grace had left home; Mother might look even older now.

Grace had seen a photograph of Gordy's ma and she looked so young and vibrant, she could almost pass for his sister. She'd had him when she was only eighteen.

In contrast, Mother had been over forty when Grace was born, at a time when, presumably, her parents had given up on the idea of ever having children.

A surprise baby then, although Mother had never said she'd been a welcome one. That wasn't the kind of thing she said.

Grace knocked on the back door. It didn't seem right to simply walk in, when they'd turned up out of the blue like this.

It was Dougie who opened the door, Dougie whose face lit up and who wrapped his good arm around her and welcomed them in out of the rain.

Mother stood up from the table, wiping her mouth with her apron. Grace could tell she wasn't best pleased; she wouldn't like to be taken unawares like this.

'So, you're back. To what do we owe this?' she asked, stern-faced.

Grace glanced at Gordy. It had been shameful but she'd managed to find the words to tell him what to expect from Mother. There was a grim satisfaction in being proved right the moment they walked through the door.

'Dougie, I think you've errands to do, am I right?' Mother said.

Dougie slipped obediently out of the room. Mother took off her apron and patted down her hair. 'You'll have to excuse me. I wasn't expecting company.'

'Mother, this is my . . . this is Gordy Johnson.' Grace said. 'He's working in the forests too.'

'Very pleased to meet you, ma'am,' Gordy said, extending his hand. 'I'm here with the CFC. The Canadian Forestry Corps.'

Mother had that chewing-a-wasp look. She wasn't really listening to anything they were saying.

Mother took Gordy's hand without enthusiasm and gave it a cursory shake. Oh, blast the woman! For once, why couldn't she be pleasant, like other people's parents? This was why Grace had never brought pals home; why she'd never actually had pals before the lumberjills.

'I suppose you'll be wanting a cup of tea,' Mother said. She heaved herself up off the chair with a sigh, to put the kettle on the stove.

Grace couldn't hold it in any longer. 'Mother, Gordy's my fiancé. We're engaged.'

There was a pause and then: 'Oh aye?' Mother didn't turn around.

'And we're getting married as soon as we're able,' Grace said, taking a seat. Gordy waited until Mother had sat back down at the table and then he sat too.

Grace's stomach clenched. She forced herself to stay calm and measured.

Mother shook her head and looked at Gordy. 'But I don't know you from Adam.'

'We know that, Mrs McGinty,' Gordy said. 'That's the reason we've come here specially today. I wanted to come and pay my respects, so you can make my acquaintance and find out a little about me. And then I'd like to ask you for Gracie's hand in marriage.'

Grace winced. Gordy was nervous: she could see the line of sweat on his upper lip.

'Gracie?' Mother sniffed. 'Her name's *Grace*.' She stood up again and busied herself making the tea.

Gordy sat a little taller in his seat. 'Well, ma'am, she'll always be Gracie to me.' Under the table, he squeezed Grace's hand and she squeezed it back. She felt a spark of hope. Whatever Mother said, she couldn't hurt them.

'And where might you be from?' Mother asked, heaving the large teapot down onto the centre of the table.

'I'm from BC, ma'am,' Gordy said.

'That's British Columbia,' Grace said, carefully. 'On the west coast of Canada. And, when the war's over, I'll be going over there, to live.'

'Canada?' Mother cried. Finally, the penny had dropped. 'Canada? Is that America? Good gracious me, noo! That's the other side of the world!' She was shaking her head, her grey curls bobbing. 'I'll no' have it! No daughter of mine is going that far away. No!'

Her voice was getting louder and Grace bit her lip. Her worst fears were coming true. She'd warned Gordy that Mother might react like this. When she was in this frame of mind, she wouldn't budge.

The kitchen door opened with a judder and Dougie came in, his eyes flitting over them. He must have heard the raised voices.

'These two want to marry and go to Canada, of all places!' Mother said. 'What have you got to say to that?'

She almost spat the words out. But it wasn't the words themselves, but rather the person she was addressing, which seemed queer. What had any of this to do with Dougie? He was only the hired help. Wasn't he?

A smile lit up Dougie's face. 'You're getting married? That's wonderful news! Congratulations. I'm delighted for you both.' He shook hands with Gordy and kissed Grace on the cheek. 'Well done,' Dougie whispered in her ear. 'Isn't this marvellous, Maura?' he said, turning to Mother.

233

"Maura"? Grace almost toppled into her cup of tea.

She remembered seeing them through the window, as she and Gordy had arrived, approaching the cottage from the road. They'd been sitting awful close. Could it possibly be true? Were Dougie and Mother courting?

The three of them waited. Mother nodded and sniffed. Was that a capitulation? Perhaps it was the closest they were going to get.

'I know it's a long way, Mother,' Grace said, firmly. 'Canada, I mean. But that's how it is. If Gordy lived on the moon, I'd follow him there. This is my life. And I want to go.'

There was silence in the kitchen. No sound but the ticking of the clock on the wall.

'"Gracie" indeed,' Mother said, finally, shaking her head.

'The other girls call me "Amazing Grace",' Grace said. 'They even sing it sometimes, in the forest.'

It wasn't the done thing to boast and "Amazing Grace" was a hymn, after all, and Mother mightn't like it being sung in that way. Grace braced herself for a ticking-off but Mother was silent, thoughtful.

'Do they, aye?' she said. 'You've got pals there then?'

Grace nodded. 'Yes, I do.' Her eyes filled with tears at the thought of them all. She'd never had friends like them. They made her feel safe; that was the only way to describe it.

Gordy squeezed her hand again under the table.

Dougie cleared his throat. 'Your lovely daughter has found a man who deserves her and they're going to build a life together, Maura. Let's hope they'll be as happy as us, eh?' he said.

So, they were a couple! Grace watched her mother's face and for the first time in her life, saw her blush.

She held her breath and felt something shift in the room.

Mother nodded. She looked down and twisted her hands in her lap as she spoke. 'I called you Grace because I'd given up on ever having a child of ma own.'

Grace kept perfectly still. Mother had never said anything like this before. She never talked about feelings, hopes or dreams or of being happy. Grace could barely believe what she was hearing.

'I'd . . . there'd been others but . . .' She shook her head. What did she mean? Babies who'd died? Grace swallowed. She didn't dare ask. She could see this was painful. If it had been anyone else, she'd have run to the other side of the table and given her a reassuring hug. But this was Mother; she couldn't. She sat perfectly still and waited.

'So, when you were born . . .' Mother looked up and smiled faintly, at the memory. 'You were a gift from God.'

Grace exhaled. 'Was I?' she breathed.

Mother's smile was broader now. 'Aye. And that's why we called you Grace. Here by the Grace of God.'

Chapter 33

'Sergeant Fraser, you were at the dance on Saturday night?'

'Yes, sir.'

Callum stood in front of Lieutenant Coomber, clenching his hands behind his back, trying to keep his breathing level. His mind was racing. He'd been expecting to get hauled in on Monday morning like this but he still hadn't decided what to say.

'Are you aware, Sergeant, that something happened, involving Captain Graham that night?'

Callum shuffled slightly. 'I had heard that, sir, yes. Word's gotten around.'

'I've been tasked with investigating the incident. I have a few questions.'

Callum nodded. He knew he should do his duty and tell everything he knew. It mightn't be too bad for Grace. There were, after all, mitigating circumstances. She'd hit the captain, sure. But it was in defence of her friend. Anyone who'd seen the state of Jean could have no doubt she'd been attacked.

But then he was swamped by uncertainty, again. They hadn't reported it – Jean had point-blank refused – and now, in the cold light of day, that looked suspicious as hell.

'You were seen leaving the hall at about nine o'clock on Saturday night. Is that correct?' Coomber asked.

Callum hesitated. 'Sure, I guess I did go outside at some point. It was real hot in there. But I couldn't be sure of the time.'

Damn it. Someone had seen him leave. Probably seen Gordy, too. It was hardly surprising. There were hundreds of people there on Saturday night.

He wondered what Graham would say had happened between him and Jean. He'd probably say it was all a misunderstanding, nothing but a bit of what they called around here "slap and tickle". No harm done. Boys will be boys.

The best he could hope for was that Graham was OK – not brain-damaged or in a coma or whatever – but couldn't remember a damn thing about the night. Worst case, he could remember everything and could name Jean and maybe him and Gordy too. As they'd put him to bed, he'd been coming round; he might have recognised them.

Even if both girls were prepared to come forward and swear on the Holy Bible that Graham had been assaulting Jean when Grace hit him, who would be believed?

Jean would have to relive the whole incident and she wouldn't do it.

Callum had no idea how the British would deal with this; or whether it would be handled solely within the camp. But even without magistrates or police involvement, he had a bad feeling that, if the truth came out, Grace would have to leave the Timber Corps. Or worse: she might be prosecuted. Gordy would never forgive him and he'd feel pretty rotten too. It was a goddamn mess and it was all Graham's fault. He should be punished but there wasn't any way of bringing him to book, which didn't implicate Grace too.

'And when you were outside,' the lieutenant continued, 'or at any point in the evening, Sergeant, did you see or hear anything suspicious?'

'No, sir.'

Lieutenant Coomber cleared his throat and glanced at his notes on the desk. 'I understand that Captain Graham had also gone outside, alone, for some air.'

He raised his eyes and they met Callum's and a flash of understanding passed through them. A tiny spark of hope lit in Callum's chest. They both knew that wasn't true.

'He was knocked unconscious with a blunt instrument,' Coomber went on. 'Probably, according to the medic, a branch or a log. Delivered with some force.'

'You're thinking one of the men hit him, sir?' Callum asked. It wouldn't be out of the question. Graham was a bully. There were plenty who'd do it if they got the chance. 'Is he OK, sir, by the way?'

He'd been a damn fool. He should have done the right thing on Saturday night and reported what had happened. Told them exactly what the captain – and Grace – had done. He'd taken the law into his own hands. Big mistake.

He scanned the lieutenant's face and asked again. 'Is the captain all right?'

Coomber sighed. 'He had concussion pretty bad but he's OK. Couple more days in the sick bay and he'll be right as rain. The question is, how did he get the blow on the head and how did he get from wherever it happened, back to his bunk? Someone tucked him up real neat.'

It was no good; Callum was going to give him something. He took a breath. 'I do know something about that night, sir. I remember going outside, sir, for a cigarette and I heard someone groaning, in the woods.'

'Someone groaning?' The lieutenant was writing it all down on a pad on his desk.

'And I found Captain Graham on the ground, sir.'

The lieutenant put down his pen and rubbed his face in both hands. When he spoke, he sounded disappointed rather than cross. 'Why are you only telling me this now?'

Callum sighed. 'Because I thought he was drunk, sir. Which, as you know, is an offence.'

The lieutenant nodded. 'Everyone knows it. The captain certainly knows it.'

It was common knowledge that fellas hid beer in the bushes and went outside for a quick swig during a dance. But not the officers. It was unthinkable.

'I didn't want him getting into trouble,' Callum went on, not meeting Coomber's eye. 'I reckon he's had some bad news from home, sir. He's not been himself lately.' Once he'd started lying, it was as though he couldn't stop.

'So, I . . . er, I got Private Johnson to help me, sir.' He didn't want to involve Gordy but they might have been seen and besides, Graham was a big guy: Callum couldn't have carried him alone. 'We hauled him back, between us, to his bunk. I didn't know he had an injury. It was dark and I could smell alcohol on his breath so . . .' Callum shrugged. 'If I'd known he was hurt, I'd never have left him.'

Coomber nodded, slowly. There was no telling if he believed him. 'I'll be speaking to Johnson, when he's back.'

Gordy was on leave today. Callum was surprised all leave hadn't been cancelled, in view of what had happened. This was serious. Captain Graham was number two of the whole camp. He sure didn't act like it – the man was a prize pig – but that was the truth of the matter.

'What did you do, when you got him to his bunk?' Coomber asked.

'We put a bucket and a glass of water by his cot.' This was true and undoubtedly the lieutenant would already have that information. 'And then, sir, we left him to it.'

The lieutenant nodded and wrote something else down on his pad.

'Will that be all, sir?'

'For now, Sergeant. But I may need to call you back, if more evidence comes to light.'

Callum saluted and marched from the room. His heart was pounding. He'd got off lightly: the lieutenant hadn't probed too deep. If it had been any of the other officers, he mightn't have got off so easily but he and Coomber had always got along.

He'd lied. That didn't feel good. The only consolation was the thought of Seffy. She'd be pleased with him; she'd say he'd done the right thing.

Only time would tell whether he had.

Chapter 34

A fortnight later, at sunset, Grace, Seffy and Gordy stood on the edge of the loch, next to a pair of wooden rowing boats. Grace peered into one. There was an inch of mucky water in the bottom.

'I'm no' getting' into that! It's leakin'!' she said.

Gordy laughed. 'That's only rainwater. I can tip it out, if you like?'

She shook her head. He was wearing his uniform; he'd only get it wet and dirty.

'You trust me, don't you, girls?' Gordy asked. 'It's not far. See the hillock on the other side? That's where we're headed. It'll take about thirty minutes. You ladies can sit back and I'll do the work!'

They were going to a dance in a village on the far side of the loch. It was the first time since the terrible, awful night, as they now referred to it, that any of the Macdonald girls had ventured out for the evening. Irene had insisted they kept their heads down. They'd been "confined to barracks"; the Canadian camp was most certainly out of bounds.

But finally, Irene had said she couldn't see the harm in going to the hop in another village.

The group of Canadian boys they knew were going and had asked, via Gordy, if the lumberjills wanted to "tag along". And even though it was a dance and Grace didn't dance, she was determined not to miss out.

Everyone was going, except Hazel and Morag. There'd been a bout of sickness in the camp in the past week. Some of the girls had been quarantined and dosed with milk of magnesia by the intrepid welfare officer, Mrs Eccles. Hazel and Morag were still feeling a little peely-wally.

'Are you wishing you'd gone in the truck with the others, now?' Seffy asked Grace. 'It's quicker, going across the water this way, rather than around the road.'

'It sure is!' They turned, to see Gordy's sergeant, Callum Fraser, striding towards them across the stony beach. He had Enid and Joey in tow.

'We changed our minds!' Enid said, her eyes widening as she saw the boats. 'Jean and Irene are going in the lorry but we thought this'd be more fun!' Without hesitation, she and Joey clambered into the second rowing boat, and the sergeant started to push it out into the water.

Grace glanced at Seffy. At the sight of Callum Fraser, she'd flushed a pretty shade of pink. She was looking anywhere but at him, toying with the edges of her coat, as though not quite knowing what to do with her hands.

Grace and Gordy exchanged smiles. For all their yelling and falling out, Seffy and Callum were a good match. But as Gordy said, they just hadn't realised yet.

'Come on then, girls, in you get,' Gordy said. 'Or those guys will get there way ahead of us.'

Gordy held Grace's hand as she stepped into the boat and it shook as she scrambled towards the wooden plank at the far end. She winced, wishing she was a slip of a thing, who didn't make boats rock. But when Gordy handed Seffy in, the same thing happened. Seffy gave a little scream, which made them all laugh. Perhaps that was simply what happened when you climbed aboard a rowing boat.

Grace had been fretting that she'd weigh the boat down too much but it slipped easily into the shallows as Gordy gave it a shove. He jumped on board after it and it glided through the water, without a problem.

Gordy sat on the middle plank, facing them, and picked up the oars.

'You've done this before, then?' Grace asked.

'Yeah but not in a while.'

For a minute, they seemed to be going in a circle. The other boat was steaming ahead of them and the girls were yelling back, telling them to hurry up, their laughter carrying across the loch.

But soon Gordy got into a rhythm and they started to cut swiftly through the water, catching the others up. The hills and woods on the other shore gradually loomed larger.

It was a little chilly now they were out of the shelter of the bay and Grace shuffled up closer to Seffy and her warm coat. The water lapped against the sides of the boat. It would be dark on the return journey but, now, it was still light.

'Isn't it deep?' Seffy said, peering over the side. 'Gosh, it's crystal clear. There are jellyfish down there. Beautiful ones. And I can see the sandy bottom of the loch. It looks an awful way down.'

It was a good thing Grace felt perfectly safe, with Gordy at the helm. She could swim, of course – or at least, she could manage a very unimpressive doggy paddle. But she'd rather not think about jellyfish or how deep the water was, ta very much.

'You've sure got some pretty lakes – sorry, lochs – here but back home, well, I reckon Canadian lakes take some beating. Our home town, Invermore, is on a lake, something like this,' Gordy said. He smiled at Grace. 'You'll see, my love, one day.'

'Does it make you feel homesick?' Seffy asked. 'Being somewhere like this?'

'Nah,' Gordy said, not taking his eyes off Grace. 'Right now, there's no other place in the world I'd rather be.'

Grace exhaled, sat back and let her hand trail through the icy cold water. Apart from that short time at Mother's, when the relief of having her approve of Gordy and give her blessing to their wedding had been so shocking that she thought she might faint, this felt like the first time she'd relaxed since that terrible, awful night.

And she hadn't been alone: the girls of Macdonald hut had held their breath with her, braced for the worst.

Every morning, Grace woke up, wondering whether this would be the day. But as each day passed, then a week, then another and nothing happened, and the reports from Gordy were encouraging – Callum hadn't "snitched" on her, for a start – she was starting to believe that everything might be all right.

'Any more news on the captain?' Seffy asked. She must have been thinking about the incident too.

Gordy's smile faded. 'Like I told Gracie, he's sticking to his story: he can't remember a thing, he went outside for "some air" that night and next thing, he woke up in bed with a sore head.'

They were silent for a minute. There was no sound but the slapping of the oars on the water.

It almost sounded too good to be true. If Captain Graham was telling the truth, surely there was a risk his memory of that night would return? Or perhaps he was lying, because it would be his word against that of two young women, who might just be believed?

Grace sighed. It was impossible to put it all behind her, just yet. But for this evening, she'd try.

Gordy was watching her, a look of concern on his face. She smiled, leaned forward and patted his hand.

'You're a good rower, Gordy Johnson.'

He grinned. 'One of my many talents, Grace McGinty! You've snared yourself a real catch in me!'

* * *

244

The men pulled the boats up onto the beach on the other side of the loch and then they all had to trudge up a steep hill to reach the village.

It was quite a climb but Seffy, in her excitement, hardly noticed. Her stupid wrist was finally free of its strapping and she'd been hugging a secret to herself all day: it was her birthday.

A couple of times she'd thought about telling the others but it never seemed to be the right moment. Grace and Gordy were, quite rightly, wrapped up in one another, while Enid and Joey were gabbling away nineteen to the dozen to Callum. Seffy was walking quietly behind them. She could hardly interrupt everyone's chatter with her "announcement". It would look as though she were trying to make the evening all about her.

Instead, she focused on Callum's long strides and the way his hobnail boots kicked up the dust on the path. She smiled to herself as he muttered, 'Hmm?' and 'You don't say?' as the girls rabbited on. It was obvious he wasn't listening. It was the first time they'd seen each other since that morning at church. She wondered whether he might glance back, once or twice, to check she was still there. But he didn't.

He could be rude and offhand at times but it didn't take anything away from the fact that Callum Fraser had done the right thing. He'd wavered but that conversation in the graveyard – when she'd practically begged him not to tell the truth – hadn't been in vain. He'd kept quiet about what had happened. He hadn't ratted on Grace and unleashed all kinds of terrible trouble. And she was grateful to him.

There were already several girls at the village hall when they arrived. Seffy didn't recognise any of them.

'Land girls,' Joey said.

One of them peered at Seffy. 'Haven't seen you lot before, have we? What farm are you from?'

'We're not Land Army,' Seffy said, breezily. 'We're Timber Corps.'

'Oh, bad luck.' The girl flashed a fake smile. 'Drew the short straw there, didn't you?'

Joey and Seffy rolled their eyes at one another.

The door burst open and dozens of new arrivals entered the hall. The truck with the Canucks, Jean and Irene had arrived. The land girls looked hungrily at the soldiers and Seffy's chest tightened.

The awful girl who'd been talking to her had already marched off, straight into the arms of one of the boys. He wasn't anyone Seffy knew but she felt a sudden surge of protectiveness for their Canadians.

But it was too late to yell "Hands off our men!" – if she'd even dared – because the gramophone had started playing a new tune – Glenn Miller – and the land girls were avidly grabbing men left, right and centre. They all looked so dapper in their uniforms, Seffy could hardly blame them.

Where was Callum? As long as no one had swooped on him. Goodness, if she couldn't get him to dance, she'd be irked if she looked round now to find him twirling one of these blasted land girls around the floor. She didn't think she could bear it.

Ah, there he was.

He was standing right in front of her, looking very tall. And handsome. There was an ironic smile playing on his lips.

'Seffy,' he said, and her stomach flipped. The way he said her name was special. He inclined his head towards the dance floor. 'Would you care to dance?'

At last!

Their eyes met. She should really tell him that she wasn't in a dancing frame of mind. Give him a taste of his own medicine. He raised his eyebrows, as though he knew exactly what she was thinking and was half expecting a refusal.

Oh, to heck with it! There was a war on, after all. She didn't have time – or the inclination – to play silly games. It was her birthday! And Callum Fraser had finally asked her to dance.

'Yes please, Sergeant,' she said, taking his outstretched hand. 'I would.'

And he held her so tenderly, up close, dancing cheek to cheek, being especially careful with her newly healed hand. Then he spun her around the floor, everyone else in the room flashing past in a blur of khaki and brightly coloured dresses. She was smiling, smiling so hard. It had been worth the wait. Oh, every minute. She felt like she was flying.

'Girls, it's gonna be mighty cold going back across that loch now,' Callum said to Enid and Joey at the end of the night. He'd cornered them by the cloakrooms, as they were fetching their coats. 'There's room on the truck going back to camp, if you wanna catch a ride. But be quick, they're about to leave.'

He smiled to himself as they nodded and thanked him and ran out of the hall. They thought he'd done them a favour but in fact, it was the other way around.

When the four of them reached the shore of the loch, Gordy was all for making the return journey more fun. 'Shall we have a race?' he asked.

Callum shook his head. 'We are not having a race, buddy. You take Grace in your boat; I'll take Seffy in mine.' He turned towards her. Her face was in shadow. 'If that's all right with you, ma'am?'

'Yes,' she said, immediately. Her voice rang out clearly in the night air.

The sky was navy blue, speckled with stars, and there was a full moon so bright they didn't need their torches. Moonlight was spilling across the loch like a silver path.

'Gosh, look at that. It's incredible!' Seffy said.

Callum was not a dreamer but it sure did look magical: like a painting, like something you wanted to keep in your mind forever.

Gordy and Grace set off in their boat and Callum took his time sorting out the oars. He didn't want to dawdle too much, in case someone turned up on the beach, hoping to hitch a ride, but he wanted to let the others get a little way ahead.

He handed her carefully into the boat and as he settled himself down on the seat facing her, he knocked Seffy's knee with one of the oars.

'I beg your pardon,' he said. Hell, what was the matter with him, all formal and awkward? They'd danced all night and it had felt like the most natural thing in the world but now they were alone, it was different. 'Say, I didn't hurt you then, did I?'

She laughed. 'Goodness, I'm not that fragile! You tapped me with the oar, nothing more. I'm a lumberjill, remember! I'm stronger than that.'

He nodded. All the girls were stronger than he'd given them credit for, when they'd first arrived. But winter was coming. He guessed that would be the real test.

They didn't speak for a minute. There was only the sound of the oars slapping the surface of the loch and water pouring off, as he pulled them up again. A cool breeze was blowing, lifting Seffy's hair off her face.

Each time he pulled back and forth, the little boat jerked forward a few more feet and they got nearer to the shoreline; nearer to the end of it being just the two of them.

'Thank you,' Seffy said. 'For keeping quiet about Jean and Grace and all that.'

He nodded. 'How 'bout we agree not to talk about that again?'

'No, let's not. Subject closed!' She smiled at him. 'It's been a jolly good night.'

'Yeah, sure has.'

The only fly in the ointment was Verne Blumenthal, who'd seemed to be watching him the whole time. Whenever Callum had looked up, or gone to fetch a drink, Verne's ugly mug was there. Who'd appointed him private eye? He might be married to Missy's sister but that didn't give him rights over Callum. He'd have a word, maybe. Tell him to back off.

'Irene seemed a little out of sorts, mind,' Seffy mused. 'She stuck to Jean's side like glue, did you notice? And she hardly danced, which isn't like her at all.'

He nodded. 'Irene and Jean-Paul have split, I hear.'

'"Split"? What do you mean?'

'I heard it on the grapevine. They ain't together no more.'

'They were never actually "together",' Seffy corrected. 'She's married, remember?'

'I remember, but sometimes I wondered whether Irene did.'

Seffy stretched back in the boat. 'It was only ever a distraction for Irene. She loves Jim. She talks about him all the time. Good for her, if she's staying away from Jean-Paul now. It'll stop the tittle-tattling.'

'Yeah, I guess.'

Seffy laughed. 'You know, I feel like I can say anything to you now and you're totally trapped!'

He shook his head, not understanding.

'Well, you can hardly march off when you're in the middle of a loch! You're always doing that: storming off when I'm talking to you. When I get too much, I suppose.'

His mouth went dry. Was that her impression of him? That he was rude and so incapable of having a reasoned argument, that he simply walked away? His mind raced, as he tried to remember the times he'd done it.

But then, Seffy changed the subject. 'When you're in the woods, do you ever think about the trees and how they've been growing there, all this time, since before we were even born?'

He laughed. 'Nope. If I thought like that, hell, I'd never be able to do my job!'

'It's nice when you laugh, Callum,' she said in a soft voice, gazing up at the moon. His insides turned to mush and he pulled the oars back too soon and missed the water. 'You should do it more often.'

And then he glanced upwards and saw it.

'Hey, what's that?' He squinted up at the horizon and stopped rowing. There was a faint green glow above them in the inky sky. And then, the weirdest thing happened: curtains of green, yellow and blue appeared.

Gordy and Grace, whose boat was just a few yards in front, had seen it too.

'Say, it's not a gun or a . . . I dunno, something to do with those darned Nazis, is it?' Gordy yelled. His voice echoed across the loch. 'Or is it the army, testing a new searchlight?'

Callum laughed softly. 'Shush, you knucklehead! It's none of those things. I know what it is: it's the aurora borealis.'

'In English, please?' Gordy shouted.

'They call them the Mirrie Dancers up here,' Callum yelled back. 'I can't believe it! Can you see it, Seffy? Hell, that's amazing. It's the Northern Lights!'

As they watched, in silence, the green light turned into wisps that billowed and snaked across the sky for the next hour or so. And even though it got cold, none of them wanted to leave the loch. It was hypnotic.

'I've never seen them before,' Callum told Seffy when the light show was finally over and he'd started rowing again. 'We have 'em back home, folks say, but I've looked and looked and I never saw them. Not 'til now.' He shook his head. 'Wow, that sure was somethin' real special.'

Seffy laughed and clapped her hands in delight. 'Oh, it was! And, do you know, it's actually my birthday today. For another—' she squinted at her watch '—fifteen minutes or so.'

'Well, happy birthday!' He was glad; it was the perfect excuse to stop rowing and make a fuss of her. He let the boat drift. It bobbed on the water and waves slapped gently against the sides. 'Why didn't you say something earlier? Too tight to buy the drinks, eh?'

She laughed. 'Ah, yes, you've caught me out. No actually, not tight, just too poor these days!'

He'd heard the British didn't earn much. Leastways, not compared to the company guys. Some of the fellas walked behind girls in the village, jangling coins in their pockets. No wonder they were so popular.

'I've never had to worry about money before,' she said. 'Honestly, we earn a pittance and they deduct money out of that for board and lodgings!' At least she could laugh about it.

'Don't your parents give you anything?' Callum asked.

'My father stopped my allowance when I joined up. At first it was a novelty, even a challenge, living on the same wages as the other girls and trying to eke out the shillings and pence. But now it's simply a drag. Being poor isn't fun! Oh, but please don't feel sorry for me. I'll survive!'

He was only teasing about buying the drinks. As if he'd let a lady do such a thing. As it was, they'd hardly had a drink all night; they'd danced so much, there hadn't been time. And yet, he'd felt – and still felt – totally intoxicated.

'Why didn't you say something? About it being your birthday?' he said again.

Seffy shrugged. 'I'm not sure. It's actually my twenty-first! Key of the door and all that. If I'd been at home, there'd have been a huge celebration. A hundred guests, cake, champagne, the works.'

Callum gave a long low whistle. 'So much? What about rationing?'

'Oh, you can get anything you want, if you ask the right questions. Also, my father's had a case of Beaujolais laid down for my twenty-first since I was born.' She caught her breath, as though regretting her words. 'But I've had a super time. I haven't missed any of that. The dance tonight and now these – what did you say they were called?'

'The Mirrie Dancers.'

'Yes, those. It's been fantastic. You know, I used to hate green, but after that sky tonight, it's officially my favourite colour! I can honestly say, the Northern Lights really were the icing on the cake!'

He laughed, taking up the oars again. 'The icing on the non-existent birthday cake?'

'Exactly.'

Fifty yards before they reached the shore, where Gordy and Grace had already pulled up, Callum dropped the oars, leaned forward and brushed his lips gently on her cheek.

'Happy birthday,' he murmured again, sitting back down.

Oh, darn it. He leaned forward again and kissed her properly this time, firmly on the lips, putting his hands gently around the back of her neck, breathing in the sweet scent of her. As the little wooden boat rocked on the water, Seffy kissed him back. Those Northern Lights had sent him crazy; she'd sent him crazy.

'Sorry,' he said, taking his seat again. 'Couldn't help myself.'

'Don't be.' Her voice was encouraging, as though she'd like him to do it again. But it was too late. The moment was over. They'd reached the shingle beach and Gordy was splashing through the shallows, to help bring them in.

Chapter 35

In the canteen, Callum could hear Gordy on the next table telling the fellas about the Northern Lights. His fist closed tight around the water glass he was holding. He wished he'd shut the hell up.

Saturday night had been somethin' special: a once-in-a-lifetime experience and he wanted to keep it private: just for the four of them who'd been there. But now it was being tossed around the room and guys were asking dumb questions and Gordy was making jokes and it was spoiling the whole darn thing.

He'd hardly slept the past few nights, replaying Saturday night over in his mind. He liked Seffy and he was getting the impression that she liked him too. When they danced together, he didn't falter and stumble, like he sometimes did with other women. They fitted together, real neat. But he wasn't free; he'd made a promise to someone else and it wasn't fair on Seffy or Missy. He was playing with fire. And he didn't wanna turn into Pa: a man who couldn't stick with one woman.

He had to stop it now, before it all went too far.

Someone was watching him. He turned to see Verne Blumenthal scowling at him across the dining room. Verne strolled over, carrying his tray in front of him, slammed it on the table and sat down on the bench, right up close to Callum. Callum continued eating, staring straight ahead as though nothing had happened.

'Gettin' mighty friendly with the little English lady, ain't you?' Verne said quietly in his ear.

He couldn't even have him up for insubordination because Verne had been promoted and they were the same rank.

Callum was aware that he was chewing faster and harder. A couple of other fellas, sensing trouble, shifted their trays and moved tables, leaving the two of them alone.

He'd tensed. He concentrated on stopping his leg from jiggling on the spot and said nothing but carried on shovelling the food into his mouth.

'Seeing stars an' all, so I hear,' Verne added, with a laugh. 'Your good lady back home might have summat to say about that, hey? Your fiancée?' He emphasised every syllable of the word.

Callum's chest tightened. He pushed back; the chair scraped on the wooden floor. They both stood up simultaneously, so they were face to face. He could smell Verne's baccy breath, see his nostrils flare and his eyes, full of hate.

'Oh, pardon me,' Verne said. 'Perhaps the English girl ain't even aware of your little lady back home?'

'Get outta my face,' Callum muttered.

Around them, the air had changed, like the atmosphere before a storm. Two of Blumenthal's pals came over and persuaded him to leave with them.

Gordy was suddenly there. 'What was all that about?'

'Nothin',' Callum said. He dropped back down into his seat and mopped up the gravy on his plate with a hunk of bread. It wasn't nothin', though. It was something. Something bad. His heart was beating like crazy.

When he left the canteen, Verne was waiting for him in the clearing outside. Before he could get the first punch in, Callum hit him hard, once, in the stomach, sending him sprawling to the ground. His fist hurt but it had felt real good. He wasn't sorry.

* * *

Lieutenant Coomber paced the office, hands behind his back. His face was grave, his voice, when he spoke, was edged with disappointment.

'Sergeant Fraser, here we are again. This time, hitting a fellow officer. What in hell's name is going on?' He jabbed his finger at Callum. 'Think hard before you answer. It'd better be good!'

Callum didn't know what to say. It'd sound pretty damn feeble to say "Women trouble, sir". He squirmed at the thought. Pathetic! He was pathetic, after all the warnings he'd given his men, too.

Verne had cottoned on to how he felt about Seffy almost before he knew himself. As Missy's brother-in-law – and, it turned out, her self-appointed protector – it was only a matter of time before Verne passed the information on. It was a mess.

'Bad news from home? Is that it?' Coomber asked.

Callum shook his head. Bad news usually meant you got an easier time for a day or two. Allowances were made. But he couldn't lie.

'Homesick?' Coomber asked.

'No, sir. I like it here.'

'Even the warm beer? And the strange natives?'

They smiled at each other.

'Yeah, well make the most of it, Sergeant. For now, you are still sergeant but there's always the possibility of demotion; you know that, right?'

Callum felt sick. He'd never forgive himself if he squandered this chance to make something of himself, if he went backwards instead of forwards.

'This ain't like you. It ain't like you at all. I put you forward for special weekend manoeuvres with our sister companies but now, I ain't so sure. And you've got leave coming up before Christmas, right? You don't wanna lose that, Sergeant.'

'No, sir.'

'So, this fight. What was it all about? Women?'

Callum bit his lip. 'We fell out, sir. We don't get on, me and him. But I won't let it happen again.'

The lieutenant nodded. 'Good to hear.' He lowered his voice. 'And make the most of Scotland because we won't be here forever.' He tapped his nose. 'OK, enough of this nonsense now. Actions have consequences, understand?'

'Yes, sir.'

Before Callum could salute and leave the lieutenant's office, Coomber cleared his throat and moved his head, as though checking the door was closed.

'That business a couple of weeks back, with Captain Graham?'

'Sir?'

'I reckon you know more about that night than you're saying.'

He said it sympathetically but Callum's heart started to pound. He tried to keep his face impassive.

'But I like you, Fraser. You put duty first. You're good with your men and I trust you. So, whatever you're covering up, I guess you're doing it for the right reason. Provided you don't get yourself in any more trouble, we'll say no more about it, d'you hear?'

Callum saluted.

That sealed it. He was risking everything for an English girl who . . . hell, who even knew if she liked him or was just killing time? The end. No more. It'd be tough but he had to stop whatever it was, before he got in too deep.

Chapter 36

It was Saturday afternoon, two weeks since their trip across the loch. Most of the girls were relaxing on their beds, writing letters and flicking through magazines. Seffy stumbled as she came back into the hut with her washing and dropped half of it on the floor next to Irene's cot.

Irene tutted. She was in an awfully bad mood these days and complained constantly of headaches. Seffy was praying a letter would come soon from Jim, to cheer her up.

'What's got into you, Dolly Daydream?' Irene asked, making no move to help pick up Seffy's smalls. 'You've no' been the same since you saw those lights in the sky. They've cast a spell on you!' She nodded down the hut, towards Enid and Joey. 'And you've sent that pair doolally.'

'Aww, don't, Irene!' Enid wailed. 'We missed out good and proper and I'll never get over it!'

Irene rolled her eyes and flopped back down on her bed.

Enid and Joey had been out every night since the dance, scouring the sky in vain, hoping to catch sight of the Northern Lights and cursing their bad luck for not going back in the boat.

Seffy bit her lip and said nothing. She wasn't sorry the girls hadn't seen the lights. Everything would have been very different, had they been there.

She placed her washing around the wood-burning stove to dry. She wasn't quite herself these days, it was true, but it was nothing to do with the Northern Lights. Callum Fraser had put a spell on her. She couldn't stop thinking about him. He hadn't been at the village hop last week, which had been a blow, but nothing could dampen her cheerfulness for long. She was dying to see him again, to make sure she hadn't imagined what had happened between them.

She touched her lips with her fingertips. That kiss! Not the first; that had been the kind of kiss that Teddy gave her, sweet and chaste. But the second one had had an urgency to it. Gosh, her stomach swooped away at the thought of it. It had been passionate; she'd never been kissed like that before. The little boat had rocked as Callum put his hands gently around her neck and pulled her towards him and she'd kissed him right back. Oh goodness, it was quite shocking, how instinctively she'd responded.

'Somethin's burning!' Irene yelled across the hut.

Seffy yelped, pushed a stick into the stove and pulled out a pair of her knickers, charred and smoking.

She held them up, making the girls giggle.

'Och, Miss Mills!' she said, doing her best Miss McEwen impression. 'How did they ever get in there? Are ye trying to burn the place down?'

Everyone, except Irene, laughed.

The door to the hut opened and Jean came in, carrying a huge parcel.

'It's for you,' she said to Seffy, as she placed it down on the floor. 'Fortunately, it's not as heavy as it looks.'

Seffy frowned. She wasn't expecting anything. She winced as she checked the label: "Lady Persephone Baxter-Mills". Thank goodness Jean had brought the parcel in and had diplomatically chosen not to comment on her title. If Irene had seen it, there'd be no end to the ribbing.

Maybe it was from Callum? It was almost too much to hope for but perhaps he'd sent her something? A late birthday present?

'Maybe it's a food parcel!' Joey said, hopefully.

Seffy shook her head. She'd dismissed the idea of asking Mummy to send food when she wrote her very first letter. The food hadn't improved but they'd got used to it and the Canucks often took pity on them and gave them food from their camp kitchens.

The girls had gathered around.

'Come on, then,' Irene said. 'Open it!'

Seffy knelt down, pulling off the string and then the brown paper.

Everyone gasped. It was a bundle of beautiful cream material.

'It's parachute silk!' Seffy said. She held it up with both hands and felt the folds of soft fabric spill out onto her lap. There was only a momentary stab of disappointment that it wasn't anything for her. 'Gosh, there's reams of it! My brothers must have sent it!'

She'd written to the boys, not really expecting that they'd be able to help. But here it was: they'd come up trumps.

'It'll make the most wonderful wedding dress, Grace,' Seffy said. 'And Irene, you'll make it, like you promised, won't you?'

Irene sighed and Seffy glared at her. She might seem a little more enthusiastic.

Irene gave a weary smile. 'Aye, Grace, of course, I'll sew it for you, hen.'

They unravelled the material and the girls draped it endlessly around Grace, marvelling over the fabric and the gorgeous colour and imagining all kinds of derring-do that must have been required, to obtain it.

But Grace was quiet.

'What's the matter?' Seffy asked her. 'You don't mind that it's from a parachute, do you?'

She shook her head. 'No, I'm pleased, really I am. It's only . . . I cannae help being superstitious. I'm fretting that it's all going too well. Mother's given me her blessing and now, I'm to have a beautiful dress.' She wrung her hands. 'I cannae help thinking something's going to go wrong before I walk down that aisle.'

'Now if you don't stop mithering,' Joey said, 'we'll have no choice but to sing "Amazin' Grace" at the tops of our voices. Isn't that right, girls?'

Grace groaned and covered her ears; she always pretended not to like it when they sang her song.

'You need to be more like Jolly Jean!' Hazel said.

Jean grabbed Grace's hands and looked at her in mock-exasperation. 'Repeat after me, Grace McGinty: "Everything's going to be all right!"'

Seffy smiled. It had been a few weeks but it was good to have the old Jean – "Jolly Jean" – back, once more looking on the bright side.

Her thoughts drifted back to Callum. It was the first Sunday of October tomorrow. Church parade. She would go down to the village and, fingers crossed, he'd be there.

Chapter 37

Irene rubbed her wet hair with a towel as she walked into the drawing room at Ballykinch House.

She felt a wee bit better after that warm bath. The crushing headache she'd had for the last few days had finally lifted.

Seffy was still sitting on the sofa where Irene had left her half an hour earlier, stroking the dog. There was no sign of Grace.

'Ma God, she's never still being interrogated?' Irene threw herself down in an armchair next to the fire and made a turban of the towel. 'We should've asked Jock. He'd have done it in half the time. It's only a letter, after all.'

Seffy sighed. 'My aunt likes to do things properly. She'd only agree to vouch for Grace's character if she could interview her first.' She glanced at the clock on the mantelpiece. 'I'm sure they won't be much longer. You head on back to camp, if you like.'

Irene shook her head. 'Och no, I may as well wait. I'll catch pneumonia if I go out there with wet hair. It's freezing.'

'And there's bound to be tea and cake before we go,' Seffy said. 'I smelled something delicious coming from the kitchen as we arrived.'

Irene's stomach heaved. 'I cannae face cake. But a cup of tea, aye, that wouldnae go amiss.'

'Oh, here,' Seffy picked up something from the seat beside her. 'Marigold's borrowed this from someone at the WI. What d'you think?'

She tossed the Simplicity pattern to Irene. She caught it and examined the picture of the bridal gown on the front. It had a sweetheart neckline and a long, pleated train. She nodded. 'Aye, if Grace approves, I could manage that. Suppose I'd better make a start. They'll be setting a date soon.'

Seffy smiled. 'She's going to look a picture. I know Grace is awfully worried about something going wrong but—'

'No, they'll be fine,' Irene said, firmly. 'That incident in the woods is in the past now. Your fella, the sergeant, did the right thing.'

She looked up. Seffy was blushing.

'He's hardly "my fella",' she said. 'I mean – gosh, I haven't seen him for weeks. Not since the night of the Northern Lights. He wasn't at church parade last Sunday and, well . . .' She gave a hollow laugh. 'I've practically forgotten what he looks like!'

Irene frowned and sat forward in her seat. Goodness, the girl was clearly heartsore. Irene had been so wrapped up in herself these past few weeks that she'd completely missed it. But wait, she already had a fella, didn't she?

'What's his name, that beau of yours in the RAF?' Irene asked.

Seffy's eyes widened. 'Who? Oh, Teddy.'

'Aye, that's it. And has he made you any promises, this Teddy?'

Seffy bent down and stroked the dog's head, not meeting Irene's eye.

'No, if you must know, he never has. It's always been an expectation, I suppose. An assumption. Our parents are lifelong chums and everyone's simply taken it for granted that we'll marry one day.'

Irene sighed. It was hardly love's young dream. It sounded more like a business contract. But she wouldn't say it; Seffy would take the hump. But she couldn't stay quiet: she had to say something.

'I'll let you into a little secret,' she said. 'If a fella is really mad about you, you know. So, this Teddy fella. Does he make your insides melt? Or your stomach turn somersaults?'

Seffy laughed. 'Goodness, this sounds like one of those quizzes in Enid's magazines!' She pursed her lips, thinking. 'No, he doesn't. And to be honest, I'm thinking of—'

'Throwing him over? Am I right? But not for that Fraser fella?'

She could see from the expression on Seffy's face that she'd hit the nail on the head.

'Och, no, hen,' she said. 'Stay well clear of those Canadian boys.'

'What, like you did?'

It was Irene's turn to blush. That affair with Jean-Paul was the biggest regret of her life and she'd spend the next forty years making it up to Jim. If, God willing, she was given the chance.

She sighed. 'Look, I'm no' proud of myself. He was lonely; I was lonely. It started out as something harmless. It was never meant to . . . go that far. It was a mistake and I feel terrible.' Her eyes were swimming as she looked across the room at Seffy. 'Don't get involved with any o' them, hen. They're all just out for a good time.'

Seffy smiled. 'Except Gordy.'

'Aye, Gordy's a good 'un.'

The drawing room door burst open and Grace appeared, grinning and brandishing a letter. 'I've passed!' she said. 'My good character is duly vouched for!' She glanced from Irene to Seffy. 'What's the matter with you two?'

'Nothing, hen,' Irene said. 'We were just saying, you've got yourself the best man in that company.' She held up the sewing pattern. 'Now, come here and tell me what you think of this dress.'

Chapter 38

Dear Teddy,

I hope you are well.

Thank you so much for your last letter. There's no need to apologise for not writing. You're probably frightfully busy. As am I, of course.

I hope it's warmer wherever you are. It's freezing here now. Some mornings we wake up to ice on the inside of the windows. Brrrr!

It was a month ago now but yes, I had a lovely birthday, thank you. Not quite the big bash I'd have had at home but I spent it with some good friends and I couldn't have asked for more.

Gosh, this was hard work. Did it sound awfully stilted? She should probably say something about wishing she'd spent her birthday with him and their chums, somewhere like The Ritz.

But it wouldn't be true.

Dancing with Callum, seeing the Northern Lights and kissing him in the middle of a loch had made it the best birthday she'd ever had.

She sighed and picked up her pen again.

Teddy, I've been thinking perhaps we should cool things off a little. Given the international situation and the topsy-turvy nature of the world. Goodness, we don't know what's going to happen from one month to the next! Perhaps it's for the best if we say, for the time being, at least, that we are simply friends, with no further obligation to one another. What do you think? Awfully good friends, but nothing more than that.

Do let me know your thoughts.

Keep well and safe.

With all best wishes from,

Seffy

She felt awfully guilty, signing off with "best wishes" instead of "love". But she was trying to let him down gently. Whatever happened between her and Callum Fraser, meeting him had made her realise one thing. Teddy Fortesque was a dote, he really was. But he was undoubtedly not her one true love.

Chapter 39

It was almost the end of October before Seffy saw Callum again. By now, it was bleak and cold, and Jock had warned the girls it was likely to snow any day.

Morning tea break had just finished, Irene was blowing the whistle to call them back to work and the girls were reluctantly moving away from the warmth of the fire.

Seffy was sitting on a tree stump, knocking back the dregs of her tea, when Callum approached from behind and tapped her on the shoulder. She turned, not recognising him for a second, in his great coat and cap.

'Oh! It's you!' She couldn't keep the delight from her voice. 'Have you been avoiding me, Sergeant?' She laughed, to show she was joking and that she wasn't one of those girls who keeps tabs on her chap.

He didn't smile. 'I've been away, on weekends. Manoeuvres. But there's something I need—' He stopped and frowned. 'Can I have a word?'

Goodness, that sounded serious. Seffy nodded and looked around for Grace, who was heading back to the larch they'd been working on. She held up five fingers, to indicate she'd be just a few minutes.

266

They waited until the other girls had picked up their axes and saws and drifted back into the woods. Seffy was dying to ask him straight out what all this was about, but she'd have to be patient. Perhaps he'd been reflecting during the five weeks they'd been apart and now he was going to do something awfully North American and ask her to be "his girl"? Oh gosh, if it was that, she'd better not giggle.

She looked up at him. No, he was too agitated; this wasn't going to be anything good. He'd taken off his cap and was twisting it in his hands and stamping his feet against the cold.

Finally, the last lumberjill had disappeared.

Seffy stood and faced him. She'd rather hear this standing up. His eyes didn't seem blue anymore: they looked grey, like the cloud-covered sky.

'That time, last month, on the boat,' he started.

'When you kissed me? Twice?'

'Yeah.'

Seffy tilted her chin. 'What about it?'

He shook his head. 'It was a mistake. I mean, I shouldn't have done it. I'm sorry.'

A *mistake?* Seffy's heart plunged.

He spread his hands. 'Look, I've got a girl, back home. We've been together pretty much since we were kids.'

'So?' She fought the pain in her chest and shrugged as though she couldn't care less. 'I've got a beau, myself.' That was a lie, of course. She'd broken things off with Teddy by letter just a few days earlier.

The news that she had a boyfriend seemed to knock the wind out of his sails. 'Sure, you'll have a fella,' he said. 'A girl like you . . .' He paused. 'OK,' he said, finally. 'I didn't want you to get the wrong idea, that's all.'

She was stung. For the past five weeks she'd spent every waking moment – and some of her dreams, too – thinking about this man. When she'd been working in the woods, she hoped he'd suddenly appear, loping towards her. She'd kept her eyes peeled for woodsmen as she drove the lorry up and down to the station and the sawmill. With every glimpse of khaki uniform or the sound of a Canadian accent, a little flame of hope had flickered in her chest.

But she'd got it utterly wrong. He didn't like her in that way, at all. He'd simply got carried away. Their kisses had meant nothing. He had a sweetheart back home and his heart belonged to her.

Oh, but she couldn't give him up. Not so easily, not like this. 'But you and I—' she started.

He was backing away now. 'No. There is no "you and I!"' His face was grim. 'I'll keep away from now on, Seffy. That's for the best. I'm sorry.'

'Callum!' she called after him but he'd gone, dodging through the trees, so that she occasionally glimpsed his broad back until there was nothing but the sound of a squirrel scurrying in the trees above and the gentle cooing of a wood pigeon.

She sat back down on the tree stump for several minutes, too miserable to move.

Finally, she heard footsteps approaching. Perhaps it was Callum, come to find her, to tell her he'd changed his mind?

But it was Grace.

'Here you are,' she said. She took one look at Seffy and brought a handkerchief out of her overall pocket. 'It's clean, mostly.'

Seffy took it, smiled gratefully and blew her nose.

'He came to tell me that there couldn't be – that there isn't – anything between us,' she said.

'Aw, that's a pity. I thought you two had something, you know?'

Seffy nodded and dabbed her eyes. 'My aunt told me once that I was a "spoilt little madam". And apparently, I was a horrible child. So, it's probably done me some good, not getting my own way for once.'

Grace sighed. 'Aye, that's as may be but I don't suppose it feels like that right now.'

Seffy shook her head violently. 'It feels like hell!' she said.

Chapter 40

Bracing, cold showers, Seffy discovered over the following week, were a good way of forcing herself not to think about Callum Fraser. She couldn't stand the pain of the icy water without shrieking but afterwards, sitting inches from the wood burner and ignoring Morag's warning of chilblains, she felt better: invigorated.

This evening, she'd assumed she was alone in the washroom but as she emerged, shivering, from the shower and wrapped herself in a towel, Seffy heard the sound of crying coming from one of the cubicles.

Oh, goodness, it must be Hazel. She'd seemed much perkier recently but perhaps she'd simply been putting on a brave face? Seffy tapped on the cubicle door. 'Is everything all right? Hazel, is that you?'

There was silence, followed by the sound of someone trying to dry her tears. Then the door opened and Irene emerged, deathly white and shaking.

'Goodness!' Seffy said. 'You look shocking. You must still have that bug. I'd go to straight to bed if I—'

Irene pushed past her, shaking her head. She ran a tap and rinsed her mouth out. When she finally turned around, she was agitated, chewing the nails on one hand. Then she hugged herself and started to pace the floor. Goodness, what a state!

'What in heaven's name is the matter?' Seffy asked. Her teeth were chattering and she wanted nothing more than to get back into the relative warmth of the hut.

Irene shushed her and beckoned her nearer. 'Summat terrible's happened,' she whispered.

It wasn't like Irene to be so dramatic. It must be something to do with Jim. Bad news.

'Promise you won't tell a soul.' Irene's eyes darted constantly to the washroom door. Cocksure, feisty Irene was a wreck. But why was she telling her? Surely her pal Jean would be a better confidante?

'Of course,' Seffy said, with a sinking heart. What else could she say?

'I'm—' Irene stopped, closed her eyes, as though summoning up the courage, then with a firm nod, she said, 'I'm having a bairn.'

Seffy gasped and in the next moment, Irene's hand was clamped firmly over her mouth. 'Shut up!' she whispered. 'No one must know!'

Seffy nodded and Irene removed her hand.

'But, I don't understand.'

'I'm having a baby,' Irene muttered. 'Do ye understand, now?'

'But how can you be? Are you absolutely sure? Sometimes, with a change of lifestyle—'

'I'm sure,' Irene said, bitterly. 'I'm always regular as clockwork.'

Seffy's head was spinning; she leaned against the sink. Never mind Irene, she felt sick herself, now. This couldn't be true, could it? How could that have happened? Oh and why, of all people, did Irene have to land the news on her? She already had enough to worry about.

Seffy glanced at Irene's middle. 'How far along are you?'

'A couple of months.'

Two months! They'd been here since June. That was . . . Seffy did a quick calculation: not quite five months. 'Look, this might be one of those false alarms,' Seffy said, trying to disguise her shock. She'd heard a girl at school discussing a similar situation in hushed tones once and she'd used that expression.

If Irene really was in the family way, then the father, surely, was Jean-Paul, the blonde French-Canadian. What did he have to say about it? Oh, but wait, there was someone much more important to think about: Jim.

Irene was sobbing into her hands now and Seffy held her towel up with one hand and put the other arm around her.

How could Irene – a married woman – have let this happen? She was older but clearly not wiser than anyone in Seffy's circle of friends. Everyone there knew that girls must keep themselves tidy for their future husbands. If there was even the slightest rumour about a girl's reputation, her marriage chances would be nil.

Even the chaps were aware of the need to behave, although the handy ones – those branded NSIT (not safe in taxis) or MTF (must touch flesh) – had to be reminded every so often.

'Try not to take on so, Irene. You're going to make yourself really poorly,' Seffy said.

Could you be much more poorly than pregnant, though? Seffy didn't dare ask the most obvious question: what in the world was Irene going to do?

Chapter 41

The girls were lined-up, sitting on two of the beds, gazing at Seffy. Irene had finally said she could tell the others about her condition and Seffy had asked them to meet her in the hut after supper. It would be a relief to finally unburden herself. It had been hard work, keeping Irene's secret for the past fortnight.

She felt cross with Irene, as well as sorry for her, for landing all this on her. Other girls might have been more sympathetic or had good advice to impart. Seffy, after all, knew nothing about this kind of thing.

'What's the matter?' Jean asked. 'Where's Irene? Is she leaving the corps or something?'

Seffy bit her lip. 'Not yet,' she said, carefully. 'But she will be, at some point.'

The girls groaned and sighed and wanted to know why and when. Irene was popular and she was their leader girl. Poor Jean looked as though she might burst into tears.

Seffy waited until they'd quietened down. She took a deep breath. 'The things is, Irene's . . .'

'What?' Morag asked. 'She's not ill, is she?'

'She's having a baby.'

Little Hazel gasped but, otherwise, there was stunned silence in the hut.

'Preggers? She can't be!' Jean said. 'She hasn't seen Jim for months!'

Seffy rolled her eyes. *Work it out, Jean,* she thought.

Morag nudged Jean hard. 'Don't be daft. It can't be his then, can it?'

The penny dropped and Jean gaped. 'Gosh,' she said. She'd gone quite pale. 'She hasn't been herself for a while now but I . . .' She started to bite her fingernails, deep in thought.

'You can catch it from sitting on a lavatory seat,' Flora piped up. 'And – well, I kissed a boy once and I fretted for weeks after, in case, you know.'

Seffy and Jean exchanged glances.

'Flora,' Seffy said, 'you and I need to have a little chat after this, I think.'

Flora shrugged. 'All right, then. I don't mind.'

Joey said, 'I know Irene's a terrible flirt and all but – well, I'm shocked, truly I am.'

'Who's the father?' Morag asked.

Seffy shook her head. 'I don't know. It's none of our business.'

'I bet I know,' Grace muttered.

'It's awfully bad luck,' Seffy said, trying to sound business-like.

'Aye, well luck's got nothin' to do with it,' Morag said. 'Irene's been playing with fire and she's got well and truly burned. "Keep your hand on your ha'penny", that's what my ma always says and it's good advice.'

Oh goodness. If this weren't so tragic, it would be droll. Seffy was surprised by the girls' reactions. Well, perhaps not Morag's. But she'd expected the others to be more sympathetic.

'What'll she do?' Joey asked. 'They'll throw her out of the corps once the welfare officer finds out. It happened to a land girl I knew.'

Which was why, Seffy explained, they had to keep quiet about

Irene's condition. With a bit of luck, she wouldn't start to show for a few weeks yet. They'd have to try to cover for her and not let her lift anything too heavy.

'But all the work's heavy!' Morag said. 'Except stripping bark and snedding.'

'Yes,' Seffy agreed, 'but she can do that and make up the fires. I managed it when I hurt my hand. If word gets out, she'll be sent away immediately and none of us wants that, do we?'

Morag sniffed. 'I thought Irene had more sense.'

'I rather think there were two of them involved,' Seffy said, blushing. Who'd have thought she'd end up fighting Irene's corner? 'And that's not particularly helpful, Morag, if I may say. Let's be kind, shall we, and try not to judge? Irene's dreadfully upset.'

This really was a calamity of the highest order. There were worse things, of course: the Nazis winning the war or Teddy or the twins not making it back. She had to close her mind to those possibilities every day, or she'd go stark, staring mad. But for Irene, this must feel like the end of the world.

The hut door opened with a creak and Irene peered in. She tried to smile. 'She's told you, then? I can tell by your faces.'

'You won't try anything awful, will you, Irene?' Jean asked.

'What, like bleach or gin or a hot bath? No, I won't. Anyway, the water at Seffy's auntie's isn't hot enough.'

'She's joking,' Seffy said, quickly. It was hardly a laughing matter but sometimes, in the bleakest of moments, a quip or two helped. It was probably why people told jokes as they sat in shelters, wondering if a bomb was about to wipe them out.

'Here, come and sit down,' Joey said, moving along the bed.

'Thanks, hen,' Irene said. 'But I'm not poorly, mind. Though I felt like death those first few weeks, I'll admit.'

'I was thinking,' Joey said. 'Couldn't you write and tell your Jim you've found out you're expecting and . . . I don't know, lie about the dates?'

'But she hasn't seen him for two years!' Jean exclaimed. 'That might work if Irene were an elephant but human babies only take nine months to cook!'

'And in any case,' Irene said, 'I could nae do that to him. My Jim's a good man. He deserves better than me.'

'Does the father know?' Grace asked, quietly.

'Aye. He knows but he doesn't want to know. That's what happens when you get involved with a boy. And yes, I am certain about the father, in case you were wondering.'

Gosh, this was excruciating; it was as though Irene were on trial. She was twisting her hands and looking most uncomfortable. Seffy's heart went out to her.

'God knows,' Irene said, 'I've been no angel, but there's only been one man for me here. I lost my heed, once and only once. I swear on my life.'

Chapter 42

Aunt Dilys frowned, her teacup held aloft. 'What kind of a pickle are we talking about?'

Seffy, Marigold and Dilys were sitting in the drawing room at Ballykinch, in front of a roaring fire.

'The worst possible pickle.' Seffy took a deep breath. There was no easy way of saying it. 'One of the lumberjills, Irene – you know her, Aunt – the dark-haired, pretty one? She's expecting.'

Marigold and Dilys' eyes and mouths opened wide.

'A baby?' Dilys asked.

'Mm. And she can't possibly keep it because she has a husband.'

'The baby is not—' Aunt Dilys waggled her hand '—not her husband's?'

'Gosh, no. She hasn't seen him for years!'

Dilys and Marigold looked even more astonished.

'Are the lumberjills in the habit of producing babies like this?' Dilys asked.

'Oh, no!' Seffy said. 'She's the only one! At least, so far.' Oops. That was hardly the best way of putting things.

'I see. So, she's a silly little ninny who's lost her head over a man. This is hardly going to do the corps' reputation any good! It'll put you back months.' Dilys tutted and put her cup down.

276

'Such a shame. From what I've heard folk were starting to have some respect for you.'

Seffy was torn between distancing herself from Irene and defending her.

'The thing is,' she said, 'I've got an idea. I wanted to discuss it with you.'

The perfect solution to Irene's predicament had come to her last night.

'Go on,' Dilys said. 'I'm all ears.'

'I thought you could take it on. The baby, I mean. Adopt it and bring it up here. It would have a wonderful life! And you'd have a baby!'

Marigold stifled a giggle. 'It's a good thing you're sitting down, Dilys,' she said.

Aunt Dilys blinked, as though she were thinking hard. Seffy held her breath.

'Did your pal put you up to this?'

'Heavens, no. She doesn't even know I'm here.'

Dilys nodded, thoughtfully. At least she hadn't said no straight away. 'I did hanker after a baby once, I'll admit. But that ship sailed a long time ago. Look at me, I'm ancient!'

'Hardly!' Seffy said.

'No, she is,' Marigold said. 'We both are.'

But Seffy didn't agree. Aunt Dilys might be middle-aged but she still had an awful lot of vim. She could definitely manage a baby.

'Obviously,' Dilys said, 'I never had a child of my own and for those months that you stayed with us, Persephone, it was jolly nice.' She sniffed and folded her hands into her lap. 'I was actually rather down – for a day or two – when you returned to your parents.'

That was something, at least. As a child, she hadn't been completely awful. Dilys had liked her and missed her.

'Anyhoo,' her aunt said, briskly, 'back to the matter of this unfortunate child. I can't do what you're asking, Persephone.

No, it's completely out of the question. When this blasted war is finally over, Marigold and I are going on a grand tour around Europe – if there's anything left of it – or perhaps across the Atlantic. Those charming Canadians have invited us to drop by and I rather like the idea. Sounds like a wonderful place. And I'm sure they don't all chew gum. But we couldn't go travelling with a baby. Really, dear, I sometimes do wonder if you've got the brains you were born with!'

Seffy felt a thud of disappointment. She supposed it had been rather a long shot.

'But what will Irene do?' she asked.

Dilys shrugged. 'That's hardly my problem. Nor, I should think, yours.'

'And perhaps,' Marigold ventured, blushing furiously, 'she should have thought about that when she was, you know . . .'

Dilys raised her eyebrows. 'Yes, quite. What does the father of this child have to say? Presumably he knows?'

'He wants nothing to do with her. Or the baby.'

Dilys bristled. 'We'll see what Major Andrews has to say about that!'

'No, please! Irene doesn't want any fuss. It's going to be a big enough scandal, as it is, when the news leaks out. And besides, it's not as though he can marry her.'

'Can't he?'

'No, I told you, she's already married. And she really loves her husband.'

Dilys sniffed. 'The war makes people behave in awfully strange ways, I must say. Perhaps I do have a tiny smidgen of pity for your friend.'

'You do?'

'Not enough to take on her child, mind. But—' she held up a finger '—there might be something else I could do.'

* * *

As Seffy walked slowly back to camp from Dily's place, a truckful of Italian POWs roared past. The chaps weren't quite as excited as they'd been the last time she'd seen them, back in the summer. They looked rather jaded and they clearly weren't in the mood for throwing out billets-doux.

She felt rather sorry for them. They were just boys, after all, a long way from home.

Seffy raised her arm in greeting and a few of them raised their hands back.

'Bella!' one shouted, but goodness it was rather half-hearted.

The truck disappeared around a bend in the road and Seffy's thoughts returned to the conversation she'd just had with her aunt. Dilys had offered to find adoptive parents for Irene's baby.

'I have a feeling that, even though he's not the father, Irene's husband would still have to give permission for an adoption,' Dilys said. 'I know, it's quite ridiculous but that's the law. So, it'll need to be a less formal adoption, shall we say. Don't look at me like that, Seffy. What other option does she have? I'll find a nice couple to take the child. And I promise, I'll keep my eye on him, or her.'

Dilys proposed that Irene would nurse the infant for a couple of weeks and then give the baby up. It would, no doubt, be one of many "little packages" left behind by the Canadians when they eventually returned home.

Later, Seffy explained all this to Irene, who nodded, silently.

'And once you're better—'

'Better?' Irene scoffed. 'You don't get over it, you know, Seffy, like the measles!'

'No, sorry. I meant, once you've recovered from the birth, maybe they'll have you back in the Timber Corps?'

Irene frowned. They both knew that was jolly unlikely. Miss McEwen had left their camp now, so that was one less hurdle to cross but Mrs Eccles, the welfare officer, would scream blue murder when she found out Irene was in the family way.

'But even if you don't come back to the corps, you could still save your marriage,' Seffy said. 'Oh and there's something else. When I told my aunt you were thinking of going to a mother and baby home in Inverness, she wouldn't hear of it. She said you could stay with her and Marigold, until the baby's born and it's . . . and it's adopted. Oh and Marigold said to tell you to get your pregnancy confirmed by a doctor. Apparently, if you've got a certificate, you can get extra rations: milk, orange juice, cod liver oil. You need it, Irene, for a healthy child.'

Seffy sighed. Perhaps everything would turn out all right. The baby was bound to be gorgeous, with Irene for a mother and a father who, despite being a prize rat, looked like a Greek god.

Maybe, when it was born, Aunt Dilys wouldn't be able to resist it: she'd simply have to offer it a home at Ballykinch, after all.

At the beginning of December, Irene confessed her condition to Mrs Eccles and as predicted, the old dragon raged at her.

'You've let your husband down, you've let yourself down, you've let your country down,' she said.

'She's right,' Irene said, later, to Seffy. 'I deserve every word of it and if I could turn the clock back, I would. I should never – I would never—' She broke down in sobs.

Shortly afterwards, she had to leave the corps and before she went to live with Aunt Dilys and Marigold, she said goodbye to the Macdonald girls.

'It's not goodbye,' Jean said, through her tears, 'it's *au revoir*. You're only a couple of miles up the road, after all. We can see each other all the time!'

Irene turned to Seffy and fished in her bag. 'Here,' she said. 'I've something for you.'

It was the alarm clock and the whistle.

'I can't take these! The leader girl has these,' Seffy said.

Irene nodded. 'That's you, now, hen. And I cannae think of anyone who'd do a better job.'

Chapter 43

Dear Missy,

Hope you're all well there.

My news is that I got a couple of days' leave this week and I took the train down to the Borders, where Ma's folks are from.

I didn't hold out much hope, turning up like that with nothing to go on, but when I made it to the village (a long hike from the station), there was only one street and I guessed it might be the kinda place where everyone knew everyone and sure enough, I only had to ask a couple of times and folk were able to tell me where Bob – my great-uncle – lived.

When I knocked on the door and introduced myself, he hugged me real hard and told me I had the Lennox look about me and I had to have a wee dram, even before we had a cup of tea. Then my great-aunt came back and hugged me and soon the whole house was full of folk, cousins and aunts and uncles. Tell the truth, I lost track in the end of who was who, but it was a good day. And they told me all kinds of stories about my grandparents and why they emigrated and all – Jeez,

my head's swimming with them but in a good way – and I
feel like I've got some of Ma back, if that makes sense.

I guess I'm not too good at letter writing and I'm sorry for
that but I'll try harder from now on. Promise.

Love from,
Callum

There, he felt better that he'd finally written to Missy.

Of course, there were lots of things he'd missed out, like hitting Verne and getting a dressing-down from the lieutenant. He'd never told her about the lumberjills. Missy wouldn't like that, knowing there were women working nearby and coming to the dances at the camp, although the chances were, she'd already heard it all from her sister, who'd be getting letters from Verne. He hadn't told her how, as he sat in the cottage, where he had to duck to get through the doors, his Great-Aunt Aggie had asked, 'So, Callum, tell us. Do you have a pretty wife waiting for you back home?'

'No, no I don't, ma'am,' he'd said. It was true.

The old lady's face had lit up and a mischievous look flashed across her eyes. 'Good! You're saving yourself for a wee Scots lassie, I'll be bound! That's an idea, though, isn't it? Marry a local girl and you can stay here forever! Do ye have your eye on one?'

'No, no I don't,' he'd said. And then seeing her face fall, he'd added, 'But I'm keeping a lookout!'

The whole place filled with laughter.

'That's the spirit, lad!' Aggie said.

It crossed his mind that she might bring a parade of local girls in for him to choose from and he'd held his breath every time the cottage door opened – without a knock or a ring – and someone else trooped in to inspect him, but they were only neighbours, friends and more cousins.

They were all Lennoxes. Like Ma. That must be why he'd felt so relaxed with them. They were his tribe. He'd come halfway round the world and he'd found home.

Chapter 44

It was a few days before Christmas. The sky was iron grey and the air was so cold, it made Seffy's cheekbones ache. The only way to stay warm was to keep moving. It was quite an incentive to work hard.

'There's snow comin',' Morag said, ominously, as though she were forecasting the end of the world. She gazed mournfully at the sky.

'Aye,' Grace agreed. 'There's snow coming all right.'

That evening there was to be a show at the Canadian camp and everyone was looking forward to it. They wanted to get their work finished on time.

Seffy and Hazel were stacking the truck. The logs were six feet high at the back and wedged in, good and hard. Once it was full, Seffy would drive the lorry down to the sawmill. It would be the last delivery before Christmas and they were in a rush to get it done before the light faded and ice formed on the roads.

It was impossible to drive the truck in the dark: the headlamps were covered to conform with the blackout, so they emitted hardly any light. A couple of the girls had to stand on the running board to help guide the lorry. When they got back, Seffy would have to remember to drain the radiator so that it didn't freeze and then fill it again in the morning.

They still had a few more logs to load and, ideally, they'd wait for a couple more girls to help. Hazel was nimble and light and she could climb up onto the logs with ease but she wasn't as strong as some of the others.

A few yards away, they heard a commotion – a shrill whinny and the thudding of hooves on the hard ground. One of the horses that was used for dragging logs out of the forest – a big Suffolk punch, called Nelson – was playing up.

'What's the matter with him?' Hazel asked. 'Is he frightened?'

Seffy looked around. It still irked her a little that she'd never had the chance to work with the horses. 'Probably had enough of standing in the cold; wants his warm stable. And he can see the other horses are already heading back.'

Joey was struggling to control Nelson. She was dodging his huge legs as he spun around and reared up.

'Wait there,' Seffy said to Hazel. 'I'll go and help her. I'll be back in a sec'. Some of those logs need straightening up but don't you dare start without me!'

She didn't wait to hear Hazel's reply; she ran towards Joey, already calling out in a calm tone to Nelson, trying to steady him. She knew about horses. Goodness, she'd been riding since she was a toddler, after all. This was her opportunity to show them all what she could do.

Seffy had barely reached the horse and stretched out to grab hold of his harness when she heard the scream, a deep rumbling sound and then the heart-stopping crash behind her. The logs were piled up on the ground where they'd rolled off the lorry and there, beneath them, was Hazel.

Afterwards, another girl, who'd been attaching chains to logs a few feet away, told them what she'd seen.

Hazel hadn't waited for Seffy. She'd climbed up onto the lorry, pulling herself up by grabbing onto the timber. The pile of logs stacked on the back had started to move.

There was a terrible shriek and as the avalanche of timber moved, Hazel went with them. She was crushed.

They took her limp and broken body to the hospital in town. She looked deathly pale but, at least she was still alive.

Jean, Grace and Seffy sat at her bedside. 'Talk to her,' Jean urged. 'You'll know what to say, Seffy. You always know what to say.'

Seffy swallowed and shuffled closer to Hazel. She took Hazel's hand – as light and white as a handkerchief – and squeezed it gently, wishing she would open her eyes and smile. But they stayed firmly shut.

'She can probably hear you,' Jean said firmly. 'Try, Seffy, please.'

She couldn't do it. A lump the size of a tennis ball was lodged in her throat.

'I don't know,' Grace chipped in. Her voice was cracking. 'The things some folk'll do to get out of work, eh?'

Grace nodded at Seffy across the bed and that was all the prompt she needed.

'Yes, don't think this lets you off the next tug of war,' Seffy said. 'We've got a rematch coming up, remember!' It wasn't true; they hadn't arranged anything but it was something to say. She wanted to give Hazel something to hang on for. 'You've got a few weeks yet to get back on your feet and be there! We can't do it without our coach.'

There was no movement from Hazel on the bed. Her head was bandaged, her eyes closed and her face was ashen.

The girls looked around as the doctor appeared in the doorway, dressed in a white overcoat. His expression was serious.

No doubt they'd get a ticking-off. The nurse had already warned them, there was only supposed to be one visitor at a time. He'd usher them out any moment. But he didn't move and Seffy turned back to Hazel.

'You'll be up there, leading the team, Hazel, and screaming at us so hard that you'll lose your voice all over again. Don't you dare think otherwise.'

Hazel had to be there. The alternative was too awful to contemplate.

Something made Seffy look up at the doctor again. Jean and Grace had their backs to him, so they didn't see as his steely eyes met hers and he gave the smallest, slightest shake of his head. Had she imagined it? She continued to gaze at him. There, he shook his head again.

It was as though she and Hazel were the only ones in the room now. The doctor stepped forward, leaned down and whispered something to Jean and Grace. Reluctantly, they allowed him to guide them out of the room.

Seffy leaned forward. She could hear Hazel's shallow breathing. It had slowed down and there were long gaps between her breaths. Her face was as white as the sheet.

As the girls left, closing the door behind them, Seffy heard Jean sob.

But, in the room, it was peaceful.

'Hazel?' Seffy said quietly. She swallowed and gently squeezed Hazel's tiny hand again. Her voice caught in her throat and she cleared it and tried again.

'Hazel, do you remember that lovely walk you told us about, once? Your favourite walk, with your boys? With Angus and Prince?' She tried to smile but her lips were quivering. 'There were rolling green hills and the lochan's sparkling blue water?' Was it her imagination or had Hazel's eyes flickered for a second?

'Can you see that now, Hazel? The hills and the lochan and Aberdeen, way off in the distance? The sun's shining down and you're walking over the grass, your feet making a soft "whisha, whisha" noise. The sun's warm and as you come over the crest of the hill, you can see them.

'Yes, there they are, look. You can see Angus; he's striding towards you, his arms held out and he's smiling. Oh, and there's little Prince too and he's so happy; he's barking and his tail's wagging and he's running ahead and they're both there, coming to fetch you, Hazel. See? You're all going to be together again.'

As Seffy said it, she realised something wonderful had happened: she believed it.

'Can you see them, Hazel?'

Perhaps it was her imagination, but Seffy thought she felt the faintest pressure on her hand.

'It's time to go to them, my darling girl,' she said softly, bringing her mouth close to Hazel's ear on the pillow. 'We all love you so much and we're going to miss you and the forest's going to miss you too. All those trees that you've hugged: they're going to miss you. But it's time to be with Angus now and Prince. You can see them, can't you?'

The other girls were outside in the corridor, peering in through the little glass window in the door. She could feel their eyes on her and she was doing it for them too. She was glad they weren't in here, crying, because that wasn't how it should be for Hazel.

'It's time to go,' Seffy whispered, again. 'God bless, my darling girl.'

And Hazel took a final breath and died.

Chapter 45

At least, when Seffy arrived at Ballykinch House later– numb with cold and shock – she didn't have to explain anything. News of the calamity must have spread through Farrbridge because Irene, Marigold and Dilys already knew.

Irene flung open the front door and wrapped Seffy in a hug, as Dilys stormed down the corridor towards them. 'No!' she was shouting. 'Not this! I won't allow it! I will not have it!'

Seffy stared at her in disbelief. Was she cross with her, for turning up like this, unannounced? Could her aunt be any more heartless? 'I'm sorry,' she muttered. 'But I didn't know where else to go.'

Irene ushered her inside to sit by the fire and Marigold brought a mug of cocoa. Slowly, the feeling started to come back into her fingers and toes. Jock had brought the girls back from the hospital in the truck. Seffy had shrugged off all attempts to console her and had walked all the way here from the camp, slipping and sliding on the icy roads.

Dilys' strange outburst seemed to be over. She sat in silence, with the others, watching Seffy intently.

'I told her to wait for me,' Seffy said, over and over. She couldn't get the terrible images of Hazel and the logs out of her head.

Tears were streaming down Irene's face. She rubbed Seffy's shoulder. 'It's not your fault, hen. Hazel could be a wee wild thing at times. Remember her swinging across the burn? It was like she didn't care what happened to her.'

Seffy shook her head. 'I wanted to go and help with the horse. It was stupid. I shouldn't have left her.' She stood up. 'I think perhaps I should go home.' It was clear her aunt didn't want her there and she couldn't face the hut and Hazel's empty bed.

'No, you mustn't!' Dilys said, pushing her gently back down into the armchair. In a softer voice, she added, 'If you go home now, Persephone, you'll never come back to this forest! You'll be swallowed up again and your life will be nothing but frivolities and the hunt for a husband.'

Seffy nodded. That was true enough. But perhaps that was the life she was meant to lead. Being a lumberjill, attempting to be different . . . she'd tried but she couldn't do it. Look what had happened. Hazel had lost her life. Seffy put her head in her hands and sobbed.

She felt someone – Dilys – pat her back. 'There, there,' her aunt said. 'Here, blow your nose and listen to me for a minute. I owe you an explanation, Persephone.'

When Seffy had managed to stop crying and Goldie had come and rested his head on her lap, Dilys sat in the chair opposite and took a deep breath.

'When you arrived, I'd just heard the terrible news and I was in a state. Hence all the rather unseemly shouting. I apologise. I know exactly how you're feeling, my dear because something very similar happened to me.'

Seffy raised her head and looked at Dilys through tear-filled eyes. 'You?'

Dilys nodded. 'When I was in the Forestry Service—'

'See, I knew you were,' Seffy said, managing a rueful smile.

'—three girls – friends of mine – went for a swim in a local river. None of us knew it at the time but it was a notoriously dangerous spot and—' Dilys shook her head '—they drowned. All three of them. I feel terrible about it, even after all these years, I blame myself.'

'But why, Aunt? It wasn't your fault. You weren't even there, were you?'

Dilys' eyes had filled with tears. 'They'd asked me to go with them and I'd said no. I had something more interesting to do. I can't even remember what it was. But I was a good swimmer and perhaps, if I'd been there, I could have done something. I could have helped them ...'

'What did you do? After it happened, I mean?'

'I left the Forestry Service, I couldn't stay and I – I went to Switzerland.'

Switzerland? Why on earth had Dilys gone there? But before Seffy could ask any more, Marigold interrupted. 'Come on now, dear. That's enough talking. I think we need to put you to bed with a hot water bottle. You're worn out. See if you can get a little rest, eh?'

Seffy felt numb and helpless. Perhaps going to bed was the answer. If she could sleep, she could at least blot everything out.

She nodded and let Marigold guide her upstairs.

The next week passed in a blur. Seffy was racked with guilt and desperately sad about what had happened. Even though everyone told her it wasn't her fault, she blamed herself for Hazel's death.

What could she do? She needed to *do* something.

'I'm leaving the Timber Corps,' she told Dilys, finally. 'I can't stay. Not now. How can I ever face the girls – or Jock – again? I shouldn't have left Hazel. I might have known she wouldn't wait for me, that she'd start trying to move those logs herself.'

Dilys' face was a mask. 'You're leaving? What'll you do instead?'

'I shall join one of the services.'

'If you think you can simply walk out of the WTC and join the WAAF or whatever, you're very much mistaken.'

Seffy's chest tightened. Even in the midst of all this misery, her aunt couldn't manage a kind word. 'I wasn't planning on walking,' she said. 'My father will send a driver for me. Or at least, he will, if I telephone him.'

Dilys folded her arms. 'No, you misunderstand me. You are not permitted to leave. You signed to that effect when you enlisted. Perhaps you didn't read the application form properly, Persephone, but when you signed up for the WTC it was on the understanding that it was for the duration and that you could not leave. I'm right. Trust me on this.'

Seffy shrugged. 'Well, I'm leaving in any case. I'll go somewhere else. I'll go home!'

'You can't simply run away!' Dilys said.

'You did! After that – after it happened to you, you went to Switzerland!'

There was silence. Goldie jumped down from the sofa and slunk out of the drawing room. Seffy rather wished she could do the same but she was locked in battle now. Dilys was frighteningly calm.

'I didn't go to Switzerland voluntarily,' she said. 'Your father – my brother – arranged it. I know he thought it was for the best—'

'Where did you go?'

'To a sanitorium. An institution. That's why I couldn't let Irene go to one of those dreadful mother and baby homes.' Dilys shook her head. 'I wasn't quite right, after the girls drowned. Your father thought I was insane. Perhaps I was, a little. But I can never forgive him for putting me in a place like that. Never!'

She gazed forlornly out of the window.

'So, that's why you don't visit us,' Seffy said.

'Yes.' Dilys turned to face her again and her eyes were full of sorrow. 'You could say your father and I had something of a falling-out.'

'And Mummy? Did you fall out with her too?'

Dilys face softened. 'I have no gripe with your mother. She's always been very sympathetic and over the years she's done her best to heal the rift. I've lost track of the number of times she's invited me for Christmas. But when all this happened, she took your father's side, of course. That's what wives do.'

Was it? Did wives subvert their own opinions and feelings for those of their husband and in doing so, become shadows of themselves? Seffy had never considered it before.

'He was always rather controlling, your father,' Dilys said. 'Our parents had died and being the older brother and therefore "head of the family", he thought it his duty to see me safely married off. *In loco parentis* and all that. But I had other ideas. When I came back from Switzerland, I moved up here, with Marigold. And he cut me off without a bean. Oh, I had my mother's jewellery but nothing more. Everything else had been left to your father in our parents' will.'

'Heavens!' Seffy said. 'There must have been some misunderstanding, surely? Father wouldn't have done that, would he?'

Dilys' mouth twisted. 'I'm afraid he would. And he did.'

Marigold was standing in the doorway in her artist's smock. There was a streak of blue paint in her hair. Seffy looked at her questioningly and she nodded.

'Your father probably thought that by withholding money, I'd be forced to find myself a rich husband,' Dilys said.

'But you didn't,' Seffy said. 'You found Marigold.'

Dilys twisted in her seat to look at Marigold and the two women smiled at one another.

Seffy's mind was racing. Everything she thought she knew about Father had been turned on its head. She'd always worshipped him, she thought he was perfect. He wasn't the man she'd thought he was.

'But at least,' she said, to Dilys, 'you had the castle.'

Dilys frowned. 'What?'

Seffy waved her arm around the room. 'This place?'

Her aunt stared blankly for a moment, then she burst out laughing. 'Oh! My dear girl, is that what you think?' She slapped her thigh. 'No, you've got it all wrong. Ballykinch doesn't belong to me! It's Marigold's! This is Marigold's castle!'

Marigold laughed then too and Seffy managed a smile. All this time, she'd thought Marigold was a paid companion or a member of staff. Goodness, how wrong she'd been. She'd been wrong about Father, wrong about Marigold. What else had she been wrong about?

'And I'm sure,' Dilys said, 'that if you'd only change your mind about leaving, Marigold would be only too happy for you to stay here a little while longer. Isn't that right?'

'Aye, it certainly is,' Marigold said. 'You and Irene and the baby, when he or she arrives, are welcome to stay as long as you like.'

'Will you stay?' Dilys asked. 'For a little while longer? We'd rather like you to.'

Seffy nodded. 'I will,' she said.

Chapter 46

It was mid-January and there was a thick layer of snow on the ground.

Seffy was sitting cross-legged on the settee, flicking through a copy of *Country Life*, without taking anything in. Goldie was curled up beside her, which was usually strictly forbidden but Aunt Dilys had turned a blind eye. Irene, who was often tired these days, was upstairs, having a lie-down.

'There's someone at the door for you,' Aunt Dilys called, from the hallway.

Seffy raised herself up – ouch, her foot had gone to sleep – and stumbled out into the hall, Goldie running in front of her. She hadn't been in the frame of mind for visitors for a while but something must have shifted. The thought of seeing someone other than Irene, Dilys and Marigold was suddenly rather appealing.

She opened the door to find Grace, Enid, Morag, Joey and young Flora. Only Jean was missing. They were dressed in overalls and jackets, their cheeks flushed with good health.

'Now, we're not here for a bath,' Grace said, without any preamble. Anyone would think they'd only seen each other yesterday, when in fact, it had been weeks.

'Not this time,' Joey said, sounding wistful.

'Hello, everyone,' Seffy said. Oh, it was nice to see them. 'Where's Jean?'

'She's away somewhere, staring at trees,' Morag said. 'She's well enough.'

Dilys was loitering in the hall. 'Aren't you going to invite your chums inside, Persephone? It's chilly, standing on the doorstep.'

Seffy started to pull back the door but Enid put up her hand. 'Och, no. We don't have time, sorry. Jock's piling the work on these days. Right now, we're out delivering logs and doing a collection. Joey's driving the lorry and—'

'Joey?' Seffy asked.

Joey laughed. 'Don't sound so surprised but aye, Jock's been teaching me. I've given him a few more grey hairs.'

'She's terrible!' Morag said. 'We almost ended up in the ditch on the way here. Twice!'

Seffy's heart missed a beat as she imagined the girls riding on the logs in the back of the lorry. *Do be careful*, she wanted to say but stopped herself. As Aunt Dilys had told her, during one of their recent chats, if you considered all the awful things that could go wrong, you'd never do anything. Sometimes, Dilys had added, bad things happen to good people. It was just an awfully hard lesson to learn.

'Of course, you mourn,' Dilys had said, 'and you're never quite the same again.' Marigold had reached for Dilys' hand and squeezed it. 'But you brush yourself down and carry on. You have no choice.'

'How are you, Seffy?' Grace asked now.

'She's well, aren't you, dear?' Aunt Dilys said.

Perhaps if you told yourself over and over that you were perfectly well, after a while you'd start to believe it.

Seffy nodded. 'I'm . . . better, thank you.' They'd all lost a friend too. And she hadn't been there. She felt guilty about neglecting the girls, on top of everything else. 'It's so nice of you to come and see me. How are you all getting on?'

'Jock said we're doing very well,' Morag said. 'We've "exceeded all expectations".'

'We thought he must've had a funny turn,' Jean added.

The girls smiled.

'And Major Andrews has gone, from the Canucks' camp!' Enid said.

Seffy's stomach plunged. She'd been trying not to think about the Canadians.

'Aye, no one knows why,' Morag said, 'but it means that pig, Grabber Graham, is in charge of the camp now. Acting major.'

Seffy winced. It was a good thing Jean wasn't here to be reminded of that awful man.

'But otherwise, you're all well?' she asked.

'We're tickety-boo,' Flora confirmed.

'It's not the same without you, though, Seffy,' Joey said.

Seffy swallowed and did her best to make her voice sound natural. 'Are you en route to the station or the sawmill?'

'We've dropped the logs at the station; we're on our way back,' Grace said. 'And now we're making a special collection.'

'It's you, Seffy,' Joey said. 'We need you back. Our leader girl, our friend. Will you come?'

Seffy heard footsteps behind her in the hall. Marigold and Irene were there now too, watching and waiting.

Irene smiled at her. 'Go, on hen,' she said. 'It's time.'

Chapter 47

A week after her return, the whole lumberjill camp was going to a dance at the Canucks' barracks. A truck was being sent for them, on account of the snow, that was still lying thick on the ground

Seffy was staying behind. She didn't care for dancing. Or for seeing Callum Fraser again, if the truth be told. She couldn't bear any more hurt or disappointment.

'How will you all fit into one truck?' Seffy asked the girls, laughing.

Joey wrinkled her nose. 'We'll be all right. We've done it before. It's a squash and we have to sit on each other's laps but it's a good way of keeping warm!'

'And I'll keep the wood burner alight, so it'll be toasty when you get back,' Seffy said. 'I'll be fine here on my own. I've got my knitting to do.'

She'd unravelled one of her sweaters and was knitting a blanket for Irene's baby. She was slow but she found knitting rather calming. It required total concentration and there was no denying, it was satisfying, watching the little rectangle grow, slowly but surely, rather like the baby itself.

*   *   *

As he strode out of the village bar, Callum almost collided with an old boy with a walking stick, who was making his way inside. It was dark and he'd hardly seen the fella.

'Beg your pardon, sir!' he said, steadying the man with one hand on his shoulder. 'Didn't spot you there!'

The fella chuckled. 'Turning to drink now, are ye, lad?'

Callum smiled and gave a "what can you do?" shrug. There'd been times, over the past few months, when he'd sure been tempted by the idea of coming down here in the evenings for a wee dram. Or two or three. He wouldn't be the only off-duty Canuck standing at the bar, drowning his sorrows. But he didn't want to turn into Pa. Drink was not the answer.

He'd only been in the bar this evening for a short while, sorting out a debt on behalf of the CFC. There'd been a scuffle between a couple of the guys last night – the kind of thing that happened once in a while – and he'd been smoothing the waters. He'd paid the landlord handsomely for the table and chair that had gotten smashed and the landlord had accepted the apology and the money. Everything was fine and dandy. If only Callum could fix the rest of his life that easy.

The sound of a vehicle's engine roaring as it struggled through a heap of snow, made him look up. He recognised the truck. It was loaded with lumberjills – chattering and laughing loudly – headed to the dance at the camp.

Seffy was probably amongst them. He'd heard from Gordy she was back now. He hoped that meant she was feeling better after that awful accident. He had no intention of going to the dance tonight. He wouldn't get in her way and spoil things. Let her have a good night out with her pals.

'Oh!' a woman cried out nearby, as she slipped on a patch of ice on the sidewalk and almost fell.

Callum ran forward and steadied her. 'All right, ma'am? You take care. It's awful slippery.'

She looked up at him gratefully. Her eyes were troubled. 'You haven't seen my daughter, have you, sir? Flora? She works in the woods; you might know her?'

Callum nodded. 'Flora, yeah. The young lassie? But I haven't seen her tonight.'

'We had a terrible row. Again. I cannae control her these days. Her father's not around. She's run away!' The woman wrung her hands. 'And I've left the wee boys on their own back at the house. I'll need to get a neighbour to mind them but—'

'Any idea where she might've gone?'

'No. Wait, yes! The girls' camp. She said she hated all of us and she wanted to stay there instead.'

Callum frowned. The camp was two miles up the road. It was getting darker and colder by the minute and there was likely to be another heavy snowfall tonight.

'But there's no one at their camp right now,' he said. 'That was them, in the truck that just passed. Everyone's gone to a dance.'

'Oh, no! And she's not even wearing an overcoat!' the woman wailed.

'I'll go look for her,' Callum said. 'That's my truck, right there. You go home, in case she turns up. The weather's coming in real bad but Flora's smart. She's probably realised it ain't a good thing to be out in this. She'll be home soon, you'll see.'

The woman grabbed Callum's arm. 'Would you do that? Oh, thank you!'

'If she's out there, ma'am, I'll find her. You go home now and look after those wee laddies and don't worry. Go careful on that ice!'

He hastened across the road to the truck he'd requisitioned for the trip into town. He didn't feel as confident as he'd sounded.

As he climbed into the driver's seat, the snow started to come down in big, swirling flakes.

He pulled out onto the road, skidding a couple of times. With the bright snow on the ground, visibility was slightly better than normal but the lights on the truck were half-covered and as he left Farrbridge and headed out towards the lumberjills' camp, it was almost pitch-black. He was driving blind.

The hut door burst open, making Seffy jump and letting in a swathe of freezing air.

'Flora? What are you doing here? I thought you'd gone home hours ago,' Seffy said, putting down her knitting. 'Is it snowing again? Where's your coat?'

The girl's boots were covered in snow, there were snowflakes in her hair and she was soaked through and shivering.

'I've come to live here!' she announced, flouncing in.

'Have you, indeed? Well, would you mind closing the door? Where are your things?' As far as Seffy could see, Flora had arrived with nothing but the clothes she was standing in. This certainly hadn't been a planned move.

'I hate my mother and I hate my brothers!' Flora threw herself down face first on Jean's bed and pounded the pillow with her fist.

'Hmm. I used to hate my brothers too.'

Flora stopped pummelling and looked up. 'Did you?'

'Yes. When they were born, my nose was put right out of joint. My parents thought I might hurt them and they sent me away.'

Flora's eyes widened. 'And would you? Would you have hurt them?'

'No! I was just jealous. And actually, now that they're all grown up, I like them. A lot.'

Flora sat up, frowning. 'Do you? Really?'

'Yes. They're doing their bit in the RAF and I'm jolly proud of them. Like a good Bordeaux, brothers improve with age. Yours will too, mark my words.'

Flora scowled. She didn't look convinced.

Seffy patted her bed. 'Look, come and sit here, next to the

wood burner. We'll put some more logs on and get you dry. Your mother will be frantic.'

'She won't. She doesnae care tuppence about me!' In a smaller voice Flora added, 'I miss my daddy.'

Seffy felt a pang of sympathy for the girl. Her father was serving, no doubt.

'Yes,' she said. 'I miss mine too.'

Father wasn't perfect, she realised that now. The way he'd treated Dilys, his own sister – cutting her off and putting her in an institution – was abominable. But Seffy still loved him. That was the thing about love; you loved people despite their faults.

Flora was still sitting on Jean's cot. She looked around the hut. 'That's Irene's bed, isn't it? She's no' here anymore, so I can take that.'

'You can sleep there tonight but you can't have it on a permanent basis,' Seffy said, firmly. The girls were still holding out the hope that Irene might come back to the corps, once she'd had the baby.

Flora tilted her chin. The girl was really acting like a spoilt little madam tonight. Had she been like that, at her age?

'Then I'll take Hazel's bed,' Flora said. 'Which is it?'

Seffy dropped the log she was about to put on the wood burner. 'You'll do no such thing! Don't you dare even think about it!'

Flora glared at her. 'Then I'll sleep on the floor!'

Oh, for goodness' sake. So much for a quiet night in with her knitting. Seffy wasn't in the frame of mind for a row but any mention of Hazel still felt like a stab to the heart. Her nerves were on edge and the thought of anyone trying to take Hazel's place, was too much.

She took a deep breath and tried to sound more reasonable. 'Look, you can't go back out into that terrible weather, so sleep in Irene's bed tonight but you can't live here, Flora. It's out of the question. You're too young. First thing tomorrow, you must go home and apologise to your poor mother for all the worry you've put her through!'

Flora was marching towards the door. 'I shan't!' she yelled. And disappeared back through it.

Callum was driving slowly up the lane, peering out into the dark, looking from side to side. It was snowing more heavily now. The windshield wipers were struggling to keep up. This was useless; he could hardly see a thing. If the girl was out there, he'd probably not even spot her. He gritted his teeth. But he had to find her, safe and sound. Hell, the lumberjills couldn't cope with another tragedy; it would break them.

He'd been away on leave when Hazel's accident had happened. He'd never forget coming back into camp and Gordy running out to tell him, 'There's been an incident. At the girls' camp. It's real bad.'

He'd nearly hit the deck. His first thought had been: Seffy. She was so darned accident-prone. Nearly getting struck by a tree, nearly breaking her wrist in the tug-of-war. He thought his heart would break, thinking she was gone forever and that the last time they spoke he'd told her there could never be anything between them. That there was no "You and I".

The relief was overwhelming – but the guilt too – when he found out it was little Hazel who'd been killed. He could only imagine how upset the girls must be. Seffy had been there when it happened, by all accounts. He wanted to go comfort her but he was probably the last person she'd want to see and. besides, Gordy told him she'd gone away. She wasn't at the lumberjills' camp anymore.

Callum braked. He'd seen something up ahead, at the side of the road. A shadow? No, a girl, running towards the truck. Flora! Thank God. No, it was too tall for Flora. His stomach flipped over, his heart soared: it was Seffy. It was as though he'd conjured her up.

302

He opened the cab door and jumped out into the swirling snowstorm and she was there, panting, frantic. 'Flora's gone!' she said and he wondered for a second if she even realised who he was. 'I was cross with her and we rowed. She was in the hut but she's run off! We have to find her!'

He'd never seen her in such a state. He was momentarily taken aback. Then he pulled himself together. 'What makes you think she's come down the road? I've crawled all the way up from the village and I haven't seen her.'

Seffy shook her head. 'I followed her footsteps for a while with my torch. She was heading this way. But then they disappeared.'

'She must be in the forest. Here, come on, take this.' There was another overcoat on the seat of the truck. He reached in and grabbed it and draped it around her shoulders, then he took her torch and shone it into the trees. The snow gave everything a strange purple glow. The bows of the trees were heavy with it and it fell, with a heavy thud, every few seconds.

'Flora!' he yelled. 'FLORA!'

He slammed the truck door and took Seffy's hand, as though it were the most natural thing in the world. 'Come on, hold on to me, so we don't lose each other.'

They started walking into the woods.

It was hard work, wading through the snow, barely able to see where they were going, as the snowstorm swirled around them. There were deep snowdrifts in parts of the forest and they had to lift their legs high to get through them.

Finally, Callum said, 'I was so sorry to hear about Hazel. I know you were there and that's real tough. What you girls are doing – and not getting much credit for, as far as I can tell – is a risky business. But you're doing a good job.'

Seffy stopped walking. She was out of breath. She smiled at him, as snowflakes settled on her eyelashes. 'Goodness! Finally, a vote of confidence! My parents think the work's too dangerous. They want me to give up the Timber Corps and go home. Which

I wouldn't do, even if I were allowed. So, thank you. Thank you for saying you believe in us.'

They found Flora in the bothy. Thank goodness she'd had the good sense to head there, when she realised the weather was too bad to find her way home.

Seffy remembered the place from that first evening in the Highlands.

'This is exactly what it was made for,' she breathed, when they spotted Flora's footprints outside. 'Sheltering in bad weather.' Callum pushed open the door and there she was, huddled in a corner, crying and cold but otherwise unharmed.

It was such a relief. And Seffy couldn't be too cross with the girl. After all, her silliness and tonight's escapade had brought her and Callum back together.

There was dry wood in the fire, kindling and a box of matches on the side. Clearly, this place had been used, recently. Callum busied himself making up a fire.

'Reckon we're gonna get snowed in here tonight,' he said, shining the torch through the window. The snow was still coming down in huge flurries and it was settling.

A little while later, the fire was crackling and Flora lay asleep on the floor between them. Callum put his coat over her.

Seffy looked down at her. 'Remember what it was like to be that age? You're all mixed up inside, trying to work out who you are.'

He nodded. 'Don't reckon that gets any easier, the older you get. I'm still trying to work that one out.'

Their eyes met. It felt as though he were apologising. Or trying to say something.

'I tried to come see you,' he said. 'When I found out you were at your aunt's? I knocked on the door one day but she wouldn't let me in.' He shook his head. 'There was no getting past her. She couldn't be bribed with bananas or lemons.'

Seffy giggled, imagining the conversation.

How had she not known about this? She'd thought Callum wanted nothing more to do with her but in fact, he'd come to Ballykinch House to try to speak to her.

'I was enclosed there, like a nun in a convent. "Healing", my Aunt Dilys called it,' she said. 'But to be fair, I don't think I could have been anywhere better.'

He nodded. 'I should think Mr Churchill's war cabinet would do well to have your aunt on their side. I can see where you get your determination.'

They dozed for a while, until the fire went out and they woke up again, chilly.

As Callum built up the fire with more wood, Seffy asked him, 'Do you miss home?' What she really meant was, do you wish you weren't here? Do you want to go back to your girl, across the Atlantic, thousands of miles away?

'Sometimes,' he said. 'But mostly, not.' He sat back down on the floor, on the other side of Flora, who was still asleep. 'But there's something else I have to tell you, Seffy. I'm—'

Oh please, not married. She would die.

'—engaged. My girl back home, well, she's my fiancée.'

Seffy gritted her teeth. She was getting used to pain these days. But ouch, that did hurt rather. Because now Callum Fraser was definitely out of bounds.

'You should have told me,' she said, quietly. 'I'd have stayed clear of you.'

'How could I tell you I was engaged? For weeks, you couldn't stand the sight of me! What, was I supposed to march up to you and say, "By the way, for your information, I'm engaged to be married"?'

She gave a rueful smile. He was right, of course. She hadn't been interested. She'd dismissed him from the very first time she'd seen him, as "not her type".

How awfully shallow she'd been. Like someone who goes out

to a restaurant for dinner and always picks the same dishes from the menu because it's safe and it's what everyone else is eating.

'Look,' Callum said, 'I want to explain about the girl back home. About Missy.'

Seffy nodded. Now that she had a name, the girl seemed awfully real.

'My pa was . . . He shook his head and stared at the stone floor for a second. 'He wasn't a good man. Even before she got sick, he made my ma's life a misery. And then, when she'd gone, he must've been sorry because he drank more, hollered more and belted me and my brothers, some.'

He shrugged. 'But it was too late then, of course; to be sorry, I mean. I don't want to turn out like him, Seffy,' he said, gently. 'I want to do the right thing.' He stretched his fingers towards her and she took his hand. She squeezed it, to show she understood. And they sat there together, like that, all night.

In the morning, once Callum finally managed to push open the bothy door – there was a drift of several feet of snow against it – they emerged into an alpine fairyland. The snow was thick on the ground and the trees looked like brides, their branches weighed down with it. Seffy huffed and made smoke into the icy air. It was fresh and still, and all the sounds were muted and muffled. It was magical.

'Come on, ladies, let's get out of here,' Callum said, linking arms with them.

Flora looked decidedly sheepish. 'I've caused so much bother.'

'Yes,' Seffy agreed. 'Your poor mother's probably out of her mind with worry. We're going to take you straight home and put her mind at rest.'

A few days later, when Dilys and Marigold heard the whole story, Marigold said, 'And your honour is still without question, my dear!'

Seffy shook her head, not understanding.

306

'The young girl! Flora, is it? She was there all night with you. So, you might have spent the night with a man who wasn't your husband but – you had a chaperone!'

Seffy supposed she was right. Flora had actually been asleep all night, so her chaperoning skills might have been called into question, but it was true – she and Callum hadn't been completely alone. But it had been the next best thing.

'Anyhoo, what's the name of this Canadian of yours?' Dilys asked.

'Oh, he's hardly mine. He's engaged to be married.'

'Ah.'

'And one day he'll go back to Canada and . . .' Seffy shrugged.

'That's the nature of war, Seffy. Your paths cross with the most wonderful people. People that you'd never have otherwise met. It's perhaps the only good part of living through a war,' Dilys said.

'And the bad part is that they leave.'

'Yes, that's true. They drift in and out. But remember this—' Dilys put her hand gently under Seffy's chin and tilted it towards her '—you're not the same person as you'd have been without them.' She smiled. 'You're better. They leave their mark.'

Chapter 48

In the spring, Aunt Dilys announced that she and Marigold would be holding a ceilidh at Ballykinch House.

'It's my birthday on April 1st. Yes, before you say it, I've always been an old fool. This birthday is a "rather significant one". Not everyone's been as fortunate as me, in reaching this milestone, so a party seems appropriate. Goodness knows, we all need cheering up. And it's been years since we had a shindig here.'

There would be a band with fiddlers and a caller for the Scottish jigs and reels. All the lumberjills were to be invited, together with some of the villagers and the Canadian boys too.

'Not all of them, of course,' Dilys said. 'Goodness, there are dozens; they won't all fit. I'll let you girls choose who comes.'

Seffy started to draw up the list immediately in her head.

Callum, of course. It would be the first time she'd seen him since the night at the bothy. And Gordy and some of the other fellas they knew. The nice ones. Definitely not Captain Graham, nor Jean-Paul.

Dilys was right: everyone needed cheering up. And not only because of what had happened to Hazel. The dark, cold miserable days of January and February had seemed never-ending. It had been a long, bleak winter. The girls had suffered from chilblains, sniffles and cold sores. There had even been a couple of cases of pneumonia in the other huts.

But now spring was coming, with its warmer days and lighter nights and they were all still here. Yes, that was definitely worth celebrating.

If hers was a family that hugged, Seffy would have wrapped her arms around Aunt Dilys when she announced the ceilidh but instead she simply smiled. 'It's a marvellous idea. The girls will be so happy. Something to look forward to! Oh, but what on earth will we wear? None of us has anything suitable for a ceilidh.'

'Ah, I may be able to help with that. Bring the gals here after church on Sunday, will you? And I'll show you what I mean.'

On Sunday, a procession of lumberjills, as well as Irene, Marigold and Goldie the dog trailed behind Dilys down unfamiliar corridors at Ballykinch House. Finally, she stopped outside a door, hesitated for a moment and pushed it open. It was shrouded in shadow and smelled musty. The shutters were closed and the furniture was draped in dust sheets. Some of the girls started to cough.

'It hasn't been touched for years,' Dilys said. 'I'd almost forgotten it was here.'

'Gosh it's like Miss Havisham,' Jean said. 'You know, *Great Expectations?*'

'Open the shutters someone, will you?' Dilys asked and once the light flooded the room, she threw open the doors of a huge mahogany wardrobe.

The girls gasped.

Tightly packed on the rail and sweeping down to the floor, were dozens of evening dresses, in taffeta, silk, velvet and satin, in every colour imaginable and adorned with sequins, pearl buttons, feathers and velvet trims.

'It's like a princess's wardrobe!' Enid said. 'May I?'

'Be my guest, dear!'

Enid carefully extracted a green satin gown and held it up against herself. It was too long but the colour was perfect. The girls murmured their approval.

'These are your debutante dresses, aren't they?' Seffy asked.

Dilys smiled. 'Of course, you were a debutante too, dear, so you recognise the uniform. Yes, believe it or not, I used to be a lady! I was presented at court and I did the season and all that.' She mimed a yawn. 'Actually, it was rather good fun but I didn't get a husband out of it, much to your father's disgust, Persephone. Engagement by the end of the season was everyone's aim!'

As the other girls pulled the dresses from the wardrobe and examined them in delight, Jean wanted to know everything about being a debutante.

'I had to go with my mother for a special lesson in the exact procedure for presentation to the king and queen,' Seffy said.

'Ooh!' Jean gasped. 'Tell me!'

'You had to approach the throne, curtsey twice and then retreat backwards.'

'Oh yes,' Dilys said. 'All the time, hoping and praying one wouldn't trip over one's train, which had to be exactly three and a half feet long.'

Grace rolled her eyes. 'Never heard anything so daft in all my life.'

Aunt Dilys laughed. 'Quite right. The whole thing was completely ridiculous. Now, how are you getting on with the dresses, girls? Found any that might suit?'

'No offence,' Morag said, turning to Dilys, 'but these dresses are too big for most of us.'

'I was bigger in those days,' Dilys agreed. '"Big boned", my mother called it.'

Seffy could see Jean raise her spectacles and gaze at Dilys from head to toe. She was measuring her, as though she were a tree.

'I was about your size, Grace dear,' Dilys said. 'Come along, have your pick of any of them. They'll probably fit you like a glove.'

310

Grace blushed and Seffy's heart went out to her. Dilys could be very tactless at times. But the other girls had already started arguing about which dress would be best for Grace.

It was all jolly exciting. Seffy stroked the bodice of a sumptuous ivory gown. She couldn't remember the last time she'd worn anything so extravagant or feminine. It had probably been when she was doing the season; a lifetime ago.

'There are more in the other wardrobe on the far side!' Dilys said. She was animated, clearly enjoying this trip down memory lane. 'You know, some of the debutantes in my day had seventeen-inch waists if they breathed in! I could never manage that but it didn't bother me. If a chap wanted a waif, well there were plenty who fitted the bill. Not me!' Dilys waved a hand towards the dresses. 'Anyhoo, they're there if you want to do something with them.'

'There's a stack of long white gloves around the place too,' Marigold said. 'You might find them in a bag at the back of the closet.'

'I can do the alterations, if you like,' Irene said. She was pressing a hand against her back and leaning on the doorframe.

Marigold jumped up from the chair. 'Here, come and sit down, dear, you look done in.'

'Irene, do you mean it?' Seffy asked. 'That would be marvellous.'

'Sure. I won't be dancing at the ceilidh, will I? Not like this! I look like one of those barrage balloons!'

It was true that in the past few weeks, Irene had got much bigger.

'Ouch.' She put her hand onto her stomach. 'The wean's kicking me now. She's heard you all laughing and it's woken her up. Do you want to feel? Here.'

Irene took Seffy's hand and placed it on her stomach. Immediately her hand was kicked away and Seffy's eyes widened in astonishment.

'Goodness!'

311

'Aye, well just imagine how it feels from the inside! She's awful lively!'

'You think it's a girl, then, do you?' Dilys asked.

Irene's face clouded. 'No. I mean, there's no telling. I'm not thinking too much about it.'

'Have you thought about names?' Joey asked. 'Perhaps, if it's a girl you could call it—' She stopped herself just in time. Seffy guessed she'd been about to say "Hazel".

There was an uneasy silence. It wasn't merely because Joey had almost said their friend's name. She should be spoken of, after all. No, it was because Irene wasn't in any position to name the baby. She was giving him – or her – away and the new parents would name the child.

'It's awfully good of you, to say you'll do the alterations, Irene,' Seffy said, quickly changing the subject. 'I'm sure we're very grateful, aren't we, girls?'

They shouldn't talk too much about the baby. It would only remind Irene of what lay ahead. Not only the birth but the giving away part. That was going to be rather horrid.

But then, at least Irene could get on with her life. And, God willing, there'd be other babies, in the future. Babies that she could keep. Jim need never know the truth about what had happened up in the Highlands. It was an awful secret to keep from him but if it saved Irene's marriage, perhaps it was for the best.

Chapter 49

On the night of the ceilidh the fireplace was ablaze in the great hall, sending shadows dancing up the stone walls and illuminating the tapestries and crossed pikes. The fiddlers were warming up at the far end of the hall, as the guests started to arrive.

'In normal times we'd have burning braziers at the gate and here at the door too, of course,' Dilys said. 'But we can't jeopardise the blackout so we've put them on the inside instead. I just hope no one tall catches alight!'

There was a strange noise coming from along the corridor.

'What on earth's that terrible racket?' Seffy asked. 'It sounds like someone strangling a—' She put her hand to her mouth and stopped herself just in time.

Marigold giggled. 'It's the bagpipers,' she said.

When the Canadians arrived and poured into the great hall, the girls, who were standing at the top of the stairs, couldn't believe their eyes: the boys were wearing kilts, of various tartans. They must have borrowed them from the villagers.

There, at the front, was Callum, dressed in a dark green kilt with a white shirt. Seffy's heart lifted. He looked incredible.

'I wasn't sure if this would be disrespectful to the kilt,' she heard him call out to Aunt Dilys, 'because although some of us have Scottish ancestry, we're not true Scotsmen.'

'Oh, fiddlesticks, no one cares about that,' Dilys said. 'Our castle, our rules. Now is that all of you? Come on in. Let's close the door, against the cold.'

'Look at them!' Jean said shaking her head in wonder. 'We thought they looked good in their uniforms but now…! They're showing us up!'

'Yes, we were supposed to be the belles of the ball,' Joey said.

'Nonsense, we look super,' Seffy said. 'Come on, let's go down – and remember, hold up your dress, no tripping over. Be ladylike!'

As soon as the Canucks saw them, the whistling started. They'd only ever seen the lumberjills in overalls, with dirty fingernails and muddy boots or wearing day dresses at the local dances. They'd never seen them in anything like these gowns. It was hardly any wonder they were so impressed.

The music started up and the dancing began, traditional Scottish reels: Strip the Willow, the Dashing White Sergeant, the Gay Gordons ('Hey, Gordy, this one's for you,' someone yelled).

Seffy danced with each man in turn and then back to her partner, to Callum. They were wheeling and turning, shouting and slapping their thighs and the kilts flew and girls' dresses billowed and she was spun around, a sea of faces flashing in front of her

She stopped finally, laughing and breathless. She'd never had so much fun in her life.

Irene leaned over the banister on the minstrel's gallery as far as she could, with her belly the size it was.

Aye, the girls certainly looked the part in their party frocks. Although she said so herself, she'd done a good job.

She watched the dancers below, whirling and wheeling. She tapped her foot in time to the music and scoured the faces.

It didn't take her a moment to spot him: Jean-Paul. Seffy had promised he wouldn't be invited but he must've sneaked in, which was typical of him. She could look at him with no feeling at all, now. He meant nothing to her. He may have had her body but he'd never had her heart.

He was galloping and turning, putting his arms into an arch with the girl opposite, to allow another pair of dancers to go through. Arms behind his back, joining a circle now, throwing his head back and laughing. He looked as though he didn't have a care in the world. And probably, he didn't.

Irene was the one with all the worries. He was able to carry on his life as though nothing had happened. It wasn't fair. Aw, well, to hell—!

Ouch! She clutched her stomach as a pain ripped through her. There it was again: a sharp stab in her middle. She took a deep breath. *Don't be daft,* she told herself. It was one of those things with a queer name. A practice contraction. That was all. She'd probably overdone it today. She'd been busy since this morning, doing the final fittings and alterations for the girls' dresses. She was tired. She'd find a quiet corner somewhere and put her feet up.

After all, the baby wasn't due for another month.

She gasped and grabbed the banister tightly and felt like she might collapse: there was warmth and wet and something trickling down her leg. This couldn't be happening: it was too soon.

Her waters had just broken.

Once she'd heard the news, Seffy searched out Jean-Paul and yelled in his ear, 'Irene's having the baby!'

She enunciated each word carefully, so there could be no mistake. Perhaps impending fatherhood would jolt him into taking an interest or showing some concern.

He cupped his hand over his ear. 'What's that?'

He'd heard her well enough; the band wasn't that loud. And heaven help him if he was pretending not to understand English.

Seffy pulled him by his sleeve out into the hallway. The sound was muted now; there was no excuse. 'The baby! It's coming!'

He shrugged. 'Nothin' to do with me, ma'am,' he said. He turned and walked back into the hall. She heard him let out a whoop before he was even through the door.

Seffy's fists were clenched.

'Whatever's the matter?' Dilys said, trotting down the stairs. 'You look like you want to kill someone.'

Seffy narrowed her eyes. 'The father of the baby's here, uninvited.'

Dilys frowned. 'What does he look like?'

'He's very blonde and very handsome,' Seffy said, through gritted teeth. 'You can't miss him.'

Dilys nodded, 'Right, I shall eject him, forthwith. Oh, you're wanted, upstairs, by the way. The medical officer's been dragged in to help but Irene says she wants you there. No one else will do.'

Seffy gasped. 'But I'm a complete scaredy-cat! I can't stand the sight of blood. I'll be a liability.'

But Dilys wasn't taking no for an answer. She ushered Seffy upstairs. 'Never mind all that. There's a baby on the way. Come now, be with your friend, help her.'

Gosh, childbirth was a noisy, messy affair and it took forever.

There were an awful lot of groans and grimaces. Seffy focused on Irene's face and doused it with cool flannels and allowed her hand to be squeezed hard, until she wanted to scream but Irene was doing enough of that for both of them.

Finally, after hours of pushing and panting and long after the ceilidh had finished and everyone had gone home, there was a faint mew and then a louder yell. A baby!

Seffy dared to look around. The doctor was holding it up and smacking its behind. It was long and bloody, like a rabbit in a butcher's window, although, just before she fainted, Seffy remembered thinking she'd never tell Irene that was her first impression of her child.

And then, everything went black.

* * *

316

The next day, the girls visited Irene and the baby at Ballykinch House. She'd had a boy, five pounds two ounces – not a bad weight, considering he was a month early.

Irene was pale but she was smiling. She looked happy.

'Was it terrible? The birth?' Enid asked. 'No, don't tell me.'

'It stung a wee bit, I'll no' lie,' Irene said. 'But he was worth it, every moment.'

'Look at you, little man. Oh, he's got hair.' Joey put her finger out and the baby grasped it. 'Gosh, he's strong!'

They laughed.

Seffy thought all babies looked like Winston Churchill. She definitely preferred puppies. But she had to admit, Irene's little chap was rather sweet. She would even forgive him for making his appearance during the ceilidh and thus depriving her of many hours of fun.

'He's perfect, Irene,' she said, hoping Irene wasn't getting too attached.

The baby was to be given away for adoption in two or three weeks. There was a couple waiting to take him. But now wasn't the time to remind Irene of that sad fact. Let her enjoy her short time with her baby, while she could.

Chapter 50

A week later, when Seffy returned to the hut from visiting Irene and the baby again, Grace was crying and the other girls were gathered around, consoling her.

'The company's leaving, Seffy,' Jean said, solemn-faced. 'In three weeks' time.'

Seffy's knees almost gave way. 'What do you mean, leaving? Not back to Canada?'

Grace blew her nose on a hankie. 'No. But they're leaving the forest. Gordy reckons they're joining the combat troops in England.'

Seffy tried not to show her shock and dismay. There had always been a chance this would happen. The Canucks' military training at weekends had become more intense over the past few months. It must have been a build-up to this.

She tried not to think about Callum. This was a bigger problem: Grace and Gordy weren't married.

'But what about the wedding?' Seffy cried. 'You need to get married before Gordy leaves!'

Grace shook her head. 'It's no use.'

'You can get a special licence and you've got your character reference from Aunt Dilys, haven't you?' Seffy said.

The other girls looked at one another.

'It's not that simple,' Morag said. 'Captain Graham has to sign off the final paperwork and give his permission, since Major Andrews isn't here. And he's dragging his heels.'

'Do you think he knows it was you that hit him, Grace?' Seffy asked, hardly daring to hear the answer.

Grace blew her nose and nodded, slowly. 'Yes. That's what Gordy thinks too. Graham's known, all this time – and now, finally, he's getting his revenge. He won't give permission. There won't be a wedding before the boys go. Gordy'll be sent to England and then Europe and then – God willing, if he's still in one piece – he'll be sent back to Canada. I'll never see him again.'

Seffy wanted to tell Grace none of that was true but she couldn't.

'And he won't listen to any of us, of course,' Grace said. 'So it's no good us begging him or asking him to help. He hates us all!' She burst into tears again.

'We must be able to do something!' Seffy said. 'Grace, you need to help me. Find out from Gordy everything he knows about Captain Graham, do you hear?'

Later, Grace reported back, but there wasn't much to tell.

'Gordy says, unless you've got a hundred pounds or something, to bribe him, then we've got no chance. Graham's a bully.'

Seffy sighed. 'Yes, we know that. What else? There must be something. What's his Achilles heel?'

Grace wrinkled her nose. 'There is something. Oh, but it's nothing.'

'Tell me! Anything!'

'Right, well he's an out-and-out snob.'

Seffy's shoulders dropped. Grace was right, that wasn't anything useful.

'When Lord and Lady Lockhart came to inspect the company, last year, Captain Graham missed out. And he was furious.'

'What do you mean, missed out?'

'The major met the laird and his good lady, of course, and then they carried out the inspection but Graham was passed over. He'd been looking forward to meeting gentry – he thought it was the next best thing to meeting the king and queen themselves – but it didn't happen. He was fuming. For weeks, he was in a worse mood than ever.'

'Right,' Seffy said. Her mind was racing. She must be able to do something with that information. She just had to work out what.

Chapter 51

'Is that you, Irene? Seffy asked.

She closed the door of the hut gently behind her and stepped out into the dark. It was early morning, icy cold, and the sun was just peeping over the horizon.

Seffy had heard a faint tapping on the window above her bed and she'd slipped out of the dorm, to find Irene there, her baby in her arms, fast asleep.

'Aye, it's me. Look, I couldn't leave without saying cheerio.'

'You're leaving? Come into the washroom a minute,' Seffy said. She was already shivering. 'We'll freeze out here.'

'The car's up on the road, waiting for me,' Irene said when they got inside. 'I don't want any bother, so let's not wake the others, eh? Your Auntie Dilys is running me – us – to the station to catch the train.'

'You're keeping the baby, then? He won't be adopted?'

'No, I'm taking the wean back to Glasgow wi' me. My ma'll see us right. I couldn't bear to leave him behind. He's ma flesh and blood, when all's said and done. I cannae leave him.'

Seffy nodded. She could understand that. But there was still another problem. 'What about Jim?'

Irene took a deep breath. 'I read something in one of Enid's magazines. It said "if serious problems arise, honesty is the best policy" and that, when the war was over, "everyone should think about forgiveness and fresh starts". She shrugged. 'I thought, maybe ma Jim would be prepared to do that now.'

'So you've written to him? To tell him about the baby?'

'Aye. If I'm taking the baby home, then I have to let him know. There are neighbours and relatives who'll tell him before me, otherwise. Isn't it better if he finds out from me? I didn't want to write but I had no choice. I've mithered about it for months. I've said, if he cannae bear to come back to me, then I'll understand. And, Seffy, there's something else I wanted to tell you.'

Seffy's heart plummeted. What now? She didn't think she could take any more drama or secrets.

'Jim and me, we've been married almost ten years. And we don't have bairns, as you know. We're from big families and we wanted the same. But it didn't look like it was going to happen. We said perhaps we weren't a good match and if we went our separate ways, we might be able to have children with someone else. He said I could leave him and I said he could leave me. But we couldn't do it.' Irene smiled.

'Because you love each other,' Seffy said, nodding.

'Aye. So, anyway, I think, deep down, I thought it could never happen to me. D'you see?'

Seffy understood. Irene thought she couldn't have a baby.

'Jim'll be home on leave soon. Don't be afraid for me, Seffy. He's a good man. I've only realised it, seeing how I've been treated by . . . by others here. It'll break his heart, of course but I had to be honest.' She looked down fondly at the baby in her arms. 'I cannae give up my bairn.'

'Good luck, Irene,' Seffy said, giving her a hug. Goodness, she'd thought Hazel, Jean and Grace were brave but Irene Calder was perhaps the bravest of them all.

'Say farewell to the other girls from me, won't you?' Irene said. 'I hope Grace and Gordy manage to marry before the company leaves.'

'I'm going to do my very best to make sure they do.'

Irene took a deep breath. 'I was awful mean to you when we first arrived.' She glanced around the washroom. 'In here, once. Do you remember?'

Seffy stroked her hair and winced. 'Yes. You called me a witch.'

'Aw, I'm sorry, hen. I don't think you're a witch no more. In fact, I think you're a wee angel!'

They laughed.

Irene shifted the baby in her arms. 'You could've taken yourself back to your easy life when I made things hard for you, but fair play to you for sticking it out. You're gutsy, Seffy and classy. You're a classy lady. Aye, you should be proud o' yourself.'

They hugged again, careful not to wake the baby. She was sad to be losing Irene like this – and worried for her, too – but Seffy's heart was soaring. She was "gutsy" and "classy." Those were the nicest things anyone had ever said.

She pulled back and stroked the top of the baby's head. 'Will you be all right, you and – does he have a name, yet?'

Irene's face clouded. 'No. The name I have in mind is James. But it depends on what Jim says. Or doesn't say.'

'How long do you think it'll be? Before you hear from him, I mean?'

Irene shrugged. 'It can take weeks for the post to come – you know that. I'll just have to be patient and wait.' She bent her head and kissed the baby softly. 'And hope for the best.'

Chapter 52

'Aunt, do you know the Lockharts?' Seffy asked.

Dilys frowned. 'The laird?'

'Hmm. And his good lady.'

'A little. Lady Lockhart sits on some of my charity committees. But if you mean, am I part of their set, then the answer is no.'

'We lead a very quiet life here,' Marigold said, with an apologetic shrug.

'Why do you ask?' Dilys asked. She shot up out of her seat. 'Blast! Did I shut up the chickens, Marigold? That darned fox'll have them.' She ran from the drawing room.

'Is something the matter, dear?' Marigold asked.

Seffy sighed. 'I need to get someone horrible to do something gracious. For some very dear friends of mine. I don't have much time; and I haven't got the foggiest idea how to do it.'

Marigold looked at her with sympathy. 'Oh dear. If there's anything we can do, you only have to ask.' She leaned across and patted Seffy's hand. 'But I have every confidence in you.'

The next day was Sunday. Seffy dressed carefully – not in her Timber Corps uniform, for once – and she accosted Lady Lockhart as she walked down the steps of the church, after the service.

'Your ladyship, I do beg your pardon, I hope you don't mind but my mother's asked me to pass on her very best wishes.'

Lady Lockhart looked blankly at Seffy, clearing not remembering her from the summer fete. 'How lovely. Remind me again, who your mother is?'

When Seffy told her – throwing in the name Dalreay Castle, for good measure – Lady Lockhart's face lit up. 'Of course! Do send your mother my very best regards in return. And your name, my dear?'

Seffy told her and gave a little bob – almost a curtsey – to show in how much regard she held her ladyship.

'You must come for tea, dear,' Lady Lockhart said, preparing to walk on.

'When? Might I come next week? Say, Wednesday? I won't be in the area much longer and I'd love to see Blantyre before I leave. I hear it's the finest castle in Morayshire!'

It was terribly forward of her and she'd thrown in a couple of lies for good measure but as Irene would say: "If you dunnae ask, you dunnae get."

Her ladyship smiled graciously. 'Wednesday it is. Shall we say three o'clock? I look forward to it.'

'Thank you!' Seffy said. 'I'll bring a friend, if I might? Lovely! Thank you so much!' She gave a little wave and slipped away.

She exhaled. Part one of her mission was now complete. But there was still a lot to do.

Dilys had been talking to the rector and was turning away. Seffy took her arm and steered her towards the cover of a large monument in the graveyard.

'If you wanted to forge a document, Aunt Dilys—' she said, quietly.

'What kind of document?'

'Oh, a letter say, or an invitation. And you needed headed paper to make it look authentic, what would you do?'

Dilys frowned. 'I'm not sure I like the sound of this. But, if your question is purely *theoretical*—'

'Oh, it is!'

'Then, the answer's simple. I'd ask Marigold. Marigold's an artist, didn't you know? She can draw anything.'

'There,' Marigold said. 'I've drawn a picture of Blantyre Castle from memory at the top of the page and I found the Lockhart crest in a book in the library. What do you think?'

Seffy thought it looked marvellous.

'But you're not thinking of sending out any invitations, pretending to be her ladyship, are you?' Marigold asked, pulling back the sheet of paper. 'Because I'm fairly sure that's a crime.'

Blow! That was it then. Marigold wasn't as game as Seffy had thought.

'But—' Marigold hadn't finished '—I have got another idea. Before the war, when one received an invitation to a garden party at Buckingham Palace, it never came directly from the king himself.'

'Didn't it?'

'No. It came from one of his lackeys. The Lord Chamberlain or someone. It said, as far as I can recall, "His Majesty has commanded me to request the pleasure of your company", blah, blah . . .'

Seffy clapped her hands in delight. 'That's it! Let's do that, then.'

Dilys was walking past the drawing room, covering her ears. 'I don't want to hear any of this. I want absolutely nothing to do with it and, Marigold, think very carefully before you get involved!'

Marigold and Seffy smiled at one another.

'It is all in a good cause, isn't it, Seffy?' Marigold said. 'I do trust you. You don't have to tell me any more than that.'

Dear Captain/Acting Major Graham,

I am commanded by the Laird (Chief of the Clan) and Lady Lockhart of Blantyre Castle to request the pleasure of your company for High Tea at 3 p.m. on Wednesday 14th April

1943, to mark the occasion of No.34 Company's imminent
departure from the Estate.

Transportation to and from the Castle will be supplied at
2.40 p.m. precisely.

There is no requirement to respond to this invitation.

Her Ladyship and His Lordship look forward to making
your acquaintance.

Yours sincerely,

J Ferguson

Head of Household

Captain Graham was standing outside his office in the Canucks'
camp on Wednesday afternoon, clutching his invitation, when
Seffy arrived to pick him up.

She'd pinned up her hair and put on a day dress and heels
and steadfastly ignored the girls' questions about where she was
going. She couldn't tell them anything, yet, in case it all fell flat.

She walked smartly up to him, praying that none of the boys
in the camp would recognise her, and asked, 'Captain Graham?'
as though she'd never seen him before.

'Erm, yes,' he said, glancing at his watch. 'I'm actually waiting
for someone. A driver's being sent for me from the Lockhart estate.'

'Yes, that's me! Lady Persephone Baxter-Mills at your service, sir!'
She waved towards the road. 'I've got transport. It's parked out on
the lane. Do come along; we mustn't keep her ladyship waiting!'

It was the lorry, of course. Captain Graham's eyes widened in
surprise when he saw it and he hesitated for a second before climbing
aboard. As Seffy had hoped, he was too polite to say anything.

They set off down the road, jerkily. Every time she jolted him
in his seat or crunched the gears, so that he winced, or braked
so hard that he almost hit the windscreen, Seffy apologised and
smiled to herself.

'Would you like me to drive, young lady?' Graham asked, after
a few minutes.

'Oh no, sir. I'm sorry but that's not allowed. You wouldn't be insured and it's awfully tricky, what with all the complicated gear changes and driving on the left. No, please, sit back and leave it to me. We're almost there now.'

She swung the wheel carelessly to the left and he bounced in his seat, banged his arm on the door and cursed. That one was for Jean, Seffy thought.

When they arrived and Graham climbed out of the lorry, he looked rather green around the gills but he did brighten at the sight of the magnificent castle.

Lady Lockhart, the darling thing, even though she had no idea of her part in the deception, played her role perfectly and came out onto the steps to greet them.

Lord Lockhart wasn't here but hopefully the captain would be happy with her ladyship's attention. He was blushing, straightening his collar and pulling down his tunic. He cleared his throat and stepped forward to shake her hand.

'So kind of you to invite us, your ladyship,' Seffy muttered, hoping that the captain was so overcome by the grandeur of the castle he was about to enter, that he wouldn't pay any attention to what she was saying.

Lady Lockhart smiled. 'Not at all. Are you two—?'

'Warm enough? Yes, absolutely fine, thank you. May I introduce Captain James Graham from Number Thirty-Four Company of the Canadian Forestry Corps, your ladyship?'

'Ah yes, indeed, I recognise the uniform, of course. Delighted to meet you, captain. Soon to be leaving us though, sadly, I hear. How will Farrbridge cope? Your men have brought such glamour to the place. Not to mention how hard you've all worked in the forest, of course. You'll be sorely missed.'

They were walking through into the orangery now and her ladyship was saying all the right things. Seffy couldn't have coached her any better.

The tea was a little delayed, so once they were seated in

the orangery, overlooking a magnificent formal garden, Lady Lockhart rang a little bell and then apologised and left the room.

'Say, shouldn't you be gettin' along, young lady?' Captain Graham said gruffly to Seffy. 'This is my invite, my high tea.'

Oh goodness, of course. She hadn't thought this through. Graham had, naturally enough, assumed she was staff – perhaps a lady-in-waiting – and she was ruining his unique experience.

As Lady Lockhart re-entered the room, Seffy stood up. 'Excuse me, your ladyship, but might I be excused?'

'Of course. Just along the corridor. Someone will show you.'

Seffy stayed away as long as she dared. What if Graham showed her ladyship his invitation? She wouldn't put it past him to ask her to autograph it. Then the game really would be up. She didn't dare leave them alone for a second longer. She hurried back. As she slipped in through the orangery door, Lady Lockhart looked rather relieved; Graham merely scowled.

Seffy accepted a cup of tea, poured by a butler.

'There's going to be a wedding, your ladyship,' she said. 'One of the gals working on your estate – a lumberjill – is engaged to one of Captain Graham's men.'

Her ladyship swallowed the piece of cake she was eating. 'Oh, I'm not surprised! When my husband and I inspected the men I was struck by how tall and handsome they – *you*,' she corrected herself, nodding at Graham, 'looked in their uniforms. The only surprising part is that more girls haven't declared themselves in love!'

Seffy laughed. 'Quite!'

Captain Graham was frowning.

'But of course, as you know, your ladyship, the troops are moving out,' Seffy said.

She surprised herself by how easily and matter-of-factly she could say those words. As though the company's departure meant absolutely nothing to her.

'Yes of course. My husband's most upset. You're going to miss the Highland Games, Captain. And of course, there's still plenty of felling to be done in the forest.'

'We – I mean, I'm sure the Women's Timber Corps, can take up the slack,' Seffy said.

Graham harrumphed. She was on dangerous ground here: of course, he wasn't exactly a fan of the lumberjills. Heaven help her, if he realised she was one.

'Oh I'm sure,' Lady Lockhart said. 'The girls have been doing a sterling job, from what I hear.'

The captain was reaching for more cake. He said nothing. He was clearly not interested in the Women's Timber Corps or their achievements.

Seffy steered the conversation back to the wedding.

'I hear that Number Twenty-Two Company are going to be the first CFC company in the area to have a wedding in their camp!' Seffy said. It wasn't true, of course, but she knew there was rivalry between the various companies and sure enough, Captain Graham frowned when he heard the news.

'I was wondering whether Number Thirty-Four Company might beat them to it,' Seffy continued, 'if, say, a wedding was arranged, at the camp, before the company moves out? Then Thirty-Four Company would hold the record. For the first wedding?'

Graham's brow became even more furrowed in concentration. Goodness, she could almost see the cogs working.

'You'd still have to read the banns,' her ladyship said.

'True, but there's time for that. Perhaps the company chaplain could conduct the wedding? They could get a special licence. All it needs, I understand, is the approval of the commanding officer.'

The two women looked at Captain Graham. He shifted uncomfortably in his armchair.

'You'd come to the wedding, wouldn't you, Lady Lockhart? And bring the laird? And the local paper would be there, I'm certain. Maybe even the nationals?' Seffy said.

She was ambushing them, giving neither of them chance to reply.

She could see Captain Graham out of the corner of her eye, shift in his seat and gaze at her curiously. He was clearly wondering who she was. He didn't strike her as being the brightest of chaps but even he must be starting to get suspicious by now.

'More tea?' Seffy asked, whisking his cup away. 'I'll be Mother, shall I?'

Later that afternoon, as they left the castle and walked towards the lorry, Captain Graham burped. Seffy pretended not to hear.

'Oh but the transport is this way!' she said cheerily, as he turned in the wrong direction.

'You know what?' he said. 'It's a fine afternoon. I think I'll walk back to camp, ma'am. But thank you all the same.' The simpering tone that he'd used all afternoon with Lady Lockhart was gone.

'Oh but it's miles!' Seffy said, wide-eyed. 'And it looks like rain. Are you absolutely sure, sir?'

He'd already set off. 'Hell, I've never been more sure of anything in my life!'

As Seffy drove past him in the lorry and he squeezed in tight to the verge, clearly worried that she was about to ram him, Seffy beeped out a happy little tune on the horn and waved madly.

Captain Graham raised a hand, rather half-heartedly.

The next day, Gordy had permission to marry Grace.

Chapter 53

The baby was making soft snuffling noises, sucking on his tiny fingers.

Ma had emptied a drawer from the press in the front room and Irene was using it as a crib. It would do for now. She'd lined it with a tea towel and crocheted him a blue blanket and a bonnet to keep his tiny head warm.

He smelled delicious; good enough to eat. She leaned in and breathed and felt her heart swell. How could she even have thought about leaving him? It made her feel quite faint, the thought of it. She fretted about it until she had to remind herself she was fretting about something she hadn't done. She hadn't left her bairn or given him away. She'd kept him and whatever else happened, that'd been the right thing to do.

Net curtains had twitched and people in the street had talked, as she'd known they would. But a babbie was a babbie and soon women were knitting shawls or bringing clothes their kiddies had grown out of, darned here and there but good enough.

And besides, everyone had enough to think about – their men overseas, the bombing, queuing for food – to mither too much about Irene Calder and the wean she'd brought home from the Highlands.

Ma was on at her all the while to give the baby a name, but she couldnae. Not yet. She still had "James" in mind but she had to wait until she knew if Jim was coming back.

'I have to ask ma Jim,' she'd told Ma, and received a doubtful look in return.

'He's no' coming back, hen.' Ma looked at the wean and shook her head. 'You've made your bed and you've got ta lie in it.'

This morning, Ma had gone out. 'I'm away to Mrs Atkins. See you later.' She cleaned for two women in the posh part of town. It was good, at last, to have the house and the baby to herself.

Ma was always telling her to let him cry and no' keep picking him up, or she'd be making a rod for her own back, but it felt wrong to let him cry, when holding him on her chest and feeling the soft weight of him soothed them both.

While the baby slept, Irene rinsed out a few nappies and a blouse for herself. Then she read the letter she'd had from Seffy, again. Aw, she missed those girls. What adventures they'd had. It was good news indeed about Grace and Gordy. They were good together, that pair. And Grace was going to wear the wedding dress Irene had made for her, after all. They were going to be very happy.

She put the letter down and started to do some housework. She looked up at the sound of the back door opening into the yard, footsteps on the cobbles, a man's heavy tread. Before she could look out of the window, the back door was flung open.

There he was. Jim. In his navy uniform, carrying a kit bag, with a neat, dark beard.

Irene dropped the duster she'd been holding and wiped her hands on her apron. 'You didnae tell me you were comin'.'

He shook his head and stepped inside. He took off his cap. 'I didn't like to send a telegram. Gi' you a heart attack. You'd think the worst.'

She nodded.

They looked at each other, uncertainly. It had been a long time.

'Come here, then,' he said. She ran into his arms and they hugged, hard. She breathed him in. She could smell the salt of the sea and the wild winds on him.

Her mind was racing. What was he going to say? And then she pulled back, as a sudden thought hit her. 'Did you get ma letter, Jim?'

He frowned and scratched his whiskers. 'What letter?'

Her heart plummeted but in the next moment, he was smiling. A small, wan smile. 'I'm teasing, hen. I got it.'

Irene put her hand to her chest. 'Now THAT near enough gave me a heart attack!' She took a breath and looked him in the eye. 'But I deserve it. I deserve a lot worse than that.'

A wail came from the front room.

Irene froze.

'Is that him?' Jim asked, after a moment.

'Aye.'

The crying was getting louder now. Irene turned to go to the baby and then turned back to Jim. She didn't know what to do.

'Do you . . . do you want to see him?' she asked. Her heart was thudding in her chest.

'Aye,' he said. 'Aye.'

Chapter 54

30th April 1943

Dearest Emerald,

Wonderful news from the Highlands! I've been a bridesmaid again. (Ahem, no comments please, about "always the bridesmaid"!)

Not such a glamorous affair as your wedding of course, but, like yours, I wore green! The Timber Corps uniform. All five of us did: Enid, Morag, Joey, Jean and me. We looked marvellous, although our foreman banned us from making an arch of axes, as he thought decapitating the bride and groom as they left for their honeymoon mightn't have been the best start.

My very good pal here, Grace, married a lovely Canadian chap at the camp. Yes, you read that correctly, not in the church, which would have been first choice of course but . . . oh, it's a long story. I'll tell you one day. All a bit of a rush to get it done before the company moved out.

There was something of a bittersweet feel to the day, at times. Grace will only have been married for a few days, then her husband will be gone. We're all speculating where *that might be, but of course I can't say. Loose lips sink ships and all that.*

The bride looked exquisite in a cream parachute silk dress and there were two hundred handsome men in uniform in attendance, plus a guard of honour and a military band!. One of the benefits of holding the wedding at the barracks was the wedding breakfast, supplied by the camp cooks, which was, I have to say, Emmie, almost as good as yours, although I could have done without the spam.

The local press covered the wedding, as it was the first – and almost certainly, the last – at the Farrbridge camp. I'll show you the cuttings when we eventually meet up. I daren't send them in the post just in case. They're awfully precious to me.

More anon! Must sign off now.

Love from,

Seffy

Seffy smiled as she thought about Gordy and Grace's wedding. It had been a wonderful celebration, full of laughter and tears of joy but it had also been a farewell, to the whole company.

Everyone had been there. All the lumberjills, from all three huts, Jock, Aunt Dilys and Marigold and, as she'd promised the Captain, Lady Lockhart was in attendance, with the laird at her side.

At the wedding breakfast, Dilys spoke quietly to Seffy. 'Lady Lockhart told me you'd come for tea at the castle, with your beau? Is that right?' she asked.

Seffy almost choked on a cheese sandwich. Oh, goodness, as she'd suspected, Lady L had thought she and Grabber Graham were an item. It was hilarious and mortifying all at the same time. Especially, as halfway through the tea at Blantyre he'd mentioned the actual "Mrs Graham", too.

Someone might have warned her that Graham was married. What must Lady Lockhart think of her, brazenly bringing her "married lover" to tea?

Later, Seffy had talked to Grace's mother.

'Was it marvellous, seeing your daughter get married, Mrs McGinty?'

The older woman sniffed. 'I'd have preferred a church but, I know—' she held up her hand '—it was here or nowhere. And at least she was married in white. So many lassies get married in uniform these days. She did that part properly, anyhow.'

Seffy smiled. 'She certainly did.'

Her favourite part of the whole day had been when Gordy read out the telegrams. One had arrived from Irene.

The girls exchanged worried glances. There'd been no word from Irene for weeks, although Seffy had written and told her about the wedding.

Gordy read out Irene's telegram.

'It says, "WISHING YOU MUCH JOY. LOVE IRENE, JIM AND BABY JAMES".'

James! Baby James! The girls cheered and hugged one another. That told them everything they needed to know.

Chapter 55

The day before Number Thirty-Four Company moved out, a Highland Games was held on the fields outside the village. None of the Canadians were there. They were busy packing up their camp. They were under strict orders to leave the place shipshape.

'I've challenged the land girls to a tug of war rematch,' Jean announced, that morning.

'No!' Seffy was adamant. She couldn't face it. Not after the last time.

'But remember, we promised Hazel?'

'Jean's right,' Joey said. 'We have to do it, for her.'

And one by one, they all agreed.

'Come on,' Jean said, 'You're leader girl now, Seffy. You need to rally the troops.'

Grace and Gordy had been away on a two-day honeymoon but they were back and the new Mrs Johnson agreed to revive her position on the team, as anchor. It would be a distraction, she said, from thinking about Gordy leaving.

Seffy asked around in the other huts and soon got two more girls to make up their team of eight.

They lost the first round. It was all over in seconds. Even wearing their gloves this time. The land girls pulled hard from the off and took them by surprise, so that the rope was pulled over the halfway line before the lumberjills even had chance to dig in. They landed in a humiliating heap on the grass and Seffy heard a few guffaws in the crowd.

Blast! They might as well give up now.

They got up, rubbing themselves down. They had grass stains on their knees and were already feeling dejected. The land girls had got the edge; there was no getting away from it.

'You're doing it all wrong!' It was Aunt Dilys, shaking her head. 'I watched that last attempt and – if you like – I can give you some advice. Do you want it? Or am I simply an old biddy who needs to keep her nose out?'

'No, please!' Seffy said. 'We'd like your help, wouldn't we, girls?'

'Aye!'

'We would indeed!'

'Right, firstly, the anchor woman: Grace. You need to pass the rope around your waist on the right, then up over your left shoulder. Here, let me show you.'

The girls watched as Dilys rearranged the end of the rope. The judge checked his watch and tapped his foot on the grass.

'Now, all of you, keep your feet forward of your knees, at an angle. And move as one,' Dilys said. 'It's all about teamwork! Don't waste energy on short tugs and let your thighs take the strain!'

Gosh, Aunt Dilys made an impressive coach. The girls didn't dare disobey.

They won the second pull.

It was the best of three. The next pull would be the decider. As they were about to start, Seffy glimpsed her parents and the twins, in their RAF uniforms, standing near the front of the crowd. What on earth were they doing here?

They waved at her across the meadow but, as pleased as she was to see them, Seffy couldn't wave back: she had to concentrate.

'Pull, Timber Corps!' Dilys yelled. Her voice rang out over the field.

339

As she leaned back, pulled and gritted her teeth, Seffy pushed everything else to the back of her mind and gave it her all.

The other girls had clearly done the same because they won. They did it!

The land girls were good sports, apart from their captain, who shook hands with a limp wrist and jolly bad grace before stomping off.

'Never mind her,' one of her teammates said. 'We told her you were bound to beat us. You're all as strong as oxen!'

The lumberjills laughed.

It felt rather nice, to be this fit and strong, Seffy thought, looking round at her pals. It gave you confidence.

They stood on the rostrum to receive their medals from Lady Lockhart.

'Wonderful!' her ladyship said. 'I know one should be impartial but I did so want you lumberjills to win. My husband's awfully impressed with your work in the forest. And so am I, for that matter! God bless you and your efforts!'

The girls grinned at each other, then Jean shouted, 'One, two, three!' and they all raised their heads and blew a kiss up to heaven, to Hazel.

'It's doing you a power of good, that forest, young lady,' Aunt Dilys said, when Seffy showed her and Marigold the medal. It was the closest Dilys would ever get to saying "Well done" but it was enough.

'Mummy! How lovely to see you!' Seffy said, kissing her mother on the cheek. 'Did Lady Lockhart ask you to come?'

To Seffy's surprise, Mummy hugged her. 'Oh, I've missed you so much, my darling!' She pulled back and gazed at Seffy, shaking her head in admiration. 'But look at you! Standing there so tall and proud. No more slouching!'

Seffy laughed. It had been worth all those months toiling in the forest: her mother was finally pleased with her posture.

'But why are you all here?' Seffy asked. A sudden terrible thought struck her. 'Nothing's wrong, is it?'

Mummy shook her head and glanced around. 'We simply wanted to come and see you, darling. It's been so long. And Miss Mackenzie invited us!'

Seffy shrugged. She had no idea who that was.

'Oh and you'll never guess!' Mummy said. 'I've joined the WVS. You inspired me!'

'Gosh, did I? Have you?'

She'd never been so surprised by anything.

'Yes, I find it helps. To do something, you know. I felt quite hopeless when you all went off to war.' Mummy pulled out her bottom lip. 'But rather than sitting around worrying, I am keeping cheerful and busy!'

Seffy had never really thought about Mummy's life and whether she was happy or fulfilled.

'Well, I'm very proud of you,' she said. 'Good for you.'

It was all adding to her conviction that being a "Mrs" wasn't the be-all and end-all. She wouldn't say that to newly-wed Grace or Emerald, of course; it would sound like sour grapes. She'd like to be married, one day. But perhaps not until she was twenty-four or -five. And that was yonks away.

'Oh, look!' Mummy said. 'Here they come now! Dilys and Miss Mackenzie.'

Her aunt and Marigold were walking across the meadow towards them, with Goldie on a lead.

'Did you—?' Seffy asked, pointing to Dilys and then to Father, who was standing a little way off, watching the caber toss. 'Is this—?'

Marigold smiled and nodded. 'Yes, all my doing. It was me.'

Mummy and the two women greeted each other warmly, then Father turned and spotted them, standing together. Mummy started to twist her handbag strap.

Dilys spotted Father and frowned. She looked as though she might be about to walk away.

341

'You know,' Seffy said quickly, 'he trusted you with something very precious.' She braced herself for a lashing from Dilys' sharp tongue, but her aunt was silent. 'And I wonder if it was his way of saying sorry. For sending you to the sanatorium and everything. He was trying to show you that he believed in you – that he trusted you – after all.'

'What on earth are you talking about?' Dilys asked.

'Me,' Seffy said, simply. 'He sent me, didn't he? I was three years old and he trusted you to look after his precious little girl.'

Father started to walk towards them and stopped a few feet away. It looked for one horrid moment, as though no one was going to speak.

Then, thank goodness, Dilys broke the ice. 'Come here, you old reprobate,' she said. Perhaps it was a private joke from long ago because Father's eyes lit up and he gave a rueful smile. He and Dilys stepped forward to embrace.

Mummy dabbed her eyes with a handkerchief and said, 'Oh my, oh my,' a few times. A moment later, when she laughed at a quip Father made, she completely forgot to hold the corners of her eyes.

'You know,' she told Seffy. 'I always rather envied Dilys. Oh, don't tell your father, he thinks she's a bohemian. But she was so brave. She stood up to everyone you know and lived her life the way she wanted to. I admired that.'

'Hello, you,' Father said, turning to Seffy, finally. 'That was all jolly impressive, with the rope.' He nodded towards the enclosure where the tug of war had taken place. 'I didn't imagine girls could do such a thing.'

Everyone laughed.

'Oh, girls can do anything they set their minds to,' Dilys said. She turned to Father again. 'This is one fine daughter you've got, Ralph.'

'I know,' he said.

Dilys slapped Seffy on the back. 'I must admit, I used to think you were a prissy little thing, who'd swap your father's rules and care for that of a chinless wonder of a husband, produce the obligatory heir and spare and spend the rest of your days holding tea parties. You've surprised me, Persephone. And I am not often surprised.'

Seffy looked up and realised with a jolt that the two young men in RAF uniform – who'd apparently gone to watch the sword dancing and were now heading back – weren't Tol and Percy, her brothers, after all. Or at least, Percy was there but the figure she'd assumed was Tol, was actually Teddy.

Tol, everyone reassured her, was A1, perfectly fine. He just hadn't been able to get leave.

'You owe me ten pounds,' Seffy told Percy, before turning her attention to Teddy.

'Hello, old girl,' Teddy said, ruffling her hair. 'You're looking well.'

Seffy pulled him away from the others. It had been six months since she'd written to him, cooling things off and he'd never mentioned it. He'd written a letter of condolence when Hazel died, but other than that, there'd been no communication between them. Why was he here? Was this the parents' doing? She had to be somewhere else in a little while. She couldn't spend much time with him. Oh goodness, this was awkward.

'Teddy, I do hope you haven't come to ask me to marry you,' Seffy said. She was half-joking; trying to make light of the situation. She didn't really imagine he'd come to propose but then again, who knew? The war was making people behave most strangely. 'It's nothing personal', she added. 'But I've got rather a lot of things to do before I get married. I want to come out of this war a better person than when I went in. You do understand, don't you?'

Teddy gazed at her, smiling, and shook his head as though he couldn't quite believe his eyes.

'I thought you'd have changed,' he said. 'All this fresh air and outdoor life, it's bound to change a gal. And, my goodness, you have.'

Seffy grinned at him, relieved that there wasn't going to be any kind of scene.

'It's lovely to see you after so long,' she said. And she meant it.

'Percy and I had leave at the same time and when he told me he was coming up here to surprise you, I thought I'd tag along, to say hello. As "an awfully good friend but nothing more than that".'

She slapped him playfully on the arm – he was quoting her letter – and he gave a pretend yelp.

'Gosh, sorry. I don't know my own strength these days!' Seffy said.

She reached up and gave him a peck on the cheek. 'Is it all right then?' she asked.

Was she imagining it, or did Teddy Fortesque look a little wistful? But ever the perfect gentleman, he simply nodded. 'It's perfectly all right,' he said. 'Hey, where are you off to?' he added, as Seffy waved and started to walk away.

Callum was sitting at the base of a pine tree, pulling a twig apart.

He stood up when Seffy approached and pulled off his cap.

'At ease, Sergeant,' she said, laughing. She threw herself down on the ground next to him and leaned against the tree trunk.

'So, you're off then?' she said, as matter-of-factly as she could manage.

'Yeah. Tomorrow. Sorry but I can't—'

She reached round and placed a finger over his lips. 'Even if you knew, you couldn't tell me, I know.'

He lifted her finger, held it and kissed it – once, twice – longer the second time, never taking his eyes off her.

'I'm not allowed to tell you anything. Hell, I don't know much.' He shook his head. 'But—' he lowered his voice '—rumour has it we're being sent to join the combat troops.'

'Where?' She leaned in closer. 'I know you can't say but, is it the red rose?'

It was their code, for England.

'Yep. Red rose, so they say.'

Seffy's stomach twisted. She'd never considered the possibility that Callum would have to go and fight. He was a lumberjack, a woodsman. But she'd seen him in his uniform, serious and smart. He was a soldier, too.

She didn't know much about the progress of the war. She stayed away from newspapers and the wireless because it was bleak and never-ending and she'd rather not know. But one thing was absolutely clear: she and Callum Fraser were going to be parted and there was absolutely nothing she could do about it.

'It's been a blast,' Callum said, nodding slowly.

'It's certainly had its moments,' Seffy agreed. 'Oh, by the way, we just won the tug of war.'

'Good for you!' He picked up her wrist and shook it. 'No injuries this time?'

'No injuries!' she confirmed. Only her heart, which was broken in two.

It felt as though all these months in the Highlands had led to this moment: a boy and a girl, alone in the forest, trying to tell each other how they felt.

'Another time, another world ... you and me.' Callum shrugged. 'Who knows?'

'But we've only got this time, this world,' Seffy replied, softly.

She sighed. This was really starting to feel like goodbye. She felt hollow inside.

'Will you write?' she asked and then in the same breath. 'No, don't.'

'You mightn't still be here,' Callum said. 'Even if I wrote, you mightn't get the letter. You'll get moved around, I guess, in due course. You'll meet different folk.'

Seffy shook her head. She didn't want to be moved around or meet "different folk". She wanted everything to stay the same.

'Anyway, look at you,' Callum said pointing at the new badge on her sleeve, 'all responsible and sensible. Leader girl!'

'Who'd have thought it?' Seffy agreed.

'You're going to be amazing,' he said.

'You already are.'

Callum looked down at his hands. 'I can't make you any promises, Seffy. Hell, I don't even know what's going to happen tomorrow or the next day. None of us does. The world's gone plum crazy.'

She felt stronger than she'd imagined she could be. She'd cope with this; she wouldn't break down and make it harder for them both.

'That's all right,' she said, slapping his leg. 'Remember? "There is no you and I".'

'—no you and I.'

He'd said the line at the same time and they laughed.

'Why is that so funny?' Seffy asked, when they'd finally stopped laughing.

'Because I sounded like a pompous ass when I said it and—' He shook his head. 'Because it ain't true.'

Seffy tilted her face up towards his and he kissed her gently on the lips. Finally, slowly, she pulled away. She wouldn't say goodbye. That kiss could be their farewell.

Without a word, she got up and walked slowly away through the trees. She could feel Callum watching her but she didn't look back.

She walked on a little further, shielding her eyes against the dappled sunlight until she saw them, standing by the burn, waiting for her. The other girls, the lumberjills.

They welcomed her with smiles; they asked if she was all right. Seffy nodded and thanked them and said that she was.

Then the girls linked arms and walked away, off into the forest, into their future.

A Letter from Helen Yendall

Thank you so much for choosing to read *The Highland Girls at War*. I hope you enjoyed it! If you did and would like to be the first to know about my new releases, you can follow me on Twitter, Facebook or via my website. (Details below.)

Like many people, I had never heard of the Women's Timber Corps, until I stumbled across a newspaper article about the lumberjills.

I was astonished that the story of these thousands of brave women and their wartime work in the forests of Britain was not better known. As the WTC was part of the Women's Land Army, there was, sadly, no official recognition of the lumberjills' efforts during WW2. They were, in effect a "forgotten Corps".

The article I read inspired me to write a 4000-word short story ("Blood Sisters") which was published – rather appropriately, given my characters' love of magazines – in *Woman's Weekly* in 2015.

At the time, a kind reader commented that my story "could have been a novel" and when I was starting to think about my second book, writing about the lumberjills seemed an obvious choice.

Through my research, I also discovered that, in WW2, thirty companies of the Canadian Forestry Corps (CFC) – almost 7000 men – answered the British government's call for help from overseas woodsmen. Many of them worked in Scotland, alongside the lumberjills.

And there I had it: my setting, my characters (or at least, their occupations and nationalities) and the small beginnings of a story (a sapling, if you like). It took a lot of time and effort to shape those initial ideas into the final novel.

I found many inspiring lumberjill accounts in Joanna Foat's excellent book *Lumberjills: Britain's Forgotten Army* (The History Press) so if you'd like to learn more about these amazing young women – some of whom were as young as fourteen – then I can highly recommend that book.

As I put the final touches to my novel, I planned to visit the Scottish Highlands. I wanted to walk in the forests where so many CFC servicemen and lumberjills had worked. I also wanted to see the official memorial to the WTC – a bronze lumberjill statue – that was finally unveiled in the Queen Elizabeth Forest Park near Aberfoyle in 2007.

However, having avoided it for two years, the dreaded Covid got me at around that time and put paid to that visit. But I will make a pilgrimage to the Highlands as soon as I'm able to rearrange it. And if you're in that neck of the woods (if you'll pardon the pun), do go and see the area for yourself. My character Hazel would be delighted to see how the trees that were so essential to the war effort have been replanted and how the forests are carefully managed.

I hope you loved *The Highland Girls at War* and if you did I would be so grateful if you would leave a review. I always love to hear what readers thought, and it helps new readers discover my books too.

Thanks,
Helen Yendall

Twitter: @Helenyendall
Website: www.blogaboutwriting.wordpress.com

A Wartime Secret

England, 1940. Can Maggie keep her family – and her secret – safe? An emotional and heartbreaking wartime novel for fans of Diney Costeloe, Dilly Court and Mandy Robotham.

When Maggie's new job takes her from bombed-out London to grand Snowden Hall in the Cotswolds she's apprehensive but determined to do her bit for the war effort. She's also keeping a secret, one she knows would turn opinion against her. Her mother is German: Maggie is related to the enemy.

Then her evacuee sister sends her a worrying letter, missing the code they agreed Violet would use to confirm everything was well, and Maggie's heart sinks. Violet is miles away; how can she get to her in the middle of a war? Worse, her mother, arrested for her nationality, is now missing, and Maggie has no idea where she is.

As a secret project at Snowden Hall risks revealing Maggie's German side, she becomes even more determined to protect her family. Can she find a way to get to her sister? And will she ever find out where her mother has been taken?

Acknowledgements

Thank you to my agent, Robbie Guillory at Underline Literary Agency, for his continued encouragement and support. We will meet somewhere other than Zoom, one day, I'm sure!

And many thanks to the team at my publishers, HQ, particularly Dushi Horti, Abi Fenton and Helena Newton, who edited my manuscript with tact and skill. Your suggestions for improving the book always made sense and were much appreciated. That first draft was very "first draft-y" and it's a credit to you that you didn't panic (at least, not to my face).

Many thanks to my Canadian friend Carole Mann, who very kindly checked my Canadian characters' dialogue and to the Friends of the Canadian Forestry Corps Facebook group, who answered some of my (many) questions.

And much love and thanks to my own "Weegie", my husband, Alan, who read the manuscript and pointed out where I had too many "ochs" and "ayes" (amongst other things).

Any remaining "dialect errors" are all mine.

Writing a novel isn't, of course, as tough as felling trees in a harsh Scottish winter but it does take a lot of work. I've been a party pooper (and a recluse) this year, as I buckled down to write and I've had to turn down so many invitations.

Big apologies to those friends (if, indeed, you still are my friends), who I had to let down. It wasn't you, it was definitely me and I promise to do better in future!

Dear Reader,

We hope you enjoyed reading this book. If you did, we'd be so appreciative if you left a review. It really helps us and the author to bring more books like this to you.

Here at HQ Digital we are dedicated to publishing fiction that will keep you turning the pages into the early hours. Don't want to miss a thing? To find out more about our books, promotions, discover exclusive content and enter competitions you can keep in touch in the following ways:

JOIN OUR COMMUNITY:

Sign up to our new email newsletter:
http://smarturl.it/SignUpHQ

Read our new blog www.hqstories.co.uk

🐦 : https://twitter.com/HQStories

📘 : www.facebook.com/HQStories

BUDDING WRITER?

We're also looking for authors to join the HQ Digital family!
Find out more here:

https://www.hqstories.co.uk/want-to-write-for-us/

Thanks for reading, from the HQ Digital team